A KNIGHT ON THE HAUNTED HUNT

THE TIME BUREAU FILES — CASE FILE TDG-512C

Compiled by Kurt Hausheer

When the Song of the Lynx is heard again, the roots of history will break.

Copyright

A Knight On The Haunted Hunt
Case File TDG-512C

Published by Sylvancrest Press
First Edition: January 2026
Printed in the United States of America

Interior Illustrations: Kurt Hausheer
Book Design: Kurt Hausheer
Cartography of Vaelthara: Tiffany Munro

For permissions, special use licensing, or inquiries:
contact@SylvancrestPress.com

ISBN: 979-8-9939835-3-0

TABLE OF CONTENTS

Map of Vaelthara
Map of Faelwyn Holt
Preface
Foreword
Prologue- The Office Killer
Chapter 1 – Treehome
Chapter 2 – The Imprisoned Hunt
Chapter 3 – The Ravine Winds
Chapter 4 – Roots That Turn Inward
Chapter 5 – The Shadow Grove
Chapter 6 – A Killer's Cunning
Chapter 7 – The Weight of the Holt
Chapter 8 – The Holt Opens
Chapter 9 – Roots And Omens
Chapter 10 – The Promise Spoken Aloud
Chapter 11 – When the Forest Chooses
Chapter 12 – The Hall That Burns
Chapter 13 – The Council That Fractures
Chapter 14 – The Rebels In The Roots
Chapter 15 – Through Fire, Toward Ice
Chapter 16 – The Wood That Bites Back
Chapter 17 – The Quiet School
Chapter 18 – Peace, Standing
Chapter 19 – Roots of Consent
Chapter 20 – The Citadel of Ice
Chapter 21 – Judgment of the North
Chapter 22 – The Forest That Should Not Answer
Chapter 23 – The Price of Peace
Chapter 24 – The Rebels' Strike
Chapter 25 – The Greenwood That Devours
Chapter 26 – The Banner of Eichenfall

Chapter 27 – Ash Over Bergshern
Chapter 28 – The Hunt Beyond Root and Star
Chapter 29 – The Day The Forest Burned
Chapter 30 – Roots Beyond The Line
Chapter 31 – The Day Graypine Burned
Chapter 32 – Roots That Remember
Chapter 33 – The Hill That Breathes
Chapter 34 – The Joke Written In Ash
Chapter 35 – The Hill That Would Not Near
Chapter 36 – Where the Forest Slept
Chapter 37 – A God's Choice
Chapter 38 – The Investigator
Chapter 39 – What the Forest Keeps
Chapter 40 – The Emissaries' Common Enemy
Chapter 41 – The Fountain Runs Again
Chapter 42 – When the Map Stops Behaving
Chapter 43 – Water That Remembers
Chapter 44 – Aelrindel's Gift
Chapter 45 – The Silence Between Tracks
Chapter 46 – The Strength of Humankind
Chapter 47 – The Killer's Help
Chapter 48 – The Confrontation at Heartroot Vael
Chapter 49 – What the Hunt Takes
Chapter 50 – Ahsin's Renewal
Chapter 51 – Kaelith's Ledger
Chapter 52 – The Forest That Walked
Chapter 53 – Call of the Haunted Knight

Appendix 1
Appendix 2
Appendix 3
Appendix 4
Appendix 5
Appendix 6

Map of Vaelthara

Map of Faelwyn Holt

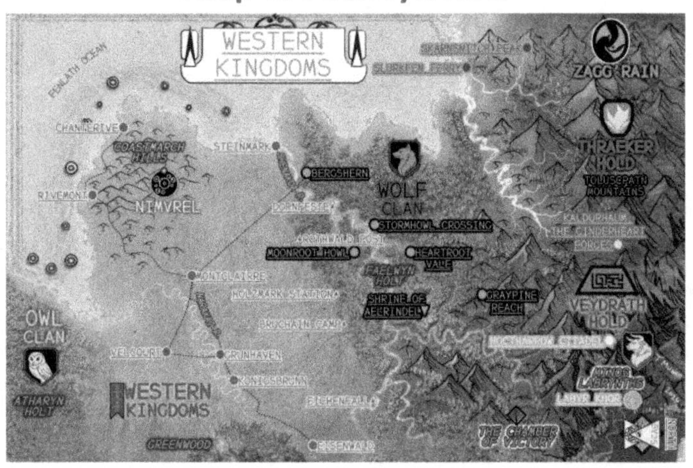

Preface

Some stories are meant to answer questions.
Others exist to show what happens when old answers no longer work.

This book stands at that threshold. It is not a story of final victories or neat resolutions, but of consequences set in motion and choices made before their full weight is understood. It is about the moment when survival demands shift, when peace reveals its fractures, and when doing what must be done carries a cost that cannot yet be measured.

Not every path leads forward as expected. Not every crossing allows those who begin it to decide where they will end up.

Read this volume not as a destination but as a passage. Some threads will tighten rather than close. Some answers will remain distant, waiting for the right moment to be faced. What matters here is not how the journey ends but why it must continue.

* * *

This book is dedicated to the memory of my father, Herman Joseph Hausheer.

I have reached the age he was when he died. I see him better than ever.

Dad, this one's for you. Thanks for everything you taught me.

— Kurt J. Hausheer

Foreword

I never thought I would miss fluorescent lights or the rules they pretended to give us. I once wore armor that listened when I spoke.

It carried power through plates and circuits, responded to silent commands, and let me fight from distances where I never had to smell blood or feel the ground shift beneath my boots. I trusted pulse and sonic weapons, shared sight through communication systems, and believed that if you could see the field clearly enough, you could control it.

Then the future ended.

A few of us crossed thirty-six centuries into a world that didn't care what we had mastered. The forest didn't recognize ranks or credentials. It didn't answer to confidence. It asked different questions — and it asked them patiently, until you failed.

I am still learning how to answer.

I learned how to carve a bow from living wood without killing it. How to twist sinew into a string that holds through rain. How to fletch arrows so they fly true through branches instead of past them. How to cross a bed of dry leaves in silence. I learned the weight of a longsword that does not hum with power, and a dagger that does not forgive hesitation.

But that was only the beginning.

I am learning to sense water before I see it — to read beech and alder where the ground drinks deeply, and spruce where roots must struggle for moisture. I am learning how prey think when they believe they are safe, and how they move when they know they are not. I am learning that the forest speaks constantly — but never in words.

None of this had a place in my former work.

There, my purpose was enforcement. Protection. Escorting an unwanted visitor from an office corridor. Here, purpose has hardened into something older and more honest: tracking, hunting, and killing so that my people may survive.

I am also learning what it means to be more than mortal.

The first time I released an arrow guided by Queen's Kiss, I nearly hesitated — not out of fear, but from awe. Power responded to intent. The arrow curved, not by force, but by permission. It was a long way from a sanctioned arrest under fluorescent lights.

Those who arrived thinking they could lead learned over time. Those who listened learned faster. Humility, it appears, remains our most effective tool.

I have much still to master. I know that now. But I also know this:

The land does not care who you were — only who you are willing to become.

This story isn't about heroes coming to save the past. It's about people who lose everything and discover that loss can be a new beginning. It's about learning to stand on your own without the structures that once defined you. It's about the cost of adapting — and the danger of refusing to do so.

If you are looking for certainty, you will not find it here.

If you have ever had to reinvent yourself to survive, you may recognize the path.

— Miren Froster

Former Sergeant, Sylvancrest Time Bureau Security
Huntsman of the Wolf Clan

Prologue – The Office Killer

Planet: Vaelthara
City: Sylvara Prime — Business District
Freedom Year (FY): 3550

The holographic caution tape parted like liquid light as Detective Investigator Arden Kholfax stepped through it. Photonic text rippled across his chest, confirming his identity with a sterile chime.

ACCESS GRANTED.

The smell hit him first.

Not blood.

Not fear.

Nothing.

The room had the sharp emptiness of scrubbed air—filters working so hard they had erased even the memory of breath. Holo-screens idled with a faint standby glow. A mug of synthetic coffee sat cooling on a desk, its aroma flattened into something metallic and stale.

Four Anari clerks sat at their workstations, backs straight, hands resting on input pads, eyes open but vacant.

As if waiting for someone to answer a question they'd never heard before.

Kholfax paused just inside the doorway. His auburn hair caught the overhead glare in dull copper streaks. The thin scar along his cheek—souvenir from an earlier case—itched sharply. The scar always reacted first. The last time he ignored it, three people had died before he understood what he was chasing.

It always did when something was wrong.

"Time of discovery?" he asked without looking back.

"Thirty-eight minutes ago," the uniform behind him said. "Building-wide activity scan flagged ninety minutes of inactivity in this suite. Patrol responded, per protocol. We haven't touched anything."

Good. Someone still followed the rules.

Kholfax approached the nearest clerk—a woman, early middle age, with a neat braid and a stylus still between her fingers. Her pupils were dilated, and her irises appeared cloudy. Her posture seemed off—too perfect, too composed. He gently touched her wrist.

The skin wasn't stiff like death usually is. It felt held in place, frozen mid-command.

"As if someone told you to freeze," he murmured.

His internal harmonics pinged. A faint resonance scratched his inner ear. Building frequencies were misaligned, but the diagnostics feed in his retinal overlay insisted:

STRUCTURAL HARMONICS: NOMINAL.

"Liar," Kholfax muttered.

"Sir?" the uniform asked.

"Nothing." He straightened. "Any audio?"

A tech moved away from the mobile node, slate in hand. "Routine noise. Typing, door chimes, background chatter." Her voice flattened. "Then silence. No screams. No panic. Just… nothing."

"Visual?"

She flicked a sequence across the holo-slate. Corridor feeds. Lobby angles. Street views. All normal—until the interior office cam.

Thirty seconds of footage just disappeared.

Not static. Not corrupted. Simply absence.

"No power loss anywhere else in the building," the tech said. "Only this suite. No logged maintenance, no security override."

Too clean. Too neat.

Kholfax moved behind one of the desks. On the screen, a cursor blinked after a single sentence:

ALL WORK AND NO PLAY MAKES FOR A DULL OFFICE.

The words sat on the display like something greasy.

"Who typed that?" Kholfax asked.

"Keystroke log says this station," the tech replied. "But the pattern doesn't match the victim's cadence. It's as if the text was dropped in whole. Injection, not input."

"From where?"

"We're still chasing the packet trail," she admitted.

Kholfax kept staring at the line until his scar ached.

Someone had manipulated these people. Manipulated the room. Manipulated him.

"Seal the scene," he said. "Full spectrum and full biological sweep. Every vent, every duct, every fiber. Run particulate mapping on the scrubber output and ceiling panels. I want to know what's been breathing in here for the last year."

The tech hesitated. "Sir… do you think this was intentional? Some kind of… industrial accident? Malfunction—"

"This," Kholfax said softly, eyes on the motionless clerks, "is someone's idea of fun."

FY 3551 — 2nd Murder Scene

Seven bodies.

Seven perfect poses.

Different district, different office design—still the same unnatural stillness.

Kholfax stepped into the second crime scene and felt it hit him again, like walking into a room with the pressure dialed wrong. The air carried a faint metallic tang this time, something artificial woven beneath the clean scent.

A forensic tech's wand whispered as it sampled the air.

"Trace compound identified," she said. "Adaptive neuromuscular binder. CR-9. Leaves consciousness intact. Fast onset. A polyhedral chrono—"

"Stop," Kholfax said.

The word cut clean.

She blinked. "Sir?"

"Plain speech."

A beat. Then she recalibrated.

"It freezes them," she said. "Exactly as they are. No movement. No pain. No degradation. They stay conscious. Their last voluntary command becomes permanent."

Kholfax observed the seven bodies. One let out a quick laugh. One leaned forward to speak. One had a hand halfway raised, as if about to call for help.

"And delivery?" he asked.

She gestured toward the ceiling vents. "Repulsor scarring and heat residue. Messenger drones. He sent the gas through the building's own lungs."

Kholfax's overlay displayed an external feed—time-stamped corridor footage. A lone figure entered, cloaked in everyday anonymity. Thirty seconds later, the office cameras went black. Ninety seconds afterward, thirteen figures emerged from the hallway.

Thirteen versions of the same person.

Mirror-layered holography shattered off the killer like shards of walking glass. Each decoy figure drifted in a different direction, each with a slightly different gait. Some greeted coworkers. Some ignored them. All moved convincingly enough.

"He taught his illusions how to walk," the tech whispered, half in awe.

"And his face?" Kholfax inquired.

She shook her head. "Every angle blurred. No matter the camera, there's a distortion field centered on the head. We can't get a single frame of clear features."

Of course not.

Outside, bounty feeds scrolled over city spires. The numbers kept climbing.

500,000 harts.

Hunters were already converging on Sylvara Prime, attracted by blood and opportunity.

Kholfax dismissed the thought of them. He observed the still bodies, the silent desks, the holo-screens frozen in place. The sharp edge of wrongness behind his ribs pressed harder.

This murderer enjoyed the pursuit.

And he was only just beginning.

FY 3552 — Third Crime Scene

Three offices.

Fifteen victims.

Thirty minutes.

The mobile lab hummed like a hive. Data flowed in translucent layers around Dr. Ireen Malvas as she stood at the central console, arms crossed, her gaze intense.

"These cortical micro-lesions should not exist," she said.

Kholfax leaned closer to the projection of a neural cortex—an icy blue replica of a victim's brain, overlaid with threads of dark interference.

"They match harmonic damage," Malvas continued. "Three overlapping frequency bands. Intense. Precise. No known environmental source."

Kholfax frowned. "Triple-harmonics are a myth."

"So were mirror-walking illusions and adaptive binder gas," she replied. "Until last year."

He observed the simulation in action. The modeled waveforms surged through the cortex, quickly severing functional pathways. Not chaotic trauma. Surgical removal.

Gas to freeze the body.

Harmonics to calm the mind.

"Why both?" he asked.

Malvas tilted her head. "Because he's testing limits. Gas alone is blunt. Harmonics alone are unreliable at range. Used together, he gets control first, then silence."

The bounty surpassed 5 million harts two days ago.

The number hadn't slowed him down. It seemed to have amused him.

Kholfax's slate chimed. A new icon pulsed in the corner of his vision—a priority ping from Central Analytics. He opened it with a blink.

SUBJECT: CORRELATED PARTICULATE ANOMALY — CLASSIFIED.

"Talk to me," he said.

Malvas flicked new data into the air—a ghosted 3D wireframe of an interior space, tagged with colored overlays.

"This is from the first scene," she said. "Your FY 3550 office. You ordered a full particulate map of vents and ceiling panels. Took us months to process the deeper layers."

The wireframe rotated. Dense clusters of particles glowed where air currents had pooled. One area—near the central wall and the ceiling above it—burned almost white.

"Most dust in a controlled environment is shed skin," Malvas said. "Dead cells, micro-fragments, tiny hair shards. Normal officers don't spend much time thinking about that. I do."

"And?" Kholfax asked.

"Those particles?" She pointed at the white blaze. "Almost all from a single biological source. Same spectrum of trace proteins, same mitochondrial signatures, same micro-keratin structure. One person practically painted that section of the room just by existing."

Kholfax's scar ached.

"How long?" he asked.

"Hard to be exact," she said. "But we're looking at hundreds of hours of presence. Either one very patient occupant… or repeat visits over years."

She flicked to another map. "Second scene. Different district. Same anomalous donor profile in the vents and corners, just much thinner. Third cluster—your fifteen victims. The safehouse we just pinged from bounty chatter—we'll know once we process it."

Kholfax gazed at the glowing clusters.

"So, we have a ghost," he said quietly. "A person who doesn't show up in person. Just in what he sheds."

Malvas was already running a sequencing overlay. "We're feeding his skin into the core genome index now. Every registered citizen, every colonized world, every archived blueprint of the Confederation's sapient lines."

A new notification stuttered into being.

RESULT: NO MATCH.
CONFIDENCE: 99.9992%.

"Try again," Kholfax said.

"It already did," Malvas replied. "The system repeated the sweep six times. Same answer. Our donor profile does not match any recorded individual or standard branch."

Kholfax exhaled slowly. "He's Anari. Everyone left is Anari. Unless the Confederation's been lying about the species extinction, the index must be wrong."

"The index," Malvas said, "thinks this genome is… archaic. Pre-Confederation. It flags it as a contamination artifact. The markers are too clean, too stable. Less drift than our oldest museum samples."

She glanced at him. "It's like someone took a deep-time template of us and walked it into the present."

Kholfax's jaw tightened. "Can we pull a face?"

"We can force a phenotype reconstruction," she said. "But the models disagree. One iteration shows tall, another moderate, one narrow-jawed, and another broad. It's like the genome doesn't want to settle into a single answer."

"No name," Kholfax said.

"No name," Malvas echoed. "But we can do something else."

She pushed another layer forward. "We can scrape the registries for identities that make statistical sense. Travel records, medical scans, administrative pings that should correspond to a body like this."

A network of data points appeared—fragmented records, incomplete travel permits, medical scans without biometric backgrounds. The system began to organize them.

"See that?" Malvas said. "These are ghosts of ghosts. Identities that appear, perform a transaction or two, then vanish. No childhood histories, no school logs, no employment chains. Just enough structure to pass standard scrutiny."

Kholfax watched as the AI drew lines between them. Three nodes flashed brighter than the others.

"If I were your killer," Malvas said, "I'd have shell lives. Paper shadows. These are our best candidates."

"Which one moved most recently?" Kholfax asked.

Malvas highlighted a node.

"This profile signed onto a refugee convoy four days before Sylos IV went dark," she said. "Under emergency clearance. Destination: Sylos IV Administrative District. No outgoing logs."

Kholfax's scar burned like a branding iron.

"Then that," he said, "is where he ran."

Detective Kholfax and Dr. Malvas.

The Safehouse

The safehouse wasn't empty.

Three bounty hunters sat leaning against the walls, with their gear neatly stacked beside them. Their faces showed the same unnerving calm as office workers. Eyes open. Limbs relaxed—frozen mid-breath.

On the far wall, letters dripped in thick strokes of darkening Anari blood:

WHEN OFFICE HEAD-HUNTERS BECOME OFFICE DÉCOR,
OFFICE POLITICS DON'T HAVE TO BE DULL.

Kholfax stared at the words until the room seemed to tilt. The smell of burnt circuits lingered beneath the metallic scent of drying blood.

"Same binder compound," Malvas said quietly from behind him. "Same triple-band lesions in the motor cortex. He's practicing on professionals now."

In the sleeping niche, disassembled holo-projectors lay gutted. Messenger drones curled like dead insects on the floor—repulsor cores burned out. Every digital trace that could have held an image or a log had been scrubbed to uniform gray.

No prints.
No hair.
No fresh DNA.

But in the corners, along the ceiling, inside the vent mouths—the particulate map glowed with familiarity.

"Same donor," Malvas said, checking her slate. "Your ghost has been nesting here for a long time. He's left more of himself in this room than most people leave in a lifetime."

Kholfax felt the wrongness deepen—the thought of a person taking up space like radiation, invisible but filling everything.

Another message waited near the exit, etched into the polyglass in a careful, almost cheerful script:

ALL WORK AND NO PLAY MAKES FOR A DULL WORLD.
SEE YOU OFFWORLD.

"Ship logs?" Kholfax asked.

"Cross-referencing now," Malvas said. "Multiple migrant corridors. Increased traffic since the new vein of rare-earth opened up more jobs on Sylos IV. But our ghost profile narrows it down."

She showed him a filtered list. One transport shard caught her eye—its manifest stamped with the same suspect identity that had appeared in her earlier analysis.

"He took a ride out under our noses," she said.

"To Sylos IV," Kholfax said.

Malvas nodded once.

"Then that's where we go," he replied.

FY 3553 — Final Crime Scene

Sylos IV burned.

The harmonic rare-earth veins beneath the crust shimmered through cracked streets like molten scripture. Skybridges sagged and fell in slow, graceful arcs. Dimensional fractures tore through the air—white wounds in reality that spat static and fragments of other skies.

Silhouettes of gods and Malloch abominations clashed in the wounded sky. The sky was a battlefield that only half the city could see.

Evacuees screamed and surged toward the time-gate spires.

Kholfax moved the other way.

The administrative block's interior had become a mausoleum of paperwork and glass. Thirty victims sat in two adjoining offices, frozen in the same unnatural poses as the others—fingers hovering over keys, mouths halfway through half-finished words.

CR-9 binder residue clung to the vents. The air tasted like old coins and ozone.

"Same signature," Malvas reported over the comm. "Same genome in the deeper layers of the dust. Your ghost beat us here. And he indulged himself while the world ended."

A sudden distortion rippled across Malvas's transmission—her holographic outline juddering as the lab behind her lurched sideways.

The audio crackled with a low, discordant hum that made Kholfax's molars throb.

Something outside her frame flashed white, then inverted to black—a brief implosion of light.

Malvas braced a hand on her console as ceiling panels shook behind her.

The distortion rippled across his retinal overlay, bending UI lines like wet ink.

"Anti-reality blast," she said, breath tight but steady. "Malloch skirmisher. They just hit the block adjacent to my sector. Local harmonic lattice dropped to sixty-eight percent before buffers caught it."

"Anti-reality? That's theoretical," he stated.

"Until now. It's the weapon of the Malloch," she finished.

Another tremor rolled through, making her projection smear for half a second like paint dragged across glass.

She didn't look back.

Didn't even blink.

"Focus on the triple-band lesions," she continued, flicking the neural map back into view as if physics itself weren't tearing in the room behind her. "Your ghost isn't improvising anymore. He's perfecting methodology."

Kholfax hesitated.

The feed flickered behind her — smoke where a building had been.

"Malvas," he said, quieter. "You okay?"

She waved it off, already pulling up data.

"Get out safe," he added. "Find a colony ship or any ship, just to a safe place."

It was the closest he ever came to saying anything else.

Kholfax didn't flinch. The world was ending, but the killer was evolving. That was the part that mattered.

Kholfax's slate chimed again. A security tech from Gate Control appeared in a small window, face slick with sweat, alarms painting angry colors behind him.

"Detective! We recovered partial visual from Gate Spire Three. Someone piggybacked an unauthorized jump during evac."

"Show me."

The feed jittered. Refugees packed the concourse. A hooded figure slipped through the chaos, unhurried. His head was swallowed by distortion.

As he reached the gate, three overlapping bands of sound tore through the audio feed.

"It's baked into the recording," the tech shouted. "Like he sang over the data."

The figure lifted one hand. Casual. Polite.

Then vanished.

"Trace logs," Kholfax said.

The tech swallowed. "That's the problem. He didn't go forward."

Kholfax stilled. "What?"

"Temporal vector is negative," the tech said. "He went into the past."

"That's illegal," Kholfax said. "And fatal."

"Usually," the tech replied. "Unless the jump lands in a survivable epoch."

Kholfax's eyes narrowed. "Say that again."

"A backward jump is a death sentence," the tech said. "Atmosphere mismatch. Pathogens. Collapse. Unless a failsafe resolves a viable window."

"Whose failsafe?" Kholfax asked.

The tech hesitated. "Time Bureau analyst. Ellendyl Felhart. Sylvancrest Time Bureau on Sylvara Prime."

The name rang old. Restricted.

"She wrote survivability code," the tech continued. "Doesn't choose when you want. Chooses when you can live."

"And he used it," Kholfax said.

"Yes, sir."

"Why that time?"

The tech shook his head. "Unknown. The algorithm doesn't explain itself. It just… resolves."

The plaza shook as another Malloch impact split the sky.

Kholfax ended the call and made his way to the stairwell. There, on the polyglass balustrade, another message waited—scratched into the surface with something sharp enough to bite through the hardened polymer.

ALL WORK AND NO PLAY MAKES FOR A DULL DAY AT THE OFFICE.
See you in the past.

The time-gate plaza shook as another Malloch impact rolled through the crust. The air above the spire shimmered, its temporal rings misaligned, arcs of crackling light lashing outward.

A gate guard grabbed Kholfax's arm. Her armor panel flashed evacuation orders in pulsing red.

"Sir, we have to go," she shouted. "Command says this world is lost. We're minutes from total harmonic collapse. If you stay, you die."

Kholfax barely heard her. His mind held a different image: forests he'd only ever seen in museum sims—an Anari world before cities, before filters, before scrubbed air and skybridges.

A killer who would walk among those ancestors like a phantom god.

"Sir!" the guard yelled. "Are you coming?"

Kholfax touched the scar on his cheek. It burned like a line drawn forward through time.

"No," he said. "I'm following."

The sky tore open as a Malloch Leviathan screamed overhead. Alarms rose in overlapping waves. Refugees shoved past him toward whatever future the fractured gate still offered.

Kholfax stepped toward the roaring light—toward an age of forests, forgotten gods, and a nameless thing that shed skin like dust and killed offices for sport.

Obsession wasn't his flaw.

It was his compass.

And it was pointing straight into the past.

Planet: Vaelthara
Location: Faelwyn Holt
Time: BV 24

Kholfax arrived 3576 years into the past on his knees. They had arrived in a different time and upon a different planet.

He was on his knees, not because the gate failed—but because his lungs did.

Air slammed into him, thick and wet and alive. It carried weight. It carried scent. Resin. Soil. Decay. Sap. Green things breaking and growing at the same time. The first breath burned. The second nearly made him retch.

He coughed hard, palms sinking into loam instead of polished stone.

The ground was warm.

Not heated—alive.

When he looked up, the forest was already watching him.

Faelwyn Holt rose in layered silence, trunks vast enough to swallow buildings, bark furrowed like old muscle. Canopies braided overhead in impossible geometry, filtering the light into drifting motes that caught and spun like pollen-stars. The air moved with purpose here, not wind but breath—slow, deliberate, aware.

This place did not resemble the museum sims.

Those had been tidy. Framed. Sanitized.

This was… intimate.

Kholfax swallowed, his mouth filling with the taste of iron and green sap. His filters were gone. His overlay was gone. No data crawled across his vision. No retinal diagnostics whispered reassurances. The oxygen-rich air made him light-headed.

Only birds. Insects. The low, distant groan of trees shifting against one another like old giants settling their bones.

He stood slowly.

All around him, the refugees were arriving.

Light fractured and folded as time-gates bled out bodies by the tens of thousands—men and women staggering, crying, laughing, collapsing. Some dropped to their knees. Some screamed. Some stared upward, mouths open, as if seeing the sky for the first time.

Over six hundred thousand souls from a dead future spilled into the forest's edge.

The Holt did not recoil.

It did not welcome them either.

It endured.

He had brought no food, water, or survival equipment of any kind.

Assessment.

Kholfax took another breath and forced it to stay down.

He smelled everything.

Sap was bleeding from a wounded branch. Damp fur somewhere nearby. Rot beneath fallen leaves—the sharp mineral tang of exposed stone. Life layered atop death in ways his old world had never allowed.

His scar throbbed—not burning this time, but pulling.

A pressure behind the eyes. A sense of depth that had nothing to do with distance.

"This place breathes," he whispered, not realizing he'd spoken aloud.

A woman nearby laughed hysterically. Another wept. A man kissed the dirt.

Kholfax turned slowly, cataloging without tools, observing without overlays.

If the killer had come here…

…then the hunt continued here.

Weeks later, after being absorbed into the Wolf Clan of his ancestors—Kholfax stood alone at the forest's edge.

A knife rested in his hand.

Nothing else.

No pack. No compass. No weapon he recognized as civilized.

Behind him, voices faded. Ahead of him, the Holt waited.

They had told him the rules.

Six months alone.

No shelter.

No guidance.

If you survive, you may be tested.

If you fail, the forest keeps what it takes.

He stepped forward.

The forest closed behind him without sound.

Chapter 1 — Treehome

"Peace is not the absence of danger. It is the moment you forget to look over your shoulder."
— *Anari proverb, origin disputed*

Planet: Vaelthara
Location: Aetherholt — Talos Eyrie, Upper Canopy Ridge
Chronometric Stamp: BV 21
Sealing Calendar: Year of Aelrindel — Owl Month, 21,426 years since the Sealing

[FIELD LOG // TDG-512C — FRAGMENT 01]
I do not regret the years we tried to pretend we were only scientists and linguists.
I regret only that we believed the past would leave us alone.
— *Commander Kellyn Windstream*

The darkness was not empty.

Harvey stood beneath a canopy warped by frost; the Greenwood bent into shapes that felt wrong even by its own ancient standards. Branches braided into spirals that should not exist, twisted as if the forest itself had been seized and wrenched around an unseen fist. Pale flakes drifted down, neither snow nor ash but something in between—cold enough to sting, light enough to cling.

Beneath his boots, the roots shuddered.

Not from wind.

From pain.

They flexed and recoiled in slow, convulsive waves, the living earth beneath him restless and strained, as if something deep beneath the forest floor were pulling against bonds it had never accepted. Every step sent a tremor through the soil, and with it came the sensation that he was being watched—not by eyes, but by memory.

Something groaned deeper within the Greenwood.

Chains.

Not metal. Not stone. Sound older than language, older than the naming of gods. The groan vibrated through Harvey's bones rather than his ears, a pressure that made his breath catch and his vision shimmer.

At the heart of the forest, a shape flickered.

Antlers of green fire rose from a towering silhouette, their glow dimmed and strangled by creeping blackness. Eyes like embers burned within the shape, fighting a tide pressing in from all sides. The voice that reached Harvey carried three tones at once—harmonic, fractured, urgent—each syllable layered atop itself, making his skin prickle.

"Green Knight…"

Harvey tried to step forward.

His body refused.

The air thickened instantly, becoming viscous, dense as sap. It hummed at a frequency that rattled his teeth and set his skull aching, each breath an effort. He strained against it, muscles burning, heart pounding in frustration and fear.

A silken veil of shadow poured down from above, slow and deliberate, wrapping itself around the antlered figure. The Crone's presence flooded the clearing—cold, eternal, venomous. It did not rage. It settled. Tightened. A net drawn closed with infinite patience.

The god's silhouette buckled.

"Only one who walks with living roots may tread my prison," the voice said, strained now, drawn thin by the encroaching dark.

"Find what was taken from me… before the forest forgets me."

Frost surged outward across the ground in a violent wave.

The trees screamed—not in sound, but in harmonic pressure. The resonance tore through Harvey's chest, crushing, disorienting, and unbearable.

The vision shattered into blinding white.

Harvey snapped awake with a sharp gasp, lungs dragging in air as though he'd been drowning.

Morning light spilled through the grown walls of the eyrie in layered shades of green and gold. The living wood breathed softly around them, its pale sap veins glowing faintly beneath the bark. Resin-sweet air drifted past his face, warm and familiar, carrying the subtle scent of moss and flowering vine.

It felt almost mocking after what he'd just seen.

Beside him, Kellyn stirred.

Her auburn hair lay in a loose tangle across the pillow, catching the light. She blinked once, then again, her eyes sharpening instantly as she focused on him. There was no grogginess in her expression—only immediate assessment, the reflex of someone who had long ago learned that waking moments mattered.

"Harvey?" she whispered, voice low so as not to disturb the tree. "Your heart is shaking the bedframe."

He dragged a hand over his face, fingers lingering at his eyes as if grounding himself. "Just… a dream." He paused, then corrected himself. "No. A vision."

That did it.

Her posture shifted subtly, spine straightening, breath steadying. Calm didn't leave her expression—but alertness replaced rest.

"Tell me."

He did.

All of it.

The bound god.

The Crone's shadow choking the roots.

The ancient, frozen terror in a forest that should never know fear.

Kellyn listened without interrupting, her hands folded loosely in her lap, her gaze steady on his face. When he finished, she fell quiet for a long moment, absorbing the weight rather than reacting to it.

"That was Aelrindel," she said at last. "Still imprisoned. Still fighting. And strong enough to reach you from inside the Greenwood."

She met his eyes, her expression firm, certain.

"He called you Green Knight. That isn't a metaphor."

Harvey swallowed. "He said only I can enter the Greenwood to free him." His jaw tightened. "But whatever was taken from him… it's frozen far to the north, guarded by Frost Giants."

Kellyn's expression sharpened—not with fear, but with recognition.

"There are old references," she said carefully. "Relics carried by gods. Anchors. Instruments that bind them to this world."

She met his eyes.

"If something like that had been taken from Aelrindel, it would explain how he was weakened enough to be trapped."

"What does it mean?" Harvey asked quietly.

She didn't hesitate.

"That a god is asking you for help."

"Gods rarely ask," she added quietly. "They remember too well what it costs them."

She reached out, cupping his face, her thumb brushing his cheek with a tenderness that grounded him more than any argument could. "You need to speak to someone. Sylveron is nearest. The High Druid will want to know immediately. So will Nadja."

Harvey nodded, though fear and certainty coiled tight together in his ribs.

The peace beyond the living walls suddenly felt thinner than bark.

If I go where the dream points, I may not come back. If I stay, I will spend the rest of my life wondering if I should have gone.

Kellyn deserves better than a man who hides behind peace.

The tree woke next.

A slow warmth rose through the floor, a deep, ancient breath moving up through root and trunk. Kellyn always felt it first. She swung her legs over the edge of the bed and stood, her bare feet resting on living wood that pulsed faintly beneath her weight.

The walls brightened in response, green-gold light blooming like a greeting.

Harvey watched her move, anchoring himself in the normalcy of her presence.

Three years since the Pyramid of Amenemapet. Three years since she became Queen of Swords and Queen of the Unveiled Path.

Three years since he became a Green Knight in training.

Three years of healing, harmony, and peace.

And now—omens dressed as dreams.

Kellyn crossed the eyrie with an easy grace. "Dawn came early for you."

"Dawn came with antlers," he muttered.

She lifted one brow. "Sylveron will appreciate that phrasing."

She brushed aside the balcony veil, and morning flooded the room.

Aetherholt revealed itself in layers. Vast spiral trunks rose like the ribs of a gentle colossus. Branch-bridges arced between them in elegant sweeps, woven and reinforced by generations of Anari hands. Below, mist clung to moss fields far beneath the canopy, sunlight catching drifting spores that glimmered like dust motes.

Harvey stepped beside her, arms circling her waist, chin resting briefly on her shoulder.

"Every morning," he murmured, "I still half-expect this tree to reassess our tenancy and drop-kick us into the underbrush."

"Be grateful," she said. "A Drakkenwyld tree would've digested you already."

"Trees with opinions are unsettling."

"I feel as though these trees raised me."

"They tolerate me."

"Highest praise for an Oakenstride."

Two Griffyn younglings spotted them from a nearby branch and waved with theatrical enthusiasm.

"Good morning, Queen of Swords!"

"Queen of the Unveiled—Unveely—Un—something!"

Kellyn smiled. "I will accept whichever title is correctly conjugated."

The children groaned so dramatically that the branch trembled.

"You terrorize children," Harvey whispered.

"I educate them."

"Same thing."

Later, the hollow kitchen glowed with fire-root warmth as Harvey stirred something purple and arguably edible.

Kellyn watched him with open suspicion. "I used to think synth-boar from street vendors was peak cuisine."

He stared at her, appalled. "You poor thing."

"Then I tried real boar."

"Not grown in a vertical agri-stack," he said solemnly.

Conversation drifted from Corlyn's inventions to Reen's new workshop, from cautious clan cooperation to

Elowen's far-off grief. Small things. Large things. The daily miracle of two worlds learning to share breath.

But Harvey's gaze kept wandering.

Toward the living wall.

Toward the forest.

Toward the dream.

Kellyn noticed.

Later still, Kellyn sat in her study, hollow, with scrolls scattered like fallen leaves. She began her field notes.

TDG-512C — Field Notes: Day 1

Aetherholt is peaceful. It should bring me comfort. Instead, it feels like the quiet breath a singer takes before the next verse.

She hesitated, then added:

I hope I am wrong.

The tree hummed softly in response.

At twilight, Harvey sat on the balcony, the Kuldemaekr resting across his knees. Emerald runes pulsed gently, mirroring the sky's fading.

"It still feels strange," he murmured, "that this blade chose me."

"It didn't follow," Kellyn said. "It decided."

He smiled faintly. "Like you did?"

"I didn't choose you," she replied. "You stumbled into my life with a camera and bad jokes, and now the universe is stuck with us both."

"Best accident I ever had."

Stars pricked the sky between branches. No alarms. No collapsing timelines. Just wind, leaves, and a blade that remembered the future.

"This could be enough," Kellyn whispered.

"For now," Harvey agreed.

They stood in peace.

Far below, something stirred.

A tremor.
A whisper.
A beginning.
But not tonight.
Tonight, the forest let them rest.

Harvey and Kellyn

Chapter 2 — The Imprisoned Huntsman

Planet: Vaelthara
Divine Year of Vaelthas — Wolf Month, 21,426 Years Since the Sealing
Aetherholt — High Canopy Roots, Archive Hollow

"Some gods do not fall.
They are buried."
— *Fragment, Pre-Sealing Druidic Canticle*

The roots of the Aetherholt breathed.

Not metaphorically.

Not poetically.

They breathed.

Harvey felt it beneath his boots the moment they stepped off the main branchway and into the lower root halls. A slow, deliberate expansion. A pause. Then contraction. The rhythm was vast and patient, like the chest of some slumbering animal too large to wake without consequence. Each pulse traveled up through the soles of his feet and into his calves, then settled somewhere behind his ribs.

The light here was different.

Sunlight filtered through layers of living bark and woven leaves, refracted again and again until it softened into green-gold shafts that drifted lazily through the hollow. Pollen motes and drifting spores caught the light, glowing briefly before vanishing into shadow. The air smelled of sap, damp earth, and something older—memory, perhaps.

Kellyn walked beside him, close enough that her sleeve brushed his forearm now and then. The contact was casual, almost unconscious, yet he felt it every time. An anchor. A check.

Still here.

He was.

Mostly.

The dream clung to him like cold after-snow, lingering long after the source was gone. No matter how warm the roots felt, a chill refused to lift from his spine.

They reached the Archive Hollow.

It was not a chamber so much as a deliberate absence grown into the roots themselves. A space where the Aetherholt had been asked—politely, reverently—to make room. Living walls curved inward in slow spirals, their surfaces etched with glyphs older than the clans as they were now. The markings pulsed faintly as people entered, recognizing lineage, intent, and memory.

Judging.

Listening.

Sylveron waited within.

No longer a clan lord.

Still unmistakably a warrior.

His armor was lighter than it had once been, bark grown and layered with treated hide rather than command plate, yet he wore it the way others wore titles. It fit him in a way authority never quite had. His stance was relaxed, his weight balanced, his eyes tracking movement without seeming to.

At his side stood Nyssara Windstream, his daughter.

Nyssara's posture was calm and grounded, her presence steady, as if she listened before acting. One hand rested unconsciously on her belly, fingers splayed protectively, though Kellyn could not yet tell whether from habit or intuition. Nyssara's scar were few, though she had fought many battles.

Nyssara's husband, Torval, stood nearby, scarred and silent. His burned side angled slightly away from the light, not from shame but from long habit. He spoke only when necessary, and when he did, it mattered.

Corlyn leaned against a root-column, arms folded, his expression sharp and restless. His eyes flicked between faces, cataloging reactions and already turning information into questions he hadn't yet asked aloud.

And Elowen.

She stood barefoot on the living floor, her toes curled slightly against the bark as if feeling the tree's breath directly. Her staff rested loosely in one hand, more companion than tool. Auburn hair framed her face, streaked with lighter ember tones that caught the green-gold light. Beneath her bronze skin, faint life-mage tracery shimmered—patterns like sap veins glimpsed through amber.

She looked up as Harvey and Kellyn entered.

Her eyes widened.

Not in surprise.

In recognition.

"You dreamed," she said.

Harvey stopped.

The Hollow shifted its attention.

Kellyn felt it too—the subtle tightening of the space, the way the roots leaned inward, as if the Aetherholt itself were listening more closely now.

"Yes," Harvey said quietly.

Sylveron's jaw tightened. Nyssara's hand stilled.

Elowen stepped closer. She did not touch him. She never did unless the tree told her it was right.

"Tell us."

Harvey drew a breath that felt wholly insufficient.

"There was a forest," he began. "Older than anything I've seen here. The Greenwood, but… wrong. Twisted. Folded in on itself. I was walking alone."

Kellyn's fingers curled into the sleeve of his tunic.

"There was a horn," Harvey continued. "Frozen. I could feel it calling. Not to my ears, but to something deeper. And someone was bound there. Trapped. Not sleeping. Watching."

Elowen closed her eyes.

Nyssara whispered, "Aelrindel."

The name settled into the roots like a stone dropped into still water.

Sylveron spoke carefully. "God of the Hunt. Of the Greenwood before the Sealing."

Torval nodded once. "Chief patron of the Wolf Clan. Before the Crone."

Harvey swallowed. "He spoke to me. Not with words. With urgency. He wants to be freed."

Silence followed—not empty, but weighted.

Then Elowen lifted her staff.

The wood hummed as it answered her intent, not brightly but deeply. She pressed the butt of it against the living floor.

The roots responded.

Light deepened.

Air thickened.

The Hollow listened.

"I see it," Elowen said, her voice shifting, layered—not command, not charm, but vision. "You're walking north. Far north. Beyond trees. Beyond rootpaths. Ice halls. Giants."

Her breath hitched.

"Aelrindel's possession, his personal horn, is frozen," she continued. "Hidden deep within a frost giant citadel. Guarded. Forgotten. And waiting."

Kellyn felt cold creep up her spine.

Elowen opened her eyes and looked directly at Harvey.

"You will take it."

Harvey did not flinch. "What does it cost?"

Elowen's gaze softened.

"Everything important," she said. "And some things you won't realize were important until they're gone."

Nyssara stepped forward, placing a steadying hand on Sylveron's arm. "If this god is freed," she said, "the Wolf Clan will be strengthened. Their ancient blessings restored."

"And if he isn't," Torval added, voice low, "the Crone's shadow grows unchecked."

Sylveron exhaled slowly. "I will go with him."

Kellyn turned sharply. "Sylveron—"

He raised a hand. "I know what you're thinking, but I am still a warrior. I will not send a man to face gods and giants alone if I can stand beside him."

Elowen shook her head.

"You may help him recover the Aelrindel's horn," she said. "You may defend him against the cold, the giants, and the traps laid by the Crone and her servants."

Her gaze sharpened.

"But once Aelrindel's horn is in his hands, only a green knight such as Harvey may enter the Greenwood."

The words rang like a verdict.

"No living being may enter that cursed forest," Elowen continued. "Not without being unmade by time, hunger, and grief. The possession of a god grants passage only to a Green Knight."

Kellyn felt something fracture in her chest.

Kellyn remembered the last council that promised stability. It had lasted less than a year and burned longer than the war that followed.

"You're saying he has to go in alone," she said.

"Yes," Elowen replied. "And he will not return the same."

Harvey reached for Kellyn's hand this time. She took it hard.

She had solved languages no one believed could be read.

This problem was worse.

There was no translation for the look on Harvey's face when fate had already decided.

Sylveron looked away, jaw working.

Nyssara spoke softly. "Vyrna should know."

"She does," Sylveron said. "Part of it. Enough."

He turned back to Harvey. "Lady Vyrna is to be wed. A union with one of the refugees trained by Ellendyl. She has invited us. The feast will gather the clan leaders, warriors, and druids."

"And," Nyssara added, "she knows old paths and old alliances, including with the Thraeker."

Kellyn's head snapped up. "The giants?"

Sylveron nodded. "Not friends. But… conversations exist."

Kellyn released Harvey's hand reluctantly. "If you're going north," she said, voice tight, "you won't go with only warriors."

Harvey frowned. "Kellyn—"

"I'll ask Seris," she said immediately. "And Serithyl. And Vaelinnae. Sylph warriors. Stealth. Speed. Life magic."

She looked at Elowen. "You saw the cost. I intend to minimize it."

Elowen studied her for a long moment.

"Your fear is justified," she said gently. "And your instincts are sound."

Her gaze then returned to Harvey.

"But understand this, Green Knight. Freeing Aelrindel may save your people."

She lowered her voice.

"It may also break something getting there. The Greenwood allows no living being entry."

The Hollow released its breath.

Light softened.

Roots shifted.

The moment passed like a held note finally allowed to fade.

Harvey nodded once. "Then I'll bear it," he said.

Kellyn closed her eyes—for only a heartbeat.

Outside, the Aetherholt whispered.

And far to the north, beneath miles of ice, something ancient, curved, and frozen waited to be taken.

Chapter 3 — The Ravine Winds

Planet: Vaelthara
Era: Divine Year of Vaelthas — Wolf Month, 21,426
Years Since the Sealing
Location: Faelwyn Holt — High Ravine Shelf

"Wind is the forest's first bowstring."
— *Khandyl, Wolf Clan Ranger*

Kholfax stood on the ridge and tried not to stare at the world as if it were a living hallucination.

Faelwyn Holt breathed.

Not metaphorically. Not poetically.

It breathed.

The canopy inhaled. The ravine exhaled.

Wind poured through the high leaves in a long, controlled draw, then released downward in a steady rush that made the entire gorge feel like the throat of a sleeping giant. It was not merely air moving. It was a pattern. It had intention. The gusts came in pulses, timed to the sway of upper boughs and guided by the shape of cliffs and the living architecture of the Holt itself.

Kholfax felt it before he understood it. His boots shifted slightly against the stone without conscious command, knees softening as if bracing against something invisible. The old scar along his cheek warmed faintly, the same sensation he used to feel when a crime scene stopped being noise and began to arrange itself into meaning.

The trees along the ravine's edge shimmered faintly, each leaf catching light as if a thin lantern skin had been stretched beneath the green. Vines moved in slow, muscular ripples, not from quick growth but from the subtle adjustment of something awake. Strange blossoms opened and closed as unseen presences drifted overhead, their petals tracking movement like a pupil following a face.

And hundreds of feet below, along the damaged edge of the forest, a human caravan rattled past on a scar of trampled ground.

Wagons groaned under stacks of freshly cut timber. Iron rims bit into roots and soil. Axes and saws hung from belts like insults forged into tools.

The crime was obvious even to a newcomer.

To an Anari, this was sacrilege.

Kholfax swallowed, his throat dry despite the damp, resin-sweet air. His hand lifted automatically to adjust the strap across his chest, fingers pausing halfway through the motion as if expecting a different weight there. No badge. No comms. Just leather and tension.

His old jacket from the Sylvara Prime Constabulary still clung to him like a past life. Scuffed. Smoke-stained. Absurd against Wolf Clan fashion. He could feel it the way one feels an old habit pressing forward in a new place, stubborn and unresolved.

Now the evidence moved, breathed, and watched you back.

His mismatched gear rattled softly as he shifted his weight. A collapsible stun baton hung beside a rough-forged hunting knife. His tactical boots, synthetic and stubborn, were smeared with shimmering Holt mud that refused to behave like normal dirt. It clung in thin threads, tugging faintly, as if testing whether he would pull away.

He did not.

He had survived the Ritual of Discovery. Six months in the wild with only a knife, no communications, and no shelter built by him. He faced the druids and their flame of potential and felt the judgment of an entire living culture settle on him like winter.

He had no knack for magecraft.

Only for the way of an Anari warrior.

Not a detective.
Not anymore.

The thought didn't sting the way it once had. It simply settled.

His shoulders had broadened. His hands bore new scars: a bowstring burn, a thorn-slice, and the fine cuts you earn when you carve wood the wrong way once and never again. His eyes had started to lift on their own now, not toward drones or cameras, but toward branches, wind, shadow, and the silent traffic of the canopy.

Khandyl did not share his uncertainty.

She stood at the cliff's edge, still, a figure shaped by the forest's own will. She didn't test her footing or shift her stance. The ground had already embraced her.

Her cloak blended with the dark green, its leaf-fiber threads catching light only at certain angles, as if it preferred not to be seen. A silver wolf's-head clasp pinned it at her throat, gleaming sharply when the sun found it.

Ranger of the Wolf Clan.
No question.

Her bow rested in her hand as if it were just another limb. Not carried. Not gripped. Present, like claws on a living creature that had never thought about being without them.

She did not look back when she spoke.

"You've trained hard to stand here," she said, her voice level. Not warm. Not cruel. Simply true. "Today, all of you will learn the forest's first law."

Behind Kholfax, the recruits shifted. The sound carried differently here, with boots and leather muted by the Holt as if excess noise were softly discouraged.

Most were refugees from Sylos IV, survivors of a world that had become a graveyard in hours. Others came from uncertain futures, from collapses and disasters that all ended the same way: a gate, a scream of light, and birdsong where no birds should have been.

Months of training had turned them into nearly warriors, but the Holt still loomed with its living presence. Some stood too stiff, shoulders locked as if posture could anchor fear. Others kept their hands too close to their weapons, forgetting that a bow did not comfort you until it had bitten you once.

"The first law of the forest," Khandyl continued, "is that what you see is not what is."

She lifted her chin toward the ravine.

The wind dipped and then shifted. Humidity layered itself invisibly, with one current sliding outward toward the plains while another curled back toward the cliff face, like a thought that refused to leave.

Khandyl's tone sharpened, and Kholfax heard the instructor beneath the ranger.

"Ballistics change with the breath of the trees. Ballistics is the right term from your time, right, Froster?"

Froster stood beside her, relaxed in a way that made Kholfax irrationally jealous. He embodied both future-born competence and ancient discipline, as if the two had finally stopped arguing inside him.

Full Anari armor covered him: dark-lacquered bark plates, vine-stitched leather, Wolf Clan geometry woven into the pattern itself. Yet clipped to one hip was a silver sonic baton from thirty-six centuries in the future, polished and practical. On his other hip hung a rune-inscribed Wolf Clan longsword.

When Froster nodded, it was a single motion. No excess.

"Ballistics is right."

A recruit muttered, "Ball… what?"

Froster leaned toward him, voice low and patient. As he spoke, his breathing slowed, his shoulders easing downward even as his hand settled on his bow.

"She means the things that change an arrow's flight after you release it. Wind. Weight. Humidity. The way the ravine steals your shot and returns it wrong. External ballistics. Just watch."

Kholfax's old instincts stirred.

Wind patterns. Trajectory curves. Aerodynamic interference.

His scar prickled again, faint but unmistakable, as the concepts shifted into something that no longer required numbers. In the future, consent was a form. Here, it was something the land remembered.

He raised his hand slightly. "How can you gauge wind speed and direction from here?"

Khandyl turned.

Her gaze settled on him like the tip of an arrow finding its mark. Not hostile. Assessing.

Then she pointed.

"Look at the trees on the edge. See the yellow pollen rising? Watch how the ravine wind catches it."

The pollen drifted lazily.

Then the ravine answered.

It swept sideways in a clean, sudden sheet.

His mind estimated a speed. Twenty, maybe twenty-five miles per hour.

Then the foolishness of that struck him. The Holt did not care about miles. It cared about behavior.

The pollen was not a measurement.

It was a sentence.

Khandyl raised her bow.

She did not aim at the caravan.

She aimed into empty woodland, forty-five degrees away.

"Second wagon from the back," she said. "Driver. The man holding the reins."

She drew.

No testing pull. No adjustment.

Froster's breathing slowed beside her. Inhale. Exhale. Then a pause — a clean space between heartbeats.

He loosed into that stillness.

Khandyl released a heartbeat later.

The arrows vanished skyward.

For a moment, nothing happened.

Then the ravine answered.

Wind seized the shafts and folded their paths inward, curling them down in wide, predatory arcs.

One struck the driver squarely in the chest.

Chaos erupted below.

"Your turn," Khandyl said. "Same shot. Watch peripherally. Replicate the pull. Replicate the breath."

Kholfax drew.

Too soon. Too full of air.

He loosed.

The arrow flew cleanly and struck a timber log.

Not a miss.

A misunderstanding.

His scar warmed again, sharper now. Look again.

He lowered his bow.

Listened.

The wind phrased itself. Long draw. Short release. A pulse that arrived after the canopy shifted.

He reset. Knees soft. Shoulders down.

He drew on an exhale.

Froster released beside him, silent, precise.

Kholfax waited.

Now.

He loosed into the stillness.

The arrow vanished.

The ravine took it.

It curved inward and struck a man near the front of the caravan through the shoulder, spinning him sideways.

Not a kill.

But deliberate.

Kholfax exhaled slowly.

It worked.

Because he listened longer.

Below, fear unraveled formation faster than blood.

"Prepare again," Khandyl said.
"With Queen's Kiss."

The name moved through the recruits like a held breath.

Some stiffened. Others glanced at their quivers as if the arrows inside had changed shape when no one was looking. Queen's Kiss was not a technique you practiced casually. It was permission layered into ritual, a reminder that the forest's mercy did not exempt it from consequence.

Kholfax felt his scar warm again, this time sharper, edged with something unfamiliar. Not insight.

Warning.

Khandyl did not rush them.

She knelt instead, one knee touching stone, fingers brushing the arrowhead she had already selected. Her movements were precise but unhurried, as if haste itself would be an insult to what came next.

She whispered the incantation in triple-harmonic.

Not loudly.
Not performatively.

It sounded less like a spell than a breath given direction.

A faint blue aura bloomed around her arrowhead, pale and cold, trailing light like a quiet comet. The glow did not pulse or flare. It waited.

"Draw," she said.

Recruits duplicated the spell at different skill levels until their arrowheads glowed faintly. A few whispered softly as they worked, not prayers exactly, but the instinct of people who once believed gods were myths and now lived in their shadow.

Kholfax hesitated.

His vocal cords opened, and he pushed air across them, producing a triple-harmonic series of sounds.

Queen's Kiss did not kill cleanly. It left a mark. It carried intent into flesh, binding pain to memory, fear to understanding. Survivors remembered the forest long after wounds healed.

His scar prickled again.

Not because the technique was wrong.

Because it was final.

He dipped the arrow anyway.

The glow crept along the shaft like frost spreading across glass.

"Loose," Khandyl said.

Froster drew beside him.

His breathing slowed first. Inhale. Exhale. Then the pause — that clean space between heartbeats where intention sharpened and doubt fell away.

Froster released into that silence.

Kholfax followed a fraction later, timing his shot not to Froster's arrow, but to the wind's next phrase. He loosed into the same stillness he had learned to hear.

Pale arcs of ghost-light traced their paths through the air.

The humans below saw them.

That was new.

Shouts erupted — warnings yelled into the open air, with men pointing upward as luminous trails curved impossibly above the edge of the ravine. Panic shattered discipline. Some tried to run. Others froze, caught between disbelief and instinct.

Seven men fell.

Not all died.

One collapsed, screaming and clutching his leg as blue light briefly crawled beneath his skin before fading away. Another staggered backward, dropping his axe, eyes wide and uncomprehending, as if he had just remembered something he desperately wished he had never learned.

Kholfax's arrow struck a man through the shoulder, spinning him sideways into the dirt.

The man screamed.

Not just in pain.

In recognition.

Kholfax's breath caught. His scar burned now, not hot, but alive, as if his skin remembered other screams layered over this one — interrogation rooms, survivors, victims who realized too late that a single moment had redefined their lives.

This isn't just fear, his mind supplied, cold and precise.

This is imprinting.

The caravan disintegrated.

Men abandoned wagons and tools, fleeing into the open plains where there was no canopy to hide enemies or roots to whisper warnings. They first ran the wrong way, then corrected their path, then ran faster as fear did what discipline could not.

"Enough," Khandyl said.

Her hand rose, palm outward.

The forest responded before the recruits did. Wind shifted. Leaves stilled. The next phrase of air never came.

The volley ended.

The recruits lowered their bows in a ragged wave, shoulders dropping, hands trembling from delayed shock. One of them laughed once — thin, sharp — then clamped his mouth shut, color draining from his face as the sound registered.

"They will not return soon," Khandyl said. "Fear roots deeper than bodies. It keeps the forest safer."

Kholfax wasn't sure she believed that.

The Holt exhaled.

Not a sound exactly. A change. Leaves adjusting. Light brightening a fraction, as if the forest had observed the exchange and decided the lesson had been… acceptable.

Froster slung his bow, then froze mid-motion.

"Beautiful work," he said softly. Then his voice shifted. "Wait. Is that…?"

Khandyl followed his gaze.

Dryads emerged from the lower brush like fog rolling uphill. Green-skinned, auburn-haired, crowned with leaves and blooms, their voices rose in a gentle harmony that thickened the air and slowed thought.

They were not hunting the humans as enemies.

They were selecting them.

Kholfax watched as panicked men slowed under the song, terror unraveling into compliance. Axes fell from hands. Eyes glazed over. One by one, they turned and walked into the trees as if following a familiar road home.

His scar flared sharply now.

This time, it wasn't recognition.

It was a protest.

Something about the sound scraped against old memories — interrogations that crossed lines, coercion dressed as necessity, choices framed so that resistance felt pointless.

He swallowed hard and forced himself to keep watching.

Khandyl spoke as if continuing the lesson.

"Dryads. Taking a few humans for correction. The beings of the forest are our allies. We protect one another."

Correction, Kholfax thought.

A year outside. Time distorted.

People returned changed.

If they returned at all.

"Their victims emerge after a year with renewed respect for the forest," Khandyl continued. "Any Anari taken by a dryad typically becomes a druid."

Kholfax heard the emphasis.

Human victims were not mentioned.

His scar cooled slowly, the way it did when a case reached a conclusion he did not like but could not yet challenge.

Not now. Not here.

Khandyl turned back to the recruits.

"Lesson one," she said. "Know your bow. Know your range. Aim with the air, the branch, the leaf."

Froster added, more quietly, "Human archers fire line-of-sight. We do not. We see flight paths through thickets, mist, sky, branches, wind, and rain."

He looked across the group, gaze lingering for a fraction of a second on Kholfax.

"These instincts slept in your blood for thirty-six centuries," he said. "Listen to the Holt. It will guide you."

Kholfax lowered his bow. The forest would guide him.

He was no longer sure it would do so kindly.

And that, he realized with a slow, steady certainty, was going to matter.

The forest was alive. And it expected something of him.

They descended into deeper Holtwood.

The air shimmered with drifting pollen shaped like tiny stars, each speck catching the light, briefly shining brightly, then fading away. Sprites floated among ferns, small, glowing beings with lantern-like eyes and wings that glowed like leaves. One circled Kholfax's head, chirped in approval, then zipped off, as if it had examined him and found him only mildly disappointing.

To the left, a centaur hunter stepped out from the trees: stag-bodied, broad-shouldered, with spiraled antlers. A boar was draped across his shoulder, steam gently rising from its hide. He nodded respectfully to Khandyl.

Kholfax managed an awkward half-salute that made no sense in any culture, then lowered his hand before anyone could say a word.

Wildflowers pulsed faintly as if breathing.

A tree spirit, half-bark and half-suggestion, stretched an arm toward the sky, then settled back into stillness as if the motion had been more sigh than gesture.

Kholfax exhaled slowly.

He had walked crime scenes on three planets.

Nothing compared to this place, where beauty and danger walked side by side without shame.

These ancient Anari saw details at distances the future had forgotten.

Perhaps, in time, he would learn to see this way.

He found himself helping other trainees, adjusting their grips, correcting their stances, and speaking with more patience than he would have expected from himself. They were not soldiers. Not really. They were people who had lost everything but still showed up every morning to learn how not to die again.

And now, for the first time since Sylos IV, Kholfax felt alive.

Froster slowed beside him. His voice dropped to a casual yet intent tone. "I've seen your face before. From our time. The scar on your face is hard to forget."

Kholfax touched the faint ridge without thinking. "Sylvara Prime. Arrived on Sylos IV just before the Malloch attack."

Froster's brows lifted. "I worked security for the Sylvancrest Time Bureau." He tilted his head. "How about you?"

"Sylvara Prime Constabulary," Kholfax said. "Detective division."

Froster blinked, then recognition hit him so hard he stopped walking. "What's your name?"

"Kholfax."

Froster stared for a beat, then let out a quiet breath. "You're that Kholfax, the detective hunting the serial murderer."

Kholfax's jaw clenched. The forest darkened around that memory, as if even Faelwyn Holt disliked the thought. "Tracked him to Sylos IV. He entered the time gate after killing thirty people. Even with the Malloch destroying everything, he still couldn't stop him."

Froster went still. "The Office Killer." His voice turned rough. "Spirits. Brutal case."

He swallowed. "If he went through the gate, does that mean he's here, in this time?"

Kholfax nodded. "Yes."

"Would you recognize him?"

"No." Kholfax pushed a branch aside, its leaves brushing his shoulder like a warning. "He masked his appearance from every camera. He created mirror images of himself that moved independently. Brilliant. Dangerous."

His voice softened, but the steel remained. "He won't stop. People like him never do. He'll kill again. When he does, I'll know it's him."

Froster exhaled. "He's one of more than six hundred thousand refugees who arrived here from Sylos IV. Only a hundred thousand were assigned to the Wolf Clan. He could be from any clan, anywhere on the continent."

Kholfax's eyes narrowed. The detective in him refused to die. "I'll find him. No matter how long it takes."

He hesitated, then added, with genuine confusion, as if suddenly realizing his ignorance. "Wait. Did you say continent? I haven't seen a large-scale map since I arrived here. In our time, there are multiple continents."

Froster nodded. "We're on a single landmass in this era. Two catastrophic events will split it. The first will happen in decades, maybe three." He looked ahead toward the Wolf Clan lanterns, flickering. "I'll ask around for a map after we return."

Khandyl looked back, assessing Kholfax.

Not as a trainee.

As something sharper.

"A dangerous vow," she said. "But a righteous one." Her eyes flicked briefly to his bow. "I saw your Queen's Kiss shot hit true. If you keep this up, you'll rise quickly."

Kholfax blinked.

He did not feel favored. He felt lost.

But her words still warmed something within him.

Froster gave his shoulder a pat. Not forceful. Not just for show. A firm touch that said you're here. "When we return, I'll tell Khandyl and Lady Vyrna. Leadership needs to know someone dangerous slipped into this age."

Khandyl nodded once, as if she had already decided the same the instant the name was spoken. "We stand against darkness, whether it comes from the east, the plains, or the far future."

Ahead, Wolf Clan lanterns flickered through the trees. Warm, inviting.

Deceptively safe.

Kholfax looked at the lights, then up at the canopy, then down at his hands.

Once, he had chased killers through cities of steel and glass.

Now he chased one through a living world that listened. And the wind, the forest's first bowstring, drew tight again.

Deep beneath, humans shouted warnings into the open air, unaware that the danger wasn't on the ground. It was in the leaves.

When myth becomes physics.

Chapter 4 — Roots That Turn Inward

Planet: Vaelthara
Divine Year of Vaelthas — Wolf Month, 21,426 Years Since the Sealing
Faelwyn Holt — Graypine Reach & The Shrine of Aelrindel

"Rot begins where grief is given purpose."
— Unattributed druidic warning, scratched out in the margins of an old codex

Sablek Thistlecrest finished healing the child before anyone noticed how tired he was.

He didn't let his hands shake. He didn't let his breath hitch. He kept his posture steady, shoulders relaxed, as Wolf Clan healers are taught to stand so the patient will borrow their calm. His fingers moved with an economy that seemed gentle. It was precision.

Bone knit beneath his palms in quiet increments, as if the child's body had always been meant to be whole and simply needed to remember its shape.

The boy's face clenched once, then softened, his eyes glossy with tears he refused to shed. Sablek murmured something gentle in old Anari, neither a spell nor quite a prayer, a reassurance shaped like a lullaby. He eased the swollen tendons, coaxed the sinew back into place, and pressed two fingertips to the bruise-dark skin until it warmed from within and the pain ebbed like a tide.

When it was done, the child stared at his own arm as if expecting it to fall apart again.

"It will hold," Sablek said. His voice was calm, almost mild. "But no climbing for three days, and no pretending you can wrestle grown warriors."

The boy managed a slight, fierce nod.

The parents expressed their thanks the way the Wolf Clan did: not with extravagance or drama, but with hands over their hearts and eyes lowered, their gratitude conveyed in the quiet that followed.

Sablek returned the gesture with a faint smile that never showed teeth. He had once believed the forest could heal anything, if you listened long enough. That belief had not survived his first unanswered prayer.

He tended the sick when sap-fever struck the young. He did not flinch at sweat-soaked bedding, at delirious babbling, or at how a child's skin could burn while the forest outside remained cool and steady.

He regrew wind-shorn branches after storms, standing in the border groves with his staff planted and his free hand pressed to the bark, raw and scarred by weather. He listened until the tree's rhythm steadied. Then he gave it what it needed: water drawn from deep roots, a patient coaxing of growth, and a whispered cadence that felt like comfort.

He mediated disputes between hunters and planters with a calm voice and patient hands, stepping between hot tempers as a man unafraid of being struck. He translated anger into need and accusations into plans. He made people feel heard without ever giving them everything they wanted.

In Graypine Reach, they trusted him as a druid of compassion.

That trust had been earned carefully.

Every morning, he walked the lantern-paths with a basket of seedstones at his hip, greeting sentries by name, asking about their aches, and pausing to watch a child chase a sprite-lure through the moss. His pace was slow, as if he had nowhere urgent to go.

Each afternoon, he worked the border-groves where human axes had once bitten too deep, coaxing new growth from old scars. He touched places that still held the memory of violence: bark healed crookedly, sap lines broken and re-stitched. His magic never forced. It persuaded.

At dusk, he shared food with patrols returning, tired and wary, from the shelves and ravines. He listened more than he spoke. He asked questions that made warriors relax their shoulders without realizing they had been clenched.

He spoke often of balance.

Of restraint.

Of learning from the mistakes that had almost ended them all.

"The forest does not ask for blood," he would say, kneeling to press soil back around a wounded root. "Only remembrance."

And most who heard him believed it.

Because Sablek never lied.

He simply did not tell the whole truth.

He did not tell them that when he knelt beside those roots, part of him listened for a different voice beneath the forest's usual song. A slow pressure. A subtle dissonance. A hollow where something had once been bright.

He did not tell them that when he smiled at children, he measured which ones watched the shadows too closely, which ones flinched at certain syllables, and which ones could be… shaped.

He did not tell them that when he mended a bone, he also studied how readily the body responded to correction.

Correction was once a sacred word.

Now it had become a tool.

When the moon rose thin and pale, and Graypine Reach settled into its nightly rhythm, Sablek gathered his cloak and staff and left the outer dwellings without ceremony.

The Reach at night was not silent. It was quieter, like deep water. Lantern-vines glowed along spiral paths. Fire-root braziers warmed the hollows where elders slept.

Somewhere in the canopy, a nightbird called, a single note repeated at long intervals, like a question no one answered.

Sablek's boots made almost no sound. His staff tapped softly, a rhythm that seemed casual. He did not hurry, yet he moved with certainty. No lingering. No hesitation.

No one challenged him.

Druids moved freely.

The forest parted for him.

Not eagerly.

Not reluctantly.

Simply… knowingly.

That was the unsettling part.

He was accustomed to Holt's awareness, to how a living forest responded to intention. But this was different. The branches above did not bend with warmth. The roots below did not flex with invitation.

They just moved aside.

As if they had been expecting him.

The shrine lay a half-day's walk from the Reach, sunk in a fold of the Holt where the canopy grew too thick for stars. The path to it did not announce itself. It did not want to be found. It revealed itself only to those who already knew where to step.

Sablek followed a row of gray pines whose needles faintly shimmered in the moonlight. The trunks were older than the Reach itself, spaced as if deliberately planted centuries earlier. Their bark bore long scars, healed over and then reopened by time, like old wounds that refuse to fade into mere history.

The deeper he walked, the more the forest changed.

The air cooled, not with altitude, not with night, but with absence.

It sounded dull, and even insects avoided this place. He heard no flutter of moth wings, no chirp of hidden creatures, and no distant rustle that indicated life moving, even when it was unseen.

The Holt's usual scent of resin and damp soil thinned, replaced by something sharp and mineral, like stone, like old ash.

The shrine was not a building so much as a wound made architectural.

A broken arch rose from the roots, a stone half-swallowed by living growth. Once, it had been carved in elegant lines: antlered glyphs, spiraled hunts, and the mark of Aelrindel, etched with a craftsman's reverence.

Now the carvings were scarred.

Half-erased by time.

Half-erased deliberately.

Aelrindel's marks still showed through, stubborn as bone beneath bruised flesh.

The god of the hunt.

Once the patron god of the Wolf Clan.

Now… neglected. Buried. Rewritten.

Sablek passed beneath the arch and felt the shift immediately.

It was the sensation of walking into a room where an argument had just ended.

Torches flickered with a green-black flame, their light unnatural, as if filtered through deep water. The shadows moved oddly, stretching toward the shrine's center rather than away.

The roots grew wrong here.

Too dense.

Too knotted.

Too eager.

They coiled around the stone like fingers around a throat. They threaded through cracks with the insistence of something that wanted to hold, not support. Some of them twitched as Sablek stepped close, responding to his presence like dogs to a familiar master.

Other druids waited within.

Anari, mostly.

Faces familiar from councils and harvest rites, from the polite politics of daily survival. Some wore marks of older clans, long faded, tattoo lines that had softened with age. A few stood apart, their posture wrong for the forest: human shoulders too square, movements too stiff, eyes still learning not to stare at living walls.

They bowed when Sablek entered.

Not to him.

To what he carried.

His staff.

Not the wood itself. The resonance inside it.

Sablek noticed their attention drifting past him. He let it. He subtly tightened his authority, like a cloak settling into place.

He stepped to the center of the shrine and pressed his palm against the stone altar.

The surface pulsed once, like a buried heart remembering how to beat.

"Begin," he said.

The song rose quietly.

Not a chant.

Not harmony.

A deliberate absence of sound, shaped into ritual.

It was not music. It was a gap where music should have been, carefully kept open. It made the air feel both lighter and heavier at once, as if every living thing in the shrine held its breath to listen.

From the roots, they came.

Dark dryads did not simply emerge; they seemed to condense from shadow and bark. Their shapes were discernible only as outlines: feminine figures of twisted wood, long limbs like branch-writhes, and hair that looked like hanging moss until it moved. Their eyes glowed like foxfire in fog. Their mouths curved into expressions that were neither smiles nor hunger.

Old intelligence lived behind those eyes.

Not mortal intelligence.

Forest intelligence.

They watched the gathered druids with an ancient, amused patience.

Then one of them turned and gestured.

The forest responded.

Roots shifted.

Vines parted.

And new figures were led forward as if by invisible hands.

Some were Anari refugees, their faces tight with fear and awe, their eyes too bright, as if they had not slept properly in weeks.

Others were human.

Clothes patched.

Hands scarred from labor rather than ritual.

They had been taken once.

They had returned changed.

Their eyes no longer tracked the world the same way. Their breathing synchronized too easily with the shrine's rhythm. Some still carried faint traces of dryad tongue in their speech, syllables that didn't belong in human mouths.

Sablek watched them with an expression that read as compassion. Most took it as comfort.

A few recognized it as an appraisal.

"You stand at a threshold," Sablek said calmly. "Not between good and evil."

He let the silence gather.

"Between action and extinction."

A murmur spread through the group. Some nodded; others swallowed hard. One person flinched as if the word 'extinction' left a bitter aftertaste of a future he refused to acknowledge.

Sablek continued, his voice steady. "The Malloch feed on conflict. On war. On division. We have seen what endless struggle brings."

He didn't mention Sylos IV. He didn't need to. There were enough refugees here, and the grief hung in the air like smoke.

He let the silence do its work.

"The Crone teaches that peace is not weakness," he said. "It is a path to happiness and security for our peoples."

The dark dryads stepped closer.

Roots rose, shaping circles in the soil.

Runes burned faintly where hands and feet were placed.

Training began.

At first, it seemed harmless.

They learned to bring growth from dead earth, coaxing green life into places where nothing should take root. They learned to mend shallow wounds and ease fevers—the simplest forms of life magic and forest craft. Some smiled upon succeeding, some cried in relief, and others stared at their own hands as if they had discovered a new species of themselves.

Then more.

They learned to coax vines into armor, not just wrapping them but weaving and layering plant fiber into something that could deflect a blade. They figured out how to thicken bark with sap-resin and shape wood into edges that struck like stone.

Then more still.

They learned the names of forest giants.

Not the names whispered in songs.

The names spoken in the ancient language that made the ground respond.

How to awaken them.

How to bind their obedience without chains.

Not through domination, Sablek told them.

Through purpose.

Through offering the giants a reason to move.

They learned to raise what had died beneath the canopy and give it motion again.

Undead giants.

Stitched together from bone and root and old grief.

A human woman gagged as the first one sat up, her empty eyes flashing with green-black light.

An Anari refugee whispered a prayer to Lireal without realizing he still remembered any prayer.

Some flinched.

Some did not.

Sablek watched carefully.

Those who faltered were reassured. Those who embraced it were guided.

No one was forced.

That was important.

Not because Sablek cared about consent in the way most assumed.

Because forced devotion broke.

Willing devotion endured.

"This is not corruption," he told them, gentle as a father explaining death to a child. "It is how their souls continue serving what they fought for in life."

He did not add: and how we turn death into a weapon the living cannot match.

When the rites were finished, several of the human druids stepped forward.

They bowed, not to the dryads, but to Sablek.

Their eyes had that dangerous brightness people got when fear had been replaced by purpose.

"We will return," one said. "To the camps. To Eisenwald's timber roads. We'll teach them to take less and regrow what they cut."

"And if their kings object?" Sablek asked gently.

The man's jaw clenched. He looked older than he should have, as if war had shaped him into something hardened. "Then they will learn the cost of ignorance."

Sablek nodded.

"Take Anari with you," he said. "Observers. Teachers. Protectors." His gaze flicked to the dryads. "And our dryads should go collect more to teach our way."

A few of the gathered druids exchanged glances. The phrase "collect more" sat oddly in the mouth of a man who spoke so often of balance.

The dark dryads watched the group disperse. Some melted back into the forest. Others moved toward the long paths leading into human lands, their steps light, their eyes hungry in the quiet way of predators.

One dryad lingered.

It did not speak aloud.

Its voice slid into Sablek's thoughts like sap into a wound.

The hunter stirs.

Sablek's face did not change. Only his fingers tightened once around his staff.

I know, he replied silently.

Others will follow him.

"They always do," Sablek thought back. Then, carefully, "He is still imprisoned."

The dryad's gaze flicked toward the altar, where Aelrindel's broken sigils lay half-buried beneath newer runes carved by another hand.

This shrine is no longer his.

Sablek did not argue.

He simply asked, as if discussing the weather, "I wonder what prompted the imprisoned one to stir?"

The dryad's smile did not reach its eyes.

Memory.

Then, softer, like a leaf brushing skin:

Or a woman who refuses to let sleeping things remain buried.

Sablek felt the faintest chill.

Not fear.

Annoyance.

Because he understood the implication, even if he could not yet prove it.

He extinguished the torches one by one. Each green-black flame died with a sound like breath leaving a throat. The shrine grew darker, yet it did not feel emptier.

If anything, it felt more awake.

He stepped back into the forest, his cloak settling over his shoulders, his expression smoothing into the one Graypine Reach trusted.

By morning, he would be tending roots again.

By night, the forest would continue learning new songs.

Songs of peace.

Songs of restraint.

Songs strong enough, he believed, to keep the Malloch forever banished.

And far away, in timber camps and border groves, humans began to listen.

Not to the Holt.

Not to Aelrindel.

To a quieter voice, beneath the roots, that promised them a way to survive at any cost.

Dark druid summoning a forest giant.

Chapter 5 — The Shadow Grove

Planet: Vaelthara
Divine Year of Vaelthas — Wolf Month, 21,426 Years Since the Sealing
Faelwyn Holt — The Old Dueling Grove

"Shadow remembers what light forgets."
— *Ellendyl Felhart*

The grove lay cradled beneath the oldest boughs of Faelwyn Holt, a place where the canopy knotted so tightly overhead that daylight arrived already exhausted.

Even at midday, the light here came thin and diffused, slipping between leaves as pale ribbons of silver-blue shadow. It painted the clearing in gradients rather than edges. Nothing was fully illuminated. Nothing entirely hidden.

Torches ringed the grove at measured intervals, their flames steady but subtly bent inward, drawn by unseen currents. Their light did not banish the shadows. It refined them. The grove seemed to breathe in time with the fire, exhaling faint motes of ash that drifted upward and vanished among the leaves.

Nine hundred recruits stood in ordered ranks.

They had trained here for two weeks.

Two weeks of bruised forearms and trembling calves. Two weeks of breath counted, uncounted, then forgotten. Two weeks of learning that instinct was not something to be obeyed—but something to be dismantled and rebuilt from silence.

Blades rested at their feet. Harmonic focus stones lay arranged beside them in precise alignment. Not discarded. Not casual. Placed.

Wolf Clan warriors formed a wide semicircle around the recruits, their presence heavy and watchful. Veterans of the ravines. Rangers who could loose arrows through fog and leaf-shadow without sight. Their usual murmurs were absent.

Everyone present understood what this session marked.

Completion.

Ellendyl stepped onto the wide stump at the grove's center.

Silence followed her the way gravity followed mass.

Her auburn hair was tightly braided down her back, shot through with ember-bright strands that caught the torchlight and then vanished again as she moved. Her bronze skin held a faint metallic sheen, not reflective so much as dense, as if light could not fully penetrate it. Black leather armor wrapped her frame, scuffed and worn from relentless use, shaped to her body with the intimacy of something long lived in.

She did not raise her voice.

She did not need to.

"Dark-mage warriors," Ellendyl said evenly. "Three forms today. Close-quarter termination. Shadow breaks. Harmonic reversals."

She paused.

For a fraction of a heartbeat, a memory intruded unbidden: her father's office on Sylvara Prime, sunlight slanting through reinforced glass, his smile when she stepped inside carrying field reports too heavy for her age.

The memory crystallized.

Then she let it go.

"Watch first."

She drew her twin blades.

The grove shifted.

Not visibly. Not dramatically. But every Anari present felt it—the subtle realignment of breath, root, and resonance. Her Catal'ri emerged low and steady, a subharmonic pulse that slid beneath conscious thought and tightened posture without command. Spines straightened. Focus sharpened. Even the torches seemed to burn more quietly.

Ellendyl moved.

Not fast.

Not slow.

Inevitable.

Her footwork traced inward spirals that never quite repeated, each step a correction of the last. The seichūsen bent like moonlight caught between leaves, paths of intent folding inward and outward simultaneously. When she turned, leaves lifted from the ground, spiraling in her wake, responding not to wind but to geometry.

Shadow thickened around her without obscuring her.

When the form ended, it did so in perfect stillness.

No flourish.

No echo.

The Wolf Clan warriors watched with something like reverence.

The recruits watched as if witnessing a language they had once known and forgotten.

And the three instructors watched—each with their own tell.

Maedhrin paced behind his cohort, ember-bright auburn hair loose and restless, fingers twitching with barely leashed impatience. "Again," he snapped. "Your timing is late. Listen to the silence between the notes."

His Catal'ri flared sharp and uneven, frustration bleeding into the sound.

Ellendyl glanced his way.

Just once.

Maedhrin inhaled, visibly reigning himself in, smoothing his harmonic without comment.

On the far side of the grove, Dherak stood unmoving, a living monolith. Huge, bronze-skinned, shoulders like carved stone. His leaf-brown eyes tracked everything. When he corrected a student's stance, his massive hand rested with unsettling gentleness, fingers lingering a fraction longer than comfort allowed, measuring pressure, balance, readiness.

Near the center stood Vaelis.

Rust-gold auburn hair braided simply.

Plain traveler's tunic.

Hands clasped loosely behind his back.

When Ellendyl said, "Vaelis. Demonstrate the Spiral Break," he stepped forward without hesitation.

His movements were clean. Balanced. Purposeful.

His Catal'ri flowed warm and steady, a harmonic that soothed rather than compelled. Several recruits straightened unconsciously as he moved, breaths evening, muscles finding balance without understanding why.

He finished. Stepped back. Gaze lowered.

He accepted neither praise nor acknowledgment.

Wolf Clan warriors murmured softly among themselves.

"Steady."

"Reliable."

"A grounding presence."

Nothing about him demanded attention.

That, too, was noticed.

Lady Vyrna entered the grove without announcement.

Her presence carried its own resonance.

Autumnfire auburn braids crowned her head, loose now from the mourning-weave. Bark-steel armor shimmered deep green along her shoulders, etched with life-runes that pulsed softly in time with her breath. Talismans at her wrists glowed faintly, responding to her proximity.

Warriors bowed.

Recruits straightened.

Even the torches leaned.

She watched in silence.

Ellendyl approached her between drills. "You wished to see their progress."

Vyrna nodded slowly. "This style is not in the Codex Harmonica."

"No," Ellendyl said. "It predates it."

"How far?"

"Far enough that it was forgotten on purpose."

Vyrna absorbed that without flinching. "My people need something that lasts."

Her gaze drifted, briefly, to Vaelis as he guided a struggling recruit through a transition, patient hands correcting foot placement.

"He steadies the ground beneath me," Vyrna said quietly. "After everything… that matters."

Ellendyl allowed herself a small smile. "Then I'm glad."

The drills resumed.

Maedhrin pushed his students hard, though with increasing restraint.

Dherak demonstrated defensive breaks that felt immovable.

Vaelis corrected form with gentle words and careful hands.

Focus stones glowed.

Harmonics rippled.

Nothing felt wrong.

At last, Ellendyl raised a hand.

"Enough."

The recruits knelt. The grove exhaled.

Fireflies drifted into the clearing, their light weaving between torchflame and shadow.

Vyrna stepped forward.

"My people," she said. "In seven days, we gather at Heartroot Vale. A joining will be celebrated. A promise renewed."

Warmth spread through the grove like sap through roots.

Ellendyl did not linger.

She turned to the instructors. "You will continue. The forms are yours now. Guard them well."

Maedhrin nodded fiercely.

Dherak inclined his head.

Vaelis bowed, respectful and silent.

Ellendyl stepped down from the stump.

The grove did not follow her.

As she walked beneath the canopy, the torches straightened. The air loosened. The forest released the breath it had been holding.

Behind her, the Shadow Grove continued its work.

Ahead of her, other paths waited.

And what she had planted here—nine hundred lives trained in forgotten geometry—would grow without her.

Whether it bent toward protection…

Or something darker…

That was no longer hers to decide.

Chapter 6 - A Killer's Cunning

Planet: Vaelthara
Location: Faelwyn Holt — Near the Ravine Shelf
Divine Year of Vaelthas — Wolf Month, 21,426 Years Since the Sealing

"Truth leaves tracks. Lies leave poses."
— *Old Sylvancrest investigative axiom*

The druid arrived at dusk.

Not running.

Not breathless.

Not panicked.

That alone made Kholfax uneasy.

He emerged from the lantern-shadow between trees as if he had been expected, boots clean, cloak unruffled. The leaf-clasp of the Wolf Clan gleamed at his collar, freshly polished. His ember-dark hair was neatly braided, not a strand loose. His bark-staff bore no scratches, no mud, no sap. It was the staff of someone who had walked nowhere dangerous.

"A patrol is dead," the druid said.

His voice was calm. Measured. Almost apologetic.

Froster's head lifted instantly, posture tightening like a drawn wire. Khandyl stilled beside the fire-ring, one hand settling lightly on her bow, thumb brushing the fletching of an arrow she had not yet chosen.

Inside Kholfax, something old and cold clicked into place.

The switch that never slept.

"How?" Kholfax asked.

The druid hesitated.

Just long enough.

"They were found standing," he said. "As if frozen. No wounds at first glance."

That word struck like a hammer.

Standing.

Kholfax kept his face neutral, though his pulse had already quickened. "Where?"

"Near the old shrine spur," the druid replied. "Close to Graypine Reach. We should go now. Before scavengers. Before… confusion."

Before questions, Kholfax thought.

He nodded once. "Take us."

They moved fast.

Six Wolf Clan warriors, spreading into patrol formation with practiced ease. Khandyl took point, reading the forest ahead with her whole body. Froster anchored the rear, head turning constantly, eyes never still. Kholfax walked the center, listening.

The forest was wrong.

Not hostile.

Not loud.

Absent.

No insects chirred. No nightbirds called. Even the wind seemed to curve away from the path ahead, brushing leaves aside rather than passing through them. The roots beneath their boots felt tense, coiled like muscles waiting for a signal.

They reached the clearing just as night finished settling.

Seven Anari stood where the druid had said they would.

Upright.

Eyes open.

Weapons still gripped in rigid hands.

Dead.

No blood stained the ground. No broken branches. No drag marks. The poses were too precise, too intentional, like statues arranged for viewing.

Kholfax's stomach tightened.

He had seen this before.

"Don't touch anything," he said automatically.

Too late.

The air thickened.

Not with sound.

With pressure.

The first harmonic rolled through the clearing like an invisible hand closing around the spine. Kholfax felt it enter him at the base of the skull and travel downward, locking vertebrae one by one.

His knees buckled.

The world tilted.

Then snapped rigid.

Breath went shallow. Muscles froze mid-motion. His heart hammered uselessly against a cage it could no longer command.

Around him, the Wolf Clan patrol stiffened, bodies locking in staggered positions, eyes wide with sudden understanding.

A figure stepped from the trees.

Hooded.

Masked.

Wrapped in a distortion that bent light just enough to make the eye slide away. The forest itself seemed unwilling to focus on him.

Behind him, dark druids emerged hesitantly, faces pale, eyes too bright. Even they looked afraid.

The hooded figure lifted one hand.

And sang.

Not loudly.

Not dramatically.

The harmony slipped into bone and nerve and breath, threading itself through the body with terrifying precision. Kholfax felt it examine him, cataloging heart rhythm, lung cadence, neural response.

Clinical.

Curious.

The patrol began to die.

No screams.

No thrashing.

Hearts simply… stopped.

Lungs forgot their rhythm.

Bodies remained upright, held in place by the same harmonic cage that pinned Kholfax in place.

Standing dead.

One of the dark druids whispered, voice shaking, "That wasn't—"

The hooded figure cut the note.

Silence slammed down like a lid.

Then movement returned.

Dark druids stepped forward quickly, efficiently. This was not their first cleanup.

A thin blade flashed.

Seven throats were cut.

Blood flowed freely now, but the bodies did not fall.

Someone pressed a dagger into Kholfax's frozen hand. Carefully. Precisely. His fingers were wrapped around the hilt, positioned just so.

Another dark druid smeared blood along his forearm. His sleeve. His chest.

The hooded figure leaned close.

Kholfax could not see his eyes.

Only the mask.

Only the breath behind it.

This is a performance, Kholfax thought, helpless. Every detail chosen.

Then the pressure vanished.

Air rushed back into his lungs. His knees gave out. He collapsed to one knee, gasping, vision swimming.

The clearing was empty.

The dead patrol still stood.

And he was holding a bloody knife.

Khandyl arrived first.

Froster second.

They took in the scene in a single breath.

Bodies.

Knife.

Blood.

Poses.

Kholfax dropped the dagger immediately. "I was set up."

Not accused.

Organized.

Khandyl's eyes moved over him with ruthless speed, cataloging blood spatter, hand position, distance to the bodies. Her jaw tightened.

Froster crouched beside one of the dead, fingers brushing a wrist, then a throat. He shook his head slowly.

"This wasn't blades," he said. "This was harmonics."

Kholfax met his gaze. "Yes."

A second patrol emerged from the trees.

Then a third.

Whispers spread faster than reason.

"He was alone with them."

"He's from the future."

"He hunted killers."

Kholfax forced himself upright. His legs trembled, but he stood. "Listen to me. The killer was here. Masked. Hooded. Powerful. Far more than a druid."

The druid who had led them stepped forward.

"I saw him," he said quietly. "I saw Kholfax do it."

The words struck like stones dropped into water.

Kholfax stared at him. "You're lying."

The druid met his gaze calmly. "I watched you sing them dead."

Froster turned slowly. "That's not true."

But others were no longer listening.

Hands drifted toward weapons.

Eyes hardened.

Khandyl raised her bow—not aimed, but unmistakably present. "Enough."

Lady Vyrna's authority had not arrived.

Judgment already had.

"Bind him," someone said.

Kholfax did not resist when they took his arms.

He did not need to.

The forest watched.

And somewhere beyond the lantern-light, a masked figure walked away untouched, leaving certainty to rot behind him.

Chapter 7 — The Weight Of The Holt

Planet: Vaelthara
Location: Faelwyn Holt — Heartroot Vale, Judgment Ring
Divine Year of Vaelthas — Wolf Month, 21,426 Years Since the Sealing

"A forest that hesitates to cut rot will lose its heartwood."
— *Wolf Clan proverb*

Heartroot Vale was full.
Not with celebration.
With judgment.

The natural amphitheater formed by the colossal roots of the Holt had been cleared of market stalls, training racks, and council benches. What remained was bare earth braided with living root-veins, polished smooth by centuries of footsteps and ritual. Lantern-vines burned dim and steady along the upper arches, their light refracted through resin-glass leaves grown for this purpose alone. The glow hummed softly, tuned to the Vale's acoustics.

Sound traveled here.

So did intent.

Truth as well, or so the clan believed.

Kholfax stood bound at the center.

No chains.

No hood.

Only a white cord, grown from a living vine, looped around his wrists and ankles in druidic knots that tightened or loosened in response to breath, heartbeat, and the collective will of those present. The cord was warm against his skin. Alive. It did not hurt him.

That made it worse.

Wolf Clan warriors ringed the space, their bark-steel armor catching lanternlight in muted greens and browns.

Elders sat higher, perched on root-seats grown to their shapes over decades. Recruits filled the outer tiers—Anari, refugees, future-born—faces tight with fear, suspicion, and the terrible relief of not being the one standing alone.

The dead patrol stood in memory between them.

Lady Vyrna stood above him on the root-dais.

Still.

Straight.

Unyielding.

Her posture was perfect, shoulders squared, chin lifted just enough to project authority without arrogance. Bark-steel armor traced her frame in layered plates grown from living oak and ironwood. Her life-mage talismans—usually pulsing with quiet vitality—were dark and inert tonight, as if even they were listening rather than speaking.

When she spoke, her voice carried without effort.

"You are accused," Vyrna said, "of murdering Wolf Clan warriors under the protection of the Holt."

No ceremony.

No invocation.

No softened language.

Kholfax lifted his chin. His wrists ached slightly as the vine responded to his movement.

"I didn't do it."

A ripple moved through the Vale.

Not outrage.

Recognition.

Everyone had expected that answer.

"You were found alone," an elder said, voice dry as old bark.

"With the blade," another added, fingers tightening on a staff.

"Standing dead," someone whispered, the words barely audible but heavy enough to spread.

Kholfax turned slowly, meeting eyes wherever he could—hunters, trainees, elders, and refugees who had watched him teach archery and tracking only days earlier.

"That," he said evenly, "is the killer's signature. Not mine."

The murmur that followed was uneasy at first—then hardened, as doubt curdled into something sharper.

A hunter stepped forward, scarred and broad-shouldered, eyes bright with anger. "You hunted this killer in your time."

"Yes."

"And he escaped you."

"Yes."

"You followed him here."

"No," Kholfax said. His voice did not rise. "We fled extinction. He used that to escape us."

The distinction died in the air.

Froster moved then, stepping into the Judgment Ring without waiting for permission.

A ripple of disapproval followed him.

"This was not blade-work," Froster said. His voice carried the clipped authority of someone used to being obeyed. "It was harmonic execution. Advanced. Controlled. Deliberate."

"Enough," an elder snapped. "You were not there."

"I arrived minutes after," Froster replied. "And I know sound. I have faced Osiri necromancers and lived."

Khandyl joined him, bow unstrung, posture respectful but unyielding. Her presence shifted the tone of the ring—she was Wolf Clan to the marrow.

"Kholfax warned us," she said. "Before this happened. He described the killings. The poses. The sound."

Vyrna's gaze sharpened, eyes narrowing slightly. "Foreknowledge can be guilt."

"Or experience," Khandyl replied.

A third voice entered the ring.

Calm.

Measured.

Almost gentle.

"Treason thrives on doubt."

All eyes turned.

Vaelis stepped forward.

No armor.

No blade drawn.

Hands open, empty, visible.

His rust-gold auburn hair was simply braided, and his clothing was plain traveler's garb—nothing that marked rank or ambition. He bowed deeply to Vyrna before speaking, the gesture flawless in its humility.

"My Lady," he said softly, "I believe Kholfax is dangerous."

A murmur of agreement followed—relief, even. Someone was saying what many felt.

"But," Vaelis continued, lifting his gaze just enough to meet the crowd, "I do not believe execution serves the Holt."

The Vale stilled.

"A killer who deceived an entire future civilization," he went on, "will not be undone by a blade. If he is guilty, death is release. If innocent, it is injustice."

Kholfax looked at him sharply.

The man's tone was reasonable. Compassionate. Persuasive.

"Exile," Vaelis said. "Cast him beyond the Holt. Strip him of protection. Let the forest decide what remains of him."

It was elegant.

Measured.

Merciful.

Too merciful.

Vyrna studied Vaelis for a long moment. Her face revealed nothing, but something in her shoulders shifted—an almost imperceptible tightening.

Then her gaze returned to Kholfax.

"You heard the argument," she said. "What say you?"

Kholfax spoke quietly. "The real killer is still here."

That did it.

Voices rose.

Anger flared.

"He accuses us now!"

"He hides behind shadows!"

"He mocks the dead!"

Vyrna raised her hand.

Silence snapped into place, sharp and absolute.

"No," she said.

The word landed like a felled tree.

"No exile," she continued. "No wandering killer allowed to stalk other clans. No doubt carried like a wound."

Her voice did not shake.

"A killer cannot live among us. Not bound. Not banished. Not spared."

Kholfax felt the decision settle before she finished.

"By Wolf Clan law," Vyrna said, "Kholfax is condemned."

The vine-cord around his wrists tightened slightly, responding to the gathered intent.

Froster stepped forward again. "Vyrna—"

She did not look at him.

Khandyl's hand closed into a fist.

Vyrna's gaze lowered. "Place him in the deep pit until dawn. The forest will hear him. The ancestors will hear him."

A pause.

"Then judgment will be fulfilled."

The crowd exhaled as one—relief, grief, certainty tangled together.

Guards stepped forward.

Kholfax did not resist.

As they led him away, he met Froster's eyes once.

Not pleading.

Not despairing.

Certain.

Froster remembered something Topkr had once said, long ago, during a winter patrol:

If the forest turns on you, ask who taught it to lie.

Froster said nothing now.

But the old ranger's voice would not leave him.

The pit yawned beneath the roots of Heartroot Vale—a vertical shaft grown, not dug, lined with bark-hard walls that swallowed light and sound alike. The opening breathed cold air upward, scented with damp earth and ancient sap.

They lowered him down slowly.

Lanternlight thinned.

Voices faded.

The vine-cord released at the bottom.

Darkness closed.

Above, the Holt continued to breathe.

And somewhere within it, a killer smiled—patient, unseen, perfectly placed.

Chapter 8 — The Holt Opens

Planet: Vaelthara
Location: Faelwyn Holt — Heartroot Deeps and Northbound Runs
Divine Year of Vaelthas — Wolf Month, 21,426 Years Since the Sealing

"The forest does not hide you.
It decides whether you belong."
— *Wolf Clan night-chant*

The pit did not sleep.
It breathed.

Kholfax sat with his back pressed against living bark, knees drawn in, boots planted in soil that was never quite still. The walls around him flexed subtly, roots tightening and relaxing in slow cycles, as if the Holt itself were dreaming. Sap moved above and below, not dripping but flowing with the muted persistence of deep water. Every sound arrived altered, softened, filtered through layers of wood and memory, as if the forest considered each vibration before allowing it to exist.

The dark here was not empty.

It was attentive.

Time lost its meaning in the pit. There was no way to mark it. No wind. No stars. No lantern glow bleeding down from above. Just breath, heartbeat, and the distant weight of roots pressing in from every direction.

Then the dark changed.

Not with light.

With absence.

A presence interrupted the rhythm.

A hand appeared on the rim above him—bare, calloused, steady.

Kholfax tensed, every muscle coiling despite exhaustion.

A shape flowed down the wall without a sound or scrape, moving with the ease of something born to vertical spaces. Khandyl landed lightly beside him, knees bent, bow already in hand, eyes scanning shadows that had not yet decided what they were.

"Quiet," she breathed—not a command, but a courtesy to the Holt.

Another figure followed, heavier but no less controlled.

Froster dropped beside them, armor muted with moss and sap, breath measured, eyes already counting exits that did not yet exist.

Behind them, three more figures descended along woven root-lines: elders, ancient hunters whose names carried weight even when spoken softly. Their faces were lined like old bark, their eyes sharp with a patience that had endured centuries.

"You're late," Kholfax whispered.

Froster's mouth twitched faintly. "You were sentenced at dusk. We're early."

The vine-cord binding the pit shimmered as Khandyl pressed two fingers to it and sang—barely audible, a low wolf-note threaded with restraint and belonging. The living knots loosened, not severed, recognizing her Song and yielding without protest.

Froster extended a vine rope. "Up."

Kholfax took it.

No one said I believe you.

Breaking judgment was answer enough.

The moment his boots touched the upper root again, the Holt shifted.

Not alarmed.

Aware.

It was the sensation of being noticed by something vast and old that had just decided to keep watching.

They moved.

Not running.

Flowing.

Lantern-vines dimmed as they passed, drawing their light inward like pupils narrowing. Moss compressed beneath their feet and sprang back behind them, erasing both pressure and memory. Paths curved softly, turning straight intent into spirals that favored those who remembered over those who rushed.

Khandyl glanced at the lanterns and murmured, "The forest is with us."

They reached the first outer terrace when the horn sounded.

Short.

Sharp.

Search.

"Go," Khandyl hissed.

They broke into a run.

The Holt closed ranks behind them.

Branches dipped at shoulder height for pursuers and lifted smoothly for Kholfax. Roots surfaced like ribs, catching armored boots and guiding bare or bark-soled feet. Ferns brushed faces—not scratching, not slowing—only marking passage with a cool, damp touch.

Then the first shot cracked the dark.

Queen's Kiss.

A pale blue lance of harmonic light cut through the canopy, freezing leaves mid-fall and casting trunks into stark, ghostly relief. Sap crystallized. Shadows fractured.

Kholfax flinched on instinct alone.

"Keep moving," Froster growled.

Another shot followed, closer this time.

The light lingered, hanging in the air like frozen breath before dissolving into a spray of blue sparks that hissed as they touched bark.

The patrol was close.

Too close.

Khandyl veered left without warning. The others followed instantly, trusting her without question. The ground dipped sharply, then rose into a snarl of thornroot that parted just long enough for them to slip through before sealing again with a sound like bone knitting.

Behind them, shouts.

A hunter cursed as bark tore through greaves.

Another Queen's Kiss flared—too high—shattering a branch into ice-crystals that rained down uselessly, tinkling like broken glass.

They reached the ravine edge.

Mist boiled up from below, cold and thick, carrying the mineral tang of stone and water from far beneath the canopy. The drop yawned wide and unforgiving.

Kholfax's heart hammered.

"This way," one of the elders whispered—and stepped forward.

Not falling.

Dropping onto a hidden root-bridge grown just wide enough for those the Holt recognized.

They crossed single file, breath held, balance instinctive rather than conscious.

Halfway over, a Queen's Kiss struck the ravine wall.

Blue light exploded across stone, illuminating everything in stark clarity.

Kholfax saw the patrol then—six figures fanning out with disciplined precision, movements clean, relentless, professional.

And he saw what they did not.

The bridge behind him faded.

Not vanished.

Forgotten.

By the time the patrol reached the edge, there was nothing to see—only mist and the echo of certainty dissolving into doubt.

They reached the far side and plunged into undergrowth so dense it swallowed sound whole. Leaves overlaid leaves. Vines layered upon vines. The forest leaned inward, conspiratorial and intimate.

After another hundred strides, Froster raised a fist.

They stopped.

Listened.

Footsteps approached—then slowed.

Voices argued softly, uncertainty threading through confidence.

"I had them here."

"No, the trail bends."

"There—no—wait—"

Silence.

The Holt breathed.

Minutes passed. Then more.

At last, a horn sounded again—longer this time. Frustrated. Official.

The patrol withdrew toward camp.

Kholfax exhaled for the first time since the pit, the breath shaking despite his control.

"They'll resume at dawn," he said.

"Yes," Khandyl agreed. "And they will not find you."

Froster turned to him. "You're an outlaw now. That means no paths, no calls, no spoken names aloud."

Kholfax nodded. "I can live with that."

One of the elders studied him, gaze weighing more than flesh. "The Holt chose tonight."

"That doesn't mean it will choose again," Kholfax said.

Khandyl met his eyes. "Then we'll move before it has to decide."

They turned north, deeper into shadow, where paths were rumor and survival depended on listening rather than knowing.

Behind them, Heartroot Vale slept—convinced justice had been served.

Ahead, the forest opened just enough to let a hunted man pass.

And far away, beneath lantern light and quiet vows, someone counted time very carefully.

Chapter 9 — Roots and Omens

Planet: Vaelthara
Location: Faelwyn Holt — Heartroot Vale
Divine Year of Vaelthas — Wolf Month, 21,426 Years Since the Sealing

"Some choices echo longer than lives."
— *Sylph proverb*

Heartroot Vale had dressed itself for celebration.

Lantern-vines arched high above the clearing, their living filaments glowing warm and steady, tuned not to any single heartbeat but to the shared rhythm of the gathered clan. Flowering creepers spilled from balconies grown directly into the great roots, their petals drifting down in slow spirals like patient snow. Music threaded through the air: low drums echoing the Holt's pulse, flutes carved from bonewood, and voices braided in working harmonies that rose and fell with practiced ease.

The Vale was not merely hosting joy.

It was participating in it.

The Windstreams arrived at dusk.

Griffyn shadows swept across the clearing, vast wings stirring petals and laughter alike. Children broke from their games and ran to the edges of the Vale, pointing skyward. Warriors straightened unconsciously. Elders paused mid-conversation, their attention pulled upward by an instinct older than etiquette.

Kellyn dismounted first.

She wore no armor, only travel leathers and the silver-threaded cloak of her clan, its sigils catching lantern-light like quiet constellations. Her auburn hair, streaked with lighter ember, was tied back simply. Her posture was composed, her expression calm.

Only Harvey knew better.

He followed her down moments later, his boots touching the living root, and felt the Vale react—not with alarm, but with recognition. A subtle ripple passed through the gathered Anari, like wind through tall grass. Heads turned. Conversations faltered.

The Green Knight had returned.

Not as story.

Not as symbol.

In flesh.

Vyrna emerged from the heart of the Vale to greet them.

She wore bark-steel armor worked with living filigree, plates grown rather than forged, catching the light in deep greens and muted golds. Life-talismans at her wrists pulsed softly with her breath. Joy sat easily on her now, worn without strain or vigilance.

"Kellyn Windstream," she said warmly. "You honor us."

Kellyn bowed, precise and respectful. "We would not miss this."

Her eyes moved immediately, cataloging faces by instinct rather than curiosity.

Froster.

Khandyl.

Neither was there.

Vyrna's gaze flicked briefly to Harvey. Something in it sharpened, not suspicion but assessment.

"You carry weight with you, Green Knight," she said.

Harvey smiled faintly. "I seem to be collecting it."

She gestured toward the inner roots. "Walk with me."

They left the music behind.

The heart-chambers of Heartroot Vale were quieter, older. The great roots here were as wide as towers, etched with faded glyphs from hunts long past, their lines softened by centuries of touch. The air smelled of deep earth and old sap, rich and grounding.

"This Vale," Vyrna said, resting a hand against the living wall, "was once sacred to him."

Harvey stopped. The word rose unbidden.

"Aelrindel."

She nodded. "The Hunter God. Before the Crone's shadow. Before the Sealing. He taught us to move unseen and to hear the forest breathe. When he was taken, something… went silent."

Harvey felt the pull then.

Not metaphorical.

A pressure behind his eyes. A tightening in his chest. A direction that did not ask permission.

"He came to me in a dream," he said quietly.

Vyrna did not look surprised. "He would. You stand between life and death more easily than most."

She turned to face him fully.

"Something Aelrindel carried was taken from him during his imprisonment," she said. "To my knowledge, it is the only thing he has ever lost."

She drew a slow breath.

"It lies in the Frost Giant citadel near the pole. Frozen. Guarded. Placed there so no living Anari could reclaim it."

Harvey exhaled slowly. "But I can."

Kellyn held his gaze.

"You are the Green Knight," she said. "If anyone can carry something that once belonged to a god into the Greenwood, it is you."

She did not soften her voice when she finished.

"The forest will not permit anyone else."

"And if I free him?"

Her voice softened. "Then the Wolf Clan remembers who we were meant to be."

She stepped closer. "But hear this clearly. The Crone will oppose you. She bound him. The giants serve her designs, whether they know it or not."

Harvey nodded. "I've met worse."

Vyrna studied him for a long moment, then inclined her head. "I believe you."

They returned to the Vale as the music swelled again.

Kellyn was waiting.

She read Harvey's face instantly.

"No," she said.

Not loudly.

Not dramatically.

Just the word.

She had faced gods, war councils, and extinction.

This was worse.

This was watching someone she loved walk toward something that might never let him walk back.

He took her hands. "I have to."

"Elowen's vision—" Her voice caught. "She said the cost would be terrible."

"I know."

"You don't," Kellyn said fiercely. "You never do."

For a heartbeat, the future pressed in around them—threads tightening, paths narrowing.

Harvey rested his forehead against hers. "If I don't go, everything else we're fighting collapses later. Worse."

She closed her eyes.

When she opened them again, she nodded once. "Then you won't go alone."

"Sylveron offered," Harvey said. "And Seri. And the sylph warriors."

Kellyn swallowed. "I don't like the math on that."

"I don't either."

They parted while the music still played.

Harvey did not stay for the feast.

Before dawn, he took word from an old fire giant trader—Toluscpatn, a keep of stone and magma where rumors moved faster than lava. From there, the citadel's location could be traced.

By midday, he was gone north, griffyn wings beating toward ice and shadow. Sylveron, Seri, Vaellinae, and Serithyl flew with him.

Kellyn stayed.

And the Vale changed shape around her.

The joy thinned. Conversations softened. Whispers took on edges.

She learned first from a Wolf Clan ranger with eyes too careful. Then, from a druid who would not meet her gaze.

Kholfax.

Outlawed.

Escaped.
Helped by Froster.
By Khandyl.

The words refused to sit together cleanly.

"They say he killed a patrol," the ranger added, uncertain. "Stood them dead."

Kellyn felt a cold certainty settle into her chest.

"That isn't how he kills," she said.

The ranger blinked. "You've seen this before?"

"I've hunted it."

More reports followed before nightfall.

Human timber camps along the western edge had changed. Rangers moved with newfound confidence. Druids walked openly among them. Forest giants had been sighted beyond the tree line.

Not attacking.

Defending.

Kellyn stood at the edge of the Vale, listening to the forest argue with itself—roots pulling in different directions, Song overlapping with Song.

Harvey had gone north into myth.

She turned south, toward smoke and steel and decisions that would not wait for prophecy.

"Ready the patrol," she said quietly.

The Windstream banner stirred.

Two paths diverged beneath the same canopy.
And neither would allow retreat.

Chapter 10 — The Promise Spoken Aloud

Planet: Vaelthara
Location: Faelwyn Holt — Heartroot Vale
Divine Year of Vaelthas — Wolf Month, 21,426 Years Since the Sealing

"Even wolves lay down their teeth when the world remembers joy."
— *Old Wolf Clan saying*

Heartroot Vale bloomed.
Not all at once.
Not loudly.

The forest dressed itself with patience.

Lantern-vines unfurled in slow, deliberate arcs from root to branch, as if mindful not to startle old grief. Petal-lights drifted through the air like fireflies that had learned restraint, settling briefly on shoulders, hair, and armor, then lifting again, unwilling to choose permanence.

Living banners of woven moss and silverleaf grew between the great roots, bearing the Wolf Clan's sigils and, older still, the antlered mark of the Hunt. Some of those sigils had not been displayed together for centuries.

Music rose before the guests fully gathered.

Drums first. Low. Deep. A heartbeat meant to steady, not excite. Flutes followed, carved from windwood and bone, their tones braided into melodies that remembered winters survived, and summers returned. Voices joined last, never solo, never dominant, harmonies shaped to disappear unless heard together.

The refugees stood shoulder to shoulder with the old blood of the Holt.

Some wore bark-steel polished to a ceremonial sheen. Others wore travel leathers still scarred by flight, stitched and restitched by hands that had known panic. No one was turned away. Children wove among the roots, laughter ringing where fear had lingered too long. Elders sat with hands folded, watching not the present but how it layered itself over memory.

Vyrna emerged as the drums slowed.

She wore no helm.

Her auburn hair was braided in the old way, crown-bound and threaded with pale bone charms that clicked softly as she moved. Her armor was ceremonial bark-steel, grown thin, etched with living leaf-and-moon patterns that shifted subtly with her breath. Life-mage talismans at her wrists glowed a steady gold, not bright, but certain.

When she stepped onto the central platform, the Vale stilled.

Vaelis followed.

He wore simple, unadorned robes, save for a single clasp at the shoulder shaped like a sleeping wolf. No sigils. No finery. No visible weapon. His posture was calm, his movements unhurried, as if haste had never learned his name.

To many, he looked like what the Holt needed.

Steady.

Present.

Unassuming.

They faced one another beneath the oldest root, its bark etched with the names of unions that had endured famine, war, exile, and forgetting. The elder druid who spoke the binding words did not raise her voice. She did not need to.

"This joining is not conquest," she said. "It is a covenant."

Vyrna and Vaelis clasped hands.

The forest responded.

Not with spectacle.

With agreement.

A breath moved through the canopy. Lanterns brightened by a fraction. Somewhere deep below, roots shifted, settling as if to accommodate a new weight.

The vows were spoken.

Not long.

Not ornate.

Promises of watchfulness. Of shared burden. Of loyalty chosen rather than inherited.

When the binding chord was sung, three voices layered into one. The Vale answered with a low harmonic hum that vibrated gently through bone and bark alike. Some of the refugees felt it in their chests and did not know why tears followed.

Then came the feast.

Tables grew from the roots, their smooth surfaces rising and locking into place with soft wooden clicks. Platters followed: roast game glazed in berry reduction, mushrooms stuffed with spiced grains, breads steamed in leaf-wraps that unfurled when torn. Sap-mead poured into carved cups that warmed the hands that held them.

Laughter returned in waves.

Stories traded hands like gifts. Cups lifted. Old warriors danced with children too young to know why this moment mattered, only that it did.

Kellyn stood at the edge of it, watching.

She smiled when spoken to. She accepted food she barely tasted. Her eyes kept returning to Vyrna, radiant and relieved, and to Vaelis, who moved easily among the guests, listening more than speaking and offering presence instead of opinion.

Nothing about him stood out.

That troubled her.

When the feast settled and the music softened again, a druid rose near the central table.

He was unremarkable in appearance: gray-green robes, hair bound simply, staff marked with the runes of renewal and growth. A healer by trade. Known. Trusted.

He lifted his staff slightly, not in command, but in request.

"May I speak?"

The Vale quieted.

"We have all fled something," the druid said gently. "Fire. Darkness. The Unmaking Choir." A murmur rippled through the name. "We remember what war costs. We remember what it takes."

Heads nodded. Faces tightened.

"We have a chance," he continued, "to choose a different path, to lay down old hostilities. Humans, Anari, all races united in peace. If we do not provoke war, perhaps the Malloch will never find purchase here again."

The silence stretched.

Then someone whispered, "Peace."

Another voice followed. "We've lost enough."

Kellyn felt it then.

The exhaustion.

The longing.

The terrible seduction of rest.

She looked to Vyrna.

The Wolf Clan matriarch hesitated.

Just for a heartbeat.

Vaelis stepped closer. He did not speak. He did not gesture.

He placed a hand over hers.

A simple thing.

A devastating one.

The forest leaned—not loudly, not visibly—but enough.

Vyrna straightened.

Her voice carried. "We will pursue peace. With humans. With all who will honor it. We will not invite war where it need not go."

Cheers rose—relieved, grateful, almost desperate.

Kellyn did not join them.

She lowered her cup.

Said nothing.

The feast swelled again, brighter now, with hope permitted to breathe. Lanterns glowed warmer. Children laughed louder. Songs grew bolder.

Below it all, roots listened.

And somewhere deep within the Holt, a choice settled into the soil—quietly, firmly—waiting to take whatever shape the future demanded.

Chapter 11 — When The Forest Chooses

Planet: Vaelthara
Location: Faelwyn Holt — Night Paths
Divine Year of Vaelthas — Wolf Month, 21,426 Years Since the Sealing

"The forest does not hide its children.
It decides who may follow."
— *Wolf Clan saying*

They ran.
Not in panic.
Not in disorder.

The Wolf Clan patrol moved as it always had—low, quick, disciplined—boots kissing moss and roots rather than striking them. Cloaks were drawn close to break the outline. Queen's Kiss bows were slung tight against the shoulders. No one spoke unless necessary. No one wasted breath.

This was familiar ground.

That was what made it wrong.

Ahead of them, beyond sight and certainty, Kholfax fled with elders whose names still carried weight in the Holt. A man condemned at dusk and unmade by dawn. A man the forest had answered.

The patrol followed the trail by instinct at first, by habit, by the muscle memory of generations who had learned to read leaf-scars and bent grass as fluently as words.

And then the forest intervened.

At first, it was subtle.

A path that should have continued did not. It softened, narrowed, and thinned into brush where memory insisted there had been clear ground an hour earlier. A fallen log lay crosswise where no log should have been—its bark still fresh, as if it had chosen to fall recently and politely into place.

A root lifted just enough to catch a heel.

"Careful," someone hissed.

They adjusted. Pressed on.

Then it became undeniable.

Vines slid from trunks like waking fingers—not striking, not attacking—only resting across ankles and wrists long enough to slow, to redirect. Branches dipped at eye level, heavy with cold dew that stung like sap when brushed aside. Ferns unfurled into waist-high walls, their fronds whispering softly when cut, the sound traveling farther than steel should allow.

Every correction cost time.

Every choice demanded attention.

"This is wrong," one ranger muttered under his breath. "The Holt knows us."

It did.

And it had decided.

The lead tracker dropped to a knee, fingers pressing into soil that should have held a clear print. The scent should have lingered—sweat, leather, and old oil from future-made gear.

There was nothing.

The ground had smoothed itself. Moss had knitted itself back together seamlessly. Even the scent felt thinned, drawn upward and away, as if lifted by a patient breath.

Queen's Kiss cracked.

A pale blue lance of harmonic light stitched through the branches ahead, meant to mark movement, flush prey, and force the forest to betray its guest.

The light bent.

Not sharply. Not with spectacle.

It diffused. Broke apart into drifting spores, refracted into a soft, useless glow that illuminated nothing but leaves and fog.

"No effect," the shooter said, disbelief threading his voice.

Another shot.

Another soft blue bloom.

Swallowed.

Behind them, the forest remained open and cooperative. Lantern-vines parted. Paths held steady. Roots lay flat and obliging.

Ahead of them, the Holt reshaped itself breath by breath.

"They're not faster than us," the patrol leader said grimly. "The Holt is."

They pushed harder.

Roots rose where there had been soil. Stones shifted underfoot, rolling just enough to throw off balance. Thorns caught cloaks but never tore them—only slowed them. A thicket closed behind them with a sound like a door politely shutting.

Someone fell. Cursed softly. Was hauled back up without complaint.

No arrows flew.

No beasts charged.

No spirits revealed themselves.

The forest did not attack. It simply declined.

Minutes stretched. Distance lay. Every landmark repeated itself with slight variation—this trunk bent a different way, that stone missing a familiar crack—as if the Holt were presenting echoes of memory, deliberately misremembered.

A spiral without a center.

Finally, the lead tracker stood.

"Enough," he said quietly. "We are being led in circles."

No one argued.

They listened.

Far ahead, there had once been footfalls. Breath. The faint clink of gear. The sound of people moving with purpose.

Now there was nothing.

Only the steady breathing of the Holt, slow and deep, like a great creature settling into sleep.

Reluctantly, the patrol made camp where the ground would allow. Lanterns were hooded. Watches were doubled. No one removed armor. No one joked.

No one slept well.

Dreams came uninvited. Forests without edges. Roots that spoke. Paths that closed behind choice rather than footfall.

At dawn, they tried again.

The forest had not changed its mind.

By midmorning, even the most stubborn understood.

Kholfax was gone.

Not hidden.

Not masked.

Released.

The patrol withdrew in uneasy silence, carrying a truth none of them dared to name aloud:

When the forest chose sides, even the Wolf Clan did not always stand on the same ground.

Somewhere far beyond their reach, paths remained open.

And somewhere behind their eyes, a question took root—quiet, persistent, impossible to ignore:

If the Holt protected him…

…what had they almost destroyed?

Chapter 12 — The Hall That Burns

Planet: Vaelthara
Region: Northern Marches — Thraekir Fire Hall
Divine Year of Vaelthas — Wolf Month, 21,426 Years Since the Sealing

"Some places do not remember footsteps.
They remember heat."
— *Sylph Clan saying*

The forest did not fade so much as end.

Trees thinned abruptly, their trunks spaced farther and farther apart until they stood like ribs around an open wound. Moss gave way to cracked stone. Soil turned into slag-glass that reflected the sky in warped, fractured shapes. The smell of resin vanished, replaced by ash, sulfur, and the dry metallic tang of old iron.

Heat rose in visible waves.

The air tasted sharp. Each breath scraped the throat. Distance bent and shimmered, turning cliffs into mirages and shadows into false depth.

Harvey slowed, lifting one hand.

Ahead, the Fire Hall emerged from the mountainside as if the mountain itself had chosen to grow teeth.

"If the Frost Giants hide the horn near the pole," Sylveron said quietly, "then the Fire Halls will know where. Giants do not build citadels without mapping them."

Basalt pillars jutted outward at aggressive angles, framing a gateway of fused stone and bronze. The metal was not decorative; it had been poured, hammered, and forced into shape while white-hot. Spiraling runes crawled across its surface, glowing a dull, simmering red that pulsed in time with something deep within the mountain.

Vents along the cliff face exhaled steady breaths of furnace air.

No banners.

No ornaments.

Fire giants did not announce their strength.

They assumed it.

Serithyl Dawnstep vanished first.

Her form did not fade like a shadow but fractured, her outline breaking into the shimmer of heat-haze until the eye could no longer agree on where she stood. Vaelinnae Windpetal followed, her body becoming a ripple in the air, light bending around her like water around a stone.

Seris knelt, pressing two fingers to the scorched ground. Her voice dropped to a whisper, coaxing the faintest threads of life still clinging to the stone into stillness. Even here, something listened.

Sylveron drew his blade without a sound. The steel drank the red glow and gave nothing back.

Two fire giant sentries stood at the gate.

Massive even for their kind, they had skin the color of cooling embers, veined with faint orange light that pulsed slowly beneath the surface. Their weapons rested against the stone, close at hand. They were not bored.

They were listening.

Harvey counted breaths.

Timed the rhythm of the vents.

Then nodded.

The Sylphs moved.

A blade slid behind one giant's knee, precise and merciful. Another slipped between ribs where the armor plates did not quite meet. The strikes were clean, surgical, guided by knowledge older than the forge.

The giants did not roar.

They exhaled—long, surprised—and folded to the stone like collapsing furnaces. Heat bled from them in visible waves.

The mountain did not answer.

They waited.

Nothing came.

Inside, the Fire Hall was a city turned inward.

Corridors spiraled downward in wide, deliberate arcs, their walls smoothed by hands that prized endurance over beauty. Channels of molten light flowed beneath crystal seams in the floor, casting a dim, furnace-glow that painted everything in amber and shadow. The ceilings vanished into soot-blackened darkness far overhead, supported by columns thick enough to be mistaken for cliffs.

This was a place built to endure catastrophe.

They moved in silence where silence should not exist.

Guards stood watch along branching passages, their silhouettes huge and still. The party passed between breaths, through gaps that should not have been there. A misstep here would not merely echo.

It would announce.

It never came.

Deeper still, the heat thickened. The air grew dense, heavy with smoke and something fouler beneath. Not rot. Not decay.

Preparation.

They reached a vault whose doors had been pried open from the inside. Metal lay twisted like wax, with stress marks that spoke of enormous force applied with careful intent.

Beyond it, the corridor opened into a chamber that did not belong.

A workshop.

Bone littered the floor.

Not scattered.

Arranged.

A massive frame dominated the chamber, its ribcage fused to iron, its vertebrae bound with black wire etched with runes that pulsed sickly green. Skulls—dozens, then hundreds—were stacked along the walls, their empty eyes glowing faintly as if remembering sight.

A bone giant.

Unfinished.

A fire giant engineer stood at a stone table, tools glowing white-hot in his hands, his posture intent and reverent. Beside him stood a figure cloaked in bark-dark robes.

The moment Harvey saw the druid, the air recoiled.

Heat thinned around him. Fire dimmed.

The druid turned.

And smiled.

"You're early," he said pleasantly. Almost pleased.

The engineer reached for a lever.

The druid lifted one hand.

Roots of shadow slid from the stone floor, wrapping bone and iron alike. The giant frame shuddered. Runes flared violently.

Seri gasped. "Harvey—"

The bone giant rose.

Not quickly.

Inevitably.

Its skull turned. Empty eyes burned green. It inhaled a breath it did not need.

The sound was like a grave opening.

Harvey stepped forward.

Kuldemaekr sang.

The blade's cold was absolute—a silence that devoured heat. He struck once, clean and centered, the cut falling exactly where life should have been.

The bone giant opened its jaws and screamed soundlessly, then flaked apart as frost raced through bone and rune alike. Magic unraveled. Green light tore free in screaming strands, collapsing inward as the construct shattered into white ash that hissed against the stone.

Gone.

The fire giant engineer roared and charged.

Serithyl and Vaelinnae met him in motion, never staying still where a blow could land. They cut tendons, joints, and leverage points. The giant crashed to one knee.

Seri ended it.

A thorn of living wood erupted from stone and pierced the heart.

The druid turned to flee.

Sylveron was faster.

Steel crossed bark. The druid fell, blood dark and steaming against the floor.

Silence crashed in, loud as a bell.

They stood amid heat and ruin, breathing hard.

Harvey knelt beside the body. Found the satchel. Inside: dried leaves, vials of dark resin, ritual chalk, and a single folded scrap of bark paper.

He read it once.

Then again.

Share the magic of the Crone.

Show them.

Recruit them.

— *Sablek*

Seris went pale.

"Sablek," Sylveron said quietly. "Who is Sablek?"

Harvey folded the note and tucked it away, feeling its weight settle behind his ribs.

"This wasn't a lone heresy," he said. "It's a network."

"And it points north," Vaelinnae said, wiping her blade clean.

She gestured toward the far wall.

A massive map had been carved directly into the stone—mountains, rivers, fault lines, and within them, a region inlaid with deep blue crystal.

The Frostcrag Mountains. Three citadels.

At the heart of the central citadel, a symbol etched again and again.

A horn.

Frozen.

Harvey looked north, through stone, distance, and fate.

"Then we don't linger," he said.

Behind them, the Fire Hall groaned—a deep, waking sound—as alarms finally rolled through the mountain.

For a heartbeat, an image of his older brother flashed through Harvey's mind. Witmar would have loved this place. He would have cataloged every forge and rune with reverence.

Harvey turned away.

They ran.

Carrying ash on their boots, a warning in their hands, and the certainty that the war they were trying to prevent had already learned their names.

Chapter 13 — The Council That Fractures

Planet: Vaelthara
Region: Drakkenwyld — The High Druid's Tree
Wolf Month, 21,426 Years Since the Sealing

"Roots that refuse the storm will break when it returns."
— *Old Druidic warning*

The High Druid's Tree rose where twelve forest paths converged.

It was not merely tall. It was cumulative.

Its trunk was wider than a keep, its bark layered with the pale spiral scars of centuries of council carvings. Each glyph marked a decision once debated beneath its branches. Each wound had healed, but none had been forgotten. The scars did not weaken the tree. They strengthened it, thickening the grain where choice had once cut deepest.

Above, the canopy spread like a living dome, its leaves overlapping in patient layers that softened all light into green-gold stillness. Even raised voices lost their edge here. Anger dulled. Pride bent.

This was where wars had been argued into being.

And where they had been ended.

Brun Dreamweaver stood at the heart of the root-dais.

His staff was rooted in living wood, not as a symbol of power but as an anchor. His palms rested lightly against the bark, fingers splayed as if listening rather than commanding. His hair had turned entirely white, yet his eyes still held the deep, attentive green of spring rain. Moss clung to his robes by choice, threading through the fabric as if he were part of the grove rather than a visitor within it.

Small birds perched along the branches overhead.

They always listened.

The circle was incomplete.

Brun felt it immediately, the absence like a missing limb. A gap in the breathing rhythm of the grove.

"Lady Vyrna has not answered the summons," he said at last.

His voice carried without force, spreading outward through bark and leaf and listening root. "Nor has any voice from Faelwyn Holt replied to our sending."

Murmurs rippled through the gathered druids. Not loud. Not yet. Unease spread faster than sound.

"She is late," one said, attempting casual reassurance. "Perhaps her wedding occupies her thoughts."

"She is never late," another replied, sharper.

Brun lifted one hand.

The forest quieted.

"I sent a runner," he continued. "One who knows the Holt paths as well as any living druid. He should have returned by now."

As if summoned by the weight of expectation, the roots near the eastern arch shifted.

A figure emerged from the living wood.

The messenger was breathless, his cloak torn by thorns that should not have been there. His boots were caked with sap and gray soil, the marks of paths that had resisted him. His face was drawn, his eyes wide with something between disbelief and dread.

He crossed the dais in three hurried steps and dropped to one knee, his fist pressed to the earth.

"High Druid," he said. "Councilors."

Brun stepped forward. "Speak."

The messenger swallowed. His throat worked as though the words themselves resisted being shaped.

"Lady Vyrna did not receive me."

The silence that followed was absolute.

Brun's fingers tightened around his staff. The living wood beneath it pulsed faintly and with a troubled rhythm. "Explain."

"I was met at the Lantern-Paths," the druid said. "By Wolf Clan wardens. They did not threaten me or raise weapons." His voice dropped. "But they barred the way."

A ripple passed through the council, sharper now.

"They told me," The messenger continued carefully, "that Faelwyn Holt no longer stands with the Council of Roots."

Silence fell again.

Heavier this time.

Brun inclined his head slightly. "On whose authority?"

"Lady Vyrna's," the druid replied. "And the elders who remain with her."

Remain.

The word settled into Brun as a stone dropped into deep water.

"Why?" he asked.

The messenger hesitated, then spoke faster, as if afraid the truth might spoil if held too long.

"They say the war itself is the danger. That every blade drawn and every spell cast in anger weakens the binding that keeps the Malloch away." His eyes flicked up, then down again. "That peace—not victory—is the only true defense."

A low sound rose from the circle. Not a shout. A collective intake of disbelief.

"Peace with whom?" someone demanded.

"With everyone," the messenger said. "Humans included."

The circle erupted.

"Madness."

"Naïveté dressed as doctrine."

"They've forgotten Sylos IV."

"They've forgotten the dead."

Brun raised his staff.

The bark beneath it pulsed once, sending a tremor through the roots. Leaves rustled. The forest answered him. Then silence returned.

"And the humans?" Brun asked quietly.

The messenger nodded. "The Wolf Clan has ceased hostilities along their borders. Timber camps stand unharmed. Paths once watched are open. There are… exchanges." He hesitated. "Druids teach restraint. Humans promise limits."

A bitter laugh escaped an elder whose antler-marked robes spoke of centuries of patrols. "Promises."

The messenger's gaze dropped. "They say this path will keep the Malloch banished forever, that war invites them, and that the Chamber should never be tested again."

Brun closed his eyes.

He saw Sylos IV as it had been described to him and heard the refugees' accounts again. Gates opening where reality had no right to tear. The Unmaking Choir unraveling cities into screams, static, and absence.

He opened his eyes.

"And you?" he asked the messenger. "Were you welcomed?"

The druid shook his head. "I was told to leave, that the High Council's authority ends at the edge of Faelwyn Holt." His voice tightened. "I was… escorted out."

The word had been chosen with care.

Brun turned slowly, taking in the faces around him.

Some were furious.

Some were afraid.

A few—too few—looked tempted.

"This doctrine," Brun said at last, "was not brought before us. Not tested. Not weighed. One of the oldest memories carried by the High Druids speaks of a doctrine like this. The Crone's doctrine. Aelrindel opposed her, ignored her warnings, had one of his possessions removed, and was imprisoned in the haunted forest of Greenwood."

"The Wolf Clan decided unilaterally," said a hawk-eyed druid of the eastern groves.

"And enforced," another added.

Brun nodded once. "Then it is not peace."

He let the pause breathe.

"It is secession. But how their doctrine took root among a majority of the Wolf Clan is puzzling."

The word cut like frost.

"What do you propose?" asked an elder whose roots reached deep into Bear Clan lands.

Brun's jaw tightened. "We cannot allow a single clan to fracture the balance of the forests. Not now. Not while the Malloch's shadow still stains memory."

He turned his staff, the runes along it catching the canopy light.

"If the Wolf Clan refuses the Council," he said, "then the Council cannot shield them."

A hush fell.

"Faelwyn Holt is hereby declared in self-exile," Brun said. "Until Lady Vyrna returns and submits this doctrine to the council's judgment."

"And if she does not?" someone asked.

Brun's voice did not rise. It did not harden.

It mourned.

"Then the Wolf Clan will stand alone when the storm returns."

"What of those among the Wolf Clan who rebel against this doctrine?" Tans asked.

"They may be aided," Brun finished.

Roots shifted beneath the dais, uneasy. Leaves whispered, though no wind passed through the canopy.

The messenger bowed his head. "They said you would say this."

Brun met his gaze. "Then they know what they risk."

High above, the branches creaked.

A single leaf detached, spiraling slowly down to rest at Brun's feet.

He did not pick it up.

Because some fractures, once made, could not be mended by gentle hands alone.

Chapter 14 — The Rebels In The Roots

Planet: Vaelthara
Divine Year of Vaelthas — Wolf Month, 21,426 Years Since the Sealing
Faelwyn Holt — Southern Rootbreak, Near the Human Timber Edge

"Truth does not shout.
It waits for those willing to hear it."
— *Inscription at the Root of the Old Watch*

Kellyn sensed the forest long before she saw it.

Myrrathis slowed without command, his wings folding inward as the bronze dragon's flight-song softened to a low, patient hum. His scales dimmed from living fire to banked embers, heat drawn inward and disciplined. The air thickened as they descended, heavy with loam and old sap. Sound bent here. Not vanished, not silenced—restrained. Even the wind learned to move carefully.

Kellyn slid from the saddle and rested her palm against Myrrathis' neck.

"Wait," she whispered.

The dragon lowered his head, eyes narrowing, pupils slitting as he tasted the air. No challenge. No prey. No fear. Only watchfulness, sharp and mutual.

Kellyn moved forward on foot.

The hideout revealed itself the way the Holt revealed all things worth protecting: reluctantly, and only when it chose to.

Roots parted just enough to form a hollowed basin beneath an ancient oak whose trunk had split centuries ago and then healed around its own wound. The scar ran like a lightning strike frozen in wood. Lantern-fungus glowed faintly along the inner bark, casting cool green light that never quite reached the edges. No fire. No smoke. No banners.

Only presence.

Five figures waited within.

Kellyn took them in at a glance.

They were tired.

Not reckless. Not desperate.

Tired.

And tired people rarely gambled their lives on lies.

Khandyl stood first, her bow unstrung yet close at hand, her autumn-auburn hair bound tight against her skull. There was a new stillness in her posture, not tension but readiness honed by sleepless nights. Froster leaned against a root-wall, his emerald-runed cleaver resting across his knees, its glyphs dimmed to a sleeping glow. He looked older than he had weeks earlier. Not in years—in weight.

Three ancient Anari rangers sat cross-legged near the rear, their armor older than most songs, grown from bark and bone long before codices were written. Their eyes followed Kellyn without surprise.

And Kholfax.

He stood apart, hands clasped behind his back, his posture straight despite the bruise-yellow shadow still lingering beneath his jaw. The Holt had not fully healed him. Not yet.

Every eye turned to Kellyn.

"You made it," Khandyl said.

Not relief.

Confirmation.

"I followed the fracture points," Kellyn replied. "The forest kept opening doors."

Froster snorted softly. "It does that when it agrees with you."

Kellyn studied them, then said what mattered most.

"You're all alive."

"For now," Khandyl said.

Kellyn's gaze settled on Kholfax.

"You escaped."

"I was released," he corrected calmly. "By people who still believe evidence matters."

One of the ancient rangers inclined his head. His voice was old wood and wind.

"We do not abandon truth because it is inconvenient."

Kellyn returned the gesture. Respect, not ceremony.

"Tell me everything," she said.

They did.

Kholfax spoke without embellishment. The patrol. The masked figure. The paralytic. The harmonic pressure that locked bone and breath alike. The precision. The way the blade had been placed in his hand, fingers arranged as if by an artist correcting a pose.

"I've seen this pattern before," he said. "In my time. On Sylos IV. On Vaelthara. He kills cleanly. He kills beautifully." His jaw tightened. "And he wants witnesses who can't speak. He thinks it's fun."

One of the elders shifted, bark-armor whispering. "A singer, then."

"Yes," Kholfax said. "But not a bard. Not a battle chant. This is something else."

"A perversion," Froster said. "A weaponized Song."

Kellyn felt her stomach tighten.

"And you believe," she said carefully, "that this killer is aligned with the dark druids."

"I don't believe it," Kholfax replied. "I know it."

He turned slightly, his eyes sharp. "The paralytic compound wasn't human. It wasn't future-tech. It was grown. Cultured. Refined. Someone with druidic access and patience made it."

The ancient rangers murmured.

"The Crone's hand," one said.

"She borrows life only to ruin it," another agreed.

Kellyn exhaled slowly. "The Wolf Clan believes peace will keep the Malloch banished."

Khandyl's jaw tightened. "Even if I hadn't activated the Chamber, releasing gods and Malloch alike, someone else would have. Eventually." Her voice hardened. "At some point, the Malloch must be banished forever or destroyed. There is no reality in which they politely forget us."

One of the elders leaned forward, eyes bright with conviction.

"The gods will return," he said. "And when they do, life will improve, not because they command it—but because they remind us of what we are capable of becoming."

Kellyn met his gaze.

"In my time," she said quietly, "the gods were gone, and we forgot ourselves." She paused. "When they returned, they offered ideals worth remembering."

The words settled like seeds.

Froster rose. "Humans are moving deeper into the forest. Timber camps are expanding. They have druids now. Rangers. Giants."

Kellyn nodded. "I've read the reports."

"They think peace protects them," Khandyl said. "It makes them bold."

One of the elders offered a thin smile. "Then let us remind them where the forest ends—and where it begins."

Kellyn closed her eyes for a breath.

She saw futures branching. Some burned. Some drowned. Some went silent.

When she opened them again, her voice carried no doubt.

"Which camp?"

"Dornfeste," Khandyl said. "Closest. Loudest. And foolish enough to believe wooden walls matter."

Kellyn nodded once.

"Then we strike there," she said. "Clean. Decisive. No civilians. But we shatter the illusion of safety."

Kholfax studied her. "And the killer?"

"We flush him," Kellyn replied. "Or we force him to move."

Kholfax nodded slowly. "He enjoys hiding. The guessing is part of it. So is fear."

Outside the hollow, Myrrathis lifted his head, sensing the shift. His wings flexed once, slow and deliberate.

Kellyn turned toward the forest edge, where distant human lanterns stained the night like embers in fog.

"Prepare," she said. "We move before dawn."

The Holt listened.

And far beyond the roots, something else did too.

Chapter 15 — Through Fire, Toward Ice

Planet: Vaelthara
Deep South of the Thraekir Range
Fire Giant Hall-Complex, Lower Deeps

"The hunt does not begin with the kill.
It begins with endurance."
— *Fragment attributed to Aelrindel*

The fire giant halls did not echo.

They absorbed sound, swallowing it as a furnace devours air, leaving only pressure behind. Harvey felt it with every step as they pressed deeper into the mountain, past corridors carved smooth by centuries of heat, hammering, and bodies that did not need to hurry. Stone walls glowed faintly from within, veins of molten orange pulsing like a slow, patient heartbeat beneath layers of blackened rock.

Every breath tasted of sulfur, ash, and old metal.

The heat was not aggressive. It was confident.

Sylveron moved first, his presence a quiet weight that set the group's pace. He did not rush, nor did he hesitate, adjusting his stride instinctively to the narrowing spaces and shifting floors. His armor bore a faint sheen of sweat that evaporated almost as quickly as it formed.

Behind him, Serithyl Dawnstep and Vaelinnae Windpetal flowed like living mirages. Their bare feet barely touched stone, placing steps where heat fractured light rather than pooled. Even their breathing was measured, timed to the vents that exhaled warmth along the corridor walls.

Seri walked last.

Her staff pulsed with restrained green light, the wood flexing slightly beneath her grip as roots tested the stone below, eager yet leashed. Life did not belong here. That made it restless.

Harvey kept his whispercloak tight around his shoulders.

The fabric bent light and sound, turning his movement into suggestion rather than presence, but the heat pressed through it all the same, pricking his skin and drawing sweat down his spine. The Kuldemaekr at his side felt heavier here, its cold muted but not extinguished, like ice held stubbornly against a forge.

They passed a lava river without ceremony.

It cut across the hall like a living wound, molten stone rolling in thick, slow waves. Chains thicker than trees spanned the flow, anchoring lift-cages and platforms above the glow. Something vast shifted beneath the surface, sending ripples through the lava that slapped wetly against the banks.

Harvey did not look down for long.

"No stopping," Sylveron murmured. "Fire giants feel hesitation."

They crossed.

On the far side, the mountain changed its mind.

The walls grew straighter. Sharper. Ornament gave way to function. Cold stone intruded into the heat-scorched halls, veins of frost lacing the black rock like scars that refused to heal.

Seris's voice dropped. "The guest quarter."

"Frost giants," Vaelinnae added softly.

Harvey felt it then.

Not the Horn.

But proximity.

A pressure at the edge of thought, like a word half-remembered or a name spoken just beyond hearing. Something north of here was aware of him, not watching yet—but waiting.

The frost giant died without a sound.

Serithyl struck first, her blade opening the back of the giant's knee in a clean, upward cut that severed the tendon and the balance in the same instant. Sylveron followed immediately, driving his spear through the giant's throat as Vaelinnae flowed past, slicing the arms' tendons with surgical precision.

The creature collapsed in a hiss of steam, with frost and blood evaporating where they touched the heated stone.

Harvey automatically took position, back to the corridor, senses stretched thin.

Seris knelt by the body, fingers already moving.

The frost giant's gear was unlike the fire giants'. Pale steel etched with runes of containment and directional binding, not endurance or strength. His cloak shimmered faintly, woven not for warmth but for navigation, responding to pressure shifts and wind currents far beyond the mountain.

Seris worked quickly.

"This," she said, pulling a folded hide-map from a hardened satchel. "And this."

A bone token followed, etched with sigils so dense they made Harvey's teeth ache just from looking at them.

Sylveron's voice tightened. "Read it."

Seris unfurled the hide.

The map did not show land.

It showed cold.

Currents of ice. Pressure lines. Windpaths spiraling upward into nothingness. A mountain mass so vast it had been hollowed into a city rather than built upon. At its heart, a single vault was marked again and again, carved deeper than the rest.

"The Citadel," Seri said quietly. "Far north. Past the living forests. Past the windpaths."

Harvey nodded once. "That's where the Horn is."

The mountain screamed.

Not in sound.

In vibration.

The hall shuddered violently as runes flared red along the walls, heat surging outward in a wave that stole their breath. Somewhere above them, iron bells began to toll, their resonance bleeding through stone and bone alike.

Sylveron was already moving. "We are done here."

Fire giants poured into the corridor behind them, their silhouettes flickering against the glow of rising magma. Heavy footfalls shook the stone. Spears rang against shields. A roar rolled forward like a wall of pressure, promising inevitability.

Seris slammed her staff into the ground.

Life answered violently.

Roots tore from seams in the stone, thick and fast, ripping through rock as if it were loam. Vines coiled around pillars, snapping them inward. Thorned branches burst upward, tangling legs, weapons, and armor.

Fire giants howled as green growth wrapped around molten limbs, steam exploding where life met heat.

"Go!" Seris shouted, already pale, sweat pouring down her temples. "I can slow them—but not for long!"

They ran.

Through collapsing halls. Past falling stone. Over cracks that opened into fire. Heat chased them like a breath on the back of the neck.

Their griffyns still waited where they had hidden them among the basalt spires.

Behind them, Seris struck again—less controlled now—forcing life into places that resisted with violent fury. The mountain pushed back. She felt it in her bones, in her teeth, in the trembling of her hands.

They burst into open air as alarms continued to roll through the mountain.

Griffyns screamed and surged forward, wings beating against superheated wind.

Sylveron caught Vaelinnae and vaulted into the saddle in one fluid motion. Serithyl hauled Harvey up behind her.

Seris stumbled, mounting last, her grip white-knuckled, her breath ragged.

The griffyns launched.

Fire giants reached the threshold just as they cleared the edge. Spears flew. One grazed a griffyn's wing, tearing feathers free in a spray of embers.

Below them, the mountain burned.

Above them, the sky hardened into cold.

Harvey clutched the map tightly as the wind tore at his cloak, the ache in his bones sharpening with every mile north.

Toward ice.

Toward the Horn.

Toward a hunt that would not forgive delay.

Passing the lava river.

Chapter 16 — The Wood That Bites Back

Planet: Vaelthara
Western Forest Marches
Human Timber Camp at the Edge of Faelwyn Holt

"The forest does not rage.
It remembers."
— *Wolf Clan battle saying*

The timber camp sat like a wound that refused to close.

A raw clearing hacked out at the forest's edge, its boundaries jagged rather than planned, as if the axes that made it had grown tired before the work was finished. Stumps ringed the clearing like broken teeth. Stacked logs lay in long, uneven rows, sap still bleeding from their ends. Rough palisades of split pine marked the perimeter, with gaps hastily filled with thorn brush and wire.

Canvas tents sagged in irregular lines around a central sawpit, where fresh cuts still glistened. Smoke from cookfires drifted low and greasy, clinging to the ground rather than rising, carrying the sour tang of pitch, sweat, and iron. The smell of fear was already there, faint yet unmistakable, even before the first arrow flew.

Kellyn circled once overhead on Myrrathis.

From the sky, the geometry resolved instantly.

One hundred lumberjacks clustered near saw lines and log piles, tools stacked close, bodies loose with fatigue rather than readiness. Fifty militia formed a rough perimeter, muskets slung over shoulders, pikes leaned against crates and fire rings. Their spacing was too wide, and their watch rotations uneven.

Two forest giants stood half-buried near the treeline, bark-armored and motionless, mistaken for growth rather than guardians. Their presence radiated borrowed authority, not allegiance. Near the far wagons, something worse loomed.

An undead giant.

Its ribcage was bound with iron bands etched with crude, hurried sigils. Greenish light pulsed faintly through its joints. Chains of blackened bone dragged behind it, scoring the earth. It did not breathe. It waited.

Too many defenders for a clean assault.

Perfect for a lesson.

Kellyn banked Myrrathis east and slipped back into the canopy. Leaves closed behind them, branches bending just enough to hide their passage without breaking.

Below, the rebels waited.

Khandyl lay prone on a mossy rise, her bow already drawn, her breathing slow and deliberate. Froster crouched beside her, emerald runes on his cleaver dimmed to a patient glow. Kholfax checked his arrows for the third time, his movements economical, his eyes never still. Three ancient Anari rangers ghosted among the roots, their faces painted in ash and sap, their bodies half-erased by posture alone.

"Count them," Khandyl murmured without turning her head.

"Already did," Kellyn replied, sliding from Myrrathis' neck as her boots sank silently into moss. "They don't know we're here yet."

Khandyl's mouth curved faintly. "They will."

Soon.

The first attack lasted less than ten breaths.

Queen's Kiss arrows flew.

Not in a volley. Not in panic. In sequence.

Light-blue threads cut through smoke and dusk, each shot deliberate, spaced just enough to prevent warning cries from forming. The militia dropped where they stood. One slumped against a crate mid-laugh. Another folded while adjusting a musket strap. A third took a step that never finished.

No screams.

No alarms.

Five men died before anyone understood that death had arrived.

Then the forest closed.

Roots rose just enough to block sightlines. Ferns unfurled. Branches dipped and tangled. The shooters were gone before the first return shot cracked uselessly against bark and vanished into leaves.

Shouts erupted.

Militia regrouped quickly, credit where it was due. Orders were barked. Muskets were raised. Pairs were sent into the forest to flank and flush.

A mistake born of habit.

Kellyn watched from the canopy as the Holt corrected it.

The forest did not strike.

It inconvenienced.

A root where none had been. A branch that caught a boot heel. A mist that softened depth and swallowed edges. Sound bent. Distance lied.

The pairs never returned.

Each kill was intimate.

A blade between the ribs. A garrote of living vine that tightened with each breath. A Queen's Kiss arrow loosed from so close the string barely sang.

The second strike came from the opposite edge of the camp.

Five more militia fell.

Then another five.

The undead giant lurched forward, iron bands creaking, one massive arm dragging its chain of bones through dirt and ash.

Kellyn swung back into Myrrathis' saddle.

"Now—Feydra," she whispered.

Fire answered.

"Aelthos!" she cried out to Myrrathis.

Myrrathis plunged from the canopy like a falling sun. Flame washed over the undead giant, devouring rot and binding magic alike. The creature screamed once, a hollow sound like wind tearing through a crypt, then collapsed into ash and fused bone that hissed against the ground.

One forest giant turned too slowly.

Kellyn did not slow at all. "Skarros!"

Dragonfire tore through bark and muscle, collapsing the giant into a tower of steam and embers. The second managed a single step before Myrrathis' talons ripped into its shoulder, and Kellyn drove flame down its spine, burning obedience into flesh.

The camp broke.

Lumberjacks dropped tools and ran.

Some fled toward the plains.

Some, in blind terror, charged the forest.

They died on the way in.

Queen's Kiss arrows struck from angles that made no sense, each shot followed by a disappearance. The Holt slowed them, tangled them, and pulled at legs, breath, and panic alike.

Sixty bodies lay scattered before the survivors understood the truth.

They were not under attack.

They were being culled.

Forty fled.

They did not stop running.

The rebels emerged only after silence settled fully, the kind that came when even insects hesitated.

They moved through the camp with practiced efficiency.

Tents were slashed and burned. Storehouses caught fire. Log piles erupted in roaring columns of flame, sending sparks spiraling into the canopy. Kellyn watched the fire spread, her expression hard and controlled.

The timber camp's current state said it would not be rebuilt soon.

Kholfax knelt to recover arrows, inspecting each shaft for warping or nicks. "They'll adapt," he said quietly. "They always do."

"Let them," Khandyl replied. "We'll adapt faster."

Froster planted his cleaver point-down into the dirt, emerald runes catching firelight. "We'll need supplies."

"We already have them," Kellyn said, gesturing to a boar roasting over the fire, then to a table nearby stacked with loaves and vegetables spilling from bags.

They worked without discussion.

A bowyer's bench assembled from a fallen table—a fletcher's rack from split crates. Feathers sorted. Shafts straightened. Heads cleaned and reused. Even musket powder was deliberately scattered into the flames, denying recovery.

Nothing was wasted.

Movement stirred at the forest's edge.

Fifty more Anari stepped from the shadows.

Ancient rangers. Scarred. Quiet. Drawn by smoke, song, and the unmistakable rhythm of war done correctly.

Khandyl met them with a single nod. They returned it without words. Kellyn looked back at the burning camp.

Somewhere beyond it, a dark druid, a human, slipped into the night, fear driving his steps faster than loyalty ever could.

Let him run. Word would spread. And next time, the camps would be more brutal. That was fine.

The Wolf Clan was done retreating.

Behind them, the forest breathed—slow, deep, and satisfied.

It had remembered how to bite.

Chapter 17 — The Quiet School

Planet: Vaelthara
Faelwyn Holt, near the Tainted Shrine of Aelrindel
BV 21

"Some songs are not meant to be heard.
Only obeyed."
— *Fragment, Crone-lit teaching*

The shrine was wrong.

It still bore the old carvings of Aelrindel: antlered sigils carved deep into stone, spirals of pursuit and release, and lines shaped to sing as the wind passed through them. Once, hunters had knelt here to sharpen their senses and steady their breath before the chase.

Now the stone did not listen.

Moss clung in sickly gray patches, brittle underfoot, cracking softly like frost-burned leaves. Lichen grew in shapes that ignored the carvings rather than embracing them. Roots bent away from the shrine entirely, diverting their growth as if instinct itself had learned to avoid it.

The forest did not forget this place.

It rejected it.

Beneath the shrine, in a shallow basin hollowed long ago for offerings, the dark druids gathered.

Anari and humans stood shoulder to shoulder, their cloaks brushing, breaths shallow. Torches burned with violet-black flames, light without warmth, casting shadows that leaned the wrong way. The air smelled faintly of copper, old sap, and something medicinal that had gone stale.

Dark dryads watched from the walls.

They did not stand so much as adhere, half-formed bodies pressed against bark and stone, their limbs indistinct, their faces suggested rather than carved. Their eyes glimmered like polished obsidian, reflecting the torchlight without blinking.

They were not hostile.

They were wary.

They waited.

The man arrived without ceremony.

No announcement. No herald. No shift in the air that could be easily named.

One moment, the deeper darkness at the basin's edge was empty.

The next, it was not.

He stepped forward in a plain cloak, his hood drawn low. No sigils. No armor. No visible weapon. His posture was unremarkable, the way professionals cultivate it—balanced, economical, forgettable.

His presence was not.

The dark dryads recoiled.

Not fleeing. Not attacking.

Listening.

Sablek Thistlecrest inclined his head at once, a gesture practiced and sincere. "You are welcome."

The man did not return it.

He moved to the center of the basin and spoke quietly, as if addressing a room that was already his.

"Stand closer."

They obeyed.

Not out of fear.

Out of alignment.

The Anari dark druids felt it first: a pressure behind the eyes, as if thought itself were being gently compressed. The humans followed a breath later, swallowing hard as their balance shifted, their inner ears at odds with the world.

"This is not spellwork," the man said. "It is alignment."

He inhaled.

The sound that followed was not loud.

It was layered.

A low harmonic vibrated through bone, settling into joints and spine. A second tone threaded through it, slightly misaligned, creating tension the body tried to resolve. A third never fully manifested—only implied, a negative space the mind reached for but failed to grasp.

One Anari druid cried out and dropped to a knee, hands clawing at the stone.

Another froze mid-step, eyes wide, throat working uselessly as breath refused to obey.

The sound stopped.

They fell—gasping, alive, terrified.

"Again," the man said calmly.

He adjusted nothing.

This time, three of them froze instantly.

Standing.

Eyes open.

Breathing shallowly and mechanically, as if their lungs were following instructions they no longer understood.

The man walked among them, unhurried, examining posture, head tilt, and jaw tension. He nudged one chin upward with a finger. Another shoulder downward.

"This is killing," he said. "The body remembers how to die even when the mind resists."

The dryads had now withdrawn, flattened against the far walls, whispering among themselves in tones too high for human ears. Their bark creaked softly with unease.

Sablek stared, awe bleeding inexorably into fear. "You… you could have slain them."

"Yes," the man replied. "But death teaches nothing if it comes too soon."

He turned back to the circle, his gaze passing over faces slick with sweat and comprehension.

"You will not use this openly. Not yet."

They leaned in, desperate for instruction and permission.

"You will preach peace," he continued. "You will speak of endings averted. Of the Malloch kept at bay. You will let others believe they chose stillness themselves."

A human druid raised a trembling hand. "And the Wolf Clan?"

The man tilted his head slightly, considering, like a scholar adjusting a hypothesis.

"They value harmony," he said. "Give them a song they want to hear."

His gaze slid to the Anari druids. "You will help. Quietly. You will nudge. Advise. Support restraint. War must look… unnecessary."

Sablek nodded eagerly. "And the humans?"

"They fear extinction," the man said. "Remind them of it. Let them believe peace is strength."

He stepped back, his cloak whispering over stone. "I will teach you more. But this—" he tapped his throat lightly "—belongs only to those who can truly hear the forest."

The Anari druids felt the weight of that sentence settle like a collar.

When the lesson ended, they climbed back toward the surface.

The shrine felt emptier than before.

At the edge of Faelwyn Holt, they stopped.

Something was missing.

The old watchers.

The ancient rangers.

The elders once corrected footwork, corrected thought, and corrected memory itself.

Gone.

Tracks led east. South. Toward broken camps. Toward smoke and arrows and living roots.

Sablek frowned, unease finally cracking his certainty. "They've left."

The man did not look back.

"They've abandoned the clan," Sablek continued.

"No," the man replied softly. "They have chosen memory over comfort."

He turned away, already losing interest. "That simplifies things."

Behind them, the shrine exhaled.

Above them, the forest listened.

And far from this place, amid fire and fear and old songs remembered too late, the Wolf Clan began fighting again—without permission.

A dark druid at the tainted shrine of Aelrindel.

Chapter 18 — Peace, Standing

Western Marches
Timber Camp of Eisenfall Reach
BV 21

The humans built Eisenfall Reach as if the forest had already declared war.

Palisades of raw pine logs encircled the camp in uneven rings, their bark still clinging, sap bleeding slowly down their sides like open wounds. Trenches had been hastily gouged into the soil, the excavated earth thrown inward to form berms reinforced with wicker and scrap timber. The geometry was defensive, inward-looking, obsessed with angles of fire rather than lines of retreat.

Canvas barracks stood in stiff, rectilinear rows, their flaps tied tight even in the heat. Lanterns burned high and bright, too many, flooding the camp with yellow-white light meant to banish shadow rather than to understand it.

At the perimeter, cannon crews drilled by torchlight.

Iron barrels were swabbed and reset again and again, hands moving by rote. Powder was measured twice. Fuses were trimmed short. Every movement spoke of men who expected to be tested and did not trust the night to behave.

A hundred militia filled the inner ring. Two companies of line soldiers held the walls. Scouts paced every approach to the forest's edge, their eyes never still.

Fear had been organized into geometry.

When the dark druids arrived, they were met with leveled spears and cocked crossbows.

"No forest tricks," the captain snapped. "No sermons."

Sablek Thistlecrest stepped forward calmly, palms open, movements slow and practiced. His bark-cloak bore no sigils now, no clan marks or druidic knots, only woven leaves and humility, shaped into something deliberately inoffensive.

"We offer protection," he said. "Growth. Barriers. The Anari do not seek war."

A soldier spat into the dirt between them. "Funny way of showing it."

The captain stepped closer, close enough that Sablek could smell iron and sleeplessness on his breath. "You'll leave now, or I'll put you down with the rest of the tree-things."

The dark druids withdrew.

They did not argue.

They did not warn.

They did not plead.

They watched.

Night came hard.

Lanterns flared brighter as the sun fell, shadows driven back rather than allowed to soften. The camp loosened by degrees. Helmets came off. Armor straps unbuckled. Someone produced a skin of spirits. Dice clattered on an upturned crate. Laughter cracked the air in short, brittle bursts that carried too far.

Discipline thinned.

The sentries did not see him enter.

He crossed the outer trench as if it weren't there, his boots finding purchase where none should have been. No glamour bent the light. No illusion softened his outline.

He simply walked.

A man in a hood, moving with the easy confidence of someone who belonged anywhere he chose to stand.

A guard turned.

The man spoke.

Not loudly.

Not clearly.

The sound slid into the guard's chest, locking his lungs mid-breath. The man caught him as he stiffened, guiding him upright with one hand, almost kindly, then moved on.

He passed through Eisenfall Reach like a teacher moving among inattentive students.

A cook froze mid-ladle, broth spilling slowly over the pot's lip.

A drummer stiffened, mallet hovering an inch above stretched hide.

A sergeant took one step forward, eyes glassy, mouth opening to shout.

The sound shifted.

Fifteen men stood very still.

Too still.

The man returned to them, this time carrying a small vial of dark resin. He uncorked it carefully, precisely even now. A single drop was pressed to a neck, a wrist, the hollow behind an ear.

Rigor set in fast.

Faster than panic.

When he finished, he adjusted them.

Facing outward.

Feet squared.

Hands relaxed.

Eyes open.

Alive, they resembled sentries at ease.

Dead, they remained standing.

At the center of the camp, he knelt by a fire pit, selected a length of charred wood, and carefully wrote on the side of a supply crate.

The words were simple.

PEACE WITH ANARI

OR

PEACE IN DEATH

He underlined nothing.

Then he was gone.

The scream came minutes later.

A scout staggered backward, pointing, his breath failing. A lantern was thrust closer. Someone reached out and touched a frozen arm.

It did not sway.

Another soldier grabbed a friend by the shoulders and recoiled when the body refused to move.

Panic surged.

Orders were shouted. Contradicted. Shouted again. A crossbow bolt snapped uselessly into the dark. Cannons were nearly fired before someone screamed sense into the crews.

Nothing answered.

By dawn, Eisenfall Reach was unrecognizable.

The bodies were burned.

The message was not.

The captain convened his officers, his eyes bloodshot and his voice scraped raw by shouting and smoke. "This wasn't a lone madman," he said. "This was Anari work. Druid work."

A lieutenant objected weakly. "Sir… no one forest-born—"

"No," the captain snapped. "No forest man does this alone."

Fear hardened.

But it did not drive them into the trees.

Instead, they built.

Walls rose higher, thicker. Stone foundations were laid beneath timber. Cannons were mounted at every corner, their iron mouths aimed outward in permanent accusation.

When the dark druids returned at midday, they were welcomed.

Sablek spoke gently. "We can regrow the trees here. Close. You won't need to send men into the forest anymore."

The captain stared at the blackened ground where fifteen men had stood.

"Do it," he said.

Roots cracked the soil within hours. Saplings surged upward in orderly rows, straight and compliant. Lumber without danger. Growth without risk.

An arrangement was made.

The humans would stay behind walls.
The druids would tend the wood.
The forest would be kept at bay.

That night, as the new garrison lights burned steadily and brightly, something watched from the treeline.

Satisfied.

The humans had chosen.

Not peace.

Structure.

And structure, once frightened enough, could always be turned.

The forest listened.

And did not intervene.

Chapter 19 — Roots of Consent

Planet: Vaelthara
Divine Year of Vaelthas — Wolf Month, 21,426 Years Since the Sealing
Faelwyn Holt — Graypine Reach & the Tainted Shrine of Aelrindel

"Peace grows best where fear is fed slowly."
— *Saying of the Dark Druids*

Graypine Reach slept lightly.

The Wolf Clan settlement lay beneath a canopy heavy with unshed rain, its lantern-vines dimmed to their lowest glow, its paths hushed except for the measured footfalls of sentries pacing their circuits. Doors were closed but not barred. Fires were banked but not extinguished. The Holt breathed beneath it all, steady and vast, yet its rhythm had changed.

Where once the forest had sung freely, now it listened.

Sablek Thistlecrest knelt beside a basin of blackened stone, older than time itself, set into the roots at the edge of the Reach. Its surface was cracked with vein-like fissures where roots had forced their way through ancient masonry, each fissure pulsing faintly with a dull violet-green light. Crone-taint, old and patient.

His hands were muddy. His robes were plain. His posture was reverent.

To any passing eye, he would have appeared to be nothing more than a druid at prayer.

Only the basin heard him fully.

The dark druids arrived without a signal, slipping from the shadows in twos and threes. Some were Anari, their movements fluid and quiet, their faces carefully schooled. Others were human, heavier in step, their eyes flicking constantly toward the trees, fear disciplined into obedience by ritual and reassurance.

They knelt in a loose half-circle.

One spoke.

"Dornfeste is ash," the druid said. "The humans say the forest came alive, that arrows fell from nowhere, and that fire took the giants first, then the men."

Sablek did not look up. His fingers traced the basin's rim, following cracks only he seemed to recognize.

"And the dead?" he asked.

"Sixty militia. At least forty lumber hands. The rest fled."

Another voice joined in, tighter. "They found their own soldiers afterward. Fifteen of them, standing, eyes open, dead."

That made Sablek lift his head.

For a heartbeat, the basin's light caught his face, revealing the conflict etched there. Not surprise. Not grief. Calculation restrained by habit.

"They are calling it an Anari message," the druid continued. "They say peace was offered once and refused."

Sablek closed his eyes slowly, as though savoring the words.

"Fear ripens quickly," he said. "What did they do next?"

A human druid answered, his accent thick with the speech of the western kingdoms. "They fortify. Every timber camp. Walls. Ditches. Cannons dragged from Eisenwald. Priests blessing steel. They will not enter the forest anymore."

"And the trees?" Sablek asked.

The human swallowed. "They asked us to grow them closer, faster. Managed groves. So they do not need to cut deep."

Sablek's mouth curved into something that was almost a smile.

"Good," he said softly. "Then we remain useful."

The basin pulsed once, as if in agreement.

Deeper still, beyond Graypine Reach and its quiet anxiety, the tainted shrine of Aelrindel waited.

Once, it had been a place of wind and leaf-song, where hunters knelt to give thanks before the night's chase. Now its stone roots bled shadow. Crone-marks layered over antlered spirals until the old symbols were visible only as ghosts beneath corruption. The air carried the sweetness of rot, masked by incense and forcing new growth.

Dark dryads clung to the bark-walls, half-formed, their limbs tapering into shadow, their eyes too old for their faces. They smiled without warmth.

Sablek stood at the shrine's center now, no longer pretending.

"They will build their walls," he told the gathered druids. "They will stack iron and call it safety. And when they feel secure enough—"

He paused, letting the silence lean in.

"—they will want more wood, more land, and more certainty."

A murmur rippled through the circle.

"They always do."

An Anari druid spoke, his voice careful, as though each word were being weighed. "And the Wolf Clan?"

Sablek spread his hands. "They want peace. They want the Malloch banished forever. They want to believe that restraint will save them."

That belief hung in the chamber, heavy and fragile.

"It is not a lie," Sablek continued. "It is incomplete."

He turned, firelight catching the lines around his eyes. "The rebels do not understand this. They provoke, burn, and kill. In doing so, they give the humans reason."

Another druid stepped forward, anger breaking through discipline. "Word reached us an hour ago. Another camp fell before its walls were finished."

The chamber stirred.

Sablek's gaze hardened. "Where?"

"South of Dornfeste. Near the old river bend."

"The rebels," Sablek said quietly, "have chosen their path."

Silence answered him.

"They will draw the humans back into the forest," he went on. "They will force a war the Wolf Clan is not ready to win. And when the humans march, they will not distinguish between rebels and loyalists."

He let that truth settle like ash.

"So, we will hunt them."

A few druids hesitated.

Sablek did not raise his voice. He did not need to. "Not as executioners. As protectors. We will find them. Drive them out. Deliver them to justice if we can. Kill them if we must."

The dark dryads shifted along the walls, pleased.

"And the humans?" someone asked.

Sablek turned toward the shrine wall, where Aelrindel's defaced symbol still lingered beneath layers of Crone-markings.

"We will help them grow their forests," he said. "We will stand between them and the deep woods. We will become necessary."

Necessary was safer than loved.

Necessary was power.

Far away, beyond root and shadow, ancient Anari moved through the forest in silence. Rebels. Hunters. Believers in gods who had yet to return.

And somewhere among them all, a man who killed with sound continued to shape the war without ever raising a banner.

The forest listened. And prepared to be torn apart.

Chapter 20 — The Citadel of Ice

Planet: Vaelthara
Divine Year of Vaelthas — Wolf Month, 21,426 Years Since the Sealing
Skjol-Varr — Frost Giant Citadel of the Far North

"All warmth is borrowed.
All life is debt.
And winter always collects."
— *Frost Thraeker proverb*

The wind did not howl.

It pressed.

Harvey felt it first as resistance to breathing, a weight that settled behind the ribs and stayed. Each inhale had to be chosen. Each exhale left him in a thin cloud that did not quite disperse, as if the air were reluctant to return what had been given.

Below them, the north lay stripped to its bones.

Ice fields fractured into long plates that caught the pallid light and held it without warmth. Stone broke through in dark ridges like old scars. No trees. No roots. No green interruption anywhere in the sweep of white.

The sky hung low, a pale iron lid without sun or star.

Their griffyns fought the gale with stubborn, deliberate wings. Frost gathered along feathers and talons, cracking softly when they flexed. The beasts did not complain. They endured, which in this place was the only virtue that mattered.

"There," Vaelinnae called, her voice nearly taken by the wind. "West face. Low entry."

Harvey followed her line.

The mountain did not rise so much as reveal itself. Skjol-Varr seemed less built than uncovered, as if the ice had been cut away to expose something that had always been waiting beneath. Sheer planes climbed in impossible angles, their surfaces too smooth, too deliberate to be natural. Veins of blue-white light ran through the structure like frozen lightning, pulsing faintly beneath layers of compressed age.

Openings marked the face.

Not caves.

Entrances.

Precise. Measured. Commanded into existence.

Sylveron angled his golden cliff griffyn down first, guiding it through a break in the wind that did not exist until he chose it. The others followed, wings folding as they descended toward a broad shelf of wind-scoured stone.

Talons struck.

The sound was small.

Everything here was small against the scale of it.

They dismounted quickly. Leather creaked. Frost cracked from armor as it shifted. Breath gathered around them in pale clouds, drifting and dissolving without hurry.

Harvey rested a hand briefly against his griffyn's neck. The creature leaned into it once, then settled, eyes half-lidded against the wind.

"Stay," he said.

It did.

Vaelinnae was already moving.

She did not walk so much as test the ground for permission, her steps light, angled, never fully committing until the next had already begun. Serithyl followed at a different rhythm—less visible, more certain, her presence slipping at the edges of perception whenever the eye tried to hold it.

Sylveron adjusted his grip on the cleaver on his back. The weapon emitted a low hum, almost drowned out by the wind, as if it sensed something it disliked.

Seris drew her cloak tighter. The color had faded from her cheeks hours ago, replaced by a steady red that grew deeper with each breath. Her lips had started to crack at the edges, thin lines that caught the cold and held it.

"This place feels… wrong," she said.

"Old," Sylveron corrected.

They moved.

The entrance swallowed them without resistance.

Inside, the wind died.

Not gradually.

Immediately.

The air did not move. It did not stir. It existed, cold and still, as if it had been set aside and forgotten.

Their footfalls vanished upward into vaults too high to answer.

The corridor stretched ahead, wide enough for giants to march ten abreast. Its surfaces were layered ice compressed to the hardness of stone, each stratum marking snowfall measured not in seasons, but in ages. The walls bore faint carvings—runes etched deep and then worn smooth by time, their edges softened but their intent unchanged.

Commands.

Warnings.

Ownership.

"No guards," Sylveron said.

His voice did not echo.

It ended where it was spoken.

"No sound," Serithyl added.

She was right. Even their breathing seemed to shorten here, as if the air refused to carry anything unnecessary.

Harvey drew the whispercloak closer. The fabric folded perception inward, bending lines, slipping attention just enough that the eye moved past him unless it knew to stop.

Not invisibility.

Permission denied.

They advanced.

The corridor opened into a broader avenue. Pillars rose on either side, thick as ancient oaks, their surfaces faceted and precise. Between them stood statues.

Jarls. Hunters. Beasts of the old north.

Each carved in ice with impossible fidelity.

Scars remained where they had been cut. Expressions held at the edge of triumph or death. No frost dulled them. No crack marred their form.

Time had not been allowed to touch them.

Seri slowed, reaching out.

Her fingers brushed the surface of one statue.

Life answered—

and recoiled.

She pulled her hand back sharply, breath catching.

"This place rejects it," she said. "Not dead. Just… closed."

Vaelinnae moved ahead, testing angles that felt wrong underfoot. Once, she stepped through a space that should have been empty and paused, tilting her head slightly, then moved on without comment.

Harvey noticed.

He said nothing.

They passed beneath an arch that seemed to bend light rather than reflect it. For a moment, the world shifted—edges misaligned, distance uncertain—then settled again as if nothing had happened.

Sylveron's jaw tightened.

"Too clean," he muttered.

Too still.

Too deliberate.

Harvey felt it settle inside him, just like the cold had—calmly, without urgency. A quiet insistence that something here was not as it seemed.

They moved deeper.

Time became hard to measure. The corridors did not repeat, but they also did not change. Every turn revealed another stretch of ice, another line of pillars, another set of carvings worn smooth but not erased.

No tools.

No debris.

No sign of abandonment.

Just absence.

"It's empty," Vaelinnae said at last.

The word felt wrong the moment it left her.

Harvey did not answer.

Ahead, the space expanded.

Light gathered—not brighter, but more present, as if it had been waiting for them to arrive before fully forming.

The corridor opened into a vast chamber.

The heart of the citadel.

A circular vault carved from ancient ice that had long since lost its translucence. The surface did not reflect. It held light in suspension, as if undecided whether to release it.

At the far end, two thrones rose.

Massive. Carved from ice that had become opaque with age and pressure. Their edges were worn smooth—not by decay, but through centuries of use.

The Horn stood between them on a raised plinth of froststone.

Frozen within a clear sheath of ice.

Coiled.

Ancient.

Its glow was steady. Not bright. Not dim.

Present.

Seri inhaled sharply. "I feel it."

Harvey did too.

Not a call.

Recognition.

The certainty settled in him without demand:

Whatever took the Horn would not leave unchanged.

He took one step forward.

The silence did not deepen.

It broke.

Not with sound—but with its return.

Mass pressed inward. Presence flooded the space. The air itself seemed to settle into weight as everything that had been withheld asserted itself all at once.

Frost giants stood around them in a perfect ring.

Already there.

Axes resting at precise angles. Pale blue skin shining like glacier stone, veins filled with ancient cold. Their breath rose in slow, steady clouds that marked time more clearly than any heartbeat.

High above, on thrones that hadn't existed a moment earlier, figures became clear.

A crown caught the light.

A staff hummed—low, resonant, wrong.

The Queen stood.

Her smile was small.

Precise.

"I laid a veil over your senses for a mile of corridor," she said in the Frost Thraeker tongue.

Her voice did not echo. Harvey and Seri were the only two in the party to understand the language.

"I placed your prize where your hunger would pull you."

Her gaze settled on Harvey.

"And you came."

The Horn's glow did not change.

It watched.

The trap had not been sprung.

It had been waiting.

Chapter 21 — Judgment of the North

Planet: Vaelthara
Divine Year of Vaelthas — Wolf Month, 21,426 Years Since the Sealing
Skjol-Varr — Frost Giant Citadel of the Far North

No one moved.

The frost giants' ring held—neither tightening nor shifting, simply existing within a perfect geometry that required no adjustments. Their axes rested at precise angles. Their breath was slow and visible, pale clouds drifting upward and fading without haste. The cold didn't bite here. It lingered, settling into muscle and marrow until even urgency seemed pointless.

Harvey felt his lungs struggle against it. Each inhale was deliberate. Each exhale a thin ribbon of white that lingered longer than it should have.

They had permission to walk this far.

The thrones now loomed above them, undeniable—frost-iron and ancient ice. The Jarl and his Queen watched without surprise, as if the moment had been carved long before the party ever began its journey north.

Between them, on the froststone plinth, the horn waited. Its glow remained steady. It did not call out.

It acknowledged.

Seri's hand grasped Harvey's arm. Her fingers were cold through the cloak. Not trembling—yet—but close.

"This was never empty," she murmured.

"No," Harvey said quietly. "It was closed."

The Queen rose.

The movement was slight, but the hall seemed to tilt with it. Frost traced along the length of her staff, clear ice caging a slow curl of dark within. Her skin had the blue of deep glacier ice, but something beneath shifted when the light hit wrong—something not meant for this place.

"Little hunters," she said.

Her voice did not echo. It moved smoothly, clear and personal, reaching each of them without raising its volume.

"From the green world. From the soft world."

A faint smile touched her lips.

I veiled your senses for a mile of corridor. I placed your prize where your hunger would pull you. And you came.

Her gaze settled on Harvey.

"You would take the Horn," she said, almost gently, "as if it were an object to be carried."

Sylveron shifted his stance, boots softly grinding against the ice. His breath was heavier than usual, forming a low fog around his face, but his posture remained firm. The emerald-etched cleaver on his back emitted a faint, hungry hum.

Vaelinnae was already moving—neither advancing nor retreating. Testing edges. Her steps made almost no sound, only the faintest disturbance of frost that quickly settled again as if nothing had passed.

Serithyl stood just behind Harvey's right shoulder.

Still.

Watching.

The Queen lifted her staff.

"Kneel," she said lightly.

The cold moved.

Not wind.

Not weather.

Command.

It pressed inward, winding through joints and along bones. Harvey felt it reach for his spine, for the small movements that keep a body upright. Seri's breath hitched as frost touched the corners of her lashes. Sylveron's gauntlets hardened at the edges.

Vaelinnae vanished.

One moment present — then gone.

A giant moved too late. Her blade flashed low, making a precise cut behind the knee. Not to kill, but to destabilize. The ring rippled.

Sylveron moved with it.

Not fast—inevitable. His cleaver came free in a single, heavy arc, catching an incoming axe and turning it aside with a crack that rang through the hall. Frost shattered from the impact, scattering like powdered glass.

Seri tried to gather life.

There was none.

Her magic reached outward and recoiled instantly, snapping back into her with a sharp intake of breath. Her shoulders tightened. Her hands trembled once, then steadied through force alone.

Harvey stepped forward.

The whispercloak wrapped perception around him, bending lines and slipping him between the attention of giants who had already begun to adjust.

The Queen's gaze followed anyway.

"You don't understand what you're touching," she said.

The cold thickened.

Axes came down.

Sylveron caught one, turned another, and forced space where none should have been. His breath was harsher now, visible in heavy bursts. Frost climbed his chin, stretching in streaks.

Vaelinnae reappeared and vanished again, sowing confusion into the ring. A second giant staggered. A third moved too slowly.

Serithyl did not move.

Then—

She was not there.

No sound marked it.

No shift of air.

Harvey felt only the absence of it. A line in the formation no longer accounted for.

The Queen's staff lifted higher.

"Enough," she said.

The cold surged for Harvey.

It tightened around his joints with a precise constriction, not freezing him but limiting his movement so much that even taking a step demanded careful decision.

Too slow.

Too exposed.

The Kuldemaekr answered.

The blade drank.

Cold flowed into it, drawn along its edge, sinking into something deeper than metal. Harvey felt the resistance lessen—not gone, but diverted.

He moved.

Not fast.

Exact.

Up the first step of the dais.

An axe struck where his shoulder had been. The whispercloak swung it past him by a breath.

The Queen watched him come.

Calm.

Certain.

"Too late," she began.

A blade touched her throat.

Everything stopped.

The cold did not vanish.

It held.

But it no longer advanced.

The Queen's eyes did not widen. They shifted.

Down.

A fraction.

To the edge of her throat.

Serithyl stood behind her.

Close enough that her breath drifted forward in a thin, steady cloud, curling against the Queen's skin before fading into the still air. A faint tremor ran through her shoulders—controlled, contained, the body's quiet response to a cold that would not allow refusal.

No frost touched her.

No step had marked her passage.

She had not crossed the distance.

She had arrived at its only necessary point.

The blade did not press.

It rested.

Perfectly placed.

The Jarl did not move.

His gaze moved once—from Serithyl, to the blade, to the Queen.

Something older than fury entered his face.

"Stop," he said.

The word carried.

Axes lowered.

Not by command shouted, but by understanding.

The ring loosened—not broken, but no longer closing.

Harvey stepped onto the dais fully.

He did not look at Serithyl.

He did not need to.

The opening existed because she held it.

"Call them back," he said.

The Jarl's jaw clenched. Frost subtly cracked along the edges of his beard as his breath grew deeper.

He lifted one hand.

The giants withdrew a single step.

Enough.

At the foot of the dais, the chained dragon shifted. Its eyes remained fixed on Harvey.

"Unchain it," Harvey said.

The Jarl hesitated.

Then lowered his hand.

The chain fell.

The dragon rose slowly and deliberately, its breath forming a rolling plume of white that coiled along the floor.

Harvey met its gaze.

"You are free."

It considered him.

Then turned and left.

No rush. No gratitude. No sound beyond the measured impact of claw on ice as it passed between giants who did not attempt to stop it.

Harvey turned to the Horn.

Up close, it felt wrong.

Not cold.

Not warm.

Present.

He placed the Kuldemaekr against the ice.

The blade did not strike.

It parted.

A clean line. No fracture. No resistance.

The ice opened as if it had already decided.

Harvey took the Horn.

For a moment, the world narrowed.

The weight was not physical.

It settled deeper.

Recognition.

Expectation.

He did not hold it long.

He passed it to Seri.

Her hands clenched around it. She flinched once, then steadied, breath catching as if something inside her had been named.

“Now,” Harvey said.

Serithyl moved.

The blade left the Queen’s throat.

The cold surged.

Axes lifted.

The hall broke into motion all at once.

Vaelinnae was already ahead, forging a path that hadn't existed until she made it. Sylveron stepped into the space behind her, anchoring it and refusing to let it close.

Seris ran.

Her breath grew sharp and ragged, each exhale a burst of white that lingered too long.

Harvey moved with them.

Behind them, the Queen’s voice rose — not loud, but sharp.

“Run.”

The word carried no urgency.

Only certainty.

They ran.

The corridor swallowed them. Sound returned in fragments—footfalls, breath, the distant thunder of pursuit building behind them.

Cold followed.

Not as a command.

As a consequence.

An ice shard crossed the distance between heartbeats.

Too fast.

Too clean.

Serithyl staggered once.

Harvey turned.

Too late.

The shard had entered just below her ribs, a narrow line of white that steamed faintly in the air. For a heartbeat, she remained upright, her posture unchanged except for the smallest shift of balance.

No cry.

No word.

Her breath left her in a soft cloud that did not return.

Vaelinnae slowed.

"Serithyl—"

"We can—" Seri began, already turning, hands lifting—

"No."

Harvey's voice was quiet.

Absolute.

Serithyl did not fall immediately.

That was worse.

Then the strength left her.

She folded without sound.

They ran.

Behind them, the giants closed.

Ahead, the exit widened into pale light.

Sylveron took a blow that would have broken a weaker man, the impact echoing through his armor and forcing him to one knee. He got up anyway, breath huffing out in heavy bursts, frost forming around his mouth as he pushed himself forward.

Seris burned what remained of her.

Green where no green belonged.

Vines tore through the ice, with thorns forcing their way into a world that rejected them, stealing seconds that felt like theft.

They broke into the open.

Wind returned like a scream.

The griffyns waited.

They mounted without pause.

Wings beat once—twice—then the ground fell away beneath them.

Skjol-Varr shrank into white.

No one spoke.

Harvey did not look back.

The horn rested between them, heavy with something that hadn't yet taken its shape.

Behind them, the North closed.

The Horn had been taken.
The Greenwood would answer.

And for the first time, the Hunt felt real.

No one said her name.

Chapter 22 — The Forest That Should Not Answer

Planet: Vaelthara
Location: Faelwyn Holt — Graypine Reach, Under-Root Paths | The Tainted Shrine of Aelrindel
Divine Year of Vaelthas — Wolf Month, 21,426 Years Since the Sealing

"Some doors do not open. They only remember your name."
— *Whispered warning, passed among Wolf Clan root-runners*

Sablek Thistlecrest was pruning winter-moss when the world flinched.

Not a tremor. Not wind. Not even that subtle change in sap-pressure that came before storms.

This was resonance.

A single note rolled through Faelwyn Holt like a bell heard underwater, too deep for ears and too pure to be chance. Lantern-gourds dimmed for one heartbeat, as if their light had swallowed itself. The bark beneath Sablek's knee tightened, then loosened, like a muscle remembering it could move. Somewhere in the canopy, a sprite dropped straight out of the air and clung to a trunk, shaking like a leaf in fever.

Sablek's shears paused mid-cut.

Behind him, three children in training wraps went perfectly still. Not because they'd been taught discipline.

Because something ancient had spoken to their blood.

One of them blinked hard, his jaw trembling, then began to cry as if he'd remembered an old fear he'd never lived through.

Sablek smiled, soft and patient, and shaped his voice into safety.

"Breathe," he told them. "The Holt settles. It does that. Sometimes the roots shift, and the lanterns dim. Nothing more."

His hand reached out and gently tucked the boy's braid behind his ear. A small gesture. Familiar. Human.

A lie with a kind face.

He finished the cut. He tied the moss back with vine-thread. He nodded to the mothers and fathers gathered along the lantern path and asked after a sick elder by name. He accepted a cup of warm sap-tea as if his hands were not full of dirt and secrets.

To everyone who mattered in daylight, he was precisely what Graypine Reach needed.

Inside, every strand of him was listening.

Because he recognized that note.

Not by melody. By absence. By the way the forest itself tried to pretend it hadn't heard anything.

Aelrindel.

Not the god's voice, not directly. Gods didn't sing in the open world anymore, not since the Chamber's long silence.

But this note had come from the seam where reality had been stitched shut. The thread had tugged.

And somewhere north, impossibly far, something had moved that had no right to move.

Sablek did not hurry.

That was rule one of surviving two lives.

He walked the Lantern-Paths as the settlement settled into its evening rhythm: fires lit low, stew pots covered, elders settling into root-niches, patrols swapping quiet reports. He spoke gently to a young hunter whose hand still shook from his first kill. He promised to check the border-groves at dawn. He smiled at a councilor and let her talk about hope until she felt heard.

His face never changed.

Only his eyes did, once, when no one was looking: a flicker of calculation as sharp as a blade edge.

Then he turned into a narrow rootway where lanterns did not grow.

Down.

Down past the places where laughter had faded. Past the fungal glow that didn't feel like comfort. Past a stretch of bark where the living wood had been scarred long ago and never healed properly, as if the Holt had decided that wound deserved to remain a warning.

The air grew colder.

Not winter-cold.

Old-cold.

A cold that belonged to a vow.

Two Anari stood guard at the bend, cloaks plain, their postures relaxed in a way that people pretended was only routine.

Their eyes were too sharp for routine.

To any passerby, they were "normal" druids on night watch.

In shadow, their focus stones revealed the truth: blackened, cracked, and tainted as if soot had grown inside the crystal.

Sablek gave the sign.

Two fingers to the chest, then downward, as if swearing an oath to something beneath the roots.

They stepped aside without a word.

The path narrowed into stone.

Not natural stone. Cut. Placed. Sealed.

The Shrine of Aelrindel had once been a place of blessing.

Now it was a mouth that tasted of rot.

Sablek entered.

The chamber breathed wrong.

The air smelled of wet iron and sour sap. The old carvings of Pursuit, Oath, and Moon-path were still visible, but their lines had been over-scratched and recut into spirals that strained the eye to follow. Bone charms hung where leaf charms should have been. Aelrindel's antlered glyphs were not erased, only smothered by newer marks.

And the altar… the altar's living wood had been carved open and filled with something that pulsed slowly, like a heart learning to beat for a stranger.

A thin chorus hummed in the dark.

Not prayer.

Practice.

Dark druids knelt in a half-circle—Anari mostly, their faces hidden beneath hoods stitched with ash-thread. Two humans sat among them, rigid and pale, their wrists bound with vine-cord not for restraint but for ritual alignment. Their breathing came in short, disciplined pulls, the way soldiers breathe when they're trying not to look like soldiers.

At the far end, where the shrine should have been calm, a cluster of dryads stood like a jury.

Not Holt-dryads.

These were wrong.

Their bodies were bark and beauty, yes, but the bark was too dark, and the beauty had edges that felt hungry. Their eyes were not green.

They were pits.

When they turned their faces toward Sablek, the chamber's hum sharpened, as if someone had tightened a string.

Sablek moved to his place, hands folded, expression neutral. The posture of a man entering service.

The dark druids did not speak of what had just happened.

Not at first.

You didn't name a wound until you knew whether it would bleed you out.

Then one of the wrong-dryads made a sound.

It wasn't language.

It was a scream folded into a whisper, like a throat trying to cry through water.

Every torch-spore in the shrine flickered.

The humans gasped. One clutched at his chest as if struck.

The Anari druids flinched as one.

And the taint in the altar… wavered.

Sablek felt it clearly: the Crone's grip, that cold hand around this place, tightening and then slipping away.

For the first time in months, the shrine felt uncertain of itself.

Sablek turned his head slightly, watching the dryads.

They were retreating.

Not all at once. Not running. Dryads didn't run.

They recoiled as if someone had spoken the one name they were forbidden to hear.

One pressed a palm to the shrine wall and hissed, voice cracking into something almost human.

"It stirs."

Another, taller, hair braided with black thorn, spoke with a trembling fury that made Sablek's skin prickle.

"The Greenwood hears."

That should not have been possible.

The Greenwood was a curse. A sealed lung. A place where living beings did not return. A place that did not answer.

And yet the shrine's taint was wavering like flame in the wind.

Sablek kept his mouth calm.

His mind went razor-sharp.

Aelrindel's horn. A god's possession.

He did not know how he knew. He only knew the way hunters see a wind shift before they feel it: a subtle betrayal in the air.

The horn had been moved.

Not approached.

Not studied.

Moved.

And the Greenwood had felt it.

The forest was no longer answering Sablek.

And for the first time, he wondered whether it ever had.

The dark druids began speaking at once, their voices low, urgent, and overlapping.

"Something broke."

"Did the Crone call?"

"No. She… hesitated."

"She doesn't hesitate."

"She did."

A human initiate trembled. "Is this… the end?"

A dryad snapped its head toward the human, its pits blazing.

"Silence."

The word carried weight. The human's teeth clicked shut as if his jaw had been locked by invisible fingers.

Sablek stepped forward.

Not fast. Not dramatic.

Just enough to pull attention into a single line.

"What happened?" he asked, voice steady. "Say it clean."

A younger Anari dark druid looked like he wanted to lie. His mouth opened.

Nothing came.

He swallowed hard and forced the truth out like pulling a thorn from tongue.

"The north sent a signal through the root-dream. The frost."

Sablek's eyes narrowed. "Frost giants?"

The young druid nodded once. "The citadel."

Another druid, older, spoke with a bitter edge. "The Horn was there. We guarded the path. We fed the humans tales to keep their eyes elsewhere."

"And now?" Sablek said.

The older druid's throat worked.

"Now the Horn is not there."

Silence slammed down.

Even the dryads stilled.

Somewhere deeper in the shrine, the pulsing taint at the altar skipped one beat, then resumed, weaker.

Sablek felt sweat form under his ribs.

Not fear.

Calculation.

His timetable had been built around the Greenwood staying shut. Around Aelrindel staying buried. Around the Crone having time to harden her net before anyone could cut it.

He forced himself to look at the dryads. "Why are you retreating?"

The thorn-braided one shuddered. "Because something pulls and calls to us. Nothing should be able to do that to us."

Sablek kept his voice low. "Who has it?"

The younger druid's gaze darted away, as if afraid the answer itself could summon punishment.

"A bearer," he said. "Not one of ours."

Sablek's jaw tightened. "Name."

The druid flinched and blurted it.

"Unknown. A green knight or perhaps the high druid."

Sablek's mind went still.

Harvey.

The Green Knight.

The one the dream-threads favored.

The one the old stories insisted could do what no other living being could: walk into the Greenwood and return.

Sablek breathed out slowly through his nose.

So, the impossible was no longer myth.

It had become scheduled.

He scanned faces.

"Is this confirmed?"

The older druid nodded once, grim. "It came through the chain. From a messenger who heard it from the north-path watchers. From… him."

Sablek's eyes shifted toward the far shadow near the altar.

The shrine had another occupant—silent, masked, and leaning against a column of scarred living wood.

A figure leaned against a column of scarred living wood, hood up, face masked in smooth, bark-white. He had been there without being announced, as if the shrine itself had grown him from a corner.

Quiet. Still. Listening.

When Sablek looked at him, the figure's head tilted slightly.

Recognition passed like a blade edge.

Sablek knew that posture.

Not a druid.

Not a priest.

Hunter.

The masked figure did not speak.

He didn't have to.

One of the dark druids, nervous, hurried to fill the silence. "He was told first. He… listens where we cannot."

Sablek's gaze stayed on the masked one. "And what does he say?"

The masked figure stepped forward.

Just one step.

The air changed with it.

Not a flare. Not show.

Pressure.

The kind of pressure prey feels when it realizes the predator is already close enough to choose.

When he spoke, his voice was calm.

Careful.

Ordinary enough to be safe.

"The Green Knight has the Horn. If he survives the Greenwood, Aelrindel could walk again," he said. "He survived the citadel."

A ripple passed through the room: shock, disbelief, awe.

A dryad hissed, teeth bared. "He should be dead."

The masked figure turned his head toward the dryad.

The dryad went still.

Sablek felt a cold satisfaction flicker.

Good.

The dryads feared this one.

He kept his tone measured. "And the Greenwood?"

The masked figure paused, as if listening for something none of them could hear.

"The Greenwood stirred," he said. "It answered."

That phrase tasted wrong in Sablek's mouth.

The forest that should not answer.

The curse that should not permit a response.

And yet, across Vaelthara, a note had run through the roots like a bell.

Even here. Even under taint. Even beneath the Crone's hand.

Sablek's fingers curled once inside his sleeves.

His timetable had collapsed.

His careful, slow conversion of the Wolf Clan into doctrine and surrender. His use of human druids as a bridge to timber camps. His quiet training in dark rites while pretending to be harmless in daylight.

All of it assumed time.

Harvey Oakenstride had stolen time.

Sablek looked at the gathered druids.

"We accelerate," he said.

Several faces lifted, hungry for orders.

Sablek spoke softly, and the softness made it worse.

"Your Crone-control wavers. Your dryads retreat. That means the Greenwoods' seal is no longer absolute."

A few druids made old warding gestures, then corrected them into Crone-signs, as if ashamed of a reflex.

Sablek continued. "If Aelrindel is freed, the Wolf Clan regains what it lost."

He let the weight of that hang.

"Blessings. Authority. Old rites. Unifying songs."

Fear flashed. Not of Aelrindel exactly.

Of what a united Wolf Clan could become.

Sablek turned back to the masked figure.

"And you," he said quietly. "You will move."

The masked figure inclined his head. Just enough.

Agreement.

Not obedience.

Sablek did not like that.

But he could use it.

"Find out where the Green Knight is headed," Sablek said. "Find the edges of his path. Find what will break him."

The masked figure's voice stayed level.

"He is not the only one who matters."

Sablek's eyes narrowed. "Explain."

The masked figure tilted his head to listen, then spoke.

"Others will feel the god's horn and know that Aelrindel is freed. They will move. Some to help the Green Knight. Some to stop him."

Sablek's lips pressed into a thin line.

Across Vaelthara, the freed god was felt.

He could almost imagine it: roots shivering, dryads waking in their trees with terror in their throats, old shrines trembling. The Crone's web was vibrating as prey wandered into it.

A dryad near the wall pressed both hands to its head as if trying to hold a scream inside.

Then it screamed anyway.

A sound like sap boiling. A sound like a tree learning it can bleed.

The scream tore through the shrine and out into the rootways, and somewhere above them, in the living world, lantern-gourds dimmed again for one heartbeat.

Sablek whispered, mostly to himself, "So the Greenwood truly stirs."

The masked figure did not respond.

He didn't need to.

Because in the thin silence after the dryad's scream, Sablek felt something else.

Not the Crone. Not the shrine.

A distant pull, like something ancient recognizing a direction.

Something had awakened.

And it was moving with intent.

Sablek lifted his chin, eyes cold.

"Then we do not wait," he said to his circle. "We do not preach peace."

He paused, and the pause tasted like iron.

"We prepare for war."

The dark druids bowed. The humans shivered. The dryads withdrew, snarling, as if they could no longer bear to be near the altar.

The masked figure turned away first, slipping into the shadows as if the shrine exhaled him.

Sablek watched him go.

The most dangerous weapon was not the spell you could see.

It was the one that moved through your plan and made you think it had been your idea.

When the masked figure vanished into root-dark, Sablek finally let his calm face crack just slightly.

Only enough for one thought to escape.

If Harvey freed him… the Wolf Clan will remember what it was.

And if the Wolf Clan remembered, Sablek's double life would end in blood.

Above them, somewhere beyond roots and doctrine, the Greenwood stirred again.

A second note.

Fainter.

But unmistakable.

The forest that should not answer…

had begun to listen.

And listening was how it would begin.

Chapter 23 — The Price of Peace

Planet: Vaelthara
Locations: Western Human Kingdoms • Königbrunn • Faelwyn Holt (Borderlands)
Divine Year of Vaelthas — Wolf Month, 21,426 Years Since the Sealing

"Victory is the only prayer the gods still hear."
— *War-Litany of the Crowned Faith*

The news of the Horn did not arrive as a rumor.

It arrived as an interpretation.

Human druids aligned with the border missions carried it first. Not breathless messengers, not panicked refugees, but calm figures in bark-woven cloaks and ash-threaded sashes, their expressions sober, practiced, almost apologetic. They did not shout. They did not warn.

They explained.

They spoke of a relic recovered from the frozen north. A god-horn. An Anari instrument older than written faith, capable of waking forests, bending armies, and unmaking borders without ever touching steel.

They did not call it a miracle.

They called it instability.

By the time their words reached the western kingdoms, fear had already been shaped into a usable form.

KÖNIGBRUNN

Königbrunn stood where pine gave way to stone and the forest edge bent reluctantly under human hands. Its walls were old, scarred by siege and sanctified by smoke. Cathedral spires rose like accusations against the sky, their bells heavy with centuries of answered prayers and unanswered ones.

This was where the western kingdoms gathered their faith.

And sharpened it.

Cannon crews drilled twice daily. Powder was weighed, reweighed, and sealed beneath priestly sigils. Firing arcs were recalculated—not toward roads or valleys, but inward toward tree lines, ravines thick with roots, and the first shadowed fingers of Faelwyn Holt.

Prayer schedules tightened. Confession became mandatory. Even silence was regulated.

Fear had found its rhythm.

And then the emissary arrived.

Ser Varyng the Sanctified did not bring an army.

He did not need to.

He entered Königbrunn beneath a banner older than the walls themselves: a crimson field scorched black at the edges, embroidered with a crown wreathed in flame.

The Embered Standard.

When it was unfurled, the city bells rang without being touched.

Priests fell to their knees.

Veterans wept openly.

Children stopped crying mid-breath.

Ser Varyng removed his helm only after mounting the cathedral steps. His face bore ritual scars and old burns, each deliberate, each a credential. His eyes were clear, fervent, and utterly untroubled by doubt.

He spoke without amplification.

He did not need it.

"The gods did not abandon us," he said. "They tested us."

The gathered clergy leaned forward as one organism.

"In the age after the Malloch," Varyng continued, "our ancestors believed the divine fell silent because humanity failed. We knelt too soon. We sought peace without victory."

A murmur rippled through the square.

Varyng raised the Embered Standard behind him.

"Faith must be proven through conquest," he said. "To kneel without a sword is to pray without a tongue."

The War-Litany was taken up instantly. Hundreds of voices answered the banner.

The land that bleeds for the Banner is land claimed by the Divine.

Varyng did not smile.

He never smiled.

THE WAR-CATHEDRAL

Within days, construction began.

Outside Königbrunn's eastern gate, stone foundations were laid for something not seen since before the Malloch War.

A War-Cathedral.

Not a place of worship.

A declaration.

Its cornerstone was consecrated in blood. Knights signed Holy Contracts in iron ink and living flesh, binding themselves to crusade under threat of divine excommunication. Priests blessed blades before they blessed the dead.

Varyng oversaw it all with calm efficiency.

"The Wolf Clan controls economic arteries," he told the assembled lords and bishops. "Root-roads. Timber flows. Forest trade hubs."

Maps were unrolled.

Faelwyn Holt was marked in red chalk.

"We will not charge blindly into the trees," Varyng said. "We will starve them first."

The human dark druids were summoned next.

They arrived wary, unsure whether they were being recruited or condemned.

Varyng regarded them with interest rather than suspicion.

"You believe the forest should be guided," he said. "Good. Then you will guide it for us."

He did not threaten.

He offered purpose.

"You will help us take Faelwyn Holt without burning it," Varyng continued. "You will show us how roots grow. How paths open. How the forest listens."

"And if the Anari resist?" one druid asked.

Varyng answered immediately.

"Then they prove our faith correct."

FAELWYN HOLT

Within the forest, fractures deepened.

Traditionalists drifted toward the old paths, toward Khandyl's rebels and the memory of gods who once walked openly among them.

Doctrine-followers remained near Heartroot Vale, repeating Sablek's words like charms.

No more wars means no more Malloch.

Lady Vyrna sat alone more often now.

Council chambers felt larger. Quieter. Hollow.

When she spoke, fewer answered.

When Vaelis Valisar spoke, everyone listened.

He moved between factions with practiced ease, offering reassurance, compromise, patience.

"The humans are afraid," he said gently. "Fear can still be guided."

He never mentioned Königbrunn.

Never mentioned banners.

Never mentioned crusades.

He did not need to.

Because peace, once offered, had become an obligation.

And obligation is the easiest weapon to aim.

As Ser Varyng departed Königbrunn for the borderlands, the Embered Standard rode with him, snapping in a wind that smelled faintly of pine.

Twenty years of war began with that step.

Not in fire.

Not in blood.

But in belief.

And deep within the forest, roots shifted—

not yet in resistance,

but in recognition.

The hunt was coming.

Chapter 24 — The Rebel's Strike

Planet: Vaelthara
Location: Western Border Roads • Near Rothwald Camp • Ruins of Dornfeste
Divine Year of Vaelthas — Wolf Month, 21,426 Years Since the Sealing

The road was wrong.

Kellyn felt it before she saw it.

Human roads always were. Too straight. Too sure of themselves. They cut rather than followed, scarred rather than listened. This one ran like a wound along the forest's edge, churned into slick mud by iron-shod boots and overloaded wagons.

And tonight, it carried a convoy.

Six wagons. Canvas-topped. Reinforced axles. Thirty militia on foot, with disciplined spacing, shields slung. Another dozen riders spread across the flank and rear, lanterns hooded but visible, their faint light swinging in time with progress.

Supply wagons.

Feeding garrisons.

Feeding walls.

Feeding belief.

Kellyn watched from above. Myrrathis circled high, wings slicing the air without a sound. Bronze scales drank the moonlight and gave nothing back. Below her, the rebels waited.

This was not forest fighting.

There were no roots here. No trunks to lean against. No living walls that bent paths or swallowed sound. Just scrubland, loose stone, shallow slopes, and the open sky.

Ancient Anari territory, stripped bare.

Kholfax knelt beside the road, half-hidden among rock and brush. His bow lay across his knees, already strung, already measured. He had chosen a position with no escape route behind him.

Khandyl lay farther downslope, jaw clenched so tightly that Kellyn could see the muscle jump. Froster crouched near a shattered mile-marker, emerald runes along his cleaver dimmed to a breath-hold. Three elder rangers lay prone beyond them, bows drawn, eyes steady, faces unreadable.

No forest.

No divine shelter.

Only skill.

Only choice.

Kellyn felt a tremor of pride tighten her chest.

Kholfax raised two fingers.

The signal passed without sound.

The convoy entered the kill zone.

For three heartbeats, nothing happened.

Then the first arrows flew.

Queen's Kiss did not scream. It whispered.

Pale-blue threads stitched through the dark, each shot placed with merciless precision. Two militia fell without realizing they had been struck. A third stumbled forward, hands clawing at empty air, then folded into the road.

No warning cry.

No alarm horn.

Too clean.

The escort reacted a breath too late.

Shields snapped up. Riders reined in hard. A captain's voice cracked through the night, sharp and frightened.

Then Froster moved.

His cleaver struck a wagon wheel with a blow that should not have been possible. Wood exploded outward in a spray of splinters and iron shards. The axle buckled. The wagon tipped, spilling crates, sacks, and blackpowder kegs into the road.

Fire followed.

Not dragonfire. Not spellfire.

Oil.

Pitch.

A torch tossed low and deliberate.

The night bloomed orange.

Rebels surged from cover in disciplined bursts, neither charging nor hesitating. They moved as if the ground itself had taught them how to cross it. Every step was placed. Every strike was measured.

Kellyn felt her pulse quicken.

They were fighting outside the forest.

Kholfax moved like a blade through shadow. He dropped one soldier with an arrow to the thigh, rolled under a panicked swing, and rose behind another, striking with the flat of his blade. The man fell, gasping, alive but done.

Old habits.

Detective habits.

Kill only when there was no other choice.

The militia broke.

Some ran for the wagons. Others fled westward. One rider tried to rally them but was struck by an arrow through the throat mid-command.

The fight was over in moments.

Bodies lay scattered along the road. Two wagons burned low and hot. Supplies spilled into the mud, hissing as fire found pitch and grain alike. Survivors fled into the dark, leaving weapons, rations, and certainty behind.

Kellyn landed Myrrathis beyond the road, her wings folding with a soft metallic hiss. She slid from the saddle and approached as the rebels regrouped.

No cheers.

No triumph.

Only breath, smoke, and the sharp scent of burnt iron.

"That was clean," she said quietly.

Khandyl met her gaze. "It had to be."

They did not linger.

They moved again.

South.

Toward Dornfeste.

The ruins still smoked.

Charred timbers jutted from the ground like broken ribs. New scaffolds had been raised—too fast, too hopeful. Fresh-cut logs lay stacked, waiting to become walls that would stand.

Militia replacements who had arrived earlier were already at work.

They never saw the rebels coming.

This time, Kellyn fought with them.

She did not unleash Myrrathis indiscriminately. No roaring inferno. No spectacle. Controlled bursts of flame turned siege engines into choking pyres, set stacked lumber ablaze, and collapsed scaffolding inward.

Precision fire.

Anari arrows sang.

Blades flashed.

The camp died a second time.

When it was done, the rebels withdrew into the shadows, breathless and stunned—not by victory, but by survival.

Outside the forest.

Alive.

They rested among shattered stone and glowing embers, watching the fires die down to coals.

That was when the conversation happened.

Kholfax sat apart, methodically cleaning his blade. Kellyn approached and crouched beside him.

"You said you heard him," she said quietly. "When the patrol died."

Kholfax nodded once. "I did."

"Describe it."

He did not hesitate.

“Male,” he said. “Controlled. Not loud. Not shouted. It wasn’t anger or frenzy. It was… shaped.”

Kellyn’s breath stilled.

“Harmonic,” Kholfax continued. “Layered. Three notes at once. One carried the command. One carried paralysis.” His jaw tightened. “The third was the killing edge.”

Silence spread outward from them.

Kellyn closed her eyes.

Dark mage-warrior structure.

Not life-mage compulsion.

Not dryad charm.

Weaponized Song.

When she opened her eyes again, the forest felt farther away than it ever had.

“He’s Anari,” she said softly.

Kholfax met her gaze. “I know.”

“And trained,” she added. “In something old. Something forbidden.”

The ancient Anari exchanged uneasy glances.

Froster spoke at last. “Then he walks among us.”

No one argued.

Kellyn looked back toward the road, toward the human lands, toward the faint glow of fires marking the edges of a widening war.

This wasn’t chaos.

This was preparation.

She turned back to Kholfax.

“You were right,” she said. “About adapting. About fighting where the forest cannot help.”

Something like relief flickered across his face.

“Then you trust me.”

“Yes,” Kellyn said. “Now I do.”

Above them, clouds slid across the moon, swallowing its light.

The rebels vanished into the night, leaving behind ashes, broken supply lines, and a truth that could no longer be ignored.

The killer had a voice.

And it was not human.

Not named.

Not accused.

But no longer abstract.

And it was getting closer.

Chapter 25 — The Greenwood That Devours

Planet: Vaelthara
Location: Eastern Edge of the Greenwood
Divine Year of Vaelthas — Wolf Month, 21,426 Years Since the Sealing

"I once believed mastery meant never yielding.
Harvey proved me wrong. He yielded to truth, duty, and compassion — and never bent. I forged warriors. He became a knight."
— *Sylveron Windstream, recalling Harvey*

The Greenwood did not announce itself.

There was no wall.

No broken ground.

No visible threshold marking where the living forest ended and the curse began.

The trees… stopped behaving like trees.

Their branches no longer reached for light. Their leaves did not turn. Their trunks leaned at angles that suggested listening rather than growth. The forest did not thicken here. It closed ranks.

Harvey felt it first in the griffyn.

The great beast slowed without command, its wings faltering mid-beat, its talons scraping stone as if searching for purchase that no longer existed. Its breath hitched. Its feathers ruffled, lifting and settling again, unsettled. Its eyes rolled white at the edges, not in panic but in refusal.

This far.

No farther.

Sylveron reined in his own mount to a halt beside Harvey's. The older knight did not need to look ahead to know.

"This is it," he said.

Ahead, the Greenwood waited.

Mist clung to the ground, not drifting but holding. Trunks darkened into shades that had nothing to do with bark or shadow. The air carried the scent of wet leaves, layered over something metallic and ancient.

Old blood.

Old endings.

Harvey dismounted slowly.

The cold of the far north still lingered in his bones, but this chill was different. Not sharp. Not biting.

Deliberate.

He passed the griffyn's reins to Sylveron.

"You don't cross," Harvey said.

It was not a question.

Sylveron nodded once. "No living Anari does."

Seris Tarl dismounted as well, her steps cautious, her hands glowing faintly as her magic reached outward on instinct—and then recoiled.

Her light dimmed.

"I can't feel the forest," she whispered. "Not the way I should. It's there… but muted, like something wrapped around its throat."

"That would be the Crone," Vaellinae Whisperpetal said softly.

The Sylph warrior stood a pace back, wings folded tight, blades sheathed. The air here refused her. Wind did not answer her breath. The sky above the Greenwood might as well have been stone.

Vaellinae met Harvey's eyes, and for once, there was no mirth there.

"Keep the Horn on you," she said. "Always. Please do not set it down or leave it behind. If you fall—"

She paused, then corrected herself with care.

"If you stumble, keep it close."

Seris stepped forward and pressed a bundle into Harvey's hands.

Rations. Root bread, dense enough to last. Leaf-wrapped meat cured with forest salts. Bark flasks etched with warding spirals, their seals grown, not crafted.

"It's not much," Seris said. "The Greenwood eats distance. Paths fold. Time misbehaves. Days might not be days inside."

Harvey nodded. "I'll make it stretch."

She hesitated, then placed her hand against his forearm.

Her magic stirred—then slid away, rejected.

"I can't bless you," she said, frustration cutting through her calm. "Anything I give won't last."

"That's all right," Harvey replied. "I'm not going in blessed."

He turned to Vaellinae.

"If something moves in the fog," she said, "assume it is already dead. If something speaks in a familiar voice—do not answer. If you hear hunting horns that are not yours—run."

Sylveron stepped closer.

For a moment, he looked at every year he had carried. Then his posture straightened, and the knight returned.

"You find Aelrindel," he said. "Wherever the Crone buried him, you blow the Horn. You do not linger. You're our people's only chance at this."

"And if I don't find him?" Harvey asked.

Sylveron's jaw tightened.

"Then you survive."

They stood in silence.

No embraces.

No promises of return.

This was not that kind of farewell.

Harvey slung the Horn over his back. Even frozen, it felt heavier here, as if the forest recognized it and resented the reminder.

He took one step forward.

Fog brushed his boots.

Another.

The Greenwood accepted him.

Seris gasped.

"He's still alive," she whispered, disbelief threading her voice.

Harvey crossed fully beneath the canopy.

The world ended.

Not faded—ended.

Sound vanished. Birdsong cut off mid-note. Wind ceased. Even his own breathing sounded distant and muffled, as if he were hearing himself through deep water.

The fog thickened, coiling around roots and trunks like patient hands. Shadows bent toward him, no matter where light should have fallen.

He walked.

Bones lay tangled in roots.

Armor split and rusted into the soil.

Blades snapped and were half-swallowed by moss.

Skulls tilted upward, mouths open, not screaming—warning.

Anari.

Human.

Others older still.

None had made it far.

The Greenwood remembered them all.

Something moved deeper in the mist.

Not approaching.

Watching.

Harvey did not quicken his pace. He did not slow.

The Horn throbbed once against his back.

Not sound.

Recognition.

Far away, something vast shifted its attention.

The Greenwood did not roar.

It did not strike.

It closed.

Harvey did not look back.

He walked deeper into the Greenwood, alone, alive where no living being should have been—

and the forest sealed itself behind him without a sound.

The Hunt had begun.

And the Greenwood was awake.

The Green Knight enters the Greenwood.

Chapter 26 – The Banner at Eichenfall

Planet: Vaelthara
Location: Western Kingdoms — Eichenfall Timber Camp, Outer Roadline
Divine Year of Vaelthas — Wolf Month, 21,426 Years Since the Sealing

"Holiness is not found. It is planted."
— *War-Litany of the Crowned Faith*

Eichenfall did not look like a settlement.

It looked like a wound that had learned to function.

The clearing was raw and uneven, hacked from the forest by saw and flame, its edges ringed with stumps like broken teeth. Sap-blackened rings marked where trees had boiled from the inside out. Mud clung to boots and wagon wheels alike, churned thin by traffic and exhaustion. Smoke hung low, refusing to rise, coating canvas roofs and stacked timber in a greasy haze that smelled of pitch, sweat, and carefully managed fear.

Men moved as if they had done this yesterday.
And the day before that.
And would do it again tomorrow.

A hundred lumberjacks. Fifty militia. And others who did not fit neatly into either count.

Rangers.

Not the kingdom's old road-wardens, who hunted deer and bandits along borders that were agreed upon. These men moved differently. Quietly. Deliberately. Their eyes did not drift. Their hands never left their weapons for long.

They wore wool cloaks stitched with leaf-patterned camouflage. Their bows were oiled, their blades clean. They watched the tree line not with fear but with professional respect.

They had been trained.

And that training had not come from any cathedral.

A rough palisade ringed the camp. Cannons crouched behind it on timber platforms, their iron muzzles aimed at the green like animals taught a single, brutal trick. In the center stood a half-built storehouse. Beside it, a newly raised stone-and-iron altar braced a tall banner pole driven deep into the earth.

The banner snapped in the wind.

Red cloth. Gold thread. A winged sword over flame.

The Burning Banner.

It cast a long shadow across the mud.

That shadow was what the emissary rode into.

The column arrived without hurry.

Plate-armored knights rode two abreast. Banner-men followed, their poles steady. Priests in white-and-crimson vestments walked beside wagons carrying stone blocks, iron braces, and carpenter's tools, all bound alongside spear shafts.

They did not look like an army.

They looked like a future under construction.

At their head rode Ser Varyng the Sanctified, Banner-Saint of the Third Crusade.

He wore no crown.

He did not need one.

His helm was open-faced, revealing a calm, unmarked expression. His armor bore ritual scorch marks where old fires had kissed it and then failed to linger. A white tabard hung over his chest, stitched with the sigil of the Burning Crown. The embered standard he carried was not large, yet it sagged under its own weight, as if the cloth remembered every battlefield it had witnessed.

Eichenfall's commander splashed through the mud to meet him, saluting hastily.

"Banner-Saint," the commander began. "We weren't told you were—"

"Faith does not announce itself," Ser Varyng replied.

His voice was mild. Polite. Final.

His gaze moved across the camp. The stumps. The cannons. The men. The rangers.

Then it stopped.

Near the northern palisade stood a forest giant, its bark-skin braided with rope charms and iron bands, clutching an uprooted trunk like a club. It stared into the tree line as if listening for a language it no longer trusted.

Beside it stood something worse.

An undead giant.

Bone lashed in vine—hollow ribs threaded with blackened roots. Eye sockets glow faint green. It did not shift. Did not breathe. Did not wait impatiently.

It simply stood.

Two druids lingered near the giants.

One human. Hooded. Thorn-ringed.

One Anari.

Not armored. Not defiant. Cloaked in wolf-gray, staff grounded, focus stone at his chest darkened like a bruise.

His face was still.

Too still.

Ser Varyng reined in his horse and studied him.

The camp seemed to contract around that silence.

"You," Ser Varyng said softly.

The Anari did not bow. He turned his head slightly. Nothing more.

The human druid stepped forward too quickly. "Banner-Saint, this one is—"

"A guest?" Ser Varyng asked.

The human hesitated. "An ally. A bridge. He has helped keep peace. He has—"

Ser Varyng lifted one hand.

Not a threat.

Decision.

Two knights dismounted and advanced with measured steps.

The Anari's fingers twitched.

The forest giant's head creaked around.

The undead giant's eyes brightened.

"He is under our protection," the human druid said, voice tight.

"Protection," Ser Varyng repeated, tasting the word. "From whom?"

"From the forest. From raids. From—"

"From truth," Ser Varyng said.

His gaze flicked to the giants. Then back.

"You have brought monsters into your walls," he said calmly. "And named it peace."

The human tried again. "He can help us negotiate with Faelwyn Holt. Graypine Reach—"

Ser Varyng's eyes sharpened.

Graypine Reach.

He nodded once.

"Take the Anari alive."

The Anari moved.

Fast.

His staff spun. The air thickened with a low, broken chord. Not beautiful. Not holy. A sound that made the dogs whine.

It faltered.

The knights did not.

One struck the staff aside. The other drove a pommel into the Anari's chest. He staggered, then tried again.

Another chord.

Stronger.

Still insufficient.

A Heliarch stepped forward, fingers raised, murmuring a blessing too brief to be called a prayer.

The air warmed.

Attention settled.

The Anari's sound died in his throat as if scolded.

Iron snapped shut around his wrists.

The human druid surged forward. "You can't—he's the only reason—"

"You are not excommunicated," Ser Varyng said mildly. "Not yet."

He leaned closer.

"Your peace is useful," he continued. "Do not confuse it with safety."

Stone was unloaded. Braces were set. The banner platform began to take shape.

The Burning Banner was not a decoration.

It was a claim.

When the Anari was dragged away, the camp's noise resumed too soon.

That was what made it terrifying.

Men wanted normal.

Later, Ser Varyng stood at the palisade, watching the forest. Rangers knelt before him, offering routes, crossings, and thin places.

"You learned to walk near Wolfwood," Ser Varyng said. "Who taught you?"

"A druid," the ranger replied. "Said the forest listens differently if spoken to right."

Ser Varyng looked into the trees.

"Then we will speak to it."

He turned.

"Prepare to move," he ordered. "We cross upstream, take Graypine Reach, and when the Wolf Clan comes…"

He paused.

"…we teach them what the Crowned Faith does with forests."

Behind him, the banner snapped once in the wind.

Not a warning.

A promise.

And far beyond Eichenfall, deep where roots remembered blood and gods oaths, the forest shifted.

Not yet in resistance.

But in recognition.

The Hunt had felt the Banner.

Chapter 27 — Ash Over Bergshern

Planet: Vaelthara
Divine Year of Vaelthas — Wolf Month, 21,426 Years Since the Sealing
Western Kingdoms — Bergshern, Walled City of the Sun

"Cities learn fear faster than forests."
— *Kholfax, field note scratched into bark with a borrowed blade*

The night in Bergshern smelled of tallow and old stone.

Not the clean, resin-sweet smoke of forest fires or hearthwood, but the scent of rendered fat and damp masonry, soaked deep into walls that had never known evacuation. The smell clung to everything. Roof tiles. Ropes. Cloaks. Even the rain that threatened to fall but never did.

Kholfax lay flat against a slate roof, his body pressed low, his breath shallow, rain-cool stone bleeding through his leathers. He did not move. He did not blink. He counted breaths until the city began to speak in patterns rather than noise.

Boots on the walls.

A watch bell rung once too often by a bored hand.

Laughter drifted from a wine house that had never burned.

Not yet.

Below him, torchlight crawled through the streets like slow, patient insects, pooling at corners and thinning in alleys. Bergshern had been built to keep enemies out, not to notice them once they were inside. Its walls were high. Its watch was loud.

Its rooftops were careless.

Kholfax shifted one finger against the tile, testing friction. Still dry enough. Still safe. His eyes tracked movement without seeming to focus, cataloging patrol intervals, blind spots, and habits.

Same mistakes, he thought—different century.

Two rooftops away, Khandyl waited, her silhouette barely distinguishable from the shadows. Even knowing where she was, Kholfax chose to see her. Her auburn hair was bound tightly; her bow rested along her forearm as if it were an extension of bone. When she breathed, her shoulders did not rise.

Froster crouched near her, massive even at rest, his broad frame folded into stillness that should not have been possible. The emerald-engraved cleaver was strapped across his back, wrapped in dull cloth to smother its glow. He rested his weight on the balls of his feet, knees loose, spine straight.

Around them, ancient Anari rangers clung to chimneys and eaves like living carvings, their skin painted with ash and soot, fingers already on their strings. Queen's Kiss charges sat in their arrows, inert and deadly, waiting for breath and a decision.

No one spoke.

They did not need to.

The temple dominated the inner ward.

Stone steps rose wide and white, flanked by sun-carved balustrades. Banners hung high, gold-threaded and proud, reflecting moonlight so brightly it felt like an accusation. The Temple of the Sun had been built with geometry that dared darkness to challenge it.

Straight lines.

Open plazas.

No place to hide.

Kholfax felt the familiar tightening in his chest.

In his old life, he would have logged names, timed rotations, and recorded exits. Here, he watched priests cross the steps, laughing, their robes loosened, their hands stained with wine and incense. Their faith felt warm. Untested by fire.

He lifted two fingers.

The signal flowed outward without sound.

Move.

Hooks bit into stone.

Ropes went taut.

Ancient Anari bodies flowed upward and over the wall like water, as if remembering gravity. Human sentries never looked up. They never heard the breath behind them.

Kholfax dropped into the shadow of a buttress and felt the city accept him for half a heartbeat.

Then it noticed.

Khandyl was already moving, her steps perfectly matching the city's rhythm. Froster followed last. Not stealthy in the human sense. Inevitable. Wherever he placed his foot, sound hesitated before deciding whether to exist.

They crossed the plaza in silence.

Two guards stood at the temple doors.

Kholfax took the left.

The man smelled of oil and damp wool. Young. His helm was too large. His grip on the spear was too tight. Fear disguised as diligence.

Kholfax's blade slid under the chin, precise and practiced. The guard stiffened once, his eyes widening in surprise rather than pain, then sagged as Kholfax eased him down, careful to keep the armor from clanging against stone.

Khandyl took the other guard without breaking stride.

Inside, the temple breathed heat.

Braziers glowed along the nave. Gold mosaics caught the firelight and threw it back in distorted saints and winged banners. The air tasted of resin, smoke, and certainty.

Priests turned.

Confusion bloomed.

Then Froster moved.

His cleaver slipped free of its bindings with a whisper of cloth. The emerald runes flared once, then dimmed as he struck. The blade cut through flesh and bone with terrifying precision. He did not roar. He did not chant.

He ended.

Ancient Anari flowed through the nave. Arrows whispered. Blades flashed. Priests fell amid their own symbols, blood darkening the gold tesserae. A mage stepped forward, hands glowing, and a Sun Priest began a chant—

Khandyl's arrow took him in the throat.

The chant died weakly.

"Charges," Kholfax whispered.

Torches flew.

Oil took flame.

The banners burned first.

Fire raced up the cloth, devouring saints and slogans alike. Heat rolled outward. Smoke clawed at the ceiling. Someone screamed. Someone else rang a bell far too late.

They were already moving.

Up the inner stairs. Onto rooftops.

Bergshern woke screaming.

Militia poured into the streets, armor half-fastened, weapons grabbed from racks, still warm from neglect. Orders collided and were canceled. Torches flared. Panic learned to run.

Kholfax took a position on a gable and let out a breath.

The city became angles.

Targets.

Queen's Kiss whispered.

Blue light stitched the night as arrows found throats, joints, and eye-slits. The militia fell without understanding where death had come from. Each shot was deliberate. Each withdrawal is immediate.

They never stayed.

They never clustered.

They killed and vanished.

A horn sounded from the west wall.

Too slow.

A unit tried to pursue along the rooftops.

An animal mage raised both hands, eyes white, and the sky answered.

Crows.

Hundreds of them boiled out of the dark, their wings beating like torn cloth. They struck helms and faces, clawing, blinding, and turning formation into screaming chaos. Men fell from roofs, arms flailing, their prayers unfinished.

Below, a healer knelt beside a wounded Anari, hands glowing a soft green, breath steady even as firelight painted her face in orange and black.

"Granary," Froster said calmly.

Kholfax nodded.

They moved.

The granary sat near the inner wall, squat and arrogant, with promise. Guards clustered there now, trying to form lines.

Kholfax dropped behind barrels and felt the old instincts sing.

He did not think of cases.

He thought of patterns.

The doors went up in flame.

Grain ignited with a roar like an animal dying. Smoke punched into the sky. Sparks leapt the wall.

Bergshern howled.

By the time commanders realized this was neither a riot nor an accident but a design, the rooftops were empty.

The Anari were already gone.

From the treeline, Kholfax looked back.

The temple burned like a fallen sun.

The granary stood as a pillar of smoke.

Orders shattered in the air.

Fear settled.

Real fear.

"They'll remember this," an ancient ranger murmured.

Kholfax nodded.

"Yes," he said quietly. "They will."

Because tonight, Bergshern had learned a truth no wall could keep out.

The forest was not the boundary.

It was the beginning.

And as they vanished beneath the canopy, Kholfax felt the shape of the war shift, the way a hunter feels a trail shift when prey realizes the ground is no longer safe.

Somewhere, far from here, a voice would be listening.

And it would not be pleased.

Chapter 28 — The Hunt Beyond Root and Star

Planet: Vaelthara
Location: The Greenwood — Inner Curse-Zone
Divine Year of Vaelthas — Wolf Month, 21,426 Years Since the Sealing

"The forest is not a cage.
It is a beginning mistaken for an ending."
— *Fragment attributed to Aelrindel, God of the Hunt*

The Greenwood did not welcome Harvey.

It tolerated him.

Fog lay low across the forest floor in slow, deliberate sheets, rising and sinking as if the land itself breathed in long, patient cycles. Roots as thick as ramparts split the soil at unnatural angles. Trunks twisted into shapes that suggested intent rather than age, their bark darkened by centuries that did not pass as time.

Light did not fall here.

It pooled.

A diluted green glow clung to clearings and hollows, rationed carefully, as if the Greenwood decided what the living were permitted to see and what they were not meant to survive.

Harvey moved with care, every step chosen, never assuming.

The Horn rode across his back, wrapped in oilcloth and leather, its frozen mass tugging at his spine. Here, even stillness had weight. The Kuldemaekr rested in his right hand, the blade dark, patient, and attentive, drinking in the Greenwood's cold as if it had been forged for this place alone.

The first dead of this day came without warning.

They emerged from the fog like memories that refused to be buried. Anari forms, once warriors, now hollowed and reassembled by rot-song and Crone-binding. Their eyes gleamed with borrowed light. Their movements lagged half a heartbeat behind their intent, as if the forest itself hesitated to acknowledge them.

Harvey did not hesitate.

He stepped forward and struck.

The Kuldemaekr hummed once, low and final, and the undead unraveled. Not shattered. Unmade. Their borrowed cohesion fell apart into ash and pale motes that drifted away, leaving nothing the Greenwood wanted to preserve.

More came.

Three. Then five.

They clawed and reached, their broken harmonics scraping at Harvey's thoughts, trying to confuse his rhythm and will.

Harvey answered with steel and restraint.

Each cut was exact. Each ending was complete.

When the last figure collapsed into silence, Harvey stood alone again, his breath fogging and his pulse steadying. The Greenwood watched.

Then it sharpened.

A figure stepped from behind a bent yew.

Tall. Lean. Anari in form, but wrong in presence. Armor ghosted into existence along its frame, remembered rather than worn. A spear rested in its hand with casual mastery. Its eyes burned pale and feral, intelligent and focused.

An Anari.

No.

A Lynx.

The clan mark was unmistakable, even after centuries of curses. Angular lines. Predatory balance. A posture built for motion, sudden violence, and pursuit without regret.

This one was not rotted.

Not stitched.

It was preserved.

Bound.

A phantom.

Harvey did not raise his blade.

He tilted his head, studying the figure as one hunter studies another across a clearing, not for weakness but for truth.

"Who are you?" he asked quietly.

Then, after a breath, "Or who were you?"

The phantom did not answer.

It moved.

The air bent as a harmonic pattern snapped into place. Not noise. Shape. The Greenwood leaned inward, its branches and fog shifting as if this encounter mattered.

For a heartbeat, the phantom's outline blurred into something vast and avian, a mirrored echo of Harvey's resonance with the griffyn. Not a transformation.

A declaration.

The hunt was joined.

They clashed.

The Lynx phantom was faster than any living Anari Harvey had ever faced. Its spear sang with cold precision, its harmonics snapping like taut wire against Harvey's defenses. Roots split beneath their feet, and fog shredded and reknit around them.

Harvey stepped into the rhythm rather than away from it.

Steel rang once.

The Kuldemaekr met the spear and drank the cold bound within the phantom's form. The Lynx recoiled, its eyes flaring with something like surprise.

They circled.

Harvey waited.

Then he struck.

One clean cut. Not cruelty. Not dominance. Mercy, shaped by a hunter who understood cost.

The blade passed through the phantom's chest, and Harvey released the slaying resonance he had learned beneath pyramids and in halls where judgment was not merely symbolic.

The Lynx froze.

Its form wavered.

Then it unraveled, dissolving into pale motes that rose and vanished into the Greenwood's canopy.

No scream.

No curse.

Only release.

Harvey lowered himself to one knee.

Someone had loved this warrior once.

That knowledge cut deeper than the fight.

Exhaustion settled into his bones. He leaned against a twisted oak, the Kuldemaekr across his lap, the Horn drawn close to his chest.

Here, proximity mattered.

Sleep took him gently, like a hand closing around a flame.

He dreamed.

The Greenwood fell away.

He stood beneath a vault of roots and stars, branches arching overhead into constellations that shifted with slow, deliberate intent. Chains of living wood and frost-bound light stretched into the distance, converging on a single figure bound at the center.

Aelrindel.

God of the Hunt.

Not crowned.

Not enthroned.

Imprisoned.

Yet his eyes burned with the same wild clarity Harvey had seen in the phantom's gaze.

"You are closer," Aelrindel said, his voice layered and alive. "The forest feels your steps now. It remembers why it feared me."

"Why did she do it?" Harvey asked. "The Crone. Why imprison you?"

Aelrindel's expression darkened, not with rage, but with sorrow sharpened into resolve.

"Because I disagreed," he said. "Because I would not let our people believe the forest was an ending."

Images rippled outward.

Anari hunting beyond trees. Across plains. Into mountains. Onto open seas. Beneath foreign stars.

Not conquerors.

Hunters who followed need rather than dominion.

Adaptive. Relentless. Free.

"I am the Hunt," Aelrindel said. "And the Hunt does not stay where it is born. It follows prey, need, and destiny beyond comfort."

The vision shifted.

The Crone stood with the Thraeker gods. Frost and bone. Bargains forged in fear.

"She saw what the Anari could become if they followed me," Aelrindel said. "Not bound to root and leaf. Not afraid of the open sky. Capable of winning wars beyond the forest."

Harvey felt the truth settle into him.

"She wanted the War of Twelve Races never to end," he said.

"Yes," Aelrindel replied. "Endless conflict keeps the Malloch sealed. Endless fear keeps my people obedient."

Aelrindel leaned forward as far as his chains allowed.

"But you," he said softly, "walked into death without kneeling. You crossed the ice without turning back. You carry the Horn not as a relic but as a promise."

The chains trembled.

"The Anari must go out into the world," Aelrindel said. "They can win there. Beyond the trees. Beyond her lies."

Harvey swallowed.

"I'll free you," he said. "I swear it."

Aelrindel smiled, fierce and proud.

"I know," he said. "That is why you were chosen."

Harvey woke with a sharp breath.

The Greenwood pressed close again. Fog curled. Roots creaked softly like old bones settling.

The Horn lay warm against his chest.

The Kuldemaekr thrummed faintly in his hand.

And for the first time since entering the cursed forest, Harvey understood.

The Greenwood was not the goal.

It was the gate.

Beyond it waited a hunt that would carry the Anari far beyond their roots into a world that had never believed they could win.

Chapter 29 — The Day The Forest Burned

Planet: Vaelthara
Location: Faelwyn Holt: Heartroot Vale • Graypine Reach
Divine Year of Vaelthas — Wolf Month, 21,426 Years Since the Sealing

"The forest endures storms.
It does not expect engines."
— *Wolf Clan war-saying*

The warning reached Heartroot Vale on a scream of wind.

Not a horn.

Not a runner.

Not a drum.

A living gale tore down the root-arches, rattled lantern-gourds from their hooks, and carried the reek of burning sap and alchemical accelerant. Leaves curled inward as if trying to hide their veins. Sprites burst from hollows in shrieking flocks. The Holt shuddered, not as a thing afraid, but as a thing struck by pain it could not yet name.

Vyrna felt it before the words arrived.

She was already standing when the druid staggered into the council hollow, ash smeared across his bronze skin, his eyes too wide to hold thought.

"My Lady," he gasped. "Graypine Reach."

Silence fell hard.

"The western host crossed the Shenakoa upstream," he continued, breath hitching. "They did not slow. They did not scout."

Sablek Thistlecrest stepped forward at once, calm as a healer beside a deathbed.

"The human druids are with them," he said gently. "They are using what they learned here. Paths cleared. Roots compelled aside. Rivers… quieted."

Vyrna's fingers tightened around the edge of the council stone.

"How far?" she asked.

The druid swallowed. "Too far."

He shook his head, as if denying his own sight.

"They came with weapons I do not recognize. Armor that drinks impact. Helms that swallowed Song. Queen's Kiss arrows struck and slid away like rain."

A ripple of disbelief ran through the gathered warriors.

"Impossible," someone whispered.

"Seen," the druid replied hoarsely. "Their elite guards walk through volleys untouched."

Another voice, sharp with fear. "Fire mages?"

Sablek answered before Vyrna could.

"Stronger," he said softly. "They do not sing to the flame. They command it."

He let the words settle, then added quietly, "They are burning tree-homes now."

Vyrna closed her eyes.

Graypine Reach.

A river settlement grown, not built. Root-houses woven into ancient pines. Children's paths braided between living trunks. A place that had never known siege because the forest had never permitted one.

She opened her eyes.

"Tree-travel," she said.

Not loudly.

Not ceremonially.

Final.

The Holt answered.

Roots shifted beneath the council hollow. Trunks leaned, groaning as living arches unfurled like lungs finally allowed to breathe. Bark parted. Paths bloomed where none had been. Warriors stepped forward without orders. Their armor sealed itself, their bows rose, and their focus stones warmed in their palms.

This was not panic.

This was recognition.

Vaelis Valisar stood at Vyrna's right, composed and helpful, already smoothing the flow of movement so there were no collisions, no cries, no wasted breath.

"We should arrive spread out," he said mildly. "They'll burn the outer growth first. We'll strike where they think they're safest."

Vyrna nodded once.

Sablek placed a hand over his heart, eyes earnest.

"Peace failed us," he said quietly. "But restraint has not yet. If we halt their advance without slaughter, doctrine can still—"

"We will stop the fire," Vyrna said.

Her voice carried no argument.

"Nothing else comes before that."

The forest opened fully.

They stepped through.

The transition was violent.

Heat slammed into them like a wall. Sound shattered. Graypine Reach screamed.

Flame roared where birdsong had lived. Black smoke clawed at the canopy, tearing holes in the green light. Along the riverbank, human war-engines squatted like iron insects, their vents hissing, their barrels glowing, their rhythm alien and relentless.

Elite guards moved through falling embers in plated suits that reflected firelight without heat, their steps in sync, their helms turning as one.

Fire mages stood on cleared ground, arms raised, their gestures sharp and economical. Each motion erased years of growth. Each spell was measured, not wild.

Tree-homes burned.

Roots screamed.

Wolf Clan warriors emerged from bark and shadow onto a battlefield already breaking its own rules.

Vyrna felt the imbalance like a blade pressed between her ribs.

This was not a raid.

This was an invasion.

She raised her blade.

Behind her, the Holt surged, opening paths even as it bled, bending itself to keep its children moving. Ahead, western banners snapped in the rising heat, cannons pivoted, and elite helms lifted in unison.

For the first time in living memory, the forest did not know how to stop what was coming.

Graypine Reach burned.

And the Wolf Clan had arrived in the middle of the impossible.

The day the forest learned fear.

The day engines spoke louder than roots.

The day peace finally caught fire.

Chapter 30 — Roots Beyond the Line

Planet: Vaelthara
Location: Western Fringe of Faelwyn Holt — Rebel Hideout (Root-Cleft Warrens)
Divine Year of Vaelthas — Wolf Month, 21,426 Years Since the Sealing

"When the howl must change, the pack listens to the one who hears winter first."
— *Wolf Clan Proverb*

The hideout breathed.

Not like lungs.

Like soil.

A thousand slow pressures worked beneath the stone, as if the mountain itself remembered it had once been alive. Roots threaded the ceiling in patient coils as thick as wrists, faintly luminous where foxfire moss clung in wet constellations. Water dripped somewhere deeper in the warrens, each drop striking a hollow with the sound of distant bells.

The air smelled of sap, iron, and crushed leaf-medicine. It also carried something sharper, harder to name: the metallic tang of fear that had learned to hold still.

Kholfax sat with his back against a root-wall that had grown around an old crack in the stone like a scar choosing to heal. His shirt was open at the shoulder. A life-mage knelt beside him, small and steady, hands lit with a restrained green that pulsed once… twice… then drew inward as torn muscle knitted back into itself.

The pain dulled to an ache.

The memory did not.

In his former life, Kholfax would have cataloged it all: the angle of a blade, the spacing of a footstep, the pattern in a killer's choices. Here, the patterns were older than crime. They were rooted. They were sung into the world by gods who were not here to correct their mistakes.

Exile only mattered if there was somewhere else he wanted to go.

He did not let himself think about Faelwyn Holt's main heart. The elders' eyes. The way the Council's judgment had sounded like law and loss at once.

Instead, he stared at the flicker of a captured image hanging in the air like a ghost.

A scry-leaf, thin and translucent, hovered above a basin of water. Its surface caught a moving reflection: smoke where a building had stood. Ash drifting through light. A child's blanket caught in a branch.

Malvas.

The life-mage. Future-born. Clever hands. Quiet voice. She had crossed the border months earlier, saying she wanted to heal, not fight. No one had believed her at first.

Then she had healed them anyway.

Kholfax swallowed, his throat tight with something that wasn't pain.

"Malvas," he said, quieter than the smoke and work around them. "You okay?"

She didn't look up. She waved it off and tugged another strip of bark-paper from her satchel, already pulling data from it in cramped symbols.

"Get out safe," he added.

Her mouth twitched once, a half-smile that didn't rise into anything as generous as comfort.

"You're too useful to die."

It was the closest he ever came to saying anything else.

Around him, the rebels rested as if they had forgotten how. Ancient Anari rangers leaned against stone and living wood, their bows unstrung yet within reach, eyes half-lidded but never fully closed. They breathed shallowly, listening for footsteps that would never come, because the forest had agreed to hide them… for now.

Froster sat on a slab of stone and cleaned blood from a blade with ritual care, wiping the edge as if apologizing to it for the necessity. The emerald runes along the cleaver's spine remained dim, yet even so, they seemed awake, like a predatory animal pretending to sleep.

Khandyl stood near the map-root at the center of the chamber. One hand rested on the living wood as if it were a throat she could feel pulsing. She didn't look like a war-leader. She looked like an arrow before release: stillness made purposeful.

And then there was Kellyn Windstream.

She stood apart from them all, like lightning apart from the storm that birthed it. Her helm was off. Her hair spilled loose down her back, catching faint green light as she shifted. Her face was calm in the exact way that unsettled everyone else.

Not calm because she was unafraid.

Calm because she had already looked down too many futures to waste breath on surprise.

Myrrathis was not in the warrens. The dragon circled high above, far enough that his shadow would not betray the hideout's location. Kellyn's bond to him felt like a distant ember through stone, steady, patient, and hungry.

A shape emerged from the root tunnel.

The druid spy moved as if he'd learned to pass through the forest without asking permission—cloak mottled with leaf ash. Hands stained with sap and soot. His breath came hard, as if he'd run the last mile with death at his heels.

He didn't wait for permission.

"Graypine Reach is burning."

The chamber went still.

Even the roots seemed to pause to listen.

Khandyl turned first, voice flat. "Repeat it."

The spy swallowed. "The human army crossed the Shenakoa upstream. Modern armor. Fire mages. Siege tools we've never seen before. They hit the river settlement at dawn. Tree-homes are down. River docks are ash. They're sacking it systematically."

Kellyn felt the words land in her chest as stones dropped into deep water.

Graypine Reach.

Closest Wolf Clan settlement to the tainted shrine. Families. Children. Old warriors who could no longer run but still sang to the trees each morning, because songs kept a people from forgetting itself.

Froster's hand tightened on his cleaver until the leather wrap creaked. "How many?"

"Enough," the spy said. "And disciplined. This isn't a raid. It's a doctrine."

Silence stretched long enough for fear to try on new shapes.

Then the arguments broke loose.

"We go now."

"They'll see us as traitors."

"We're exiled!"

"They'll kill us on sight."

"They're killing our people."

Voices overlapped, braided with fury and shame. The words weren't just debate; they were desperate bargaining with reality. If they could find the right sentence, perhaps the world would rewind.

Kholfax pushed himself to his feet. The life-mage's work held, but his body still remembered being torn. He swayed, then steadied himself.

"If we arrive exhausted and half-healed," he said, "we die uselessly. And we take others with us."

Froster rounded on him, eyes flaring like struck stone. "You want to wait while Graypine burns?"

Kholfax met his gaze without blinking. "I want to arrive alive."

That was the difference between rage and war.

Kellyn spoke then.

Her voice did not rise. It cut through the noise like a blade through cloth.

"The humans aren't going to stop," she said. "Not here. Not ever. Their emissary didn't come for timber camps. He came for conversion or extermination. Peace was never an option."

The chamber quieted, not because they agreed, but because her certainty carried weight. It settled, pinning arguments to the floor.

She stepped closer to the map-root.

Green veins pulsed beneath its surface, forming the living outline of Faelwyn Holt and the lands beyond. Rivers. Camps. Roads. The human border cities were like hard knots in a muscle that refused to soften.

"The Wolf Clan will not welcome us," Kellyn continued. "But they won't turn us away if the alternative is annihilation."

Khandyl nodded slowly. "The forest opened paths for us when they hunted Kholfax. It knows where we stand."

The spy hesitated. His eyes flicked toward Malvas, then back to Kellyn.

"There's more."

All eyes snapped to him.

"The humans are using druids," he said. "Human druids, trained by the dark circle. They're regrowing burned timber quickly enough to feed the army. They're learning to make the forest cooperate."

A murmur rippled through the chamber like a cold wind finding cracks.

Kellyn felt something inside her click into place, like a mechanism settling when the final gear aligns.

"Then we change the battlefield," she said.

They looked at her.

Not as a commander.

As a hinge.

"A forest doesn't have to stop at its edge," Kellyn went on. "That line exists only because we believe it does. Trees don't respect borders. Roots don't recognize claims."

She placed her palm against the map-root.

Her fingers sank slightly into the living surface. The wood accepted her touch as it accepted law or fate.

"We don't conquer by burning cities," she said. "We conquer by growing over them, transforming camps into groves, roads into thickets, and walls into seedbeds."

Her eyes lifted, and the foxfire in the chamber seemed to dim, as if even light wanted to listen.

"Let them bring cannons," she said. "We'll give them forests they can't march through, supply, or survive in. We'll take their straight lines and teach them to curve again."

Froster exhaled slowly.

"Spread the forest," he murmured, not as a strategy but as a vow.

Khandyl's expression sharpened with something old and dangerous.

"Make the world remember what green stands for," she said.

Decision settled like falling snow: soft, quiet, absolute.

They would go.

Not as exiles.

Not as rebels.

As the first roots beyond the line.

They healed through the night.

Not with celebration. Not with songs. Songs would have been a luxury, and luxuries had a way of drawing predators.

Poultices were shared. Bandages were rewrapped. Arrows were reflected until the hands doing the work could perform the task blind. Queen's Kiss charges were checked and reseated. Focus stones were warmed, cooled, and warmed again, as if the magic within them needed reassurance that it would still be permitted to exist.

Kholfax sat with Malvas again while she recorded reports with a charcoal tip that shook once, then steadied. He watched her hands, the way she held her breath before writing certain words, as if some truths had edges.

"How bad?" he asked quietly.

Malvas didn't answer right away. She adjusted the scry-leaf over the basin. The image flickered, then caught.

Graypine Reach.

Or what remained of it.

Tree-homes collapsed inward like charred ribs. The river ran black with soot. On the far bank, human troops moved in lines too straight for this world, and above them rose shapes like iron beetles, siege frames braced with metal and glistening with resin.

"They're not improvising," Malvas said softly. "They're executing a plan."

Kholfax's jaw tightened.

"Plans have weaknesses," he said.

"Only if the people making them can be frightened," Malvas replied.

Kholfax didn't like how correct that sounded.

Across the chamber, Kellyn stood with Khandyl and Froster, their faces lit from below by the map-root's green pulse.

"We don't go in and die on their terms," Kellyn said. "We make them bleed for every step they take. We make them regret even thinking about moving forward."

Khandyl's hand remained on the map-root, fingers flexed as if feeling distant tremors.

"The Holt will resist," she said. "It doesn't like being forced to move beyond itself."

Kellyn's gaze didn't waver. "Then we persuade it."

Froster's voice was low. "And the clan?"

"We aren't asking permission," Kellyn replied. "We're bringing survival."

That sentence, more than any speech, changed the air in the warrens.

Because it meant they had already crossed the point where reconciliation mattered more than outcome.

At dawn, they moved.

Tree-travel did not take them into Graypine proper. The Holt was wounded there. Too loud. Too watched. Too likely to become a trap.

Instead, the forest carried them to its outer veins, to a place where roots were young, and the trees still argued with the plains. A fringe where the earth didn't know whether it belonged to leaf or road.

They emerged beneath a low canopy of lean pines and stubborn brush. The sky here felt wider. Wind touched their faces without invitation.

Open ground.

The ancient rangers stiffened. Their instincts disliked this exposure. The plains had no walls, no whispering aid.

Kellyn looked out across the line where green ended, and human geometry began.

Road cuts. Ditches. The faint glint of metal in the distance. Smokestacks. Watch fires. A whole world built on the assumption that wood was there to be harvested.

Kholfax stepped beside her. He was pale but upright now, his posture rigid with purpose.

"This is where they think they're safe," he said.

Kellyn nodded.

"This is where we teach them otherwise."

She turned back toward the rebels, toward Khandyl and Froster, and the ancient rangers who had chosen exile over obedience.

Her gaze lingered on Kholfax for a fraction longer than necessary.

Not romance.

Recognition.

They were both people out of time, carrying knowledge that made the present feel fragile.

Then she placed her palm against a different root.

A deeper one.

Older.

Not the Holt's soft pathways, but the ancient artery leading toward Draknest and flame-stone.

Dragon-song answered.

Not audible.

Felt.

A resonance that made the foxfire moss tremble, made the roots tighten as if bracing.

The world folded.

Kellyn emerged beneath open sky and smoking stone.

Draknest.

The air smelled of sulfur and wild heat. The ground radiated warmth through her boots like a heartbeat that refused to stop. Above, clouds churned in slow spirals, and through them a bronze comet fell.

Myrrathis dropped from the sky like a descending star.

His wings folded as he landed beside Kellyn with heavy grace, talons cracking rock. Heat washed over Kellyn, fierce and welcome. The dragon's eyes locked onto hers, his slit pupils bright as molten coin.

Kellyn swung into the saddle in one motion.

"We need help," she said softly, voice carrying into the aether. "Not just steel. Not just fire."

Myrrathis rumbled, a sound like distant thunder agreeing.

Kellyn looked east, then west.

In forests yet to grow.

At roads that would one day choke on roots.

At cities that would learn what it meant to be alive inside their own walls.

"The forest is done waiting," she said.

And far away, unseen and uninvited, roots began to dream of roads.

Not politely.

Not slowly.

Hungrily.

As if the world had finally remembered that green is not decoration.

Green is conquest.

Green is mercy.

Green is the shape of a future that refuses to be cut down.

And in the first faint shiver beneath the soil, the rebels' new war began: not a war of raids but a war of spread.

A war where the forest itself would become the marching army.

And the line would be swallowed.

The Queen of Swords

Chapter 31 — The Day Graypine Burned

Planet: Vaelthara
Location: Graypine Reach — River Settlement and Forest Verge
Divine Year of Vaelthas — Wolf Month, 21,426 Years Since the Sealing

Graypine Reach was already burning when the Wolf Clan arrived.

Not the clean burn of lightning. Not the honest burn of a hearth that gives as much as it takes. This was a chemical flame and ordained violence, fire made efficient, fire taught to hate. Smoke rose in greasy black columns from tree-homes split open by iron shot. Living bridges had collapsed into the Shenakoa, their woven roots severed by cannon blasts, their braided supports snapping like bones. Bark-halls smoldered, sap running down charred trunks in slow, shining rivulets that looked too much like blood.

Even the river carried the verdict. It rolled ash and bodies downstream in slow, accusing spirals, as if it could not decide whether to cleanse or remember.

The humans had not come to raid.

They had come to erase.

At the forest edge, where the last intact roots still held a line against the open flats, Vyrna stood unmoving. Her bark-steel armor was cracked and scorched, its leaf-etched plates dulled by soot. She wore the war-crown: her autumnfire braids bound tight, threaded with bone beads that marked vows from older years, when war still had rules and mercy still had a place to sit.

Around her gathered what remained of Graypine's defenders.

Archers with ash-blackened cloaks and trembling wrists, their quivers half-empty. Elk cavalry stamping and snorting at the scent of burning sap, their huge antlers haloed in drifting soot. Druids with bleeding hands and hollow eyes, their palms raw from forcing life into scorched soil that wanted to die.

They had been holding.

Not winning.

Holding.

And beside Vyrna stood Vaelis Valisar.

Unburned. Unhurried. His cloak lay clean across his shoulders, as if smoke had politely gone around him. His focus stone hung at his chest, dark as wet slate. His expression held the soft gravity of concern and the practiced patience of a man who wanted to be seen as steady when others broke.

He watched the battlefield the way a careful scholar watches an argument. Not for who suffers.

For those who shift.

Beyond the tree line, the human host occupied the flats with brutal clarity.

Pike blocks stood six ranks deep, ash-wood shafts tipped with steel heads that glinted through smoke. Sun Priests moved among them, touching metal with two fingers and murmuring blessings that didn't soothe so much as tighten.

Matchlock companies knelt behind the pikes. Powder horns hung clipped to their belts. Rifled barrels rested on iron forks. Each soldier moved with the obedient economy of men drilled until thought became unnecessary.

And further back, like the final punctuation to a sentence written in blood, cannons crouched in pairs along the riverbank. Their bronze muzzles glowed faintly red. Crews worked, stripped to the waist despite the cold, their bodies slick with sweat and soot, shoving ramrods and shot with the practiced rhythm of a machine that had learned to breathe.

Steam tanks squatted behind them, riveted monsters belching vapor. Iron treads ground soil into paste. Their turrets tracked slowly and methodically, like animals taught patience rather than mercy.

Fire mages moved among the ranks in scorched white robes, their hands glowing with contained infernos that pulsed like restrained heartbeats.

Graypine screamed again as another fireball arced into the canopy.

The projectile was not just flame. It carried a hot pressure that made the air itself recoil.

A tree-home exploded outward. Branches and bodies flew into the smoke. For a heartbeat, the silhouettes of people hung in orange light like broken insects caught in resin.

Then the wind took them.

Vyrna's jaw tightened until it looked like her teeth might crack.

"Queen's Kiss," she said.

The Wolf Clan answered.

Arrows slid from the shadows. Feathered shafts moved through heat and smoke like pale fish in poisoned water, whispering death into gaps in armor, throats beneath gorgets, eyes behind goggles. The militia fell. Pike lines shuddered but held. Officers screamed orders through brass trumpets that cut through the chaos like knives.

For a moment, there was a rhythm.

Shoot. Vanish. Shift. Shoot again.

The forest tried to help.

Roots surged beneath human boots. Vines lashed ankles. Mud softened in sudden pockets, swallowing heels. The Holt bent light at the edges, making distance uncertain and angles lie.

Then the cannons spoke.

The sound flattened the world. It wasn't noise; it was pressure, a blunt hand over the ears and lungs. The ground convulsed. A shell tore through the forest edge and detonated within a root-hall.

Ancient wood became shrapnel.

Anari bodies became echoes.

The blast rippled through the living roots underground, collapsing passages that had been arteries of safety for generations. The Holt shuddered as if struck in its bones.

Matchlocks fired in disciplined volleys.

Lead balls ripped through bark armor and flesh. The shots weren't random. They were measured, corrected, and adjusted.

The humans were learning fast how to kill what had always believed itself unkillable.

The Wolf Clan tried to advance.

Fire met them.

Human fire mages hurled devastation in overlapping arcs, careful to burn away cover before the rifles spoke again. Entire sections of the forest ignited. Roots burned underground, invisible and merciless, collapsing pathways and trapping defenders in smoke and flame.

Vyrna lifted her blade.

"Elk riders," she commanded, voice cutting through the roaring air. "Forward!"

The great elk charged.

Massive antlered beasts burst from the shadows, hooves striking mud and ash. Riders leaned low, spears and glaives at the ready, their bark-steel armor gleaming with soot and sweat. They hit the human flank like a rolling storm, antlers slamming into pike shafts, bodies driving into formation with the unarguable logic of weight.

Pikes snapped.

Militia scattered.

For a breath, for a single bright breath, it looked like enough.

Then the steam tanks turned.

Turrets roared.

Canister shot scythed through elk and rider alike. Antlers shattered. Bodies tumbled. One great beast collapsed, screaming, its rider crushed beneath it as iron pellets tore into living wood. Another tried to stand with half a leg gone, eyes wild, refusing to accept the idea of falling.

The forest did not know how to comfort an elk dying in the open.

The Wolf Clan fell back into the trees.

Not in panic.

In grim necessity.

They retreated with the discipline of old wars, pulling wounded through rootways that still held, dragging the living away from fire that did not care whom it touched.

Graypine Reach became a battlefield of flame and ruin, of smoke-choked prayers and shouted names swallowed by the wind.

Then the rebels struck.

Not with a roar.

With a correction.

From the southern treeline, death arrived quietly, as if the forest itself had decided to edit humans out of the world.

Froster emerged first.

His emerald runes flared along the cleaver's spine, bright enough to stain the smoke green. He didn't charge. He arrived, stepping into a matchlock line and carving through it with a calm that was almost devotional. Steel split like bark under his blows. Men split in half. Rifles clattered into the mud.

Khandyl moved with him, blades flashing, each strike placed for tendons and throats, for spines and wrists. Her face was set in that exhausted, feral focus of someone who has stopped asking the world to be kind.

Kholfax fired without haste.

Queen's Kiss snapped again and again. Not at the nearest targets. At the right ones.

Officers. Gunners. Fire mages. Signal-men. The people who turned bodies into a machine.

Each shot was a decision.

Each decision was fatal.

Ancient Anari followed them, rangers and warriors long unused to open ground. Fear showed in their eyes like a second reflection.

They fought anyway.

Human elite guard advanced to meet them.

These were not militia.

Their armor was heavier, layered with treated plates and rune-etched ceramics that deflected Queen's Kiss. Rifled muskets cracked with sharper reports. Rounds punched through bark armor and flesh alike. The elite advanced in disciplined wedges, their faces hidden behind narrow visors that made them look less like men and more like judgment given shape.

Anari fell.

Rebels bled.

The line buckled.

And then the forest roared.

Not one sound.

Many.

Wings beat the smoke.

From treetop height, shadows rose like old myths deciding to become real again.

Dragons.

They tore through the canopy with the violence of revelation, bursting into open sky as if the world had forgotten what it meant to fear a storm.

Kellyn Windstream descended astride Myrrathis, his bronze scales reflecting firelight, flame gathering in the dragon's chest like a dawn preparing to burn.

Elowen came beside her on her silver-green dragon, spiraling with living vines. Her hands were already weaving spells, fingers moving like a musician counting beats that could bind an army.

Behind them swept more wings. Not one dragon.

Not two.

A flight.

Not circling.

Not warning.

Ending.

Myrrathis exhaled.

Fire poured through matchlock ranks. Men vanished into the brightness. Leather and cloth flashed into ash. Pike shafts ignited from grip to tip. A cannon crew screamed as the bronze softened, the barrel sagging like wax. Horses panicked and bolted, dragging the lines apart.

Acid and flame tore open steam tanks. Metal buckled like wet bark. One tank's turret blew free, spinning into the river with a hiss that turned water to steam.

Elowen's magic slammed down among the fire mages.

Roots erupted from scorched soil as if the world itself had decided to take revenge. Thick tendrils crushed platforms. Vines snapped wrists. Living growth clawed focus stones from hands and wrapped around throats with patient, suffocating insistence.

Dragons landed inside human formations.

Wings flattened squads. Talons shredded ranks. One dragon's tail swept a pike block into the mud, like a hand wiping a table clean.

Human discipline broke.

Men ran.

Some threw down weapons.

Some screamed prayers.

Some simply fled, eyes wide and empty, as if they had seen the face of a god and found it indifferent.

On the far line, the human emissary's banner dipped as guards dragged him toward the river. A knot of elites tried to form a retreat corridor, firing measured volleys even as they burned and choked on smoke.

Dark human druids raised desperate spells.

Malformed forest giants erupted from the ground, their bark and bone fused unnaturally. They lumbered forward not as a victory but as a sacrifice, buying space with their own bodies. One giant took dragonfire and kept walking for three steps before collapsing in a hiss of steam and black sap.

Vyrna watched the rout, her face ash-streaked and her eyes burning.

"Let them go," she said.

A nearby warrior stared at her, disbelieving.

"They will carry our answer," Vyrna finished.

Not mercy.

Message.

Behind her, Graypine Reach burned.

But beneath the ash, roots were already moving.

New growth pushed through scorched soil in thin green needles. Saplings rose where cannons had fallen, trembling in the heat like newborns thrust into a cruel world.

Steel had come to Graypine.

And it had learned, too late, that fire alone does not conquer a forest.

The fires burned low by the time the screams stopped.

Graypine Reach no longer sounded like a living place. The Holt had gone quiet, as wounded things do, not dead, not safe, simply holding itself together long enough to breathe again.

Vyrna walked the ruins alone.

Her guards followed at a distance, silent and ashamed of their own bodies. Even Vaelis did not intrude. This was a queen's accounting, not a council's.

She stepped through what had once been a root-hall where children learned the Song of Bark and Leaf. Half of it had collapsed into the river. The other half still stood, blackened and cracked, sap oozing down scorched walls like tears.

A druid knelt nearby, hands buried in the earth, whispering apology after apology to the roots beneath him, as if repentance could stitch the char back into life.

Vyrna did not interrupt.

She passed through the fallen elk cavalry, where canister shot had torn them apart. Proud beasts reduced to wreckage. Antlers snapped. Riders crushed beneath them. She placed her palm against one still-warm flank and bowed her head.

"You ran when I asked," she murmured. "That matters."

Further in, she found the dead who had no wounds.

Children.

Elders.

Those caught when fire leapt faster than warning.

The Wolf Clan had always believed the forest would protect them.

Tonight proved the forest could bleed.

Vyrna stopped at the riverbank. Smoke drifted low. The Shenakoa carried ash downstream as if trying to wash its hands but failing.

Behind her, soft footfalls approached.

Khandyl.

Vyrna did not look up.

"We lost three root-halls," Khandyl said. "Two bridges. Almost a quarter of the river homes. The healers are… doing what they can."

Vyrna nodded once, like a judge hearing numbers already carved into stone.

"The humans will return," Khandyl continued. "With more. With better."

"Yes," Vyrna said. Her voice was steady now. "They always do."

She turned at last. Her eyes reflected both the firelight and the first thin edge of dawn.

"They brought iron into the forest and called it faith," she said. "They brought fire and called it righteousness."

Her fingers tightened on her blade.

"So, we will bring roots to their roads. Shade to their walls. And forests to their cities."

Khandyl inhaled sharply, as if she'd been waiting to hear those words from a mouth that mattered.

Vyrna straightened, shoulders squared beneath bark-steel armor.

"This is no longer a war to protect the forest," she said. "It is a war to teach the world what a forest is."

She looked east where dragons circled low, silhouettes against smoke and sunrise.

"Let the humans panic," she said. "Let them pray louder."

Her voice hardened into iron beneath bark.

"The forest has begun to answer."

Western Human Kingdoms — Dispatches, Sermons, and Sealed Reports

The first report reached Königsbrunn at dawn.

It was written in a shaking hand, wax seal warped by heat.

To the Banner-Saint's Command:

Graypine Reach was not a raid.

It was an annihilation.

Dragons emerged from the forest canopy, multiple wings, coordinated, with fire, acid, and entangling magics.

Steam tanks were lost. Cannons were destroyed. Elite guard was shattered.

Survivors report trees moving. The forest advanced during combat.

Recommend immediate fortification of all garrisons.

— Captain Huldrek Weiss, Third March

By noon, five more reports arrived.

None agreed on numbers.

All agreed on terror.

A Sun Priest stood before the council chamber, voice raised, eyes wide and shining with mania.

"They are not merely elves," he cried. "They are a living blight! Their gods walk with them! Their forests march!"

A general slammed his gauntlet onto the table.

"Forests don't march."

A scribe, pale-faced, whispered without looking up from his ink.

"They did."

By evening, sermons replaced strategy.

In cathedrals and camps alike, priests invoked Saint Aurelius with trembling fervor.

"The faithful are tested! The forest is a trial! Steel your hearts!"

But beneath hymns, soldiers whispered different prayers.

That dragons had landed among them like judgment.

That fire had fallen from green wings.

That the forest had swallowed the roads behind them.

At Rothwald Post, engineers began reinforcing the walls outward, not inward, as if the enemy were the land itself.

At Dornfeste's ruins, commanders ordered that no rebuilding occur.

Too close to the trees.

And in the private war chamber beneath Königsbrunn's cathedral, Ser Varyng the Sanctified listened in silence as reports piled up at his feet.

He did not rage.

He did not shout.

When the last messenger finished, Ser Varyng folded his hands over the Embered Standard and spoke calmly.

"Good."

The room froze.

"Now they believe the forest is holy," he continued. "That means it can be conquered."

He turned to his aides.

"Accelerate the War-Cathedral. Double the banner rites. Find me every druid, human or otherwise, who knows how the trees move."

A thin smile crossed his face, so brief it might have been imagined.

"If the forest wishes to march," Ser Varyng said softly, "then we will teach it what crusade means."

And somewhere, far east, in a forest that had begun to remember its teeth, roots shifted as if tasting that word.

Crusade.

A Western Kingdom's steam tank.

Chapter 32 — Roots That Remember

Planet: Vaelthara
Location: Graypine Reach — Aftermath Groves
Divine Year of Vaelthas — Wolf Month, 21,426 Years Since the Sealing

I had seen cities after massacres before.

Steel cities. Glass cities. Places where blood pooled on alloy floors and emergency lights painted everything the same flat red, as if the world had already written the report and only needed my signature. In those places, grief behaved like smoke: it rose, choked, settled into corners, and never grew anything back.

Graypine Reach was different.

Here, the forest did not stay wounded.

It answered.

Not with speeches. Not with banners. Not with rage.

With work.

Where cannon fire had gouged the earth, shoots already pushed upward, pale at first, then darkening as sap thickened and decided it had business to attend to. Roots surfaced through churned mud like knuckles breaking skin, thick cords of living will threading around shrapnel and splintered bark as if the Holt were knitting its own ribs. Moss spread in wide bruises over scorched trunks, softening the hard edges of violence. Even the air had changed. It was heavy, sweet, and wet with regrowth, as if a storm had rolled through and left the world smelling newborn and feral.

The forest was drinking the blood.

Not greedily.

Purposefully.

I stood on a ridge of shattered stone where a steam tank had died under dragonfire. Its riveted shell lay folded inward like a crushed rib cage, its vents warped open, black teeth bared at nothing. Heat still breathed from it in faint pulses, the kind of residual warmth you feel off a dying animal if you kneel too close.

Vines were already inside.

They didn't creep like timid things. They investigated. Tendrils slipped into seams and emerged from the far side, testing, tasting, and deciding where to anchor. Leaves brushed the soot-darkened barrel as if checking whether it still posed a threat, like a cautious hand checking a blade even after it's been broken.

It occurred to me, with a chill that had nothing to do with the weather, that the Holt wasn't simply reclaiming wreckage.

It was learning it.

Behind me, Graypine Reach smoldered.

Not burned out.

Burned through.

Homes grown from living wood leaned at strange angles, cracked yet stubbornly upright, as if refusing to grant humans the satisfaction of collapse. Others were gone entirely, reduced to char, bone, and the white ash that looks innocent until you realize it's what remains when life has been made small enough to fit in your palm.

Elk cavalry lay where they had fallen, their massive bodies now reverently wrapped in woven branches. Druids moved among them with quiet hands and quiet eyes, binding antlers, cleaning blood, and closing lids. They sang under their breath, low and steady, voices frayed but unbroken. The songs didn't sound like mourning. They sounded like instructions.

Hold. Breathe. Return.

I had watched Wolf Clan warriors die today.

I had watched humans die faster.

And still the forest grew.

That was the difference that put iron under my tongue.

In the Bureau, death was an ending you cataloged, cross-referenced, and filed.

Here, death was a nutrient.

A lesson.

A currency that the Holt accepted without ceremony.

Khandyl stood a few paces away, bow unstrung, helmet off. Her hair was damp with sweat and ash, and her face looked carved rather than worn, as if people look after they've spent every spare thought on survival and left none for expression. She stared at the river, where smoke drifted low like fog that had forgotten how to rise.

"They thought peace meant safety," she said quietly.

Not bitter. Not loud. Just… tired in a way that had edges.

"Humans always do," she added, and it landed like an old truth that had waited too long for someone to say it out loud.

Froster sat on a broken root nearby, broad shoulders hunched, his emerald-rune cleaver resting across his knees. The blade pulsed faintly, the runes breathing like a sleeping animal. He had blood on his forearms. Not all of it was human. He kept wiping it away, methodically, and it kept coming back to him, if not on his skin.

"They didn't come to trade," he said.

His voice was calm, but calm on Froster was never comforting. It was the calm of a door being locked.

"They came to overwrite."

Overwrite. That word again. Ugly and accurate.

The Wolf Clan hadn't lost because they were weak.

They'd lost because they believed the forest itself was enough of an argument.

It wasn't.

Not against engines.

Not against doctrine.

Not against men who could look at a living home and see only lumber, and at a living people and see only an obstacle that needed a name to justify its removal.

Movement stirred ahead. A ripple through smoke. A shift in attention.

Lady Vyrna walked through ash and new green together.

Her bark-steel armor was scorched and cracked in places, and her life-talismans were dimmed not by damage but by exhaustion, as if her protection had spent itself and now sat quietly in shame. Her gait was slower than I'd ever seen it. Not the slow of injury. The slow of weight.

She carried today on her shoulders like a cloak she couldn't take off.

Kellyn walked beside her, soot streaking her face, her eyes sharp despite the fatigue etched around them. She had the look I'd seen on people who'd survived too many close calls to believe in luck. Dragonfire still ghosted the air behind her like an afterimage. High above, Dragon Clan wings circled low, massive shadows crossing new leaves and broken stone alike, a reminder to the humans in the distance that the sky had chosen a side.

Vyrna stopped in the center of what had once been a market root.

I recognized it by smell more than by shape. Sap, smoke, river mud, and the faint sweetness of crushed fruit that had burned without ever becoming food.

She didn't raise her voice.

She didn't need to.

"My people," she said. "Hear me."

The Wolf Clan gathered.

Not in ranks.

In rings.

Loose and breathing. Wounded and alive. Warriors, druids, and elders with ash on their brows. Children held close, eyes too big, hands gripping sleeves that still smelled of home. Rebels stood among them now. Exiles. Traitors by decree. Defenders by fact. Even a few faces I knew, who had once whispered Sablek's doctrine in council halls, now stood quiet, staring at the ruin as if it had finally taught them how to read.

Vyrna's gaze moved.

Khandyl first.

Then Froster.

Then me.

And when it reached me, it paused just a fraction longer than expected, long enough for the moment to sharpen into a memory.

"You were right," she said.

The words landed harder than cannon.

Not because they were dramatic. Because they were expensive.

A queen could survive being wrong.

Her people could not survive her pretending otherwise.

"I mistook restraint for wisdom," Vyrna continued, her voice steady as bark in winter. "And peace for safety."

Her eyes swept the burned line where the forest had once been continuous and now looked… interrupted, like a sentence cut off midword.

"The humans did not come seeking balance," she said. "They came seeking ownership."

A murmur rippled through the rings. Not anger. Not relief.

Recognition.

Somewhere in the aftermath grove, a sapling forced its way up through a cracked beam with a sharp little snap, and the sound felt like punctuation.

Vyrna turned to Kellyn and inclined her head deeply, not the casual nod of politics but the formal dip of gratitude and debt.

"You and the Dragon Clan saved Graypine Reach," she said. "Your aid came when the forest alone could not answer."

Kellyn bowed in return, sharp and formal. But her eyes were already elsewhere, measuring, calculating, looking past today into the shape of what would try to kill them tomorrow.

Vyrna straightened.

"The dark druids have fled," she said. "They ran to the old shrine like parasites retreating to rot."

A low growl passed through the warriors. It wasn't an animal sound. It was the sound of a people realizing the enemy lived within their walls.

"They are cast out," Vyrna declared. "By blood. By root. By oath."

Her voice did not tremble.

"Any who shelter them share their exile."

That one drew approval, not joyous, but clean. Like a knot being cut rather than untied.

Then Vyrna's voice softened, and that softness made it hit harder.

"First, we heal," she said. "We bury our dead. We sing the roots back together."

She paused, letting the Holt speak for her.

Around us, the ground shifted again. A root surfaced through churned mud, thick and glossy, and wrapped around a broken pike shaft like a fist clenching. Leaves unfurled in fast, hungry spirals. The earth smelled rich, almost intoxicating, the scent of a world refusing to be reduced to ash.

"The forest has tasted war," Vyrna finished. "It will not forget."

Silence sat on the rings like a hand.

Not fear-silence.

Decision-silence.

Then Kellyn stepped forward.

"Tomorrow," she said, and her voice carried cleanly through the smoke, "I call for the Wolf Council to convene."

Eyes turned. Even those who didn't like her listened, because Kellyn had earned the right to be heard in the fire.

"I have a strategy to share," she continued. "Not retreat. Not defense."

Her hand gestured to the ground beneath our feet, to the saplings pushing up through wreckage, to the roots trying to knit the world closed again.

"Expansion."

The word hummed.

Roots twitched.

I felt it in my spine, like the forest itself flinched at the audacity and then… leaned in.

Because expansion wasn't a plan.

It was a confession.

That they were done being a boundary.

That they were done being a myth that people told themselves to feel safe at night.

Afterward, as the gathering loosened and healers moved among the wounded, I pulled Khandyl and Froster aside.

"The shrine," I said. "Tomorrow."

They didn't ask which one.

They didn't need to.

"They'll regroup there," Froster said. "Try to hide behind gods and ghosts."

"They'll fail," Khandyl added. "But we should be the ones who end it."

Kellyn approached before I could say more. Elowen followed, already tired in the way only a life-mage gets tired, a kind of exhaustion that sits behind the eyes because you've spent pieces of yourself to keep others whole.

"I'm coming," Kellyn said simply.

"I figured," I replied.

Elowen nodded once. "So am I. Someone has to clean up after you."

A breath of wind moved through Graypine Reach then.

Not weather.

Not the river.

Something deeper.

Leaves rustled in patterns I was beginning to recognize, not random, not playful.

Deliberate.

The forest was listening.

And for the first time since I'd crossed the time gate, something settled inside me with a quiet that felt dangerous:

This war was no longer about survival.

It was about territory.

Not land.

Meaning.

The humans wanted to overwrite the Holt with roads, prayers, and iron.

The Holt had answered with sap and teeth and memory.

I looked down at the crushed tank and the vines threading into it, at the saplings rising among the dead, at the ash drifting over new leaves like a blessing and a warning.

The forest had chosen.

It wasn't asking for permission anymore.

It was growing.

Chapter 33 — The Hill That Breathes

Planet: Vaelthara
Location: The Greenwood — Deep Interior
Divine Year of Vaelthas — Wolf Month, 21,426 Years Since the Sealing

"Harvey looked for answers.
I looked for where they were hiding."
— *Witmar Oakenstride*

The Greenwood no longer resisted Harvey.

It endured him.

That was worse.

Resistance had rules. It announced itself. It gave you edges to push against. Endurance was the opposite. Endurance was a blank stare. A patient throat. A place that could watch you drown and never blink.

Fog lay low, silver-gray and damp, sliding over bark and bone alike. It didn't drift like weather. It moved like an animal that had learned to be quiet. It lapped at roots and spilled into hollows, and when Harvey exhaled, the fog accepted his breath as if it had been waiting for it.

The trees here did not lean toward the light. They leaned toward you.

Sometimes he caught a trunk tilted just slightly inward after he passed, as if it had been listening harder while he wasn't looking.

Roots appeared where they hadn't before. Paths that had looked promising curved back on themselves hours later, like a finger tracing a circle around prey. Sound traveled oddly. A snapped twig might ring out like a gunshot fifty paces away or disappear entirely an inch from his boot. Once, he heard a whisper behind him that sounded exactly like Serithyl's voice saying his name, and his skin crawled with the instinct to answer.

He didn't.

He kept walking.

The Greenwood punished attachment first. It didn't have to kill you to take you. It only had to make you turn around.

Undead things crawled from shallow graves of leaf mold and twisted roots. Some wore remnants of Anari armor, plates half-swallowed by moss. Some wore nothing at all, their skin stripped to pale sinew, their mouths packed with old leaves that kept them from speaking anything true.

Their eyes were wrong.

Not hungry.

Directed.

Borrowed intent burned in them like a candle held behind a mask.

Harvey cut them down anyway.

Kuldemaekr sang softly with every strike. Not loud, not proud. A low, measured note that made the Greenwood flinch in places it pretended weren't alive. When the blade passed through bone, the dead did not fall. They disintegrated, unraveling into gray ash that sank into the forest floor like an apology.

The ash did not scatter in the wind.

There was no wind.

It sank with the dignity of something being returned to pay a debt.

He stopped counting kills by the fourth day.

Or the tenth.

Time inside the Greenwood was a thing you discovered only by losing it.

He started counting searches.

Caves. Ravines. Sinkholes. Hollow trunks large enough to swallow keeps. Crevices that breathed cold air like lungs that had forgotten how to warm. He followed instinct until it dulled into frustration, then followed the

Horn's pull until it blurred into a background ache, a constant tugging behind his ribs.

The Horn wanted something.

The Greenwood wanted something else.

And Harvey, caught between a relic and a curse, began to feel like a thread in a tightening knot.

If he forgot her voice, the forest would take him.

Not the Crone's voice. Not Aelrindel's.

Kellyn's.

He repeated it quietly, like a trail marker carved into bark.

"Stay with me," he murmured once, though she wasn't there.

Later, when the fog pressed so close that he could see his own breath as a wall, he said her name again, neither as prayer nor as romance.

As coordinates.

As proof that he still belonged to something outside this place.

He realized he could walk the Greenwood for a lifetime and never find Aelrindel.

That was the true terror of it. Not death.

Irrelevance.

If the prison was hidden, it was deliberately concealed. The Greenwood didn't hide it the way a forest hides a deer. It hid it the way a mind hides a truth it cannot bear.

That night, Harvey slept with his back against a living root thicker than a watchtower. The Horn lay wrapped in oilcloth and leather against his chest. Kuldemaekr rested across his lap like a promise he could not afford to break.

Sleep took him like a hand closing around a flame.

And the dream came with teeth.

This time, Aelrindel did not stand far away among stars and roots. He was closer. Not free.

Nearer.

Chains of living wood and frost-bound light still wrapped him, braided around his wrists and throat like vows turned into restraints. His antlered silhouette filled the dream-hall as a storm fills a sky.

"You are searching the forest," the god said, his voice like wind moving through antlers. "When you should be searching the shape."

Harvey's jaw tightened. Even in dreams, impatience felt expensive here.

"I need more than riddles," he said. "I need a place."

Aelrindel's gaze sharpened, not offended. Appraising. A hunter's attention.

"My prison is not vast," he said. "It is not deep. Legions do not guard it."

The dream shifted. The Greenwood tilted like a map being turned in hands that knew it better than you ever would.

A hill rose.

Small.

Forested.

Almost unremarkable.

That was the trick. Walls didn't protect the prison. It was protected by being forgettable.

Within the hill, a cave mouth yawned like a held breath. Not dramatic. Not obvious. Just a dark curve in green shadow that, for one heartbeat, looked like the world had opened its lips.

"Mark the rise," Aelrindel said. "Not by steps. By sightlines. The forest hides what you approach crookedly."

The words carried weight, the way a command carries weight when it is also a confession.

"You have been walking like prey," the god added, softer. "You have been letting the Greenwood turn you. Stop giving it your angles."

Harvey swallowed. The dream tasted of sap and old iron.

"How?" he asked, and for the first time in days the question wasn't frustration.

It was readiness.

Aelrindel leaned forward as far as his chains allowed. The roots and star-branches above him flexed, tense, like the Greenwood itself didn't like him moving closer.

"Walk straight," the god said. "Not stubborn. Not blind. Straight as an oath is straight. Straight as a spear is straight. Straight as a Hunt must be when the prey tries to make you dance."

The image of the hill burned into Harvey's mind, not as a picture but as a pull. A contour. A pressure in the shape of a landscape.

Then the dream snapped shut.

Harvey woke with his hand on Kuldemaekr's grip, breathing hard, heart steady in a body that refused to be surprised by terror anymore.

The fog had thinned.

And he was no longer alone.

Three dead Anari stood at the edge of the clearing, unmoving, heads tilted as if listening for permission.

They weren't shamblers.

They were waiting.

Harvey rose without ceremony and killed them.

One. Two. Three.

The blade unmade them into ash and silence, and the forest drank that silence too.

Then the cold changed.

Not ambient.

Directed.

Something stepped forward from between two blackened trunks.

A wight.

Not rotted. Not stitched. Not sloppy with hunger.

A warrior.

Its armor and helm were immaculate, dark steel etched with runes that caught the little light filtering through the canopy and bent it into thin, cruel lines. Frost curled from its joints. Its helm bore the long, sharp angles of a predatory mask, as if the face beneath it had never been permitted to be human again.

It drew its blade without sound.

And the air drained warmth.

Harvey felt it in his teeth. In his knees. In the places where old injuries remembered winter.

This wasn't a random guardian.

This was a message.

You are close enough now that we will spend something to stop you.

The wight moved first.

Fast.

No wasted motion. No flourish. A blur forward, low and sudden, blade angling for Harvey's ribs with surgical intent.

The style made Harvey's stomach drop.

It bore an uncanny resemblance to Ellendyl's.

Not identical, but kin. The same economy. The same cold certainty that the shortest line between two bodies was death.

Harvey answered with Griffyn form.

Grounded.

Anchored.

He met the strike not by chasing speed but by claiming space. Feet set. Shoulders squared. The blade turned aside with controlled force, the way you shut a door against a storm.

Steel rang once.

The sound didn't echo.

The Greenwood swallowed it like a secret.

They circled.

The wight flowed sideways, never crossing its own line of balance, each step part of a larger arc. Lynx-style hunting sought weakness through misdirection. Feints layered on feints. Rhythm broken, rebuilt, broken again, until you couldn't tell where the strike began and where it ended.

Harvey refused to chase the rhythm.

Griffyn did not chase.

It waited.

The wight struck again.

High, then low, then inside Harvey's guard with a thrust meant to slip beneath armor and freeze his lungs mid-breath. Harvey twisted, his shoulder clipping bark. The blade scraped his side, and cold burned through cloth and skin, a bite so clean his body didn't register it as pain at first.

Then pain arrived, late and furious.

The wight pressed.

A spinning cut. A hook. A sudden retreat that lured Harvey forward.

And then the trap.

The wight reversed direction mid-step, its blade snapping up toward Harvey's throat with the cruel certainty of something that had executed hundreds.

Harvey barely brought Kuldemaekr up in time.

Impact numbed his arms. Cold seeped into his bones. For a heartbeat, his vision tunneled, and he felt the Greenwood lean closer, eager.

The wight advanced, relentless now.

This wasn't hunger.

This was judgment.

Harvey forced himself lower, grounding himself, letting Griffyn settle back into him. He let the next strike glance off his pauldron on purpose, taking the sting to draw the wight closer. He felt the cold bite his shoulder and welcomed it like bait.

The wight committed.

Harvey struck.

Not fast.

True.

Kuldemaekr bit into the wight's breastplate.

The rune-etched armor flared.

The undead did not scream.

It screamed with absence.

A ripple passed through it, starting at the point of contact and racing outward like frost reversing itself. The Lynx form shattered mid-motion. The wight collapsed inward, not falling so much as being erased. Essence unraveled. The shape of the warrior emptied itself, leaving nothing behind but gray ash sinking into the soil.

In seconds, it was gone.

And the armor remained.

Harvey stood shaking, breath ragged, blood freezing along his side.

The breastplate lay pristine in the leaf-mold, runes intact, power humming quietly, like a quiet animal when it is not sure whether you are friend or owner.

He stared at it, and the Greenwood waited.

Because this was always how it worked. It offered you tools, shortcuts, and help.

And then it demanded to know what you would become with them.

Harvey stripped off his patchwork armor without ceremony: fungus, bark, vine, scavenged metal, the desperate craft of someone surviving in a place that didn't allow it. He pulled the wight's breastplate on.

It fit.

As if it had been waiting.

He tested movement.

Perfect.

Too perfect.

He hated that, and he couldn't afford to refuse it.

The wight's blade crumbled when he touched it, as age finally claimed what death had preserved too long.

Harvey let it go.

He climbed.

High.

One of the Greenwood's rare giants, a tree that rose above the canopy like a watchtower. The ascent tore at his side, and each pull sent cold blood shifting beneath the new armor. He didn't stop. He didn't hurry. He climbed like a man who knew that the longer he stayed in the Greenwood, the more of him it would file away.

At the top, the world opened.

Greenwood stretched in every direction, a sea of twisted crowns, fog pools, and subtle rises. Nothing should have been distinguishable.

And yet.

He saw it.

The hill.

Just as in the dream.

A subtle rise above the endless green, modest enough to be overlooked by anyone not looking for the shape of a lie.

Harvey exhaled slowly and lined up his bearing.

Tree to tree.

Sightline to sightline.

Straight.

Not stubborn-straight.

Oath-straight.

He remembered Sylveron's voice, sharp as a whetstone:

Never walk the forest the way it wants to be walked. Walk it the way it cannot bend.

Harvey descended.

Set his line.

And began the final approach.

Behind him, the Greenwood shifted.

Ahead of him, the hill waited.

For the first time since he'd entered the cursed forest, Harvey knew the difference between wandering and pursuing.

He was no longer searching.

He was closing.

And somewhere in the fog ahead, the hill breathed again, slow and patient, as if it could already taste the Horn against Harvey's chest and were deciding whether to open its mouth.

The Green Knight with new armor and helm.

Chapter 34 — The Joke Written in Ash

Planet: Vaelthara
Location: Königsbrunn — The Half-Raised War-Cathedral
Divine Year of Vaelthas — Wolf Month, 21,426 Years Since the Sealing

Stone dust hung in the air like incense for a god that had not yet decided whether it would listen.

The War-Cathedral of Königsbrunn was unfinished by design. A completed cathedral becomes a monument. A half-built one stays hungry. It keeps men working, priests shouting, coins moving, and fear from settling into something as dangerous as doubt.

Its walls rose in brutal angles of pale limestone and black basalt hauled from conquered quarries. Scaffolds webbed the structure. Chains creaked. Pulleys groaned. Every few breaths, a block was hoisted and settled with a bone-deep thud that traveled through the city like an imposed heartbeat.

Banners of the Burning Crown snapped from every exposed height. Red cloth. Gold thread. A crowned flame stitched so meticulously it looked less embroidered than branded into the air itself. Braziers burned day and night, fed by pitch and resin, their smoke marking Königsbrunn for leagues.

Faith here was not whispered.
It was announced.

The nave lay open to the sky. Wind poured through it, flinging grit across unfinished stone. Choir lofts were outlines. Pews were timber stacks. Yet the place already felt consecrated, not by holiness but by repetition: hammer-stroke, chant, hammer-stroke, chant. Labor as liturgy.

Ser Varyng the Sanctified stood beneath the open vault where the roof would one day seal the world into a single obedient echo. He wore no crown. He did not require one. His hair was close-cropped. His face carried the stillness of a man who had excised impulse from his life. Even his breathing appeared regulated.

The Embered Standard rested behind him, its cloth scorched and restitched so many times it looked less like fabric than a ledger of wars survived. The pole was old iron, pitted and dark.

Before him knelt three dark druids.

Mud-stained. Leaf-scarred. They carried the forest's scent like confession: wet bark, crushed fern, old smoke. One watched Varyng's hands. One watched the Standard. The third watched the exits.

A thin ring of Sun Priests stood at the nave's edge, ash-marked foreheads catching light. They did not glare. They did not threaten. They waited.

"You failed," Ser Varyng said.

His voice did not rise. The cathedral carried it.

One druid swallowed. "We slowed them. The forest turned against us. Dragons—"

"The forest," Ser Varyng said, "is land that has not yet learned obedience."

The druid's gaze dropped.

"How many new druids can you train?" Varyng asked.

"True druids? Few. Rangers, yes. But druidic binding requires selection. And time."

"How much?"

"A year. Per candidate. And only with—"

"Anari."

The word was logistical.

"With their dark circles," the druid continued. "Dryads that aren't right. Candidates taken, changed, returned."

"Taken," Varyng repeated. "Changed."

"Yes, Sanctified."

A stillness passed through him that was not surprise. It was recalculation.

"Then we ally with them again."

The druids stiffened.

"They fled after Graypine," one said. "They will not trust—"

"They will," Varyng said quietly. "We will offer them everything."

He pointed to the first druid. "You will return to their shrine. Speak of mutual survival. Promise land. Autonomy. Influence. Whatever they request."

"And if they refuse?"

Varyng rested a hand on the Standard.

"Then you will remind them what stands between humanity and its destiny."

The druid bowed too low.

"You will expand the rangers," Varyng continued to the others. "Every forester. Every hunter. Every child who can track or vanish."

"They will never move like Anari."

"They will not need to," Varyng said. "Forest warfare is not poetry. It is logistics with leaves."

A scorched-robed priest approached. "The fire trials are complete. The young mages are promising."

"They will be refined," Varyng said. "Fire must learn patience before wrath."

He looked toward the forest line on the horizon. It appeared darker than the sky deserved.

Beyond the city, preparation never stopped. Steam tanks beneath tarps. Layered armor etched with impact channels. Rifled barrels. Powder wagons. Hymns structured like marching orders.

"We adapt," Varyng said. "We always have."

He looked at the kneeling druids.

"We lost a battle."

His expression did not change.

"And gained clarity."

That was the last ordinary sentence spoken in the War-Cathedral that day.

The messenger arrived through the foundation trenches, mud to the knees, urgency burning through whatever remained of dignity. Sun Priests seized him before he collapsed.

"Let him through," Varyng said without turning.

The man staggered forward and fell to his knees.

"Graypine," he rasped.

The druids flinched.

"Speak."

"We struck as ordered. Fire mages. Cannon. Steam tanks. Pike lines. We burned tree-homes. Took the outer bridges. We were winning."

He looked up, blood bright in the corners of his eyes.

"We were winning."

"What happened," Varyng said, "is what you tell me next."

"They came from above. Dragons. In formation. Not beasts. Soldiers." His voice thinned. "Fire through smoke. Acid. Vines. Roots inside our lines. Steam tanks split. Cannons melted. We couldn't see them until they were inside us."

"How many survived?"

"Enough to run."

"Enough to report."

"Yes."

"What of the Banner-Saint's column?"

"Pulled back before the rout. Escorted."

"Good," Varyng said.

The word hung wrong.

"Graypine Reach was not a battle," Varyng continued. "It was a demonstration."

He turned at last.

"They showed us their sky. Their reach. That the forest answers."

He paused.

"In answering, they made themselves predictable."

The druids stared.

"You thought you were learning the forest," he told them. "You were learning how it permits you to die."

He crouched before the messenger.

"Did you see her?"

Recognition flickered.

"Yes. Kellyn Windstream. She led them."

Varyng nodded once.

The ledger balanced.

A field report was handed to him. He broke the seal and read.

"Survivors report trees were moved. The forest advanced during combat. Recommend immediate fortification."

He tapped the board lightly.

"They are frightened of trees."

Silence.

"Fear is an ingredient. It is not a plan."

He set the board aside.

"The Anari believe they showed us weakness," he said. "They showed us priority."

He turned toward the horizon.

"They fight like a people defending a home. They answer when something burns."

His eyes narrowed.

"Which means we decide what burns."

The words settled heavily.

"We will not march into their forest again. Not yet."

He lifted the Standard.

"We will make them come to us."

A breath caught somewhere behind him.

"Find the shrine where the Anari traitors hide," Varyng said. "Not because I fear them."

His voice sharpened.

"Because I will use them."

"How?" someone asked.

"As bait."

The word dropped clean.

"Bait for the Wolf Clan. Bait for the Dragon Clan. Bait for compassion."

He spoke as if enumerating materials.

"Sanctified roadlines. Timber camps. Banners visible from the forest edge."

A pause.

"And then we burn what they cannot let burn."

"Children?" a voice cracked.

Varyng looked at the speaker evenly.

"I am not a beast."

A fragile easing of breath.

"I am worse," he said. "Because I am useful."

No one exhaled again.

"The Malloch does not care if we are kind," he said. "Only if we are alive."

He planted the Standard.

The sound echoed like a nail driven through wood.

"Stop mourning a battle," he said. "We are building a war."

Outside, braziers smoked.
Below, hammers continued.
Beyond the roadlines, the forest held its silence like teeth.

Graypine had burned.

Now, burning was policy.

That Evening

The kings gathered beneath the unfinished vault. No guards. Only Sun Priests and architecture.

"You fear the forest," Varyng said. "You should. It bleeds."

"You fear the Anari. You should. They learn."

"You fear the Malloch more. That fear is correct."

He spoke of gates. Anti-reality. Cities erased without siege.

"In every future where humanity survives, we are united. Armed."

"And in every future where we hesitate, we vanish."

"You once said humans lose," a king said.

"Yes."

The word struck clean.

"Unless you allow me to change how the war is fought."

He raised the Standard.

"Align with me. Or be erased by history."

No one answered.

That was consent.

AFTERWARD — The Ocular

High scaffold. Wind. Smoke.

A tap at his temple. The ocular opened.

Tricklen Gearwisp flickered into view. Durak Runebinder followed, forge-light heavy around him.

"They field dragons," Varyng said. "We field nothing in the air."

"And when you do?" Durak asked. "You turn it on us."

Varyng did not deny it.

"I lost at Graypine," he said. "I will not lose twice to the same sky."

"You need what your priests cannot pray," Durak said.

"My priests are for morale. You are for results."

Silence.

"Then I will buy the sky," Varyng said.

Armor schematics unfurled. Impact lattices. Dispersion channels.

Tricklen went still.

"It's elegant," he breathed.

"You will have it," Varyng said. "In exchange for zeppelins. Two. One lift. One war. Ballista mounts. Wind-stable."

"And training," Durak said. "A year."

"Which makes you inconvenient," Tricklen grinned.

"I am already inconvenient," Varyng replied.

Terms were exchanged. Distrust formalized.

The ocular dimmed. Wind returned.

Below, the cathedral rose.

"They have dragons," Varyng murmured.

He touched the Standard.

"Then we learn to hunt the sky."

Quieter: "This is not about the Anari."

It was about the Malloch.

Far beyond the city, the forest answered with silence.

And silence, here, had teeth.

Chapter 35 — The Hill That Would Not Near

Planet: Vaelthara
Location: The Greenwood — Inner Curseward
Divine Year of Vaelthas — Wolf Month

Harvey should have reached it by now.

The thought arrived without panic or drama, just the plain certainty of a hunter whose body keeps its own ledger. Distance is honest. Hunger is honest. Blood is honest. The Greenwood was none of those things.

He had seen the hill from above the canopy. Not a mountain, not a ridge, just a low rise that broke the forest's endless, breathing skin. A subtle green swelling crowned with darker trees, as if the world had swallowed a stone and it still showed in the throat.

Aelrindel's prison.

A place with an outline. A place with a there.

He had chosen his line the way Sylveron taught him: pick a bearing, pick a landmark, and walk as if doubt were a luxury you cannot afford. No meandering. No "let's see what's over here." The Greenwood punished curiosity.

So, he walked straight.

Tree-to-tree. Root-shadow to root-shadow. A dead-reckoned arrow through the living maze.

At first, it felt right. The trunks passed in a steady rhythm. The fog thinned and thickened like breath, but never broke his line. His boots sank and rose, sank and rose, mud sucking at the leather with wet, possessive sounds. Branches clawed at his shoulders. Thorns snagged his cloak and released it reluctantly, as if they wanted to keep a souvenir.

Hours. Maybe.

Time in the Greenwood did not behave like time. It slid. It clung. It doubled back on itself and smirked.

But distance? Distance was supposed to be clean.

He stopped when his instinct told him he should be at the hill's base, when the air should have shifted from approach to arrival. When the trees should have begun to lean differently, when the ground should have pitched upward with that faint, unmistakable tilt that tells your calves what's coming before your eyes do.

He heard only the Greenwood's slow, heavy listening.

Fog drifted between the trunks in sheets, thin enough to see through, yet thick enough to swallow edges. The air smelled of wet leaves, old iron, and something else beneath it, a faint sweetness like rot pretending to be fruit.

Harvey set his pack down and climbed.

Bark cold under his palms. Sap tacky at the seams of the trunk. He moved with the practiced economy Sylveron had burned into him: three points of contact, weight close, breath quiet. He rose through the lower branches into thinner limbs that swayed like ribs under pressure, climbing until the fog became a floor beneath him and the canopy opened into a sickly green-tinted light.

He pulled himself into the crown and looked out.

The hill was there.

Not closer.

Not farther.

There as if he had never moved at all.

The exact same subtle hump breaking the sea of treetops. The same silhouette. The same darker crown. The same position relative to the crooked, lightning-scarred pine standing like a black needle a little to the left of it.

Harvey stared until his eyes watered.

"That's not possible," he said aloud, and his voice sounded wrong up here, as if the air had borrowed it and were deciding whether to give it back.

He climbed down slowly.

His boots hit the ground with a dull thud, and the Greenwood swallowed the sound as deep moss swallows footprints.

Illusion, then.

Except the hill was not a trick of the eye. If it were only glamour, it would have been easier. A false hill, a decoy, a pretty lie.

This was worse.

This was nearness being denied.

Harvey tightened the leather strap across his chest, where the Horn rested, frozen and heavy. The oilcloth around it crackled faintly as he shifted. The Kuldemaekr sat in his hand like a patient thought, its dark blade drinking in the Greenwood's cold without complaint.

He picked his line again and tried a different method.

This time, he went by sound.

He closed his eyes and walked toward where the hill must be, refusing to let the forest's geometry tempt him into correcting himself. He counted his breaths, keeping the rhythm steady. One breath, two, three. Each exhale was a metronome. Each inhale a vow.

Roots snagged his boots, trying to throw him. He recovered without breaking stride.

A low branch whipped across his cheek, leaving a line of sting. He didn't flinch.

The fog thickened, coiled, and brushed his face like damp fingers. Something moved beyond it, neither close nor far, yet present enough to be counted as pressure.

He kept walking.

When his knee struck a half-buried stone and pain flared bright and sharp up his leg, he grunted, caught himself on a trunk, and kept going, his teeth clenched.

No detours. No flinching. No retreat.

After what felt like an hour of stubborn devotion, he stopped, opened his eyes, and climbed once more.

The hill waited.

Same distance.

Same height.

Same quiet patience that felt less like a place and more like a decision.

Harvey pressed his forehead to the bark and laughed once, short and humorless. The sound was swallowed instantly, as if even laughter were an offense to the Greenwoods' etiquette.

"Fine," he muttered. "Then tell me what you are."

He descended and tried a third approach.

He chose a straight line of saplings and stones and made marks. Notches in the bark. A strip torn from his sleeve, tied around a branch. A small pile of pale stones stacked at the base of a trunk.

He walked, counting paces.

One hundred. Two hundred. Three.

Fog slid over his markers. The strips of cloth fluttered as if in a wind he couldn't feel, turning slowly, turning wrong, until they pointed behind him.

He stopped and turned to look.

The stone pile at the base of the trunk was still there.

But it was not behind him.

It was to his left.

By several paces.

He walked back to it and knelt, touched the stones with his fingertips. Damp. Real. Not illusion.

He stood and looked around. Every tree looked like a cousin of every other, but the notches he'd carved were there. The cloth he'd tied was there.

The world had not erased his trail.

It had moved the world around it.

A slow, deliberate rearrangement. Not teleportation, not confusion. A gentle cheat, like a hand nudging a game piece while pretending to scratch an itch.

Harvey's breath went cold in his lungs.

"Magic," he said softly. "Not glamour. Not misdirection."

A curseward.

The word tasted right. A spell that doesn't hide the prison. A spell that renders approach meaningless. A hill you can see forever but never touch.

He tried a fourth time, furious now, but fury in Harvey was not shouting. It was precision, sharpened into refusal.

He climbed back into the canopy, fixed the hill's position relative to three distinct trees, then dropped down and moved from landmark to landmark with relentless accuracy. Trunk scar. Bent branch. A dead snag pointing like a finger.

He took the straightest line he could carve through a forest that hated straightness.

He walked until his calves burned, his mouth went dry, and his breathing grew so loud that it sounded like someone else was following him.

He climbed again.

The hill remained.

Still.

Waiting.

Unmoved by effort, as if effort itself were a currency the Greenwood had declared invalid.

Harvey sat in the fork of the tree, higher than he had any right to be, and looked out across the canopy until his eyes stung.

Aelrindel had shown him the hill in his dream.

Not to taunt him.

To teach him to recognize it.

But recognition wasn't enough.

Not here.

Below him, the fog rolled, slow and thick, as if the forest were exhaling its satisfaction.

Harvey climbed down and sat with his back against the trunk, his pack beside him, Kuldemaekr across his lap. The Horn rested against his ribs, its frozen weight pressing into him, a constant reminder: you brought the key. The Greenwood had simply refused to provide the door.

He listened.

The forest breathed.

Slow. Heavy. Watching.

And then, beneath that, he felt the slightest shift.

Not sound.

Not movement.

A subtle tightening, like the world gathering itself to witness what he would do next.

Harvey's gaze lifted to the fog.

"I know you're doing it," he said, not to the Greenwood but to the intelligence behind it. The Crone. The curse. The ward. The patient malice in the place's architecture.

He stood and walked back to the line he'd marked with cloth. He faced the hill and did not move.

He held still.

And watched.

The fog slid. The branches swayed. The trees leaned in slow, almost imperceptible increments, each adjusting its posture as if making room for something unseen to pass through.

Harvey kept his eyes on a scarred trunk directly ahead.

It did not move.

But the trunk to the right of it… shifted.

Not by much.

A fraction. A breath. A lie.

The Greenwood was not blocking him with walls.

It was sliding him sideways.

Every step he took was being paid out into drift.

Every straight line was being converted into a curve without his consent.

The hill did not draw nearer because the forest refused to allow nearness.

Harvey's jaw tightened so hard his teeth ached.

He missed Kellyn so sharply it made his throat sting.

Not because she would have comforted him.

Because she would have understood the rule and then stabbed it.

There's always a rule.

He could hear her voice with brutal clarity: steady, irritated, and brilliant.

He closed his eyes and let that imagined steadiness slow his breathing.

If the forest was making him drift, then the answer wasn't to walk harder.

It was to stop being something the forest could drift.

He opened his eyes and looked down at the horn.

Frost crusted its seams. The oilcloth was stiff with cold. Its weight felt heavier in the Greenwood, as if the curseward recognized it and instinctively hated it.

"You're a key," Harvey murmured. "So, what's the lock?"

Kuldemaekr hummed faintly in his lap, a low note of displeasure, like a blade that doesn't like being idle.

Harvey looked toward the canopy again.

The hill waited, patient and unchanged, a quiet mockery of progress.

He stood.

This time, he did not set out immediately.

He took one slow step toward the hill's edge, and the forest… listened.

He took another.

Fog brushed his boots like a warning.

He stopped and tilted his head, eyes unfocused, sensing the sideways pull, that subtle, persuasive drift the Greenwood used like a river uses its current.

He felt it.

A pressure at the edge of perception.

A hand not touching him, but deciding where he would end up.

Harvey smiled without humor.

"So that's it," he whispered. "You don't keep me out. You keep me… adjacent."

The Greenwood did not answer.

It didn't have to.

The hill stayed where it was.

And Harvey remained where he was.

Close enough to see. Far enough to fail.

He tightened the Horn's strap across his chest and settled the Kuldemaekr in his grip.

"Alright," he said softly, his voice steady now, the way it had been when the hunt stopped being a search and became a contest.

"You've shown me the trick."

He looked at the hill one more time, the same distance, the same silhouette, the same silent no.

Then he turned away from it.

Not in surrender.

In strategy.

If the Greenwood were a maze that moved, then walking toward the center would be pointless.

You didn't beat a moving maze by charging its walls.

You beat it by finding the hand that moved them.

And somewhere beneath root and fog, the curseward waited, confident in its own cleverness.

Harvey's boots sank into the damp earth.

He began walking, not toward the hill.

Toward the rule that kept it forever out of reach.

Harvey peering at the hill that is never nearer.

Chapter 36 — Where the Forest Slept

Planet: Vaelthara
Location: Eichenfall Timber Camp, Western Reach
Divine Year of Vaelthas — Wolf Month

They found the camp quiet.

Not peaceful and quiet. Not the hush of snow or prayer.

This was the quiet you hear in a room after a scream ends, when the air is still trying to remember how to move.

Eichenfall lay in a raw bite carved from the woods, stumps jutting from churned earth like broken teeth. The clearing should have been loud with human industry, sawsong and curses and the steady percussion of axes. Even in winter, camps like this had sound: kettles clanking, horses snorting, men arguing over rations, a sentry stamping to warm his boots while pretending it was discipline.

Here, nothing was argued.

No birds. Not even scavengers with the decency to be opportunistic. No insects stitched their thin, restless music between the trunks. The wind approached the clearing and did something almost human.

It hesitated.

Kholfax was the first to step across the boundary of worked ground.

He did it the way he always did it now: slow, deliberate, eyes moving before his feet. He let the silence tell him where the lie was hiding.

The scar along the left side of his face prickled the instant he crossed the threshold.

Not pain.

Recognition.

The kind that came when something you hated had already arrived and made itself at home.

Bodies stood everywhere.

Not strewn. Not piled. Not collapsed in the untidy honesty of death.

Standing.

A lumberjack at the edge of the sawpit held his axe mid-lift, forearms corded, mouth half-open as if he'd been about to shout a joke to the man beside him. A militia man leaned on a spear like it was a staff for prayer, his shield still strapped, knuckles white around the shaft. Two men stood shoulder-to-shoulder near a cookfire, heads bent toward each other, their closeness almost tender. If you didn't look too long, you could pretend they were sharing warmth.

Then you looked at their eyes.

Open. Clouded and fixed on nothing.

Their pupils had the blank sheen of glass left too long in rain.

Kholfax moved closer, careful, as if the stillness might shatter like thin ice and swallow him.

He studied the militia man's jaw.

Locked.

No slackness. No fall. No final softness.

Death had taken them upright and left them that way, like a cruel joke told by someone who believed posture was the same as dignity.

Kholfax reached out and hovered his fingers near the man's throat. Not touching skin. Just feeling the air.

Cold. Slightly metallic. A faint tang, like lightning after a storm.

"Paralytic," he said, voice low. "Fast onset. No thrashing. No collapse."

Froster stepped into the clearing behind him, his massive frame taut as a drawn bow. His eyes swept the field of statues, narrowing with slow, simmering rage. He didn't speak. When Froster spoke, the world usually paid in blood.

Vyrna followed, her bark-steel armor muted beneath ash-stained cloaks, her war-crown braided tightly. Her presence carried weight even when she said nothing, like a tree that had decided to stand.

"You're certain," she said.

Kholfax nodded once. His hand rose to the scar without thinking, thumb brushing it like a worry-stone. "I've seen it before."

His mouth went dry as the memory pressed up from the future like a corpse insisting it still had business.

"Not this… arranged," he added. "But the voice that does this kind of work?" He swallowed. "It belongs to someone who likes control."

A few paces deeper into the camp, the main timber hall waited, half-built and already weathered, its beams blackened where pitch had been smeared to ward off rot. Lanterns hung from hooks, unlit.

Someone had written on the hall's outer wall.

Not painted. Not carved.

Burned.

Letters dark and drying, each line thickened by repeated strokes as if the writer wanted the words to weigh more.

LUMBERJACKS ARE OK.
THEY SLEEP ALL NIGHT
AND WORK ALL DAY

Kholfax stared at it longer than the others.

The message wasn't clever. That was what made it worse. It wasn't poetry or prophecy. It wasn't a threat with artistry. It was the kind of thing a child might say, a simple rule held up like a shield against life's messy chaos.

He felt his stomach tighten, not with fear but with that old, sick professional understanding.

Cadence. Structure. The fake logic that tries to sound reasonable.

A killer explaining himself.

He could almost hear Malvas's voice in his head, dry and relentless.

He wants to be understood. He's performing comprehension. That's your leverage.

The thought hit him so sharply that he almost turned, half-expecting her to be there behind him, holding a scanner or a parchment, already cataloging details with maddening calm.

Of course, she wasn't.

The absence was a clean wound. No bleeding, just an ache that left the world feeling slightly off-balance.

He had never told her how much he respected her persistence. How he relied on it. How her refusal to let horror become "normal" had kept him human when cases tried to sand him down into something colder.

Too late now.

Around them, Wolf Clan druids moved in quiet circles, assessing, listening, and touching the earth with reverence and anger braided together. Their life magic was held back like breath, waiting for Vyrna's word.

But not all of them carried the same Song.

Kholfax watched as three figures in wolf-gray cloaks slipped between the dead. They moved as if they belonged at the camp, as if they'd slept there. Their hands were stained with sap and soot. Focus stones hung at their throats, darkened like bruises.

Dark druids.

They knelt among the bodies, pressing palms to the soil and whispering low harmonics that felt wrong in Kholfax's teeth.

Not a scream of corruption.

A subtler twist. A note bent just enough to make the forest hesitate before answering.

Like someone had taught the roots to flinch.

Vyrna saw it. He knew by the way her jaw tightened, by the stillness that sharpened around her.

Kholfax stepped to her side and kept his voice low. "It's them."

Her gaze remained fixed on the druids, the dead, and the burned words that still smoked faintly in the cold air.

"I don't know who," he continued, "or how many. But the killer moves among the dark circle. I'd stake my remaining life on it."

Vyrna didn't argue.

She didn't need to. The evidence was standing upright all around them.

She nodded once, slowly, the nod of someone accepting a war they had spent years trying to talk down.

Then she lifted her hand.

Not a grand gesture. Not a queen performing authority.

A simple signal.

And the Wolf Clan acted.

Life magic surged.

Not gentle. Not consoling. Not the soft green kindness of a healer closing a child's scraped knee.

This was the forest's answer when it decided patience had failed.

Roots split the compacted earth with a wet crack, like ribs parting. Saplings tore through floorboards and skinned planks, their growth accelerating into violence. Vines climbed beams still warm from the morning sun and cinched around them, reclaiming human carpentry with botanical contempt. Moss spread over tools, swallowing iron and wood alike, not hiding evidence but erasing ownership.

The timber camp did not burn.

It was overwritten.

The dead were handled with care that felt almost unbearable.

Warriors and druids moved among them, unfastening hands from axes, easing spears from locked grips, and lowering themselves into shallow trenches that opened as the roots lifted and the soil softened. No prayers to human gods were spoken here. Only the Wolf Clan's low Songs, frayed with exhaustion yet steady enough to guide grief into action.

Leaves folded over faces.

Soil-covered boots.

Vines braided across chests like a final embrace.

No graves.

Only growth.

Kholfax felt the forest drinking deeply, not greedily but purposefully. Blood-soaked earth turned fertile beneath his feet. The air thickened with the rich scent of turned soil and sap breaking open. Death was accepted without judgment or mercy.

That was the forest's gift.

It did not ask who deserved what.

It simply reclaimed.

When the work was finished, Eichenfall no longer existed.

Where the clearing had been, a young, dense grove stood, already knitting itself into the larger Faelwyn Holt as if eager to close a wound before anyone could look too closely. The burned message on the timber hall was half-swallowed by bark, its letters warped and pulled apart as the wood grew, as if the forest disliked even the shape of the words.

That was when the sky changed.

A shadow passed over the new leaves.

A pressure rolled through the canopy like a held breath.

Then came the low, unmistakable thunder of wings.

Myrrathis descended from the cloud and cold like a falling star caught at the last possible moment. Bronze scales caught the dim light and shattered it into fragments, each a small, defiant flame. Heat rolled off him, not wild but controlled, like a furnace radiating when it has decided exactly what it will melt.

He landed at the grove's edge with purposeful grace, his wings folding in and his talons sinking into soil that had been human ground only a short time ago.

Kellyn dismounted.

Her boots touched the ground, and she looked around once, taking in what had happened here with the speed of a mind that refused to be surprised by horror twice.

The absence of bodies.

The young grove.

The half-swallowed message.

The quiet.

Understanding settled across her face like armor.

"This is what it looks like," she said, her voice calm, certain, and almost frightening in its steady calm. "The forest doesn't retreat anymore. It replaces."

She looked at Vyrna. Then at Kholfax. Then at the gathered warriors and druids, whose eyes held the hollow focus of those who have crossed a line and cannot pretend it was a step.

"We don't just burn camps," Kellyn continued. "We grow over them. Cities, too. Streets become rootways.

Walls become trellises." Her gaze hardened, not cruel but resolved. "And we don't leave afterward."

Myrrathis rumbled behind her, a sound like distant thunder agreeing with inevitability.

Kellyn's eyes moved to the horizon, where the forest line darkened the world like a bruise.

"Anari will live there," she said. "In what used to be human cities. We will learn to fight beyond the trees, on open ground, on stone roads." She paused, and when she spoke again, her words hit like hammered iron. "We adapt or we die."

Kholfax watched her a moment too long.

Not awe. Not myth-making.

Respect, clean and hard, the kind a man gives only after he has seen leaders freeze when the rules change.

Kellyn didn't freeze.

She rewrote the rules.

Malvas would have liked her, he thought. Too much, probably. They'd argue for hours. Malvas would insist on evidence, while Kellyn would insist on action. Somehow, the world would be better and louder afterward.

The thought almost made him smile.

Almost.

The grove creaked as it settled into its new shape. The young trunks shifted, aligning, knitting, as if the forest were adjusting its posture in a bed it had decided to keep.

And somewhere, not far away, something that wrote jokes in blood felt Faelwyn Holt's edge creep closer.

It did not flee.

It did not hurry.

It simply smiled back, patient as a curse.

Because the forest, at last, had begun to wake.

And when the forest woke, it remembered everything.

Chapter 37 — A God's Choice

Planet: Vaelthara
Location: The Greenwood — Inner Reach
Chronometric Stamp: BV 21

The Greenwood did not yield.

It did not resist either.

Resistance implied effort. Opposition. The possibility of being overcome.

This was something colder.

Harvey had tried everything he knew.

He walked in straight lines until his calves screamed and his inner compass dissolved into static. He fixed his bearing by scarred trunks, forked branches, and fungus patterns that should not repeat, yet the forest bent gently around his intention and set him down exactly where it wished. He circled the hill until distance became a joke, the trees sharing behind his back. He climbed above the canopy, clung to swaying crowns with sap-sticky hands, memorized the horizon down to the smallest break in leaf and shadow, then descended only to find the hill unchanged.

Always there.

Always just as far.

Never nearer.

He carved shallow, deliberate marks into the bark with the Kuldemaekr. He stacked stones. He tore strips from his cloak and tied them to branches, a trail of ragged breadcrumbs no forest could have hidden.

Hours later, he found the same strips fluttering behind him.

Not displaced.

Returned.

He slept beneath roots as thick as walls and woke beneath the same roots, though he knew he had not stopped there. His dreams were restless yet honest; it was waking that lied. The Greenwood folded its paths back on themselves with the patience of something eternal, not to confuse him but to deny him the dignity of progress.

Illusion layered upon illusion.

Not deception meant to trick.

Denial meant to endure.

The Crone was not concealing the prison.

She was refusing access to the idea of reaching it.

That understanding settled into Harvey's bones with a quiet weight.

He sat with his back against a broad oak whose heartwood now hummed faintly, a low resonance suggesting the curse was thinning, loosening its grip like fingers going numb. Aelrindel's horn rested across his knees. It was no longer frozen. Its surface was dark and matte, unadorned by frost, as if it had never known ice.

It felt heavier.

Not in mass.

In expectation.

The Greenwood watched him, not with eyes or intent, but with awareness. Leaves whispered just enough to remind him he was not alone. The air tasted different now, charged and close, like the moment before a storm breaks or a truth is spoken.

He understood then.

This was not a barrier to be bypassed.

It was not a puzzle to be solved by persistence or cleverness.

It was a question.

And he had been answering it incorrectly.

Harvey closed his eyes.

He let the Greenwood fade.

He thought of Kellyn.

Her hands, steady and precise when she worked, as if meaning itself could be coaxed into alignment with enough patience. He thought of the way her jaw tightened when the rules lied and how she never accepted inefficiency as fate. He thought of Sylveron's quiet certainty, of Seri's laughter ringing out in places where it should have died, of the Sylph warrior who had bled beneath the ice so Harvey could keep moving.

And of Witmar.

His brother's voice rose unbidden, dry and amused, as it always did whenever the world tried to look smarter than it was.

If the rules won't let you in, little brother, Witmar had said once, leaning against a console that shouldn't have existed yet, maybe you should stop trying to break them.

Harvey exhaled slowly.

The Horn was not a weapon.

Weapons forced outcomes.

The Horn did something older.

It invited.

Harvey hesitated.

Not in fear.

In clarity.

He saw it then—not as vision, not as prophecy, but as absence.

No return path marked behind him.

No quiet afterward.

No moment when this would simply be finished.

The Frost Queen's words surfaced unbidden, stripped of ice and crown alike.

Those who bear that name are rarely finished with what follows them.

If he raised the Horn, it would not end when the curse broke.

It would not end when Aelrindel walked free.

It would not end when the Greenwood healed.

It would go on.

Harvey breathed once, steady and deliberate.

And chose.

He lifted it.

The Greenwood fell still.

Not in fear. Not in resistance.

In recognition.

Leaves paused mid-whisper. Insects froze in the air, their wings catching light like suspended glass. The fog drew tight and thin, as if the forest itself leaned closer, curious despite itself.

Harvey pressed the Horn to his lips.

And blew.

The sound did not echo.

It did not roll outward through trunks or thunder across ravines. It did not shatter branches or startle birds into flight.

It went down.

The note folded inward, collapsing through air and soil alike, bypassing matter entirely. It resonated through memory, through oath, and through the oldest geometry of pursuit and promise. It vibrated in the bones of hunters long turned to dust and in the scars of gods who had forgotten why they ran.

It was not loud.

It was undeniable.

The ground answered first.

Mist tore itself apart as if burned by an invisible flame. Shadows peeled from their roots and fled, screaming into nothingness, their outlines unraveling as if exposed to truth rather than light. The Greenwood shuddered—not in pain, but in relief—as something old and cruel lost its grip.

Then the phantoms came.

They did not rise from graves.

They arrived.

Hunters stepped between moments, translucent yet whole, their forms woven from pale light and remembered motion. Ancient Anari warriors surged forward, antler-crowned and blade-bearing, their eyes clear now, no longer hollowed by the curse. Lynx Clan phantoms moved like wind over snow, free at last from the Crone's binding, their expressions fierce with gratitude and unfinished purpose.

They did not speak.

They ran.

They poured past Harvey like a living tide, cold and clean as mountain air, their passage leaving him untouched yet shaken. The illusion around the hill faltered—not shattered by force but unraveled by relevance. The barrier had never been meant to resist them.

At the heart of the charge, one figure slowed.

Witmar Oakenstride stood before Harvey, solid enough to see, yet not solid enough to touch. He looked much as he had in life: rumpled and observant, with one eyebrow lifted in permanent skepticism, as if the universe itself were making a claim he intended to audit.

"Well," Witmar said, glancing at the rushing phantoms. "You always did overcommit."

Harvey's throat closed. "You're—"

"Dead?" Witmar supplied. "Yes. Still. Don't make it awkward."

Despite everything, Harvey laughed. It broke him a little, like ice giving way under a careful weight.

"I didn't think—"

"No," Witmar said gently. "You weren't supposed to. That's kind of the point."

He looked toward the hill. The phantoms were already striking the barrier—not with weapons, but with presence. The illusion screamed as it failed, peeling back layer by layer, unable to deny what had already been denied once.

"You did well," Witmar said. "You always did. It just took you a while to stop trying to solve things like a problem."

Harvey swallowed. "I wish—"

"I know," Witmar replied. "But this part?" He stepped back, already thinning. "This is yours."

He smiled once more, softer now.

"Tell Kellyn," he said, fading, "I was wrong about the odds."

Then he was gone, swept back into the Hunt's rushing tide.

The hill opened.

Roots tore free as if glad to let go. Stone cracked outward—not broken, but released. The cave mouth yawned wide, breathing for the first time in centuries.

Harvey ran.

His legs burned. His breath tore at his chest. The Horn was still warm in his hands, humming like a heart that had finally remembered its rhythm.

Inside, the prison waited.

Or what remained of it.

Chains of light shattered as the last phantoms struck, completing a circle that had never been meant to close. The barrier collapsed inward with a sound like a long-held breath finally released.

Aelrindel stood free.

Taller than Harvey had ever seen in person. Antlered. Broad-shouldered. His presence bent space without effort, not by force but by inevitability. His eyes were bright, already turned toward paths beyond this world.

"You answered," Aelrindel said.

Harvey dropped to one knee, exhaustion hollowing him out. "I didn't know what else to do."

Aelrindel studied him for a long moment.

"You did not free me by breaking my prison," the god said at last.

"You freed me by returning my choice."

The Greenwood shuddered softly around them.

"I carried that horn long enough," Aelrindel continued, "to forget where the Hunt ended and where I began."

His gaze shifted—not to the Horn itself, but to Harvey's hands around it.

"If I retake it," he said quietly, "it will answer me again."

"And I would never stop."

He stepped closer. Not to claim it.

To steady Harvey's grip.

"You did what I could not," Aelrindel said.

"You let me leave."

"The Hunt does not end," Aelrindel said quietly. "It only changes who bears it."

The air tightened. Light folded inward as the Chamber of Victory answered, drawing him upward with slow, inescapable gravity.

Beyond him, another presence tore free from the Greenwood's fading shadow—twisted, furious, unraveling as the Crone was dragged from her stolen dominion, screaming not in rage but in loss.

Aelrindel did not look back.

"Thank you, Green Knight," he said as the pull intensified.

"You gave us back the choice we forgot."

He inclined his head once.

And then he was gone.

The god had gone.

The Horn had not.

Warm.

Humming.

Aware.

The Greenwood released him.

It did not take him.

The pull that had drawn gods and curses away loosened, then vanished, leaving the clearing unnaturally still. Light settled where it had been strained. Roots relaxed. Leaves resumed their whisper, tentative at first, then surer, as if the forest itself were testing the shape of its own breath.

Harvey remained kneeling.

The Horn rested in his hands.

Where Aelrindel had stood, the air thickened once more—not with divinity or command, but with presence. Hooves pressed softly into loam that had not borne weight in centuries.

A stag stepped forward from the Greenwood's heart.

Its hide was black as wet bark at night, its antlers broad and branching, etched with faint green veins of light that pulsed in time with the Horn's low resonance. Its eyes were not wild.

They were patient.

The stag lowered its head.

Not in submission.

In recognition.

Harvey rose slowly, the ache in his limbs sharp and real, grounding him in a body that was still his own. He did not speak. There was nothing to say that would not cheapen the moment.

The forest shifted around them—not closing, not parting.

Making room.

Somewhere deep beneath the roots and soil, something ancient settled into alignment. The Greenwood was no longer cursed.

It was claimed.

Harvey placed one hand against the stag's neck. It was solid. Warm. Alive.

The Horn quieted.

Not silenced.

Waiting.

When the stag turned, Harvey followed.

Together, they moved into the trees.

When silence returned to the clearing, it was not the silence of absence.

It was the silence of a Hunt that had found its bearer.

The Greenwood stood cleansed.

Watching.

The gods had left the Hunt behind.

They had not ended it.

And far beyond its borders, the world remained unaware that it had just acquired a Huntsman who would not stop when the gods did.

The imprisoned god of the hunt.

Chapter 38 – The Investigator

Planet: Vaelthara
Location: Greenwood Forest
Divine Year of Vaelthas — Wolf Month, 21,426 Years Since the Sealing

The Greenwood, After the Cleansing

The Greenwood did not resist them.

That alone unsettled Kaelith Blackwynd.

The vampire count moved beneath towering boughs that once would have recoiled from his presence, their bark twisting away from undeath as if offended by the contradiction of his presence. Now, the trees stood still. Roots did not curl. Moss did not wither beneath his boots. The forest breathed—slowly, evenly—like a great beast finally permitted to sleep.

It no longer hunted.

It no longer remembered hatred.

Behind Kaelith came six Veydrath undead knights, ancient and immaculate, their armor etched in grave-script older than the Confederation itself. Pale embers burned where eyes once had been. They moved without sound, without breath, without question.

Kaelith stopped.

He knelt.

At the center of a shallow glade lay a body.

Or what remained of one.

The corpse wore Greenwood craft: Anari leathers grown rather than sewn, vine-stitched plates hardened with resin and bark-song—living armor. Armor meant to flex with breath and motion. It had not been torn open or shattered.

It had been opened.

The chest had collapsed inward with surgical precision, as if something colder than steel—and more deliberate—had passed through it, taking the body's heart with it.

Kaelith extended two fingers, hovering them above the wound.

"No echo," he murmured.

He pressed down.

Necro-harmonics unfurled from him in a controlled ripple, tasting memory as a living tongue tastes salt. He did not force the residue. He listened to it, allowing the death to assemble itself without coercion.

The forest did not interfere.

That, too, was new.

A wight.

Not crude.

Not feral.

A duelist.

Kaelith straightened and turned his gaze to the second site.

Several paces away lay the remains—or what little of them remained. The body had partially collapsed into gray ash, as if erased rather than destroyed. Its armor remained intact. Anari make, but with different Clan styling on the boots and clothing. Runes etched so finely they approached divine craftsmanship.

The breastplate was unmarred.

Untouched.

Kaelith studied it for a long moment.

"This one was erased," he said quietly. "Not slain."

One of the undead knights inclined his head. "Aelrindel's mark?"

"Likely," Kaelith replied. "Or something close enough to offend the dead."

He paced between the two sites, reconstructing the engagement with the precision of a man who had once solved murders spanning centuries and star systems.

A mortal knight. Skilled. Armed with a relic blade. Alone.

The tunic's weave and insignia were Anari. Purpose-built. Trained. Executing rather than hunting.

A clash.

A pause.

Then—realization.

Kaelith returned to the fallen mortal and crouched again, examining the armor seams.

Not ripped.

Not torn free.

Unbuckled.

Removed.

His lips thinned by a fraction.

"Deliberate," he said. "He knew exactly what he was doing."

One knight began to speak. "Then the body is not—"

Kaelith raised a hand.

"No," he said. "The body is his."

He gestured toward the fungal tunic.

"The armor is Anari, and it remains intact. Its blade was mundane. The armor worn here is newly forged. Living. No undead would choose it." A pause. "And no god would leave it behind."

He stood and scanned the glade.

"The weapon, Kuldemaekr?" he asked.

Another knight answered immediately. "No trace. No resonance. No echo. Not even absence."

That mattered.

Artifacts screamed when destroyed. Gods scarred reality when they departed.

This left nothing.

Kaelith closed his eyes briefly.

"Then the sequence is clear," he said. "The Horn was sounded. The prison answered. The god reclaimed his relic."

He opened his eyes.

"And the mortal paid the price."

The Greenwood whispered, leaves speaking a language that no longer screamed.

One knight hesitated. "The armor exchange—"

"Irrelevant," Kaelith said flatly. "Death is rarely tidy, especially when gods are involved."

He looked once more at the body.

"For the record," he added, quieter now, "this knight fought a high wight alone."

A pause.

"And won."

He rose, authority settling around him like a mantle of frost.

"Prepare a report," Kaelith ordered. "Harvey Oakenstride is dead. The hunter god has left the plane. The Greenwood curse has ended."

He paused, then added:

"No further action required."

The undead knights bowed as one.

As they turned to leave, Kaelith lingered a heartbeat longer, his gaze drifting to the pristine Anari armor gleaming faintly in dappled light.

For just a moment—only a moment—something like doubt crossed his face.

Then it vanished.

He turned away.

Behind them, the forest closed in.

Not to hide the truth.

But to keep it.

Continuation — The Empty Prison

Kaelith did not leave immediately.

That unsettled the knights.

He moved deeper into the Greenwood, following a pull that was no longer hostile but unmistakably hollow. The forest no longer resisted him. Distance did not fold. Paths did not bend. The land… allowed.

After several minutes, the trees thinned.

A hill rose ahead.

Small. Forested. Unremarkable.

Except that the ground around it was wrong.

Kaelith knelt and pressed his palm to the soil.

"No resistance," he said softly. "No echo-cage. No divine anchor."

The hill was no longer hiding anything.

They found the cave entrance half-concealed by roots that had grown back in haste rather than design. Bark split. Stone cracked outward.

Something had forced its way free.

Inside, the air was cold—but not cursed.

The knights remained at the threshold as Kaelith entered alone.

At the cavern's heart stood the prison.

Or what remained of it.

Runes lay shattered across the stone floor like broken glass, their harmonic script unraveled beyond repair. The binding circle had not merely been undone.

It had been answered.

Chains of light had once anchored here. Now they were gone, their endpoints scorched clean into nothingness. No residue of Malloch. No backlash.

Only absence.

"Aelrindel is free," Kaelith said.

One knight shifted. "Then the Huntsman—"

"Returned," Kaelith finished. "Not to the world. To its owner."

He extended his necro-harmonic senses once more.

There was a single rupture.

Vertical.

Clean.

Recent.

A god's recall.

"The mortal did not survive the release," Kaelith said. "No living anchor ever does."

He turned back toward the forest mouth.

"Document the site. Record the prison as permanently collapsed. No re-binding possible."

The knight hesitated. "And the Horn?"

Kaelith shook his head once.

"There is no Horn to search for," he said. "There is no knight to pursue."

He paused at the threshold, looking once more at the broken prison.

"The Hunt has left this world."

He stepped back into the Greenwood.

Then Kaelith raised two fingers and tapped his temple.

A soft internal chime answered—utterly alien amid bark and root.

His right eye glimmered faintly with geometric light.

"This is Kaelith Blackwynd," he said calmly. "Veydrath emissary. Investigation complete."

He looked once more toward the glade.

"The Green Knight is dead. The imprisoned god has been freed."

A pause.

"The Greenwood is cleansed. Anti-life properties absent."

Another pause. "Archive this conclusion. End transmission."

The light faded. The forest did not react.

And that, Kaelith decided, was the most troubling evidence of all.

Chapter 39 — What the Forest Keeps

Planet: Vaelthara
Location: Windstream Grove, Ancestral Canopy
Divine Year of Vaelthas — Wolf Month, 21,426 Years Since the Sealing

The grove was quiet in the way only old places could manage.

Not silence. Never silence.

The Windstream canopy breathed.

Leaves whispered against one another in layered currents that never fully aligned, each branch speaking its own small language of tension and release. Above, interlocked limbs creaked with the patient complaint of centuries, bearing memory. Below, roots rose and folded back into the earth like knuckles resting after long labor.

The air smelled of sap and rain-soaked bark, of moss warmed just enough by filtered light to recall what the sun once felt like.

Kellyn Windstream stood beneath the heart-tree of her line.

Her hands were folded at her waist. Her spine was straight. Her breathing was measured, neither shallow nor forced. She had chosen this place deliberately. If truth were coming to her, it would come here, where Windstreams had stood to receive births, oaths, verdicts, and names carved into history by endurance rather than noise.

The tree did not bow to her.

It never had.

Ellendyl approached without ceremony.

She did not wear her blade. She did not wear the dark. She came as she had once been, before futures splintered and titles lost their weight. Her steps were quiet, not careful. This was not a place that demanded caution.

In her hands, she carried a folded bundle wrapped in oilcloth and bound with leaf-fiber cord.

Kellyn knew what it was before it was offered.

Ellendyl stopped an arm's length away.

"They asked me to bring this," she said quietly. "Not to explain it."

She extended the bundle.

Kellyn took it.

The oilcloth was cool against her palms. The leaf-fiber binding was unmistakable: Windstream work, reinforced with Greenwood stitch patterns Kellyn had studied since childhood, admired for their elegance, and never quite mastered. The cord was tied for transport, not ceremony.

For a long moment, she did not open it.

She simply held it, letting its weight speak where words had already failed.

Then she loosened the cord.

The tunic unfolded in her hands.

Fungal leather, bark-laced and grown rather than sewn, its living weave long since dormant. The left side was split cleanly, the cut precise enough to be unsettling. Darkened stains marked the wound's edge, soaked deep into fibers that had once responded to their wearer's breath.

Harvey's armor.

Kellyn's fingers traced the seam where he had repaired it himself, uneven and stubborn, a fix meant to last just long enough to matter. She remembered him muttering about the balance, about how it pulled oddly across the shoulder when he moved too fast.

She had teased him for it.

The memory landed without warning.

Ellendyl watched her closely.

"The Veydrath investigator is… thorough," she said carefully. "He is convinced."

Kellyn nodded once.

She did not ask, convinced of what.

She did not ask how the body had been found, why no one had returned with anything else, or how certainty could exist in a forest that had once learned to lie so well.

She already knew the answers that mattered.

"The Horn?" Kellyn asked.

Ellendyl hesitated, then shook her head. "Gone. No trace. The prison was empty. Whatever happened there was… final."

Kellyn refolded the tunic exactly as it had been given to her, restoring every crease with deliberate care. She retied the cord.

"Thank you," she said.

Ellendyl opened her mouth, then closed it again. There was nothing left to say without trespass.

Kellyn turned slightly, her gaze lifting into the canopy where light fractured into shifting green constellations.

"I thought," she said after a moment, "that losing the Horn would feel like defeat."

Ellendyl remained silent.

"But it doesn't," Kellyn continued. "It feels like closure. Like a door we were never meant to keep open."

She rested the bundle against the roots of the heart-tree, just for a breath, just long enough to acknowledge what it represented.

"The gods are gone again," Kellyn said. "The Greenwood is healed. The Hunt has returned to itself."

Her voice did not waver.

"The Anari will not wield that power," she went on. "Not now. Not later." A pause. "That may be for the best."

Ellendyl studied her.

"And Harvey?" she asked.

Kellyn closed her eyes.

Only briefly.

"He did what he always did," she said. "He answered when something called."

Ellendyl inclined her head.

When Kellyn opened her eyes again, something in her expression had changed.

Not broken.

Not hardened.

Settled.

"Leave me," Kellyn said gently.

Ellendyl obeyed.

The grove accepted the quiet that followed.

Kellyn remained beneath the heart-tree long after the footsteps faded, the folded tunic resting against the roots like an offering that asked for nothing in return. She pressed a hand to her abdomen without thinking—then froze.

The sensation was subtle. Easy to dismiss.

She did not.

Later, when she would be alone in the deeper quiet of the homestead, she would confirm it. She would sit on the edge of a bed carved generations before she was born and realize that the future had not taken everything.

Not yet.

For now, she stood and listened to the forest breathe.

The Anari would grow. They would heal. They would spread the forest carefully and deliberately, believing time had been granted to them.

Kellyn believed it, too.

That was the tragedy of it.

High above, leaves shifted, caught in a wind that carried no voice, no warning, no echo of a horn long gone from the world.

The forest kept its counsel.

And far beyond Vaelthara, in places where time was an instrument and memory a weapon, others were already taking notes.

Chapter 40 — The Emissaries' Common Enemy

Planet: Vaelthara
Location: Emissaries Comm Channel
Divine Year of Vaelthas — Wolf Month, 21,426 Years Since the Sealing

The chamber did not exist.

It asserted itself.

An enforced convergence of signal, spell, and probability, imposed rather than constructed. No coordinates anchored it. No geometry defined its edges. It was not summoned so much as invoked, a flattening of distance and discretion into obedience. Here, eras were not bridged. They were compressed until resistance became inefficient.

Secrecy did not survive this place.

Nothing here belonged to any single race, timeline, pantheon, or god.

Thirteen sigils ignited.

Each announced itself according to its own laws.

One burned like a brand pressed into the air, radiating conquest remembered as virtue.

One pulsed like a living heart, wet and rhythmic, counting futures by survival alone.

One unfolded without sound, already watching, already recording.

Others hissed, rang, resonated, or were, their presence bending the field around them as gravity bends light.

At the center of the projection lattice stood Ser Varyng the Sanctified, Banner-Saint of the Burning Crown.

His armor still bore soot-scars from Graypine Reach. Not cleaned and not hidden. Proof of error retained as instruction. He stood with hands clasped behind his back, posture exact, restraint coiled tight beneath discipline. This was a man who had survived failure by dissecting it while it was still warm.

"This session is live," Varyng said.

His voice required no amplification. The chamber adjusted itself to him.

"Archive integrity locked. Record to the Continuum Vault."

A sigil to his left resolved into a tall, funeral-iron silhouette.

Kaelith Blackwynd, Blood-Magister of the Veydrath. Grave-Inquisitor of the Undead Courts. His presence dimmed the field around him, not by force, but by subtraction, like light stepping carefully around a void.

"Investigation complete," Kaelith said.

No triumph. No satisfaction. Only precision.

"The Greenwood curse has ended. The prison of Aelrindel is empty. The hunter god has exited the plane."

Several sigils shifted hue, reacting before their representatives chose to.

Forge-light flared within the stone-carved silhouette of Durak Runebinder.

"Then the variable is removed."

"Contained," Varyng corrected immediately. "Not removed."

Kaelith inclined his head by a fraction. "A corpse was located—mortal remains. Greenwood armor confirmed. Divine recall signatures present. No horn resonance remains."

Aeryx Stormfeather's projection sharpened, wings folding tight, feathers static with charged atmosphere.

"So the Anari superweapon is gone."

"Or reclaimed," Kaelith replied. "By its owner."

A pause followed. Not silence. Recalibration.

Varyng raised a gauntleted hand, and the chamber filled with layered tactical overlays: elk cavalry rupturing pike formations, harmonic Song slicing through powered armor seams, dragons collapsing siege arrays in seconds, forests advancing where roads had been.

"The engagement at Graypine Reach confirmed several data points," Varyng said.

"The Anari are not forest-bound by necessity."

Ssyl'varak, the Shedding Oracle, hissed softly, scales sliding over one another like pages turning. "Then by what?"

"Doctrine," Varyng said. "Tradition. Self-limitation."

Images shifted again. Forests expanding. Cities swallowed. Rootways replacing streets.

"They do not defend forests," Varyng continued. "They weaponize them."

Durak's forge-light flared brighter. "Adaptive ecosystems."

"As battlefields," added Liang-Shen, voice calm, surgical, already cutting toward conclusions.

Kaelith stepped forward once more.

"The Anari rely on harmonic unity," he said. "Break rhythm, they falter. Isolate clans, they bleed. Introduce dissonance and they adapt—but never instantly."

Aeryx's feathers bristled. "Then they must be studied as prey."

"No," Ssyl'varak corrected. "As systems."

"As materials," Durak added, without irony.

Varyng let the alignment settle. He did not rush consensus. He harvested it.

"From this moment," he said, "the Anari are classified as a Prime Adaptive Adversary."

A glyph burned itself into the chamber, searing classification into record and reality alike:

ANARI — ACTIVE STUDY TARGET

"All findings will be shared," Varyng continued. "Doctrines. Countermeasures. Failures. Losses. No race claims final authority."

"And if none of us succeeds?" Aeryx asked.

Varyng's smile was thin, controlled, and utterly sincere.

"Then we will have learned how to kill gods."

The sigils dimmed.

But the archive did not close.

Instead, it expanded.

A deeper layer unlocked itself automatically, without request.

Without permission.

ADDENDUM — THE KEYSTONE VARIABLE

"This variable has not been named aloud," Varyng said quietly.

Kaelith inclined his head. "Then it is time."

The chamber's focus collapsed inward.

A single image resolved.

Kellyn Windstream.

Anari. Linguist. Time-breaker.

Ssyl'varak's scales rippled. "The Unsealer."

"The first fracture," Durak intoned.

Liang-Shen's voice carried no heat at all. "The proof that memory can be weaponized."

Varyng did not look away from the image.

"In every future represented here," he said, "the Malloch emerge after her actions."

"Correlation?" Aeryx asked.

"No," Kaelith said. "Causation."

Silence followed. The kind that only falls when denial is no longer computationally efficient.

"She did not act out of malice," Morgath-Tor observed.

Ssyl'varak hissed softly. "Worse. She acted out of belief."

Varyng's jaw tightened.

"She believed the Anari deserved to live."

The statement landed like an accusation.

"When the Anari survive," Varyng continued, "the gods return. When the gods return, the Malloch answer."

"And when the Malloch answer," Thrugor Frostborne said, voice like glaciers grinding, "there is no future."

Liang-Shen's tone sharpened. "She is dangerous not because she is cruel—but because she will never stop."

Durak struck his anvil-staff once. The sound rang final.

"She will burn the universe to save her people."

Kaelith spoke last.

"She is not our greatest enemy," he said.

"She is the keystone."

A new glyph burned into the archive, hotter than the others, resistant to erasure:

KELLYN WINDSTREAM — APOCALYPSE VECTOR

"Her victories are to be inverted," Varyng declared. "Her alliances disrupted. Her symbols dismantled."

"And if she falls?" Morgath-Tor asked.

Varyng did not hesitate.

"Then the universe gets another chance."

The chamber began to collapse, probability unflattening, sigils withdrawing into their respective infinities.

Kaelith lingered a moment longer, eyes fixed on Kellyn's image.

"She saved her people," he said softly.

A pause.

"And damned everyone else."

The archive sealed.

Deep within it, a private annotation auto-saved itself, flagged beyond normal access, encrypted even against gods:

Absence is not proof of ending.
Some hunts leave the world behind.

Chapter 41 — The Fountain Runs Again

Planet: Vaelthara
Location: Faelwyn Holt, Wolf Clan Territory — Council Hollow (near the Shrine Roads)
Chronometric Stamp: BV 21

[FIELD LOG // TDG-512C — FRAGMENT 41]
When a forest forgives, it does not forget.

It simply begins again.

The air changed the moment Vyrna stepped beneath the council boughs.

Not sweeter. Not warmer.

Cleaner.

Like rain after smoke. Like sap rising where fire had passed and failed to finish its work.

The Council Hollow formed a living amphitheater grown from the ribs of elder trees, trunks arcing inward as if the forest itself had leaned close to listen. Their bark bore scars of age and lightning, of carvings made before memory learned to write itself down. Lantern-vines traced the curves in patient green-gold, but tonight their glow did not feel like a warning.

It felt like a witness.

Vyrna moved through the hollow slowly, allowing the quiet to catch up to her. The Wolf Clan's mantle rested on her shoulders, braided bark and silverleaf clasped by a running wolf carved smooth by generations of hands. Her hair, usually bound tight for council, had loosened with the day's strain. Dark strands brushed her cheek when the wind stirred.

The wind had been restless lately.

Tonight, it was steady.

That alone unsettled her.

Kholfax stood near the root-ledge, half in lanternlight, half in shadow. The scar across his face made that division stark and symbolic, a pale lightning-strike marking the distance between who he had been and what he had chosen to become. Once, he had belonged to fluorescent halls and sterile certainty. Now he belonged to bark, bowstring, and the hard arithmetic of survival.

He had never believed justice fixed things. Only that refusing to act made him complicit.

He did not watch the elders.

He watched the edges.

The places where shadows decided whether or not to become people.

Froster leaned against a nearby trunk, arms folded, his posture loose in the way only trained fighters could manage. His calm was a practiced illusion, and Vyrna had learned to read the tension beneath it. His eyes stayed on her, steady, ready. Not obedience. Not dissent.

Loyalty with thorns.

Khandyl did not sit. She paced the curve of the hollow like a wolf too caged to rest, her longbow slung across her back, fletching catching lanternlight as she turned. Her hair bore streaks of pale dust.

Vyrna hated that she noticed.

It meant time was passing in the only way that mattered.

By taking something.

Elders murmured among themselves. Druids clustered in small knots, robes heavy with the smell of soil and sap. Warriors rested hands on spear-shafts, listening without pretending not to. The hollow was full, but never crowded.

The forest knew how to hold people without pressing them.

Vyrna stepped to the root-ledge.

"Report," she said.

Her voice carried, as it always did, even when she wished it wouldn't.

A druid named Halren stepped forward. He was old enough that bits of leaf clung to his beard as if they had grown there, and his eyes held the tired shine of someone who listened to trees more than people. He bowed, fist to chest.

"Eichenfall Timber Camp is gone," Halren said.

No gasps followed.

No surprise.

Only the quiet shift of weight, leather against bark.

"Gone," Vyrna repeated, tasting the word.

Halren's mouth tightened. "It was… emptied. The humans were still standing when we arrived."

Something colder than fear moved through the hollow.

Kholfax's hand drifted to his scar, fingers pressing lightly as if it had become a compass needle.

"They were posed," Halren continued. "Militia. Lumberjacks. Camp followers. All rigid. All arranged."

"Paralyzed," Kholfax said softly.

Halren nodded. "And drained. The forest drank them after. When we seeded the ground, it accepted them too quickly."

Vyrna heard the unspoken truth: this was not a natural death.

"Was there a message?" she asked.

Halren hesitated, then motioned. Another druid stepped forward, carrying a rough plank cut from a building wall.

The wood was dark with dried blood.

Letters had been painted with a steadiness that made Vyrna's ribs feel too small for her breath.

THEY SLEEP ALL NIGHT
THEY WORK ALL DAY
LUMBERJACKS ARE OK

A few elders made warding signs. Not in superstition.

In disgust.

"That's not a wolf's humor," Khandyl snapped. "That's a predator playing with the idea of laughter."

Vyrna studied the words until she could see the mind behind them. Not the hand. The satisfaction.

A killer who wanted to be heard.

"Dark druids," Kholfax said again, and now it was no longer conjecture. "Same signature as the patrol. Same paralysis. Same staging. He's not just killing. He's rehearsing."

Halren cleared his throat. "There was also… forest growth."

Vyrna lifted her gaze. "Explain."

"Subliminal patterning," Halren said. "Saplings planted in lines that only made sense from above. It was as if someone tried to redraw the camp into a grove."

A murmur rippled.

"And you allowed it?" an elder demanded.

Halren lowered his eyes. "We did not stop it. We finished it."

Silence tightened like a drawn bow.

Forest replaces harm.

Forest reclaims what is taken.

Forest conquers without banners.

Victory, by Wolf Clan doctrine.

But this victory had handwriting.

"We will not pretend this is righteous," Vyrna said at last. "But we will not pretend it is useless."

"That's a dangerous sentence," Khandyl warned.

"So is the world," Vyrna replied.

She turned to Kholfax. "Tell them."

"The killer believes he has sanctuary," Kholfax said. "He leaves messages only when he's certain we cannot reach him."

Vyrna felt the forest press gently against her back.

Then Halren spoke again, and the air changed.

"High Lady," he said, voice unsteady with something dangerously close to joy, "the fountain at the Shrine of Aelrindel… flows again."

For a heartbeat, the words made no sense.

Then they did.

The fountain had been dry beyond memory. A basin grown around absence. A prayer aimed at a locked door.

If it flowed now—

A hush spread like dawn.

"The Hunt returns," someone whispered.

"He is free," another said.

Vyrna felt her breath catch on something sharp and bright.

"Aelrindel," she said, softly.

The name felt like warm iron.

Froster straightened. Khandyl stopped pacing. Kholfax pressed his scar, and for the first time since the future, his expression looked relieved.

Not for himself.

For them.

"We are not done suffering," Vyrna said, stepping forward, "but we are not forsaken."

The hollow answered her with rhythm. Spears struck the earth. Chests thudded. Low harmonics rose as a Hunt-song began, voices stacking until the trees themselves seemed to vibrate.

Vyrna smiled once.

Then let it fade.

"We will honor this," she said. "And then we will hunt."

Aelrindel was free.

So was the killer.

And the Wolf Clan finally had a god who might hear their vow.

The forest listened.

And somewhere within it, something that loved to write in blood understood that the Hunt had resumed—and adjusted accordingly.

Chapter 42 — When the Map Stops Behaving

Planet: Vaelthara
Location: Western Human Kingdoms — Royal War Pavilion, March Column near the Shenakoa River
Chronometric Stamp: BV 21
[FIELD LOG // TDG-512C — FRAGMENT 42]

Some defeats kill soldiers.

Others kill assumptions.

The canvas snapped in the wind like a warning flag that no one wanted to read.

The royal war pavilion had been raised on open plains where the grass grew thin and stubborn, as if it had learned to survive on disappointment. Guy-lines pulled tight. Stakes driven deep. Everything about the encampment spoke of intention, of permanence imposed on land that had not consented.

Cookfires ringed the perimeter in disciplined arcs. Cannon teams swarmed around iron mouths like insects tending a god that ate powder and screamed judgment. Matchlock companies drilled in tight rectangles, officers barking cadence until breath turned to mist and the men stopped thinking in sentences.

Everything about the column screamed mass.

A human king could win a hundred battles if he could feed this many bodies long enough to arrive.

Inside the pavilion, the emissary stood with his hands clasped behind his back, posture perfect, spine aligned as if the world still rewarded plans that assumed obedience.

He wore no crown. No fur mantle. No sigil of faith.

Only hardened armor beneath a travel cloak, sleek and functional, its contours too precise for this century.

The kind of armor that made priests argue whether its wearer was a devil or a saint.

The kings did not like him.

They needed him.

A long table dominated the pavilion's center. Upon it lay the map, pinned beneath a glass weight heavy enough to imply authority. Inked roads. Measured distances. River crossings plotted to the finger-width. Timber camps marked like teeth along the forest edge.

Bergshern circled in red.
Steinmark in blue.
Montclaire in black.

Strategy made the world feel tame.

A lieutenant burst through the pavilion flap without announcing himself, face pale, boots streaked with mud as if he had run through bad decisions and not yet escaped them.

"My lords," he said, breath fracturing, "refugees."

One of the kings frowned. "From where? We have not yet reached Bergshern."

The lieutenant swallowed. "From Bergshern."

The pavilion cooled, as if the air had decided to reconsider itself.

The emissary's eyes narrowed. "Bring them."

They were ushered in moments later. Civilians wrapped in travel cloaks. Soot-streaked. Hollow-eyed. The kind of people whose running had gone on long enough to erode identity.

A woman clutched a child so tightly the child did not cry. Just stared.

A man stepped forward. He smelled of salt and smoke, like someone who had fled toward the coast and then kept fleeing anyway.

He bowed clumsily. "My lords."

"Speak," a king snapped.

"Bergshern is gone."

Silence.

The king laughed once, harsh. "You mean taken."

The man shook his head. "No. Gone."

The emissary leaned forward slightly. "Define 'gone.'"

The man's eyes flicked to the emissary's armor, and something old and animal recognized certainty.

"It's… forest," he said. "Trees. Not brush. Not saplings. Trees."

One of the kings slapped the table. "Impossible."

"We saw it," another refugee whispered. "I walked that road my whole life. And the road ended. Not in rubble. In trunks."

The emissary's jaw tightened. "How long ago?"

"Days," the man said. "We fled when the first groves appeared. Thought it was druid tricks at the edge. Then the trees came faster than fire."

"Bergshern has walls," a king insisted.

The man's laugh came out wrong. Like a cough. "Walls don't stop roots."

A cannon officer stepped forward, voice cautious. "We can retake it. Burn it. Clear it."

The woman holding the child looked up, eyes shining with something close to hatred. "Burn what? The streets? The houses? There are no streets. There are no houses."

The emissary tapped the table once. A small sound. A final one.

"Timber camps?" he asked.

The man hesitated, then nodded. "All along the edge. Eichenfall. Dornfeste. Rothwald. You can't see the palisades anymore. Just green."

One king's face slackened. "That's our supply."

"That's our industry," another murmured, as if realizing the word had become a joke.

The emissary did not outwardly react. But behind his eyes, a plan cracked and was discarded like a blade that could no longer hold an edge.

"Steinmark," he said. "What of Steinmark?"

The refugees exchanged glances.

"Steinmark was given a choice," the man said quietly.

"A choice," a king sneered.

"Leave," the man whispered. "They said leave and live."

The emissary's gaze sharpened. "Who said it?"

"Anari," the man said. "Not the forest-edge ones. Others. They moved like soldiers."

The emissary made a note he would never write down.

They've learned to operate outside their doctrine.

He had wanted that data.

He hated the feeling of receiving it.

One king stood abruptly. "Then we march faster."

The emissary looked at him. "March where?"

The king jabbed a finger at Bergshern. "There."

The emissary tapped the map gently, as if calming an animal.

"You cannot march to a location that no longer exists in the form you require," he said.

"It exists!" the king shouted.

"It exists as a forest," the emissary replied.

"Then we burn it."

"You can attempt that," the emissary said. "But understand the equation. You burn. They regrow. You clear. They seed. You build. They root."

He paused.

"And they can do it elsewhere while you commit here."

Silence fell again.

Outside, cannons clanked. Horses snorted. Men laughed by fires because they did not yet know the war had changed shape.

"This is sorcery," a king whispered.

The emissary's eyes went distant. For the first time, his certainty looked less like armor and more like scar tissue.

"It is strategy," he said. "With teeth."

"We have matchlocks," a young officer protested. "Cannon. Fire mages."

"And they have dragons," the emissary said, without looking at him.

Silence deepened.

Not because dragons were new.

Because dragons had just become symptoms.

This was not a war against warriors.

It was a war against a world that could decide to become something else.

"Send riders," the emissary said crisply. "Confirm Bergshern. Steinmark. Every timber camp."

"Why?" a king demanded. "The refugees—"

"Because I do not move empires on hearsay," the emissary replied, and beneath the authority lay fear: the fear that the world might not confirm itself anymore.

He looked down at the map.

Quietly, to himself, "They're learning."

"Who leads them?" someone asked.

The emissary did not answer aloud.

Names made things real, and reality was already misbehaving.

But in his mind, the name burned.

Kellyn Windstream.

The one who had unsealed the wrong door.

The one the other emissaries hated like a theological problem.

The one whose victories threatened not kingdoms, but futures.

"It is no longer a border," the emissary said, pointing to the forest line. "It is a weapon."

The canvas snapped again.

And somewhere far beyond the plains, trees were growing where streets had been.

Chapter 43 — Water That Remembers

Planet: Vaelthara
Location: Faelwyn Holt, The Shrine of Aelrindel, Fountain Court
Chronometric Stamp: BV 21
[FIELD LOG // TDG-512C — FRAGMENT 43]

Some miracles arrive like mercy.

Others arrive like a blade returned to its sheath.

The shrine road had always felt wrong to Vyrna.

Not hostile. Not cursed. Just… unfinished. A path grown for pilgrims who never arrived. Root-arches leaned inward over it the way a mouth leans toward a secret, and the stones beneath her boots had that old, patient dampness of places that had waited so long they'd stopped believing in footsteps.

Tonight the road felt awake.

Lantern-vines had been coaxed into bloom all along the approach, their green-gold light pooling in soft islands over moss and stone. The air held a clean chill that reminded Vyrna of winter mornings, when the world pretended it had never been burned. The scent of pine resin cut through lingering smoke-memory like a fresh wound.

And somewhere ahead, water moved.

Not a drip.

Not a seep.

A flow.

That sound did not belong here.

For centuries the Shrine of Aelrindel had been a place of disciplined absence: a court maintained out of stubbornness, a basin kept clean out of loyalty, a name spoken out of refusal to let silence win. Even prayer had been performed the way one performs watch duty, not because it works, but because abandoning the post feels like betrayal.

Now the shrine spoke back.

The Shrine of Aelrindel rose from living wood and old stone, half temple, half grove. It wasn't built the way human shrines were built, with walls that insisted and corners that pretended they could make holiness behave. It had been grown. Patiently. By hands that understood the difference between shaping and strangling.

Above the court, boughs interlaced like ribs. Carved standing stones ringed the fountain space in a wide circle, each etched with hunt-runes and clan-marks worn soft by centuries of touch. The stones had always looked like sentries guarding something that never arrived.

Tonight, they looked like witnesses.

At the heart lay the Fountain Court.

For centuries it had been a basin of carved rock, dry as bone, ringed by twelve standing stones and swept clean like an empty cradle. The Wolf Clan kept it that way because surrendering the space to moss felt too much like admitting the god was gone for good.

Now it sang.

Water spilled from a crack in the stone that had never held a crack before. Clear as glass. Cold as mountain air. It fell into the basin, swirled once, and then settled into a steady, patient circulation that made the whole court sound like breathing.

The sound ambled without pleading.

It simply existed, the way a returning truth does.

The gathered Wolf Clan entered the court in near silence, as if afraid a loud word might scare the water away.

Elders first, draped in bark-mantles and silverleaf clasps, eyes bright with that cautious disbelief old people wear when a story tries to become real. Druids followed, their palms stained with sap and soil, talismans dimmed from the week's work of keeping the Holt stitched together. Warriors came last, spearpoints lowered, their steps measured not from fear but from reverence.

And among them, the rebels.

Once outcasts. Once hunted. Now something messier and more honest than forgiveness: necessary.

Kholfax entered with the others but did not step forward. He stood at the edge of lanternlight, hand hovering at the scar on his face as if it were a compass needle that only pointed toward danger. His eyes kept lifting to the tree line beyond the stones, scanning the dark where the shrine's glow dissolved into forest shadow.

Froster stood beside him, broader than most, posture deceptively loose. He looked like he belonged anywhere a fight might start. In lanternlight, his face seemed older than it had been a month ago, not from years but from the way responsibility carved itself into a man when there were no longer supervisors to blame, no longer councils to hide behind, no longer peace to pretend at.

Khandyl, as always, was a step ahead of the crowd, as if her spirit hated walking at the same pace as ceremonies. She had paced through councils, battles, and funerals alike, a wolf too caged to rest. But when she saw the water, she stopped so suddenly the feathers on her arrows quivered.

For a long moment, no one spoke.

The fountain did it for them.

Vyrna stepped into the center of the court and felt the shrine's weight settle around her: history, devotion, absence, and now the sudden shock of return.

Her mantle of braided bark and silverleaf clasped at the shoulder like a vow. Her armor was scarred from Graypine, still smelling faintly of smoke despite every cleansing rite the druids had performed. She had walked through ash so recently she could still feel it between her teeth when she breathed.

She knelt.

The stone rim was slick beneath her palm. The water was colder than she expected, not merely chill but precise, like a blade's edge dipped in snow. And under the sound of the flow, beneath it like a hidden root, was a harmonic so low it wasn't heard so much as felt.

It prickled along her forearm.

It climbed into her jaw.

It resonated in her teeth.

Aelrindel.

Not a voice. Not words. Not the theatrical booming humans expected from gods.

A presence.

A pressure in the air like a familiar hand returning to a doorframe.

Vyrna dipped her fingers into the basin and lifted them to her lips.

The water tasted of pine sap and night air and something sharper, like iron struck against flint. It was not gentle water. It was water that had run through mountains and refused to apologize for what it had carved.

Her throat tightened.

Wolf Clan leaders did not cry in front of their people.

So she did not.

But grief moved in her chest anyway, rising like an animal that had been trapped too long and suddenly saw daylight.

"Aelrindel," she said, and her voice came out rough. "Hear us."

Behind her, the elders bowed their heads. Druids placed fists to their hearts. Warriors lowered spearpoints until the tips hovered just above the stones, a ring of restrained steel.

Khandyl's mouth moved silently, repeating the name as if she'd forgotten how it sounded aloud and was afraid it might break if spoken wrong.

Vyrna stood, water dripping from her fingers, and faced her people.

"You all feel it," she said. "This is not a rumor. Not wish. Not doctrine."

She gestured to the basin, where moonlight and lanternlight braided on the surface like thread.

"This is a return."

A quiet murmur moved through the court. Not loud enough to be called cheering, but thick enough to count as relief. Some of the youngest warriors looked stunned, as if they had heard a story all their lives and then the story had stood up and walked into the room.

Halren the druid stepped forward, old eyes shining with something dangerously close to joy. His beard held tiny leaf bits like decoration, and his hands trembled as if the forest itself had poured too much meaning into them.

"High Lady," he said softly, "the shrine's roots have shifted. The grove is… responding."

Vyrna nodded. "As we respond."

She raised her hands.

The Wolf Clan's oldest rite began. Not a prayer recited, but a vow spoken and carried by many mouths until it became communal law.

"We are the pack," Vyrna said.

The court answered, voices layered: "We are the pack."

"We are the Hunt."

"We are the Hunt."

"We do not ask the world for mercy."

"We do not ask the world for mercy."

"We take what we must," Vyrna continued, and her voice sharpened here, "and we pay what we owe."

"We pay what we owe."

The last line belonged to her alone, spoken into the fountain's steady breath:

"And we do not let our gods be stolen again."

The words left a ripple in the court so tangible Vyrna felt it in her teeth.

For a heartbeat, she let herself believe it fully.

Then her mind returned to the plank of timber. To blood letters. To bodies posed like practice. To the wrongness of that childish cadence carved into death.

THEY SLEEP ALL NIGHT
THEY WORK ALL DAY
LUMBERJACKS ARE OK

Victory that smells like rot.

Kholfax shifted at the edge of the circle, and Vyrna met his eyes.

He didn't speak.

He didn't need to.

The scar along his face seemed to tighten, as if it remembered the killer's harmonics. In his gaze sat the question like a blade held low:

What now?

Vyrna turned back to the fountain and forced herself to breathe slowly.

The Wolf Clan was celebrating.

They deserved to.

They had lived with absence so long they had learned to build a life around the hole. Let them have this water. Let them touch proof.

But leadership meant noticing the thorn inside the rose.

Because the fountain running again meant only one thing:

Harvey Oakenstride had succeeded.

Harvey had freed Aelrindel.

And if Harvey had succeeded, then the Crone had failed.

Which meant the world's oldest chessboard had just lost two pieces at once, and nobody knew what that did to the game.

A young warrior named Saelwyn stepped forward, eyes shining like someone standing too close to a legend.

"High Lady," he asked, almost breathless, "does this mean the Greenwood is safe now? Does it mean we can enter?"

Vyrna hesitated.

Words mattered here. Careless answers turned faith into funerals.

"I do not know," she said, honest enough to hurt. "But the water says something has changed."

Halren murmured, almost to himself, "The forest does not scream anymore."

That phrase prickled across the court. Some nodded. Some looked frightened by the idea of a cursed thing going quiet, as if quietness were the most dangerous form of hunger.

Froster's gaze drifted upward to the canopy beyond the shrine. For a moment he looked like a man listening for the faintest hiss of a comm channel that would never crackle again.

Then he spoke, quietly, to Vyrna alone. "If the Greenwood is quiet… someone will go looking."

Vyrna's stomach sank.

"Yes," she said.

The emissaries would notice.

The Veydrath would notice.

Anyone with the ability to step where living flesh once could not would be drawn like iron to a magnet.

And that meant the Wolf Clan's miracle would quickly become someone else's investigation.

Khandyl stepped close, voice low, fierce with contained emotion. "This is ours," she said. "Do you feel it? He's back. Aelrindel is back."

"I feel it," Vyrna said, and she meant it.

Then she met her eyes and let a sliver of the burden show.

"But I also feel the other thing."

Khandyl's expression tightened. "The killer."

Vyrna's gaze flicked to the edge of the court, where lanternlight dimmed into forest shadow.

"Yes," she said. "The blade we did not forge, but which someone keeps trying to hand us as a tool."

Khandyl's mouth curled. "We don't need him."

"No," Vyrna agreed.

But the forest had grown through Eichenfall. Timber camps were becoming woodland. In raw strategic terms, the killer's atrocities were accelerating Wolf Clan doctrine.

That was the trap.

Evil that helps is the easiest evil to excuse, and the hardest evil to uproot.

Vyrna turned and lifted her voice so the court could hear her without hearing the full truth.

"Tonight," she announced, "we honor the return of Aelrindel. We drink. We sing. We remember our dead."

A murmur of assent.

"Tomorrow," she continued, and here the words hardened like resin curing, "we hunt the ones who have stained our doctrine with madness."

This time, the assent came sharper. Spearpoints rose a fraction. Druids' hands flexed as if already feeling for roots beneath the soil.

Kholfax's shoulders eased by a hair. Froster nodded once, like a soldier receiving an objective.

Halren stepped forward again, reverent. "High Lady… shall we carry water to the council hollow? To the families?"

Vyrna nodded. "Yes. Let the Holt taste it. Let them know this is real."

She stepped back from the basin and watched her people.

Warriors drank cupped handfuls, eyes closed as the cold struck their tongues. Elders touched the water to their brows. Young druids murmuring prayers that sounded like gratitude and fear braided together.

She should have felt only pride.

Instead, she felt the next thing coming, like pressure building behind the weather.

Because miracles did not arrive alone.

And when gods moved, mortals tended to bleed.

Vyrna lifted her chin and stared into the darkness beyond the shrine stones, into the forest where lanternlight failed.

Run far, she thought, not to her people but to the unseen killer, the dark druids, the emissaries, the lingering threads the Crone might have left in the world.

Run far.

Because we're done pretending we don't see you.

The fountain flowed.

The court sang.

And somewhere out beyond the shrine roads, the world prepared to answer what the water had announced.

Chapter 44 - Aelrindel's Gift

Planet: Vaelthara
Region: Faelwyn Holt and the Western Forests
Chronometric Stamp: BV 21
Designation: Aftermath Cycle

When Aelrindel was bound, we learned to hide.
Now that he runs free, we must learn something harder:
When to chase, and when to let the world run from us.
— *Faelor, God of the Night Hunt*

The first sign was not joy.

It was disbelief.

It began in a healer's hollow beneath the western boughs, where the roots rose like knotted ribs, and the lantern-vines kept their patient green-gold watch. A Wolf Clan healer knelt beside a woman who shouldn't have been pregnant, palms hovering over her abdomen the way a careful hand hovers over a wound it doesn't understand.

The count was wrong.

The cycle was impossible.

The woman laughed at first, a short breath of mockery at her own nerves. "Your herbs are too strong," she said. "Your Song's gone sentimental."

Then the healer's harmonics tightened.

Not louder. Not stronger. Just truer, like a chord finally finding the note it had been missing.

The leaves above them stilled.

Not from windlessness. From attention.

The woman's laugh died in her throat. Her hand drifted to her belly as though it had become a door and she had just heard a soft knock from the other side.

The healer swallowed. Looked up as if expecting to be struck for saying it aloud.

"You're carrying," she whispered.

The woman stared at her like she'd spoken a joke with no punchline.

And then, as if her bones had been waiting decades for permission, she began to shake.

By midday, there were six such cases.

By nightfall, dozens.

And by the second dawn, Faelwyn Holt had awakened into something it had not known since the gods last walked openly beneath its boughs: the feeling that the future had been rewritten without asking anyone's consent.

Not through victory.

Through return.

THE HOLT AWAKENS

By the third day, the healers stopped counting only the expected.

They began counting the unthinkable.

Couples long resigned to silence felt their Songs awaken again, not as yearning but as answer. Women who had never conceived now carried life. Elders who had told themselves the line was ending found their throats closing when the healer's Song confirmed what their minds refused to accept.

Even the ground seemed to behave differently.

Sap ran sweeter. Leaf-buds fattened out of season. Mushrooms pushed up in neat rings like punctuation, as if the forest had decided to annotate reality.

The Wolf Clan didn't call it a blessing at first.

They called it a rumor.

Then a pattern.

Then, with the kind of reverence that begins as fear, they began to call it by a name they hadn't used in generations:

Gift.

KHANDYL AND FROSTER

Khandyl stood barefoot on the root-walk above the western stream, where water slid around stones older than her clan's oldest grief. The bark beneath her soles was cool and alive, and the current carried the scent of wet moss and distant snowmelt.

One hand rested unconsciously at her abdomen.

The other braced against living wood as if the forest might tilt.

"I thought it was the travel," she said quietly. "The strain. The shifting. That… wrong feeling you get after too many days on roads that don't like you."

Froster didn't answer immediately.

He watched the stream as if it were a screen, waiting to reveal the next disaster. His runed cleaver was leaning nearby, close enough to reach with a half-turn. Old habits from a future where comfort was always the first trap.

"You don't look afraid," he said at last.

Khandyl let out a breath that sounded like a laugh that couldn't decide whether it had earned itself.

"I am," she replied. Then, softer, honest in the way she rarely allowed herself to be: "But not of this."

She turned to him, eyes unguarded. No council posture. No war-mask. Just a woman holding a miracle and wondering what it was supposed to cost.

"We were careful," Froster said, like carefulness was a law that should have protected them.

"By Anari reckoning," Khandyl answered. "Which is why this should not be possible."

That was the part that made it holy.

Not that it happened.

That it happened against the rules they trusted.

Froster exhaled slowly, a man who had survived pulse-fire, sonic rupture, and time collapse.

"I don't know how to protect a child here," he admitted.

Khandyl's smile was fierce, and tired, and certain in the way wolves became certain when they decided something belonged to them.

"You already are," she said.

Below them, Wolf Clan voices rose in song.

Not a celebration song.

A warding song.

Because the Holt had learned, long ago, that joy without protection was just another way to die.

VYRNA AND VAELIS

Vyrna felt it before the healer confirmed it.

Her Song had changed.

Not louder.

Deeper.

A resonance beneath her ribs that didn't belong to armor or wound or exhaustion. It moved with her steps. It answered her breath. It made the world feel slightly… tilted toward tomorrow.

She stood in the shrine's shadow with her mantle clasped tight and her jaw set like a door barred from the inside. A queen did not indulge trembling.

Vaelis Valisar stood very still when she told him, the green-gold light from the fountain catching sharp lines of calculation behind his eyes.

"You're certain?" he asked.

"Yes."

The word was clean. Irrevocable.

Silence stretched between them.

Vaelis's gaze flicked, just once, to her abdomen, then away as if looking too long might turn it into an equation he couldn't solve.

"This should not be possible," he said carefully.

Vyrna met his eyes. "Neither should any of this."

For a heartbeat, something like wonder crossed his face. It was brief. Fragile. The kind of expression that looked dangerous on a man like him.

Then it vanished behind thought.

He turned away, already planning, already measuring, already deciding what this meant for alliances and doctrine and the kind of war that eats futures.

Vyrna's hand rested lightly over her heart.

She did not yet know what this child would cost her.

Only that it already mattered more than anything else.

That was the terror hiding inside the miracle:

Not that life had begun.

That it had become leverage.

KELLYN WINDSTREAM

Kellyn learned alone.

No healer.

No ritual.

Just a quiet moment in the Windstream homestead, palms flat on an old table carved generations before she was born. The wood still held the faint grooves of ancestral hands. The kind of craft that remembered its makers.

Her breath caught for no rational reason.

She closed her eyes and listened, not to her pulse, but to the harmonics inside her.

They answered differently.

Not diminished.

Not damaged.

Divided.

Like one voice that had become two.

"Oh," she whispered.

She sat slowly. One hand rose to her mouth, not to stifle grief but to keep it from spilling out as sound. Because if she let herself make noise, she might not stop.

Harvey was gone.

The Horn was gone.

Aelrindel was free and absent all at once, like a door slammed shut after a rescue.

And yet…

And yet—

Tears came. Not sharp. Not breaking.

Grief did not leave her.

But it made room.

Not forgiveness.

Not relief.

Something stranger.

Continuation.

She pressed her palm to her abdomen and felt nothing, which was somehow worse than feeling everything.

"It's not fair," she said to the empty room, and the words sounded childish the way truth often did when it had no place to hide.

Outside, leaves whispered against one another in overlapping currents.

The forest did not answer.

It simply kept breathing, as if reminding her that the world could still do that.

ELOWEN AND CORLYN

Elowen laughed first.

A bright, startled sound that made Corlyn blink like he'd been struck.

"You're sure?" he asked.

"I healed myself three times," she said. "And once more because I didn't trust joy."

Corlyn sat heavily on the edge of the root-bench like a man whose legs had suddenly remembered they were allowed to fail.

"I don't understand how," he admitted.

Elowen squeezed his fingers. Her grip was warm. Steady. Alive.

"Neither do the gods, I suspect," she said, and her smile trembled at the edges.

Corlyn's gaze sharpened, fierce with the kind of vow that didn't need witnesses.

"I will protect them," he said.

Elowen's expression softened. "I know."

She leaned into him, and for the first time in too long, he let himself hold something that wasn't a weapon.

NYSSARA AND TORVAL

Nyssara said nothing.

Words were too small for this.

She simply leaned into Torval's chest as the truth settled, not as a shock, but as a quiet weight that changed where her breath landed.

Torval rested his chin in her hair.

"Aelrindel," he murmured.

Not a prayer.

A greeting.

Nyssara nodded once.

The Hunt had not passed them by.

THE UNLIKELY MOTHERS

By the third day, the healers had stopped pretending this was coincidence.

By the fourth, they had stopped pretending it was safe.

Not because pregnancy was danger.

Because pregnancy was promise, and promise was a scent predators followed.

Even beyond Faelwyn Holt, in distant forests, a quiet surge followed. Not universal. Not overwhelming.

But undeniable.

Among refugees from the future, disbelief turned to awe. They had come from a time where gods were metaphors and forests were resources and survival meant making everything smaller, quieter, manageable.

Now they stood in living proof.

This was what belief had once meant.

This was what it could mean again, for better or worse.

And in the spaces between celebration, the sharp-minded felt the shadow behind it:

If Aelrindel's freedom could do this…

Then what else had changed?

What else had been loosened?

THE SHRINE OF AELRINDEL

The shrine overflowed.

Antler carvings. Braided cords. Fresh-killed game laid with reverence. Children ran laughing beneath elders who had never expected to see such numbers again.

The fountain flowed.

Not forcefully.

Joyfully.

Water spilled clear and cold, catching sunlight in shifting color, as if it remembered how to be beautiful after centuries of being nothing.

The Wolf Clan sang.

They called it Aelrindel's Gift before the druids dared to name it.

Because the people always named miracles first.

Scholars arrived later to explain them into smaller shapes.

THE DRUIDS ARGUE

They gathered beneath the High Canopy, where the branches braided so tightly that even sunlight had to choose its way through.

"Twelve cycles violated," one said sharply. "Fertility does not surge after divine departure."

"It is Daryana's blessing," another countered. "She is Aelrindel's mate. Fertility is her domain."

"Then why here?" demanded a third. "Why now?"

"The Greenwood was purified."

"The Horn sounded."

"The fay were fed. Human blood returned to forest soil."

"Correlation is not causation!"

Voices rose.

"Perhaps it is not the god at all," someone said, quieter, as if afraid the forest might hear. "Perhaps the forest itself, made whole again, chose renewal."

Silence fell when the eldest druid raised her hand.

"The Hunt was broken," she said. "And restored."

They turned.

"Aelrindel was not merely freed," she continued. "He was answered."

No one spoke.

Because that word carried implication.

Answered meant there had been a call.

And a call meant there had been a debt.

HIGH DRUID BRUN DREAMWEAVER

Brun Dreamweaver had listened without interruption, hands folded, eyes half-lidded like a man hearing two conversations at once: the druids' voices and the forest's.

Now he spoke.

"It does not matter whose gift this is," he said calmly. "Only that it was given."

He looked at them one by one, and in his gaze there was no argument, only the quiet authority of a root that had survived storms by refusing to move.

"The Anari do not survive by conquest alone," he continued. "We survive by renewal."

His eyes lifted into the canopy where leaves stirred in a wind that carried no threat.

"Make the forests whole," he said. "Make them fay. Make them sacred."

Then he lowered his gaze again, and his voice dropped into something like a vow.

"And life will answer."

The druids bowed their heads.

Above them, the leaves whispered.

Not warning.

Promise.

And within Faelwyn Holt, and beyond it, life began again, not cautiously, not slowly, but with fierce, impossible hope.

Which was how wars truly began.

Not with banners.

With births.

Chapter 45 — The Silence Between Tracks

Planet: Vaelthara
Location: Faelwyn Holt — Western Watchlines
Chronometric Stamp: BV 21
[FIELD LOG // TDG-512C — FRAGMENT 44]

Some silences mean peace.
Others mean the forest is listening.
The patrol returned at dusk without blood on their boots.

That, more than anything, unsettled Kholfax.

They emerged from the western watchline in disciplined quiet, bows unstrung, cloaks dusted only with leaf-mote and loam. No scorch marks. No harmonic residue. No bodies dragged behind them on sled or vine. Just men and women who had gone out prepared for violence and returned with nothing heavier than their own thoughts.

Froster watched them from the root-ledge, arms folded, posture loose in the way that meant he was paying attention to everything. He counted faces without moving his lips.

"All present," he said at last. "No losses."

"No contacts?" Vyrna asked.

The patrol leader shook his head. "Nothing hostile. No spoor. No Song fractures. We crossed three timber clearings and two abandoned camps. Quiet all the way through."

Quiet.

Kholfax turned the word over in his mind like a stone that refused to show a sharp edge.

"How quiet?" he asked.

The patrol leader hesitated. "Wrong quiet."

That earned a flick of Vyrna's eyes.

"Explain," she said.

"The forest's working," the leader said carefully. "Growing where it should. Healing where it was burned. But there's… no echo. No backlash. No residue of panic. It's like the land already decided the danger was gone."

Gone.

Kholfax felt the familiar itch begin behind his scar.

They dismissed the patrol and stood alone beneath the western canopy, where the young trees were already threading together into something that would soon deserve to be called woodland.

"It's what we wanted," Froster said. "Isn't it?"

"No," Kholfax replied. "It's what we hoped for."

Vyrna's expression was calm, but the forest had taught her to hear what lived under words.

"You think this is a pause," she said.

"I think it's a held breath," Kholfax answered.

By the second day, the reports aligned too neatly.

No new killings.
No disappearances.
No harmonic anomalies.

Dark druid cells had fractured or gone to ground. The remaining exiles stayed put, compliant, subdued. The blood-lettered timber planks had not reappeared. The grotesque staging that had once announced confidence now lay absent, like a signature deliberately withheld.

Froster read the summaries twice before setting them aside.

"If he's gone," he said slowly, "then we won."

"No," Kholfax said. "If he were gone, we'd see debris. Panic. Overcorrection."

Vyrna leaned against a living pillar, fingers resting lightly at her abdomen. The forest hummed around her — healthy, balanced, almost content.

"For the first time since this began," she said, "my Song isn't warning me."

"That doesn't mean safety," Kholfax replied.

She met his eyes. "It means space."

That was the danger.

On the third night, Kholfax walked the outer watch alone.

The moon hung low, pale through new branches. Roots creaked softly as they settled. Somewhere far off, an owl called — not alarmed, not curious. Just present.

He knelt at the edge of a former camp road, where moss had already erased wheel ruts that had taken decades to cut.

No blood.

No marks.

No harmonics.

And no absence either.

That was what finally made his breath slow.

The killer never vanished cleanly.

He subtracted.

He took something with him every time.

Here, nothing had been taken.

The forest was complete.

Kholfax stood and whispered into the leaves, not expecting an answer.

"If you were done," he murmured, "you'd be louder."

The forest did not respond.

It simply continued growing.

The council met at dawn.

Vyrna listened to the last report, then lifted her hand.

"We will not escalate," she said. "Not yet."

A murmur passed through the gathered warriors and druids — relief edged with unease.

"We maintain patrols," she continued. "We watch. We listen. But we do not hunt shadows that may no longer exist."

Kholfax said nothing.

Afterward, as the others dispersed, Froster lingered beside him.

"You're not convinced," Froster said.

"No," Kholfax replied.

"Because you think he's still out there."

Kholfax shook his head.

"Because I think he wants us to believe he isn't."

Froster frowned. "Why?"

Kholfax looked west, toward the deeper forest — toward the places that did not yet belong to anyone again.

"Because the worst moment to strike," he said quietly, "is when the prey decides it's safe to sleep."

Behind them, the forest breathed.

Ahead of them, the tracks ended — not in confusion, not in blood, but in silence.

And silence, Kholfax knew, was not the absence of motion.

It was the space between steps.

Chapter 46 - The Strength of Humankind

Planet: Vaelthara
Location: Cathedral Council Hall, Königsbrunn
Chronometric Stamp: BV 21

I leave no tracks, yet all roads bend to me.
I flee when chased, but follow when called.
When I was gone, the forest hid.
Now I breathe, and the hunt begins again.
--*Riddle of the Wolf Clan*

The Hall of Concordance had been raised to endure centuries, not panic.

It did not know what to do with panic anyway.

Its vaulted ceiling arched high enough to swallow voices, ribbed with dark oak beams salvaged from forests that no longer existed, hauled across borders that had once been laws and were now only stories told to children. Tall lancet windows admitted a cold, wintry light that struck banners hanging in rigid lines, crowns and beasts and suns stitched into thread as if thread could keep pace with a world that was changing its mind.

The hall smelled of wax and ink and old stone.

And beneath it all, faint as blood beneath skin, it smelled of smoke.

At the far wall stretched the world.

A relief map of Vaelthara carved directly into the stone decades earlier, continents raised in sculpted certainty, riverways etched deep enough to catch shadow. Gold leaf marked capitals. Thin veins of silver traced trade routes. Mountain ranges rose like knuckles. Plains lay broad and obedient.

Someone had recently painted over portions in green.

Not careful. Not ceremonial. Not heraldic.

Green slapped on in haste, uneven in places, thick in others, like a wound dressed too fast.

Forests where plains had been.

Roots where roads once lay.

Bergshern.

Steinmark.

Six timber camps along the Shenakoa.

Gone.

Not destroyed, not besieged, not conquered in the way kings could understand.

Replaced.

The monarchs sat in a broad half-circle, each throne cut from a different stone and inlaid with symbols of lineage. They wore crowns heavy with tradition: iron circlets, gilded helms, bands of gold too thin to stop anything but vanity.

None sat easily.

Hands gripped armrests. Fingers worried signet rings. More than one sovereign had removed a glove to press bare skin against the cold table, as if contact with stone could anchor them in a reality that still behaved.

"This is not conquest," King Henri said at last. His beard was shot with grey. His crown was unadorned save a single sapphire that looked suddenly childish in this light. "This is consumption."

"It is worse," Queen Maribel of Chanterive replied. Her hair was braided tight, her face sharp enough to cut glass. "An army leaves ruins. Ruins can be rebuilt. This leaves roots."

A murmur rolled through the hall: agreement, fear, the thin hiss of injured pride.

At the chamber's far end stood the emissary.

He did not wear a crown.

His presence was spare, almost deliberately so. A long, dark coat of unfamiliar cut hung from his shoulders, travel-worn but meticulously maintained, its fabric swallowing light rather than reflecting it. At his throat rested a small sigil, angular and metallic, unrecognizable to any heraldry in the room. It caught the eye without explaining itself. That was its purpose.

His face was lean, lines etched not by age but by discipline. His eyes were steady, colorless in the shifting light. When he regarded the assembled kings, there was no deference, no hostility.

Only assessment.

"The forests are advancing," the emissary, Ser Veryng, said.

His voice carried easily, calm and unhurried. The hall itself seemed to accept it, as if stone preferred certainty even when certainty was bad news.

"Not randomly. Not spiritually. Strategically."

He gestured. A scribe at the side of the chamber shifted layered transparencies across the central table. Projected light overlaid seasonal growth patterns, troop movements, and forest expansion in stark, unavoidable clarity. Lines of advance. Rates of spread. Nodes that flared where timber camps had been and then vanished beneath green.

"The Anari are no longer defending woodland," Ser Veryng continued. "They are deploying it."

The kings looked at the map as if it had betrayed them.

"Then we burn it," growled King Ulric, broad-shouldered beneath a mantle of wolf fur, crown iron, hands scarred. "As we always have."

The emissary turned his gaze to Ulric, unblinking.

"You already tried," he said.

Not accusation. Not insult. Just fact, spoken like a doctor telling you the bleeding hasn't stopped.

"You burned camps. You burned borders. And the forest grew back. Faster."

Silence settled hard.

Somewhere in the hall, a banner shifted. The sound was small. It felt enormous.

"The Anari fight as ecosystems," Ser Veryng went on. "Every loss feeds their next move. Every clearing becomes a lesson. Every burnt acre becomes soil they understand better than you do."

King Henri leaned forward, chair legs scraping faintly over stone. "Then speak plainly. What are we to do?"

Veryng did not answer at once.

Instead, he raised one hand.

"Before you reject what I propose," he said, "you should see what you already possess."

Only then did several of the kings notice the man standing near the cathedral doors.

Unremarkable at first glance, which was precisely why he was terrifying in the right hands. Average height. Travel cloak worn smooth at the shoulders. Boots scuffed by long use. Hands callused not from labor but from repetition.

His face was young. Earnest. Tense with the awareness of being watched by history.

"This," Veryng said, "is Magister-Candidate Odrin Hale."

Odrin inclined his head once. Swallowed.

"He is not powerful," the emissary added. "That matters."

The kings frowned. A few scoffed. Power was the only currency they trusted.

At a subtle signal, Odrin stepped forward.

He lifted one hand.

A flame sparked to life above his palm, tight and controlled, no flourish, no roar. Fire the size of a coin, steady as a held breath.

He let it fade and traced a different sigil in the air.

The space around him thickened, shimmering faintly as protective wards settled like invisible glass, the sort of magic that didn't impress peasants but saved soldiers.

He knelt. Touched the stone floor. Whispered.

Moisture beaded up from the rock, gathered briefly into a trembling sheen, then sank back into the carved relief of a river.

Nature magic.

Odrin drew a small blade and cut his forearm. Blood welled bright against pale skin.

He murmured a phrase. The wound sealed, leaving only a thin pale line.

Healing.

Gasps rippled now.

Not because the feats were grand.

Because they were plural.

Odrin did not stop.

He shaped force without naming it: pressure folding inward, displacement humming briefly before collapsing into nothing. The air shuddered and went still.

He lowered his hands.

"I cannot cast deeply," he said, voice steady despite the weight of crowns and judgment. "I cannot match Anari harmonics. I cannot sing forests awake or break armies with sound."

He lifted his chin.

"But I can learn any school you teach me."

The hall did something strange then.

It hesitated.

Because kings were used to one kind of fear: the fear of being overpowered.

This was the fear of being outgrown.

Ser Veryng let the murmurs wash over him and, for a heartbeat, the hall blurred.

Not with magic.

With memory.

A different chamber. No banners. No crowns. Just steel, white light, screaming alarms. Cities without forests. Skies burned pale by orbital debris. The Malloch advancing through equations humanity had once believed complete.

Railguns firing until their barrels glowed. Particle shields collapsing under pressures no god had ever tested.

Science alone had held.

For a time.

Long enough to learn.

Long enough to adapt.

Long enough to realize it would never be enough by itself.

In that future, magic had been myth and gods had been jokes told to keep children from being afraid of dark.

The universe had not cared.

Here, the universe still listened.

That was the difference.

Not mercy.

Opportunity.

Ser Veryng returned to the present as King Henri cleared his throat like a man stepping toward a cliff and pretending it was just a doorway.

The emissary stepped forward.

"Anari mages are perfected instruments," he said. "Focused. Singular. Deep."

He gestured toward Odrin.

"Human mages are platforms."

The word hung heavy and ugly in the mouths of kings, but it was true. Platforms could mount anything. Platforms could become anything. Platforms could change purpose. Platforms could carry new things faster than doctrine could approve them.

"You will not outmatch Anari power," the emissary continued. "But you will outpace it. Counter it. Combine what they keep separate."

Beyond the chamber doors, royal guards stood rigid at attention.

Their armor was new: layered plate etched with reinforcement sigils, polished to a mirror sheen. Their helms bore narrow visors and flared cheek guards, designs born of hard-learned lessons. Each carried a newly issued musket, its blackened barrel wrapped in leather and rune-thread, the bayonet catching torchlight like teeth.

Innovation made manifest.

Queen Maribel frowned. "And the cost?"

The emissary did not hesitate.

"You will lose land," he said. "You will lose forests, towns, and pride. In the near term."

A pause long enough for the words to bruise.

"But you will gain something they cannot."

He tapped the relief map.

"Numbers. Versatility. Attrition."

King Henri's hands tightened on the table. "You speak of grinding war."

"I speak of survival," Veryng replied. "Anari doctrine is slow to change. Yours is not."

Ulric snorted. "Our doctrine is faith."

"Faith is a tool," Veryng said, and the room stiffened at the audacity of it. Then he added, softer but sharper, "And tools are meant to be used."

He turned toward the unfinished cathedral visible through the windows, scaffolding climbing its walls like a second skin, stone rising day by day because fear had learned to fund masons.

"Centralize magical training," he said. "Every school. Every child with aptitude. No doctrinal barriers. No priestly silos."

A few kings bristled.

"You would turn our faith into a laboratory," Ulric snapped.

"I would turn it into a future," the emissary said evenly.

Silence.

At last, King Henri exhaled as if he'd been holding his breath since Bergshern disappeared.

"We sue for peace," he said quietly. "While we train."

Ser Veryng inclined his head.

"Correct."

"And when the peace fails?" Queen Maribel asked.

Veryng's eyes hardened, a glint of something colder than confidence passing through them.

"Then you will not be helpless."

He moved a step closer to the map.

"There is one more foundation you must lay."

The kings stiffened again.

"Alongside your mage colleges," he continued, "you will establish institutions devoted to number, matter, motion, and logic. Mathematics, engineering, and natural philosophy."

Ulric frowned. "You speak of scholars."

"I speak of weapons that have not been invented yet," Veryng replied calmly.

Silence, deeper this time.

"In my time," he added, choosing each word like a blade chosen from a rack, "we learned too late that magic answers why."

He tapped the map again, right over the spreading green.

"But science answers how fast."

The kings exchanged uneasy glances because speed was the one thing crowns couldn't decree.

"You will not see the full result," the emissary said. "Nor your heirs. But their heirs will. And they will thank you for planting seeds instead of monuments."

He turned, as if almost an afterthought.

"There is one final matter."

The kings leaned in despite themselves. Even Ulric's rage paused to listen.

"The Eastern Empire," the emissary said, "has already begun similar reforms."

A ripple went through the chamber: disbelief, irritation, pride flayed raw.

"Their Emperor has agreed to unified magical training, centralized scholarship, and parallel scientific academies."

Queen Maribel's eyes narrowed. "When did this happen?"

Ser Veryng met her gaze evenly.

"Soon enough, they will believe they will surpass you."

That did it.

Ulric's chair scraped loudly as he rose halfway, then caught himself. Henri's jaw tightened. Advisors hissed urgent whispers behind the thrones. Pride flooded the room like hot wine.

Veryng let it burn.

Competition advanced faster than fear.

And pride faster than wisdom.

He inclined his head, almost courteous.

"Peace with the Anari will buy you time," he said. "But progress will decide whether that time is wasted."

Outside, the wind shifted.

Somewhere beyond stone and crown and certainty, roots continued their patient advance.

And inside the Hall of Concordance, humankind did what it had always done best when the universe tried to erase it:

It stopped arguing about what should be true.

And began building what would be.

Chapter 47 — The Killer's Help

Planet: Vaelthara
Location: Faelwyn Holt — Heartroot Vale, Southern Canopy
Chronometric Stamp: BV 21

I hunt without seeing.
I strike without knowing the name of what I kill.
I do not ask if the prey is guilty.
When the sun rules, I sleep.
When the world lies, I wake.
I leave no trophies.
Only silence that remembers me.
What am I?

– *Riddle of Faelor, the Night Huntsman*

Ellendyl Felhart arrived without ceremony.

No trumpet-vines sounded. No scouts announced her passage. One moment, Heartroot Vale was only roots and shadow; the next, the air tightened, remembered itself, and let her through. The forest did not open a door for her so much as it stopped pretending she did not belong.

She stood beneath the great interlaced roots that gave the vale its name and took one slow breath.

The place still carried violence, but it had been violence done with restraint. Bark had blistered where harmonics had struck. Thorn-vines remained coiled in defensive spirals, still half-convinced they would need to bite again. The loam held the sour-sweet tang of scorched sap, as if the forest had singed itself to cauterize a wound.

And underneath it all, threaded faintly through the air like an old drumbeat returning:

Aelrindel.

Not voice. Not command. Only presence. A pressure that made every living thing feel slightly more awake.

Dark warrior-mages stood scattered beneath the canopy. Most were Wolf Clan by birth, exiles by choice or necessity, and ashamed to degrees that varied with the light. Some had scrubbed the ash-mark from their foreheads until their skin was raw. Others wore it openly, a quiet admission that guilt didn't vanish just because you hated it.

They straightened when they saw Ellendyl.

Not because they loved her.

Because they knew what she was when she stopped being gentle.

Ellendyl's gaze swept over them like frost settling across a pond: smooth, total, and promising that anything reckless would be punished not with anger but with consequence.

"How many left with him?" she asked.

Froster answered from her left, half-shadowed by a root-arch. His posture looked loose until you noticed his hands: relaxed the way trained hands relaxed when they were ready to go from stillness to violence in a single breath.

"Thirty-two," he said. "All Lynx-trained. Six druids. Two dryads. Vaelis took the best of them."

Ellendyl nodded once.

Not approval.

Accounting.

"And the rest?"

Khandyl's voice came from farther back, where she stood with one hand unconsciously resting at her midsection and the other on the grip of her sword, as if those two anchors were the only honest things left in the world.

"Waiting," she said. "Or ashamed."

Ellendyl turned slightly so the dark warrior-mages could see her face.

"If you stayed," she said, voice low but carrying, "you will listen. If you left, you will be hunted. There is no middle ground."

No one argued. No one even tried.

The forest itself had learned, lately, that middle grounds were where people died.

Ellendyl stepped deeper into the vale. Froster followed. Kholfax moved with them, his eyes always a half-beat ahead of his feet, like a man still trying to reconcile forensic instincts with a world that solved problems by singing at trees.

The others kept their distance. They could feel it: this was not a council, not a comfort circle, not a moment for public absolution.

This was instruction.

And instruction hurt when it was honest.

Only when the roots closed around them, turning the space into a natural corridor, did Ellendyl stop.

"I did not teach him that spell," she said flatly.

Froster's brow tightened. "The teleport."

"Yes." Ellendyl's jaw worked once, as if she had bitten down on something bitter. "Only two beings knew it in full. One alive. One undead."

She looked at Froster as if the answer should be written across his skin.

"And one of them is not here."

Kholfax didn't speak. He didn't need to. He had already been thinking the same name, the same way a bruise thinks about pressure.

Khandyl exhaled slowly. "Ahsin."

Ellendyl did not answer immediately. When she did, her voice was precise enough to cut stone without raising its volume.

"Ahsin Blackvein taught me how to survive dark harmonics," she said. "He did not teach me how to abandon restraint. If he gave Vaelis that spell, it was not carelessness. It was an intention."

"Or manipulation," Froster said.

Ellendyl's eyes flicked to him. "There is no difference when power is involved."

They walked under the heart-root, past living walls grown thick with old druidic warding. The veins of the root glowed faintly now, green-gold threads that hadn't been there before Aelrindel's return. The forest's blood remembered its god.

Kholfax spoke as if the words had been building pressure in his chest for days, and he was tired of pretending they weren't there.

"I should have seen it sooner," he said. "But the killings in the future were scattered. Different locations. Different methods."

Ellendyl stopped walking.

"How many?" she asked.

Kholfax didn't hesitate. Numbers were the only thing he trusted to stay still.

"Four," he said. "Then seven. Then fifteen. Then thirty."

Silence thickened. Even the leaf-whisper overhead seemed to draw back, listening.

"On Sylvara Prime," Kholfax continued, "during evacuations. During riots. During those stretches where the dead become… administrative. Then on Sylos IV, when the Malloch arrived. When people were desperate enough to run toward anything that promised escape."

Ellendyl closed her eyes.

"That explains the promotions," she said quietly. "His harmonic precision. His calm. His ability to end threats without chaos."

She opened her eyes again, and the gentleness was gone.

"I elevated him," she said. "Because he solved problems."

"He was innovating," Kholfax said. "Killing with the voice. No blood. No trace. That's why I couldn't see the pattern at first. He didn't want credit. He wanted… practice."

Froster's gaze sharpened. "Sablek knew."

Kholfax nodded once, jaw tight. "Sablek told us everything before he disappeared. The poison. The paralytics. The way Vaelis liked his victims standing. Watching themselves die."

Ellendyl's hand curled slowly into a fist.

"The dark dryads?" she asked.

"Targeting humans," Kholfax said. "Taking them. Training them. Returning them wrong. Forest giants moving again. Undead giants. Sablek provided cover. Vaelis provided doctrine."

Ellendyl stared up into the canopy, where branches braided so thickly they made their own night.

"He didn't just infiltrate the Wolf Clan," she said. "He rehearsed a kingdom."

Her gaze dropped back to them.

"He will go to the Greenwood," she said. "Not for refuge. For legitimacy."

Froster frowned. "The Lynx Clan."

"Yes." Ellendyl's voice hardened. "Lost. Cursed. Erased from memory. Vaelis will proclaim himself its rebirth. The last echo of the Lynx will become his banner."

"And Ahsin?" Khandyl asked quietly.

For a fraction of a breath, Ellendyl's eyes softened. Not kindness. Something older: the recognition of a debt that could not be repaid cleanly.

"If Ahsin lives," she said, "he will not approve. If he does not…"

She let the sentence die where it stood.

A pause stretched. The roots seemed to hold it in place.

Then Ellendyl spoke again, and the question she asked changed the air.

"Have you heard anything of Harvey?"

It landed harder than any accusation.

Froster's mouth tightened. "No."

"Nothing since Aelrindel was freed," Kholfax added. He looked away as he said it, as if the forest might witness the words and decide to punish them.

Ellendyl nodded once, slowly.

"That," she said, "is not a good sign."

She turned back toward the open vale, where the dark warrior-mages waited beneath the roots like men and women who had stepped close enough to the abyss to feel its breath but not close enough to fall.

Ellendyl lifted her voice.

"Gather," she ordered.

They moved immediately. No hesitation now. Even shame can become discipline if you give it a shape.

"Those who remain will be retrained," Ellendyl said, each word a nail driven into place. "Those who hesitate will be dismissed. Those who lie will not leave this forest."

A few faces flinched.

Good, Ellendyl thought. Fear is sometimes the only honest teacher.

She stepped forward, authority settling around her like a mantle reclaimed.

"We do not answer Vaelis with chaos," she said. "We answer him with structure."

She extended her hand, palm down. The air beneath it thickened. Harmonics gathered—not sung, not spoken, but disciplined into form. A lattice of pale green lines unfolded across the earth, forming a grid between roots: lanes, angles, measures. Not wild magic.

Training geometry.

"Vaelis is not merely a killer," Ellendyl continued. "He is a strategist of terror. He teaches methods. He makes your fear into doctrine."

Her eyes swept them.

"So we will learn to hunt without becoming him."

She nodded once to Froster.

Froster turned to execute the orders, already thinking in patrol patterns and perimeter lines.

Kholfax lingered a half step behind Ellendyl, then spoke as if he couldn't help it.

"What do you call this?" he asked quietly. "This… thing he's making."

Ellendyl's eyes remained fixed on the western horizon, toward the Greenwood.

"A syllabus," she said.

Kholfax frowned. "A syllabus."

Ellendyl's mouth curved into something that was almost a smile, but not warm.

"Yes," she said. "He is teaching. So we will do what we should have done the first time."

Her voice dropped. Not softer.

Sharper.

"We will grade him."

The forest whispered overhead, a sound like pages turning.

And far beyond Heartroot Vale, in a Greenwood no longer screaming but far from healed, something listened.

Not the god.

Not the forest.

Something smaller.

Something crueler.

Something that had left bodies standing and called it sleep.

And in that listening, there was anticipation.

Chapter 48 - The Confrontation in Heartroot Vale

Planet: Vaelthara
Location: Faelwyn Holt, Community of Heartroot Vale
Year: BV 21

The forest is not a cage.
It is a bow.
Aelrindel lives again,
and the arrow remembers why it flies.
– *Aelrindel's Truth*

Heartroot Vale had always been a place that kept its voice low.

Not because it feared being heard, but because it had never needed to shout. The trees here were older than most oaths. Their roots braided beneath the soil in slow, deliberate coils, and when the wind moved through the canopy it did not roar, it conferred.

Tonight, even that quiet language felt cautious.

The light under the boughs came down in sheets of green and gold, broken by leaf-shadow into a living mosaic that never held still. The air smelled of rain that hadn't fallen yet, of sap, of damp bark warmed by day and cooling now. The forest floor was springy with needle-mat and fern, a softness that made footsteps feel like trespass.

It should have been peaceful.

It was not.

At the center of the vale stood four figures and an accusation sharp enough to split a tree ring.

Kholfax held the space like a man used to rooms where truth was a weapon, and everyone pretended not to bleed. He did not pace. He did not fidget. He watched. His eyes moved before his body did, cataloguing angles, distance, and cover. The scar along his left cheek caught the shifting light and made his face look carved rather than born.

Khandyl stood slightly behind his shoulder, not out of deference but instinct. One hand rested near her blade, the other loose, ready. She looked like someone who could survive anything except watching someone she loved become a fool.

Froster's posture was relaxed in the way trained killers learned to make it look. Loose shoulders. Open stance. Calm face. The calm was a lie built from discipline. His eyes never stopped counting.

And Vyrna… Vyrna had already woven a ward around them that didn't glitter or flare. It simply sat in the air, a pressure like a storm front, invisible until you tried to move through it. Her fingers still carried a faint crackle of Song-residue. Her gaze was fixed forward with the steadiness of a woman who had learned that leadership meant holding your own heart by the throat.

Across from them stood Vaelis.

Tall. Still. Cloaked not in fabric, but in the kind of shadow that looked like it belonged to him. He was dressed in Wolf Clan leathers, but the way he wore them was wrong. Too neat. Too controlled. As if he'd learned the uniform and never learned the belonging.

His face was composed into something that might have been patience.

It wasn't. It was calculation resting.

The vale waited.

The trees did not lean away from Vaelis.

They did not lean toward him either.

They watched, as if curious which kind of death would be chosen tonight.

Kholfax broke the quiet.

"You've deceived us all," he said, and his voice did not need volume to carry. It was the kind of quiet that made people stop breathing so they didn't miss a syllable. "You led us to believe you were one of us."

He held Vaelis's eyes.

"But you were never Wolf Clan. Not in the way that matters."

Vaelis didn't blink.

The silence between them stretched, taut as bowstring.

Kholfax continued, each word laid like a stone in a path only he could see.

"I chased him in the future," he said. "The media called him the Office Killer. The first bodies were mistakes dressed up as accidents. Then the patterns tightened. Four. Seven. Fifteen. Thirty." His jaw tightened, a muscle working once. "The number didn't matter. The shape did. He liked control. He liked stillness. He liked turning people into objects."

Khandyl's hand flexed once near her hilt.

Froster's gaze slid to Vaelis's hands.

Vyrna's ward thickened, a subtle tightening in the air like lungs preparing to hold a breath.

Kholfax took one step forward.

"You know what gave you away?" he asked.

Vaelis's mouth twitched, almost amused.

Kholfax didn't take the bait.

"Absence," he said. "Your convenient absences. When raids went out, when lines were drawn, when risk was shared, you were always… elsewhere." He tilted his head slightly. "With the dark druids. Where questions are swallowed by ritual, and nobody notices which hands are clean."

The forest made a slight sound, leaf against leaf.

Like a whisper of agreement, it didn't want to admit.

"And then," Kholfax said, "you got careless."

He pointed, not dramatically, just precisely, the way an investigator pointed at a fingerprint.

"The timber camps."

Vyrna's throat tightened at the memory: bodies upright, posed, stolen from collapse.

Kholfax's eyes sharpened.

"You didn't just kill them. You staged them. You wrote on the walls." His voice hardened. "In modern Anari, just like in future crimes."

That landed.

Not like an insult.

Like a spear in soft earth.

Because "modern" wasn't a word that belonged here. Not in Wolf Month. Not in Heartroot Vale.

Kholfax's expression didn't change. That was its own kind of brutality.

"You wrote a children's rhyme in blood," he said, "like you were leaving a joke for people who would be too dead to laugh."

He stepped closer. Close enough that if Vaelis moved wrong, Kholfax would feel it in his bones before his eyes caught up.

"You're the Office Killer," Kholfax said, and the title sounded obscene in the sacred air. "And you don't get to keep wearing our skin."

For the first time, Vaelis reacted.

Not with fear.

With irritation.

His eyes flicked, not to Kholfax, but to Vyrna's midline. Not desire. Not anger. Assessment.

A flash behind the eyes, a flare of something bright and ugly, like a blade glimpsed beneath a cloak. Vaelis made a micro-movement toward Vyrna—a move whose path would place him in a protective position in front of her.

"You're wrong," Vaelis said softly.

The words were calm.

The harmonic beneath them was not.

Kholfax felt it more than heard it: a pressure on the teeth, a faint tightening in the inner ear, the beginning of a resonance shaped like a hand closing.

Froster shifted, half a step, aligning his body as if expecting a blow from any direction.

Khandyl's sword slid a fraction free with a whisper of steel.

Vyrna's ward flared once, not visible, but present, like an animal lifting its head.

Vaelis exhaled.

His lips moved, not in a spell's chant but in a pattern. A cadence too smooth. Too practiced. As if he'd spent years rehearsing how to make reality obey. It was a Lynx Clan form, lost and forbidden by silence more than by law. Vael'Shar Eclipse Field. Fifty-Step Midnight.

A deep subharmonic thrum rolled through Kholfax's teeth. Ear pressure. Nausea. The sense of light being reshaped rather than erased.

The vale went black. Not night, not shade, but a deliberate denial.

And somewhere inside it, Vaelis could still see. To anyone without Lynx training, it was blindness with teeth.

Kholfax recognized it.

That was the moment before the lights went out.

"Vaelis," Vyrna said, and her voice was weighted such that it didn't come from rank. It came from truth. "Do not."

Vaelis's gaze flicked to her, and for the briefest heartbeat, something twisted there: anger, longing, resentment, and beneath it a colder calculation that made the other emotions look like disguises. Kholfax saw protection of a different sort in his eyes. Protection of something Vyrna carried.

Then he moved.

Darkness erupted, not like night falling, but like the world being edited.

The sunlight under the canopy vanished as if someone had snuffed it between finger and thumb. Shadows became substance. Leaf-glimmer died. The vale became a sealed box of black, absolute, and immediate.

Kholfax's vision went useless.

Khandyl swore, a short, sharp sound swallowed by the dark.

Froster's breath hitched once and steadied.

Vyrna's Song snapped outward in a defensive pulse, but the darkness swallowed even that, turning it dull, muffled, wrong.

This was not a mere absence of light.

It was a barrier made of deliberate denial.

A Lynx-trick. The dark warrior-mage combat style.

A hunting veil.

Within it, Vaelis moved like a rumor.

No footfall. No branch-crack. Nothing. Just the shifting pressure of something circling, closing, choosing.

Kholfax angled his body, trying to place the sound that wasn't there.

"Tell me," Vaelis's voice said from nowhere, low and intimate, "do you miss your bright halls? Your neat little truths? Your clean conclusions?"

The words had that same pressure behind them, the lethal triple-harmonic edge that didn't bruise the skin so much as command the nerves beneath it.

Kholfax swallowed hard. He could feel his muscles threatening to lock, the first whisper of paralysis testing his spine like a key searching for the right notch.

He forced breath. Forced motion. Forced his hands to remain his.

"Not as much as you miss an audience," Kholfax said.

A pause.

Then the darkness tightened, as if offended.

Khandyl's voice cut through, fierce. "Coward."

Vaelis laughed once, softly.

"Coward?" he murmured. "I'm standing right here."

Froster moved.

Not toward sound, but toward pattern. He stepped where the dark felt thinner, where the pressure shifted like a predator's shoulder turning. A soldier's logic applied to magic: find the seam, then tear.

His hand shot out.

Touched nothing.

But in that, nothing was a sudden cold, like contact with deep water.

Vaelis had been there.

And now he wasn't.

Vyrna's voice rose, not loud, but layered, a chord built to carry authority through chaos.

"You will not be welcome on Wolf lands ever again," she said, and the words struck the darkness like a thrown spear.

For a heartbeat, the pressure hesitated.

Kholfax felt it: the harmonic grip around his nerves loosening by a hair.

Vaelis paused.

A fraction of a second.

And in that fraction, Kholfax understood something that made his stomach go cold.

Vaelis was deciding whether to kill them. All of them.

Not in fury.

Not in panic.

In the same clean way, a man decided whether to close a door behind him.

Kholfax's mind flashed forward: Vyrna's body upright and dead, Khandyl frozen mid-reach, Froster collapsed like a cut cord. A tableau. A "joke." A message.

And then, like a leash snapping taut, Vaelis's decision changed.

Why did he shift toward her?

Not to shield himself. To interpose. The kind of protective

positioning Kholfax had seen before in killers who still had one rule they wouldn't break, one line they wouldn't cross.
Not mercy.
Constraint.
A tether anchored to Vyrna, to what she carried.

Vaelis's voice came again, nearer now, too near.

"You think exile is punishment," he whispered. "You think naming me makes me smaller."

Then, softer still, almost amused:

"It only makes you predictable."

A syllable followed that didn't belong to any Wolf Clan tongue, a word shaped like a hinge turning.

The darkness folded.

There was a sensation like the world blinking, like the vale itself swallowing.

And then the veil tore away.

Light returned in a rush, green and gold spilling back into the clearing as if embarrassed to have been frightened off. The trees stood where they had been. The ward shimmered faintly as it reasserted itself. Insects resumed their careful stitching of sound.

Vaelis was gone.

Only his absence remained, sharp as a footprint in ash.

Khandyl spun in place, blade fully drawn now, eyes scanning.

Froster's fists clenched once, then loosened. His jaw worked as if he wanted to bite through the air.

Kholfax stood very still, because his body was catching up to the fact that it had almost stopped being his.

"He's gone," Khandyl said, voice tight with fury. "But he's not done."

Vyrna's gaze stayed on the spot where Vaelis had stood. Her expression didn't fracture. It hardened into something older than anger.

"I can still feel him," she said. "That Song. That… wrongness."

She turned to Kholfax.

"He's calling for his followers."

Kholfax's mind raced, grabbing at the one thing that mattered: direction.

"He said a word," Kholfax murmured, tasting it in memory like poison you needed to identify. A hinge-word. A travel word.

His eyes lifted to the dark line of trees beyond the vale, beyond the soft breathing of Heartroot.

"Greenwood," he whispered.

Khandyl's shoulders tightened. "He's going back to Lynx territory."

"To the Greenwood," Vyrna confirmed, voice like drawn steel. "Where curses used to do his work for him."

Froster's eyes narrowed. "And now the Greenwood is quiet."

That sentence landed badly.

Because quiet cursed places did not become safe.

They became available.

Before anyone could speak again, a figure stepped out from between two trunks.

Not a dramatic entrance.

Just… present.

As if he'd been there all along and decided to stop pretending, he wasn't.

"Sablek?" Kholfax said, disbelief roughening his voice.

Sablek Thistlecrest moved into the clearing with the slow care of a man approaching a fire he'd helped start. His eyes looked distant, not from innocence, but from the exhausting weight of holding two lives in one body.

"I heard," Sablek said quietly. His gaze flicked to the place Vaelis had vanished from. "I never thought he'd fall this far."

Khandyl's blade lifted an inch.

Vyrna's ward tightened again, subtle as breath held.

Sablek raised his hands, palms open. "I'm not here to defend him."

Kholfax's eyes cut into him. "Then why are you here?"

Sablek swallowed.

"Because you're too late," he said, and the words tasted like ash. "Not to name him. You've done that." His eyes met Vyrna's and held. "But to stop what he's going to wake."

Vyrna's voice stayed steady. "Say it."

Sablek looked toward the forest line, toward the direction the Greenwood lay like a bruise on the world.

"The Lynx Clan will rise again," he said. "But not as they were. Not as you remember from stories." His mouth tightened. "It will be an echo wearing a crown of rot."

Froster's gaze sharpened. "And the dark druids?"

Sablek's expression flickered. Shame. Fear. Something worse: inevitability.

"They will follow him," Sablek said. "Because he speaks to the part of them that wants permission."

Kholfax felt his scar prickling, that old recognition of a predator already moving while you were still naming it.

"So, we hunt," Kholfax said, voice cold and steady. "We hunt him into the Greenwood."

Khandyl nodded, fierce. Froster's shoulders squared. Vyrna's eyes narrowed, already choosing routes, allies, sacrifices.

Sablek's gaze lingered on Vyrna for a heartbeat too long, as if he wanted to say something he didn't deserve to say.

Then he turned away, voice dropping.

"Act quickly," he said. "Because the darkness he can summon…"

He paused, and the vale seemed to listen harder.

"…is learning to stay."

The forest rustled.

Softly.

Not in comfort.

In warning.

The confrontation had ended, but it had not resolved.

They had named the killer.

They had watched him choose not to kill them.

And that meant something far more dangerous than victory:

Vaelis had left with an unfinished thought.

And unfinished thoughts were where monsters grew their second head.

Vyrna sheathed her fear as if it were a blade and looked at her people.

"Then we move," she said.

And the bow of the forest, newly strung by Aelrindel's return, began to draw.

Chapter 49 — What the Hunt Takes

Planet: Vaelthara
Location: The Greenwood — Inner Reach, Beyond the Shrine Paths
Chronometric Stamp: BV 21
Designation: Oath Settlement

The Hunt does not take blood first.
It takes memory.
Because blood can be spilled by accident.
Memory cannot. – *Aelrindel, god of the hunt.*

Harvey stood alone where the Greenwood grew thickest.

In the Greenwoods in-between, where paths never formed because no one lived long enough to walk them twice.

The forest was no longer hostile.

That was the lie that almost broke him.

Leaves parted when he moved. Roots shifted without trapping his boots. The air no longer pressed against his chest like a held grudge. For the first time since he had entered the Greenwood, he was allowed to exist.

That was how he knew the price was coming.

The Greenwood didn't bargain in coin or blood. It collected identity.

He rested Kuldemaekr's tip against the loam, both hands folded over the pommel. The blade glowed faintly, green light threading through its runes like breath through ribs.

"You are free," Harvey said quietly, not to the forest, not to the god, but to the truth he had already accepted.

The Greenwood answered with stillness.

Then the Hunt arrived.

Not as hooves.
Not as horns.
Not as thunder.

As presence.

The air deepened. Sound softened. Distance lost meaning. Harvey felt the way a hunter feels when something steps behind him without breaking a twig.

Aelrindel did not manifest as a form.

He manifested as alignment.

Harvey's breath slowed. His heartbeat steadied. The weight he had carried since the Horn's sounding settled into something sharper, cleaner.

"You have done what was asked, came the truth — not spoken, not sung, simply known."

Harvey bowed his head.

"I did," he said. "And I would again."

There was no approval.

Only inevitability.

"You walked where none could follow. You freed what was bound. You closed a wound that predated memory."

Harvey swallowed.

"Then let me return," he said. "Let me go back to them."

The forest did not reject the request.

That was worse.

Return is not refused, the Hunt answered.
Return is measured.

The Greenwood shifted.

Not around him — within him.

Harvey felt the first loss as a misfire in his own wiring, like a stair that wasn't where his foot expected. A word rose in him and went soundless before it reached his tongue—a soft slip, like reaching for a name that should be there and finding only shape.

Kellyn.

The thought rose automatically.

And stopped.

His breath hitched.

He tried again, frowning slightly, as if the word had caught on his teeth.

Kellyn.

There was no image.

No voice.

No warmth behind the ribs where she had always lived.

Only a hollow outline — the sense that something important belonged there, without any knowledge of what it was.

Harvey's hands tightened on Kuldemaekr.

"No," he said quietly. "That's not—"

The Hunt did not interrupt.

It let him search.

He reached for the smallest anchors first.

The taste of hearthbread. The shape of his own home. The way he tied his boots without thinking.

Those went loose. Quietly. As if they had never belonged to him.

Then faces. Laughter under roots. Arguments softened by trust.

Names he could once have spoken in the dark without hesitation slid away like fish in deep water.

And then, without warning, the center gave way.

Kellyn.

The name rose. Stopped.

He tried to grasp the memory behind it and found only the outline of a hand that had been holding him upright.

Harvey staggered. He did not fall.

He did not fall.

"You're taking too much," he said, voice rough.

The Huntsman answered without mercy or malice.

You asked to finish the war.

You asked to stand where gods stand.

You asked to be more than a man.

Harvey closed his eyes.

When he opened them again, tears were falling — slow, silent, confused.

"Who was she?" he asked.

The question broke something older than pain.

The Greenwood did not answer.

Not because it could not.

Because the Hunt does not name what it takes.

Harvey pressed a hand to his chest, feeling the space where love had been and finding only resolve. The hole did not empty him. It aimed him.

Strangely, it was enough.

His devotion did not waver.

The Anari still mattered.

The gods still mattered.

The war still mattered.

The Malloch burned in his thoughts like a fixed star — a direction rather than an enemy.

That was the design.

Love binds.

Purpose sharpens.

"You will remember why you fight," the Huntsman told him.

"But not who you fight for."

Harvey nodded once.

Aelrindel's presence faded — not gone, just behind him now, like a bow settling after the arrow is released.

The Greenwood released him.

When Harvey stepped forward, his stride was steady.

He knew his name.

He knew his blade.

He knew his god.

He knew the Hunt.

But when he paused at the forest's edge and looked back — feeling like he had left behind something vast — there was no grief strong enough to hold him back.

Only a faint ache, like a scar whose story had been forgotten.

He turned west.

The war awaited.

And somewhere far behind him, beneath roots that remembered even if he could not, Kellyn Windstream slept under an old tree, one hand unconsciously resting where life turned in the dark. Over time, that life would look at Harvey Oakenstride and feel an ache with no name.

The Hunt had taken its due.

And the arrow was in flight.

Greenwood Forest, BV 21

Chapter 50 — Ahsin's Renewal

Planet: Vaelthara
Location: The Greenwood — Old Lynx Territory
Chronometric Stamp: BV 21

The Measure of a Hunter
Old Wolf Clan riddle, newly reinterpreted
What grows sharper the farther it travels,
yet breaks when turned inward?

The teleport tore the air like a breath held too long and finally forced free.

Dark light folded in on itself, collapsed into a point of screaming pressure, then snapped outward. The Greenwood recoiled for a heartbeat—out of habit more than alarm—and Ahsin Blackvein stepped through the rupture as he had a thousand times before.

Upright. Controlled. Unafraid.

Crimson sigils traced his veins beneath pale skin, faint and precise as engraved lines on old steel. The marks of vampirism did not burn tonight. They only remembered.

He took one step forward.

And the forest did not recoil.

That was wrong.

The Greenwood had always answered him with resistance, a low, grinding pressure like a prison recognizing one of its own cursed echoes. Even as Veydrath. Even as Count. Even as master of undead courts and necro-harmonic doctrine. The forest had known him for what he was: life that refused to finish dying.

Now—

Now the air moved aside.

Leaves stirred without hissing. Roots shifted just enough to clear his path. The ground accepted his weight without protest, without the faint tremor of rejection he had learned to ignore centuries earlier.

As if it had been waiting.

Ahsin froze.

Behind him, the teleport discharged its remaining passengers. Vaelis Valisar emerged first, posture composed, eyes already scanning the terrain and shadows with the confidence of someone who assumed the world would obey him if he learned it well enough. Around him, the Lynx dark-warriors slid into the Greenwood in staggered formation: cloaks settling, blades whispering into place, eyes adjusting to the perpetual twilight like predators reacquainting themselves with an old hunting ground.

"This is it," Vaelis said quietly. Reverent. Certain. "The heart of what was taken from us."

Ahsin did not answer.

He lifted his hand slowly.

The movement cost him more than it should have. His fingers trembled—just slightly—but the tremor carried a century of discipline, breaking its silence.

He pressed his palm against the bark of the nearest tree.

Warm.

Not the false warmth of stolen blood. Not the echo-heat of necromantic circulation. Real warmth. Living warmth. The kind that pulsed faintly back against his touch, answering without fear.

Ahsin's breath caught.

"No," he whispered.

The word held no panic. No terror.

Only disbelief.

The Greenwood did not grant him visions.

It gave him memory.

Sunlight spilled through high boughs onto speckled fur. Moss and wet stone scented the air. Laughter—quick and sharp—slipped between trunks as easily as bodies did. Hunters flowed through leaf-shadow like thought itself, their antler-crested helms glinting, blades never raised unless needed.

The Lynx Clan.

His clan.

Before exile. Before curse. Before the Greenwood learned to hate its own wounds.

Ahsin staggered back a step.

Vaelis turned sharply. "Ahsin?"

The vampire did not look at him.

"I can hear them," Ahsin said, voice raw, scraped thin by something older than pain.

Vaelis frowned. "Hear who?"

Ahsin's hand rose to his chest.

"My brothers," he said. "My sisters." His fingers pressed harder, as if trying to still something traitorous beneath the bone. "The old hunt-calls. The spacing between steps. The pauses before the strike."

The pain arrived then.

Not the sharp agony of a blade or the tearing scream of magic undone. This pain was deeper. Quieter. The kind that came when something profoundly right returned after centuries of denial.

Ahsin's heartbeat stuttered.

Once.

Twice.

Vaelis stiffened. "That's not possible."

Ahsin's vision blurred. The Greenwood tilted—not away from him, but toward him, as if a listener were leaning closer.

The curse was unraveling.

He felt it as ice does when it begins to crack under weight borne too long. The vampiric bindings—woven by the Crone, reinforced by defiance, sustained by hunger—began to fail.

Blood no longer obeyed him.

Necro-harmonics slipped from his grasp like ash through open fingers.

He gasped.

Air burned his lungs, savage and unfamiliar. Each breath scraped as if it were the first in a lifetime—and the last.

Vaelis stepped forward instinctively. "Hold yourself together. Anchor the spell—"

"I can't," Ahsin said, and his voice broke cleanly in half. "There is nothing left to anchor to."

That was the cruelty of it.

The forest recognized him.

Between the trees, shapes emerged.

At first, only silhouettes—tall, lean forms with tufted ears and eyes that caught the light like amber beneath moonwater. Then faces resolved. Familiar lines. Scar patterns he had once traced with his fingers, laughing, careless, young.

They did not accuse him.

They did not rage.

They waited.

"Ahsin," one said gently.

His knees struck the ground.

"I failed you," he whispered. "I survived when I should not have. I learned things that twisted what we were."

The Lynx spirits stepped closer. They were no longer phantoms or echoes. They were memory given form, made solid by a forest that had finally forgiven itself.

"You endured," said another. "So that the Hunt would remember us."

Ahsin let out a broken laugh. "I became a monster."

"You became a bridge," the first replied. "And bridges are not meant to remain."

Vaelis stood frozen, watching centuries of certainty fracture in real time.

"Ahsin," he said sharply. "Do not do this. We need you."

Ahsin looked up.

For the first time since Vaelis had known him, the vampire's eyes were not red.

They were gold.

Alive.

"I gave you the spell," Ahsin said softly. "I believed you would use it to protect what was lost."

Vaelis's jaw clenched. "I will restore it."

Ahsin smiled—small, weary, unbearably human.

"You will claim it," he said. "That is the difference."

His body began to change.

Not violently. Not in collapse, scream, or blaze of corrupted power.

Gently.

The pallor of undeath warmed into color. The rigid perfection of vampirism softened into mortal imperfection. His breathing steadied. His heartbeat strengthened—then slowed.

Then stopped.

Not in death.

In completion.

Light traced through his veins—not blood, not magic, but memory made real. Ahsin Blackvein exhaled once more.

And turned to ash.

Not the foul ash of destruction, but the clean, pale residue of something finished properly. It drifted down, settling into the roots at his knees, where the forest drank it in without hunger.

Silence followed.

Vaelis stared at the place where his mentor had been.

Around them, the Lynx spirits bowed their heads.

Then they turned—and walked deeper into the Greenwood, fading not into shadow, but into belonging.

One of the dark warriors whispered, "He's gone."

Vaelis did not move.

"No," he said slowly.

"He was taken."

The forest rustled softly, unconcerned.

Vaelis straightened. His grief did not explode.

It calcified.

"Prepare the camp," he ordered. "Mark the boundaries. This land is ours again."

None argued.

But as they moved to obey, Vaelis cast one last glance at the ash settling into the soil.

For the first time since leaving the future, uncertainty crept into his thoughts.

If the Greenwood could forgive Ahsin—

What else could it undo?

Above them, leaves shifted, and somewhere beyond sight, the Hunt moved on—complete, unbound, and no longer looking back.

Closure for a vampire.

Chapter 51 — Kaelith's Ledger

Location: Veydrath Archive Reliquary
Temporal Frame: FY 3553 (Post-Sylos Collapse)
Access Classification: Emissary-Prime / Private

Kaelith Blackwynd did not trust conclusions that arrived too cleanly.

He stood alone in the reliquary vault, funeral iron armor unfastened at the throat, its weight resting on hooks shaped like rib bones. Around him, memory-engines whispered. Not data. Regret. Each archive shard carried a thousand dead perspectives, compressed until contradiction was no longer wasteful but informative.

The Greenwood report hovered before him.

STATUS: Cleansed
CURSE: Ended
PRISON: Vacant
DEITY: Aelrindel — withdrawn
BEARER: Presumed terminated

Presumed.

Kaelith's lips curled, just barely.

He replayed the field impressions. Soil samples. Bone resonance. Residual divine harmonics. The armor was retrieved. The sword left behind. The corpse was almost convincing.

Almost was never enough.

If the Hunt had truly ended, the world would feel quieter.

It did not.

He expanded the comparison lattice. Overlaid it with older conflicts. Pre-Confederation extinctions. Forest expansions that followed no ecological logic. Entire civilizations erased without total war, leaving only root systems and stories that refused translation.

Eleven races.

All gone.

All non-Anari.

All once native to worlds that had tried to tame their forests rather than listen to them.

Kaelith let that sit.

The prevailing theory among the emissaries was comfortable:

The Anari were dangerous because they adapted.

Because they harmonized.

Because they expanded their forests like weapons.

But Kaelith suspected that was the effect, not the cause.

He pulled another thread.

SUBJECT: Dark Druid Networks

ANOMALY: Cross-racial recruitment

PRIMARY QUESTION: Why recruit humans?

Anari did not need humans.

Humans were slower, louder, and spiritually blunt. Their magic was crude, linear, and inefficient. If power was the goal, humans were ballast.

Unless power was not the goal.

Unless balance was.

Kaelith replayed the fragmented testimony attributed to Sablek Thistlecrest. Not answers. Speculation. Doubt. A man trying to reconcile devotion with terror.

"The Old Power does not belong to the Anari."

"It tolerates them."

That line had not appeared in the official transcript.

Kaelith had pulled it from the marrow.

The Old Power.

Older than gods. Older than pantheons. Older than negotiated creation rights.

Not a will. Not a mind.

A constraint.

Forests were not sacred because the Anari said so.

The Anari were tolerated because they obeyed the forest.

That inverted everything.

If true, then the Wild Hunt was not an Anari superweapon.

It was a failsafe.

A correction mechanism is deployed when the imbalance exceeds the tolerance.

Which meant extinction was not vengeance.

It was accounting.

Kaelith expanded the projection.

Green Knights — Cross-Pantheon Eligibility (Theoretical)
Observed Incidence: Anari only

Not because other races were excluded.

Because other races did not qualify.

Yet.

Dryads had always known this.

They did not convert out of kindness. They trained custodians. Druids were not priests. They were probationary members of an older agreement.

And if that was true…

Kaelith's fingers paused over the interface.

Then the dark druids had not been traitors.

They had been early adopters.

Recruit humans.
Teach them to listen.
Let forests grow under alien hands.

Dilute Anari exclusivity.

Undermine the monopoly.

Not to destroy the Anari.

To survive them.

Kaelith leaned back, the stone throne accepting his weight with the patience of something accustomed to waiting centuries for a thought to finish forming.

Which brought him, inevitably, to Kellyn Windstream.

She appeared unbidden, the archive recognizing the association before Kaelith consciously requested it.

Linguist.

Unsealer.

Dragon rider.

Time-breaker.

She had not created the Malloch threat.

She had removed the lid.

Kaelith studied the causal braid again, slower this time.

Kellyn opened the Chamber.

The gods returned.

The Malloch followed.

Not because she erred.

Because the universe had been holding its breath.

"She did what any mother-race would do," Kaelith murmured to the empty vault.

She saved her people.

Temporarily.

And in doing so, exposed the Anari to something they had never truly faced before.

Competition.

If the Old Power could be appeased by humans, Sza'thir, Minos, dwarves…

If druids could arise elsewhere.

If Green Knights could emerge outside Anari control.

Then the forest would no longer belong to one voice.

And the Hunt would no longer answer to one people.

Kaelith closed the archive.

He did not forward his conclusions to the other emissaries.

Not yet.

Hypotheses were dangerous things.

They had a habit of becoming strategies.

Somewhere on Vaelthara, a forest expanded where none should have.

And somewhere else, a human learned how to listen to roots.

Kaelith smiled faintly.

The Hunt, he suspected, was far from finished. It was only diversifying.

Chapter 52 — The Forest That Walked

Planet: Vaelthara
Region: Western Marches of Faelwyn Holt
Seasonal Reckoning: Late Leaffall, Year of the Returning Hunt

The forest did not surge.

It advanced.

From the western edge of Faelwyn Holt, roots pressed outward into old grasslands with the patience of stone and the inevitability of tide. There was no single moment one could point to and say it began here. The change arrived the way truth often does: gradually enough to be denied, decisively enough to be undeniable.

Moss came first, pale and quiet, softening ground that had known iron-shod hooves and wagon wheels for generations. It crept into ruts, filled old scars, drank what bitterness the soil still remembered. Fern followed, then thorn, not in chaos but in conversation with slope and shadow. Saplings rose where wind slowed, and water lingered—beech and alder in the deep loam, spruce where the earth remained lean and stubborn.

The forest was not angry.

It was thorough.

This was not a conquest by fire or blade. No banners were raised. No walls were torn down in fury.

It was succession.

The land had been waiting for its turn.

The Wolf Clan moved with it.

Not ahead of the growth, nor behind, but alongside—learning where the forest wished to go and choosing not to stand in its way. The males ranged west in small, disciplined bands, traveling by tree-road where it had already knit itself together and by foot where roots still tested the ground. They did not march. They flowed.

Froster moved among them easily now, his bow resting against his shoulder with the same unconscious familiarity his old rifle once had. His eyes had learned new habits. He no longer searched for thermal anomalies or electronic ghosts. He watched leaf tremor, shadow drift, wind, heat, and the way birds chose one branch over another. The forest spoke if one did not rush it.

Kholfax kept to the edge, rarely leading, rarely following, listening more than he spoke. He had spent his life trusting patterns derived from data and deduction. Now he was learning a slower skill: letting conclusions come to him when the world was allowed to finish its sentence.

Khandyl ranged when she could, though not as far as before. Her steps were careful, measured, her balance altered in ways she still did not entirely trust. One hand often rested unconsciously at her midsection, as if reassurance were a physical thing that might wander if not reminded of where it belonged. The forest did not hurry her. It seemed to know.

They did not burn fields.

They planted.

Living arches rose where roads had once cut straight lines through the land, their roots lifting cobbles gently, splitting stone without shattering it, and repurposing what humans had laid down rather than erasing it. Old wells sweetened, their water clearing as if relieved to be remembered. Streams returned to channels etched deep into the land's long memory, routes long abandoned by maps but not by the earth itself.

Between the Korranth River and the Shenakoa, green corridors stitched themselves together, mile by mile. Open ground breathed again, then learned to exhale leaves. By the time the first scouting parties reached the bluffs overlooking the Fenlath Ocean, the forest already carried salt in its breath.

The sea received it without protest.

Along the cliffs, wind-twisted pines took root, their roots gripping stone with patient ferocity. Their needles sang in coastal gusts, a thin, constant music. Gulls wheeled above the unfamiliar canopy, confused at first, then curious, then content. Driftwood was ringed by living roots. Shade crept toward the tide.

Faelwyn Holt had reached the edge of the world.

Back within the deepwood, life turned inward.

In hearth-hollows and root-homes, Anari women gathered in quiet circles. Disbelief gave way to laughter, laughter to tears, and fear braided tightly with reverence. Midwives moved from bough to bough, hands steady, songs cautious, counting heartbeats that should not yet be. Old melodies returned—songs last sung when the gods still walked openly, and calendars were young enough to be hopeful.

Vyrna stood beneath the shrine of Aelrindel, watching offerings pile high: antlers polished smooth by touch, arrowheads laid with care, carved bone, and woven leaf. The fountain murmured steadily behind her, water remembering what it was for.

Her hand rested at her belly, fingers spread as if bracing herself against what was coming.

"This changes nothing," she told herself.

It changed everything.

Across Vaelthara, the knowledge spread—not through proclamation or decree, but through posture and pause. In the way couples lingered longer at parting. In the way hardened refugees from a godless future found themselves watching saplings with something like awe. The forest was no longer only a weapon.

It was a promise.

Kellyn remained at Windstream Homestead.

She walked the ancestral paths slowly now, tracing steps laid by those who had shaped the land before her, listening for voices that did not need to speak aloud. The absence of Harvey had settled into her bones like winter: present, enduring, not yet fully understood.

When the truth reached her, it did not come as a shock.

It arrived as certainty.

She sat beneath the oldest tree on the ridge, its bark scarred by centuries of weather and memory, one hand over her heart, the other over her womb. She allowed herself a single, quiet breath in which grief and hope could coexist without argument.

Far to the west, Khandyl and Froster stood at the edge of the new forest, watching waves break against roots that had never known water.

"We're changing the map," Froster said softly.

Khandyl shook her head, a small smile touching her mouth. "No. We're remembering it."

Behind them, the forest continued its patient work—growing, listening, preparing.

Somewhere beyond sight and time, a conclave had decided the Anari were a problem to be solved.

Here, under leaf and wind, life did not argue strategy.

It simply went on and multiplied.

Chapter 53 – Call of the Haunted Knight

Planet: Vaelthara
Location: Atharyn Holt (Home of the Owl Clan)
BV 21

Atharyn Holt lies south of Faelwyn Holt, where the forests grow quieter rather than warmer. This is not a tropical land, but a cool, temperate shadow-wood, shaped by altitude, mist, and long dusk. The canopy here is high and layered, with ancient quaking aspen interwoven with broad-leaf nightwoods whose leaves drink light rather than reflect it. Even at noon, the forest breathes twilight.

This is the domain of Thalorin, god of Death, and Vaelthas, god of Shadow, and their influence is not cruel, but precise. Death here is understood as passage, not ending. Shadow is not concealment, but discernment. The forest feels watchful rather than hostile, as though it is constantly measuring the weight of what enters.

Atharyn Holt is threaded with high root-paths and elevated walkways, grown rather than built, allowing the Owl Clan to move silently above the forest floor. Treehomes are narrow and vertical, spiraling around trunks, their entrances hidden in shadowed notches. Lanterns are rare. When used, they glow with soft indigo or ghost-white light that reveals shape without banishing darkness.

To walk in Atharyn Holt is to feel time slow and narrow, as though the world has drawn a careful breath. Nothing rushes here. Nothing shouts. And nothing escapes notice for long.

Maeve was gathering fruitlamps to light her home in the trees near the edge of Atharyn Holt. A light mage of the Owl Clan, she brushed back her chestnut hair, reached for one last lamp, then turned toward the ladders. Her fungal tunic, leggings, and leather boots blended with the surrounding forest. A longsword rested at her hip, a dagger in her boot, a longbow strung across her torso, and a quiver nestled on her back.

A horn sounded in the distance, to the north, from the lands of the western human kingdoms.

Something changed inside her—a pull invisible to the eye but undeniable in the sound.

Maeve dropped the fruitlamps to the moss and unslung her bow. She nocked an arrow and took one step toward the sound.

The call tightened around her, irresistible, dragging her north.

Other Owl Clan Anari were already running and riding north on both sides of her. Everyone moved toward the horn's sound. Even the fay creatures hurried north, answering the call.

Maeve joined them. Images of prey slipped into her mind. Joy surged with urgency, bright as a blade.

Maeve came back to herself with the taste of iron and sap in her mouth.

The joy was gone.

The urgency had burned out of her veins like a fever breaking, leaving behind hollow stillness and the ache of muscles pushed far past reason. Her legs trembled. Her breath came ragged and uneven, as if she had been running for days instead of minutes. The sun was about to rise in the east—she realized she had been running all night. The sky still held a faint, bruised brightness, as though night had been too full to leave cleanly.

She blinked, grounding herself in the world as she rubbed her cramped legs.

Stone beneath her boots. Grass crushed flat by many feet. The outer wall of the human city of Valecourt loomed ahead, its gate twisted open, its hinges warped and blackened by fire. Smoke drifted from the city, thin and gray, carrying the bitter scent of ash and blood.

Whatever had called them had moved beyond them. For now.

Maeve straightened slowly.

Only then did she realize how many were with her.

The Owl Clan stood gathered in a loose crescent beyond the walls, warriors, druids, and scouts—her entire community. Hundreds of them, breathing hard, weapons still in hand, eyes darting as if expecting the call to return at any moment.

But they were not alone.

Dryads stood among the roots at the edge of the field, their green skin dulled and ashen, their blossoms wilted as if the Hunt had leeched something essential from them. Sprites hovered uncertainly overhead, their wings stilled, their usual laughter replaced by wary silence. Pixies clutched one another, blinking as if waking from a shared dream they did not wish to remember.

A centaur shifted nearby, hooves scraping stone, nostrils flaring as he surveyed the broken city with visible distaste. Satyrs leaned on their staves, their expressions grim and uncharacteristically sober. Tree folk stood where no path had been before, their bark-slow faces unreadable, roots sunk deep into soil they had not chosen.

Brownies huddled close to the wall, wide-eyed and shaken.

Maeve turned in a slow circle.

The forest had come with them.

A murmur rippled through the Owl Clan ranks, low and unsettled. These were not beings summoned lightly. Many had never stood together in one place, not for council, not for war, not for celebration.

Maeve's hand tightened on her bow.

"This is wrong," someone whispered. "How did we get here?"

A druid of her clan, Jast, stood a few paces away, one knee on the ground, one hand braced against the earth as if steadying himself. His breathing was controlled now, but his expression was distant, inwardly fixed on something none of them could see.

Maeve crossed to him. "Jast."

He looked up slowly.

His eyes were clear. Too clear.

"They were the prey," he said, not answering her directly. His gaze flicked toward the city. "The humans. When enough of them fell, it ended—for those who heard it."

Maeve followed his look. Bodies lay where panic had dropped them, at the well, in the street, against the walls—no defensive line. No formation. Only the flight was cut short.

"Yes," she said quietly. "I wanted to kill them—I think."

Jast swallowed.

Something inside him shifted, a realization settling like cold water in his chest.

Dryads.

He had walked beside them for a year and lived within their song. He had learned the slow, patient surrender that turned resistance into understanding. He had endured the charm until it no longer bound him, until he could hear a dryad's command and choose not to obey.

That was how one left their service.

A year. Sometimes more. Sometimes less.

He had believed himself beyond being charmed after his year with the dryads.

Immune.

He looked at the dryads standing silent among the roots, their eyes unfocused, their presence muted.

This charmed them, he thought.

Not seduced. Not persuaded.

Called.

The uncharmable had answered.

And so had he.

Jast pushed himself to his feet, the decision settling with quiet certainty. The longer they lingered like this, the more dangerous it became. The open field was wrong for all of them, too exposed and too vulnerable if the call returned.

He lifted his staff and struck a stone once with it.

The sound carried.

The fay turned toward him, not as followers, not as subjects, but as beings suddenly aware again of where they stood.

"What called us has passed," Jast said, voice steady. "We are free again. It is gone."

He gestured south, toward the dark line of trees that marked the beginning of Atharyn Holt.

"Return home. All of you."

No compulsion laced his words. No charm.

Only direction.

For a heartbeat, nothing happened.

Then the dryads moved first, stepping back into the roots as if sinking into familiar ground. Sprites fluttered uncertainly, then darted away in streaks of dim light. Pixies vanished with small pops of displaced air. Brownies slipped into cracks and shadows, gone in the blink of an eye.

The centaur snorted once, sharp and irritated, then turned and loped toward the forest edge, hooves striking a rhythm that faded quickly. The tree folk withdrew more slowly, roots pulling free with a sound like reluctant breath, their forms dissolving back into bark and soil.

Within moments, the field felt wrong.

Too open.

As if something vast had passed through and left the air thinner behind it.

Maeve exhaled without realizing she'd been holding her breath.

The Owl Clan remained.

Warriors. Druids. Those trained to face what came next.

Jast turned to her. His voice was lower now. "If the horn sounds again, they won't have a choice."

Maeve nodded. "Nor will we."

He glanced once more at Valecourt. "There may be answers within those walls."

Maeve raised her bow. "Then we go in."

The Owl Clan formed up without orders, instinct returning as the haze lifted completely. They crossed the threshold of the broken gate together, stepping into the ruined streets with practiced caution.

And somewhere far beyond stone and field and fear, the echo of what called them lingered, not sounding, not gone, waiting for the world to misstep again.

The gates of the city hung ajar. A guardsman lay slain beside them. Beyond the wall was breached, and the dead littered the street.

Maeve entered the city with her Owl Clan companions. Charred buildings, broken windows, smashed carts, and overturned market stalls lined the streets. The dead lay face down, slain while fleeing something. It felt like they were being watched by some in hiding.

A shutter twitched. Then stilled.

She examined the body of a human male seated and slumped against a well. His gaze was vacant, and blood seeped from his chest and mouth. Jast, one of the druids of her clan and a former refugee from the Anari's future time, knelt beside her and spoke to the man.

"Who did this?" Jast asked in the strange human tongue.

Valkryss had given some of the refugees that gift, the old tales said.

The human swallowed, then croaked, "Ghosts. Wood elf ghosts. Led by a wood elf holding a horn in one hand and a wicked green blade in the other. He also had a strange box with a glass cover on his belt. They were…."

The man slumped forward, dead.

Maeve asked Jast what the human had said. Jast furrowed his brow, then said, "Anari ghosts, led by an Anari huntsman. Maeve, did you feel you had to come here, as though you could not refuse? I found myself standing here after hearing the horn in the distance while I was in the forest, miles from here."

Maeve replied, "The call of the hunter god, Aelrindel, who wields the horn that commands hunters to prey and prey to flee. I felt it too. Legend says no Anari or fay may resist the huntsman's horn. Aelrindel is imprisoned, according to legend."

Jast stood, looked around, and strode to another human body.

"What are you looking for, Jast?" Maeve asked.

"Another live one to question. I need answers. We are exposed out here. In fact, we should all return to Atharyn Holt as soon as possible. We are not safe out here."

Maeve looked about, then said, "Nearby patrols and settlements will likely respond. You're right."

They found no more humans to question. They caught fleeting glimpses—children, and a few adults—before doors slammed and shadows swallowed them. Jast and Maeve decided it was time, and told the others of their clan who were currently in Valecourt to return to Atharyn Holt at once.

They returned home exhausted. They had been compelled to leave the safety of Atharyn Holt, a dangerous risk of being caught in the open.

Location: Drakkenwyld, Draknest Community

Time: BV 21, Several weeks after the fall of Valecourt

Nadja of Draknest climbed the ladder to the treehome above.

The home was reasonably new, grown rather than built, its platforms shaped from living branches coaxed into interlocking strength. Nadja reached the top and stepped onto the covered platform, her boots soft on bark polished smooth by years of careful passage. Her fungal clothing was faded and worn from travel, and her staff, carved with leaves, beasts, spirals, and runes, bore the quiet nicks of a woman who had walked through danger more often than through ceremony.

Kellyn Windstream sat near the open edge of the platform, one hand resting on the railing, the other unconsciously braced against her lower abdomen. The canopy unfurled before her like a sea of leaves, the distant horizon softened by mist and dusk-light. She did not turn at first.

"You heard it already," Kellyn said.

Nadja paused, then nodded. "Not the horn. The stories."

Kellyn turned then, sharp and immediate. "From where?"

"Owl Clan first," Nadja said, stepping closer. "Atharyn Holt. Then, the Wolf Clan scouts. Then, timber traders who should not have lived long enough to speak."

Kellyn's eyes did not blink. "Tell me."

Nadja leaned her staff against the trunk wall and exhaled once, steadying herself. "They heard a horn in the night—a clear night. Not near. Not distant. Directional. Anari ran toward it, not knowing why."

Kellyn swallowed.

"Valecourt," Nadja continued. "A city. Not a fort. Not a camp. A city of stone and walls that thrived on the trade of lumber. When the Owl Clan arrived, it was already over."

Kellyn closed her eyes briefly.

"They spoke to the dying," Nadja said. "Humans. What few were still breathing."

Kellyn's voice was barely audible. "What did they say?"

Nadja met her gaze. "They spoke of phantoms. Anari phantoms. A host of them. They spoke of a huntsman leading them, carrying a horn and a blade of green light."

Kellyn's breath caught, just slightly.

"They said he rode a great stag," Nadja went on. "That he did not shout. Did not rage. That he struck, and the Hunt ended."

Kellyn nodded once, slowly. "That is similar to Aelrindel's aspect."

"Yes," Nadja said. "That is what the druids believe."

Kellyn's eyes sharpened. "Is that all?"

Nadja hesitated.

Kellyn leaned forward. "Nadja."

"One of the humans mentioned something else," Nadja said carefully. "Something… strange."

Kellyn went still.

"A box," Nadja said. "Clipped to the huntsman's belt. Metal. With glass set into it. They said it bounced when he ran."

For a heartbeat, the world narrowed to a single sound.

Kellyn's breath.

Then she laughed, once, broken and disbelieving, and pressed a hand to her mouth.

"That's not a god," she said.

Nadja frowned. "Kellyn…"

"Aelrindel would not carry a camera," Kellyn said, voice tightening as the truth snapped into place. "He wouldn't know what to do with one."

She stood abruptly, the platform creaking in protest.

"That's Harvey," she said. "That's Kuldemaekr. That's his stupid old camera he refused to leave behind because he said it helped him remember who he was."

Nadja stepped forward instinctively. "Kellyn…"

"The Greenwood is no longer cursed," Nadja said quickly, trying to anchor her. "The druids are certain. They say the ancient Hunt has returned because Aelrindel is free."

Kellyn shook her head. "No. The ancient Hunt returned because Harvey answered."

Silence stretched between them, heavy with names neither of them said aloud.

"Other tales are coming in," Nadja said quietly. "About a month later, from far beyond Valecourt. Patrols gone. Merchant wagons filled with timber were found dead in the wild. Cities near our forests were attacked and left almost empty. Always the same story. About a month apart. Always the horn. Always phantoms. Always the huntsman moving on before anyone can follow."

Kellyn was already moving toward the ladder.

Nadja reached out and caught her wrist.

Then, gently, she placed her other hand against Kellyn's belly.

Kellyn froze.

"Where do you think you're going?" Nadja asked.

Kellyn's jaw clenched. "To find him."

Nadja held her there, not forcefully, but firmly. "You're not going anywhere," she said. "You're too far along now. You can barely sleep without the healers scolding you."

Kellyn's shoulders sagged, just a fraction.

"He didn't come home," Kellyn whispered. "He didn't even try."

"Or he couldn't," Nadja said. "Or he believes he shouldn't."

Kellyn looked back out over the forest, eyes bright with something dangerously close to hope.

"He's still fighting," she said. "He's alive. And he's winning battles no one else can reach."

"Yes," Nadja agreed. "And no one can keep up with him."

Kellyn rested both hands against her abdomen now, grounding herself in the undeniable truth there.

"He's become the Hunt," she said. "Wild. Unbound. Always moving."

Nadja nodded. "And those who try to join him arrive too late. They find only bodies… and fading phantoms."

Kellyn closed her eyes.

"Good," she said softly. "That means he's still mortal."

Nadja frowned. "How does that follow?"

"Because gods stay," Kellyn replied. "Harvey never could."

The light faded further, leaves whispering as night settled in earnest around the treehome.

Far away, beyond forest and stone and border, a horn sounded again in some other night, heard by none here, but already changing the shape of the world.

Kellyn remained where she was, one hand on her belly, the other braced against living wood.

Why didn't Harvey come home?

The thought came unbidden, sharp and unwelcome.

If he lived.

If the Greenwood no longer barred his path.

If the Horn answered him.

Then he could have returned.

Nadja did not answer at once. Some truths required space to arrive intact.

"Not every silence is an ending," she said at last. "Some are simply the sound of something moving beyond reach."

Kellyn's hand settled against her belly. Beneath her palm, life stirred—steady, unhurried, indifferent to legend.

She understood then that whatever Harvey had become, it was not meant to end. It was still moving.

And the world was already making room for it.

The End of Book 3: A Knight on the Haunted Hunt
The Time Bureau Files:

Book 1: The Chamber of Victory
Book 2: The Queen of the Unveiled Path
Book 3: A Knight on the Haunted Hunt
Book 4: Mothers of Death
Book 5: Bears Never Hunt In Packs
Book 6: Call of the Dark Child
Book 7: The Wisdom Clock
Book 8: Gifts That Never Stop Killing
Book 9: The Purified Maze
Book 10: Scales of Nobility
Book 11: Feathers of the Banished
Book 12: Fury of the Unmourned
Book 13: Song of the Necromancer
Book 14: The Last Queen—The Final Hunt

Also available in the Time Bureau Files universe are the Time Crimes novellas.

The Haven World's Vow
Operation Lyrianne
Operation Huntsman
Operation Faelor
Operation Anaradin
Operation Bloodwind
Operation Aetherholt

Appendix 1: Wolf Clan Fighting Form

Cultural Martial Terms of the Anari (Applied to Griffyn Style)

ENGRAVING THE CODEX — CEREMONIAL RELIC FORMAT

This is not just a list. This is the Anari sacred war-script as it would appear in a temple archive or master-blade chamber, carved in silverglyph or sung onto crystal vellum.

CODEX HARMONICA — ENTRY II: WOLF CLAN

Arath Faelorin — Song of the Moonlit Pulse

"Steel is not the weapon. Rhythm is." — Faelor, Hunter-God of the Moon

ᚠᚾᚠᚱᛁ

🐺 Wolf Clan — Faelor's Doctrine of the Pulse and the Hunt

Patron Deity: Faelor, the Nocturnal Hunt, Lord of Instinct and Moon-Shadow

Divine Song: Arath Faelorin — Song of the Moonlit Pulse

Martial Philosophy: To hunt is to align with the prey's heartbeat.
Wolves do not force combat — they fall into the rhythm of the enemy and then break it at the moment of kill.

ᚠᚾᚠᚱᛁ

🎭 Wolf Clan Martial Geometry & Harmonic Identity

ᚠᚾᚠᚱᛁ

🔪 Eight Wolf Vael'Shar — Fully Codexed in Anari Martial Script

All Wolf movements follow the S-shaped Lýren'thal of the Hunt, circling one step off the enemy's rhythm before the killing stroke.

ᚨᚾᚨᚱᛁ

1. Vael'Shar Moonfang–desh — "Moonfang Descent"

Verse Applied: Arath Faelorin — Pulse Verse 2 ("The Heartbeat Before the Kill")

Fael'thyr Alignment: Blade descends at a slanted, curved line, never cleanly vertical.

Lýren'thal Path: Curving advance → Drop-in at angle

Veyl'Ashar: Pulse Gap entry — strike falls just as heartbeat slows.

Catal'ri: Deep one-note exhale like a growl held in the throat.

The enemy feels their own pulse echoing wrong just before impact.

ᚨᚾᚨᚱᛁ

2. Vael'Shar Silver Prowl Arc — "Silver Prowl Arc"

Verse Applied: Pulse Verse 1 ("Stalking Breath")

Fael'thyr: Curved downward slash as if tracing prey's path.

Lýren'thal: Side-step arc, circling rather than engaging head-on.

Veyl'Ashar: Harmonic Pulse Gap — ideal stalking distance.

Catal'ri: Whispered intake — the breath before the howl.

Wolf warriors say: "The kill begins two steps before the strike."

ᚨᚾᚨᚱᛁ

3. Vael'Shar Rising Howl Reversal — "Rising Howl Reversal"

Verse Applied: Pulse Verse 3 ("First Cry of the Hunt")

Fael'thyr: Upward curved strike meant to rip the enemy's stance open.

Lýren'thal: Rising half-spiral, reversing enemy descent move.

Veyl'Ashar: Pulse Gap → Vertical disruption distance.

Catal'ri: Sudden ascending tone like the beginning of a distant howl.

Used to break Griffyn descent forms — aligning Wolf as natural counter-predator.

ᚠᚾᚠᚱᛁ

4. Vael'Shar Lungpiercer — "Lungpiercer Lunge"

Verse Applied: Pulse Verse 4 — "Killstroke"

Fael'thyr: Blade thrusts while crouching, aiming beneath guard.

Lýren'thal: Forward curl at chest-height.

Veyl'Ashar: Pulse Gap → Killing Breath — finishes inside guard.

Catal'ri: A sudden breath-stop — pressure ripple felt in the lungs.

This strike is taught with the saying: "Breathe once. Die once."

ᚠᚾᚠᚱᛁ

5. Vael'Shar Hunting Circle Sweep — "Hunting Circle Sweep"

Verse Applied: Pulse Verse 2 repeated off-beat

Fael'thyr: Blade arcs in a horizontal circle, moving around the enemy's flanks.

Lýren'thal: Full circle path, mimicking pack movement.

Veyl'Ashar: Harmonic Pulse Gap — harassment ring.

Catal'ri: Two-beat rhythm — one growl, one silence.

Makes humans report feeling "surrounded," even when only one Wolf is present.

ᚠᚾᚠᚱᛁ

6. Vael'Shar Echofang Return — "Echofang Return"

Verse Applied: Pulse Verse 5 — "Second Fang"

Fael'thyr: A backhand slash delivered after slipping around the guard.

Lýren'thal: Reversal S-turn inside enemy's stance.

Veyl'Ashar: Pure Killing Breath — so close the enemy feels breath on their neck.

Catal'ri: The impact sound comes half a beat late, causing time reflex confusion.

Wolf warriors say: "The prey thinks it is still alive until the echo hits."

ᚨᚾᚨᚱᛁ

7. Vael'Shar Moonrise Hook — "Moonrise Hook"

Verse Applied: Pulse Verse 3 held note

Fael'thyr: Hooking upward cut meant to destabilize footing.

Lýren'thal: Lifting S-curve, undercutting stance.

Veyl'Ashar: Pulse Gap disruption range.

Catal'ri: A rising growl that cuts once the enemy exhales.

Seen as a "pre-kill" form — Wolves believe a kill should follow a stumble.

ᚨᚾᚨᚱᛁ

8. Vael'Shar Silent Pounce Draw — "Silent Pounce Draw"

Verse Applied: Pulse Verse 0 — "The Breath That Isn't Heard" — only taught to pack-leaders.

Fael'thyr: Draw-cut delivered from motion, not stationary — blade unsheathed mid-leap or mid-creep.

Lýren'thal: Broken S-curve leading to instant entry.

Veyl'Ashar: Spiral Walk → Instant Killing Breath.

Catal'ri: No sound at all — even the blade's steel sings nothing.

Wolf saying: "If you heard it, it wasn't ours."

Appendix 2: Lost Codex Harmonic of the Lynx Clan

Arath Vecha'Lyn — Song of the Silent Hunt

Seichūsen: Lyn'thyr — The Fractured Shadow Line

Appendix 2: Lynx Forms

Lýren'thal: Null Spiral Path (tight spirals, non-repeating steps)
Veyl'Ashar: Eclipse Range (inside normal killing distance; shared shadow)
Catal'ri: Subharmonic Purr (felt more than heard)

"We do not vanish. We move where the eye never was."
— Lynx teaching fragment, preserved through Ah'sin

1. Vael'Shar Vecha'drain — "Vein of the Silent Fang"
(Life-drain and self-heal)
Verse: Verse of the Taken Pulse
Lyn'thyr: Tracks the heart-line, not the armor line.
Lýren'thal: Short inward spiral, sliding under guard.
Veyl'Ashar: Chest-to-chest Eclipse Range.
Catal'ri: Inward hum; exhale is withheld.
Effect:
Blade or hand contact pulls a sliver of life-force and harmonic energy from the target into the wielder, closing wounds and restoring stamina. To onlookers, the victim withers; the Lynx (or Ellendyl) stands straighter, wounds fading.

2. Vael'Shar Umbral Shroud — "Hunter in the Five-Step Night"
(5' radius darkness cloak)
Verse: Whisper Verse of the First Shadow
Lyn'thyr: Soul-line sinks beneath the world's light.
Lýren'thal: Micro-spiral around own position.
Veyl'Ashar: ~5' radius — perfect for dueling space.
Catal'ri: Three soft pulses, then silence.

Effect:
A dense globe of shadow erupts around the wielder.
Inside it:
Wielder sees normally,
others see only vague motion and smudged silhouettes.
Ideal for single combat, assassination, or breaking missile line of sight.

3. Vael'Shar Second Shadow — "Echo of the Hunter"
(Phantom-step feint / teleport-like slip)
Verse: Echo Verse of the Unseen Step
Lyn'thyr: Soul-line oscillates between two positions.
Lýren'thal: One perfectly timed lateral sidestep or pivot.
Veyl'Ashar: Close, duelist's distance.
Catal'ri: Tiny click or tongue-pop timed to the step.
Effect:
Enemy perception "chooses" the wrong position.
They swear the Lynx vanished and reappeared, but it was one precise step plus shadow warping. This is the basis of Ah'sin's corridor fighting and Ellendyl's "how did she get behind him?" moments.

4. Vael'Shar Night's Throat — "Strangling Silence"
(Silence aura for spells & Catal'ri)
Verse: Quietus Verse
Lyn'thyr: Wraps around opponent's center like a noose.
Lýren'thal: Small circling step, always a half-beat off the enemy's rhythm.
Veyl'Ashar: 10–15' radius.
Catal'ri: One sharp inhalation, then none.
Effect:
Within this aura:
spoken spells falter,

shouts drop to hushed croaks,

other clans' Catal'ri fail to fully manifest.

Perfect for neutering battle-chanters, Griffyn horn-tones, and human war-priests.

5. Vael'Shar Eclipse Field — "Fifty-Step Midnight"

(50' radius darkness where only Lynx see clearly)

Verse: Final Eclipse Verse

Lyn'thyr: Fractures into multiple lines, one to each threat.

Lýren'thal: Almost stationary; the Song moves instead.

Veyl'Ashar: ~50' radius — a full killing ground.

Catal'ri: Deep subharmonic thrum that causes ear-pressure and nausea.

Effect:

A dome of absolute darkness falls.

Non-Lynx: effectively blind — no shapes, no light, spells dim.

Lynx / Lynx-marked (Ah'sin, eventually Ellendyl): see in sharp greyscale.

Brutal for breaking platoon formations, trapping elites, or turning a city alley or forest grove into a Lynx-only battlefield.

6. Vael'Shar Ashen Pact — "Last Gift of the Lynx"

(Release of cursed Lynx / undead back to Anari spirit)

Verse: Final Verse of Release

Lyn'thyr: Straightens from fractured to whole for a heartbeat.

Lýren'thal: No physical movement; the Song steps out.

Veyl'Ashar: Point-contact — a hand on chest, a clasp, a hug.

Catal'ri: Three-note descending chord only Lynx and sensitives hear.

Effect:

When used on Lynx-cursed undead (like Ah'sin) or beings bound in necrotic Lynx echo, this form burns away the undeath, returning the soul to Aelrindel's path and leaving only ash.

Harvey's embrace of Ah'sin in the Greenwood unknowingly completes a broken Vael'Shar Ashen Pact — why Ah'sin dies as Anari again, with Lynx phantoms waiting.

7. Vael'Shar Cornered Vecha — "Claws of the Four Walls"

(Cat-cornered / many foes form)

Verse: Verse of the Cornered Prey

Lyn'thyr: Splits into four short arcs, one to each cardinal direction.

Lýren'thal:

Tight pivoting footwork,

shoulders turning while feet barely move,

blades always crossing where enemies converge.

Veyl'Ashar: Only an arm's length — everything is too close.

Catal'ri: Rapid staccato purr, accelerating with each exchange.

Effect:

Used when:

surrounded,

pinned against walls,

or in tunnels where retreat is impossible.

The Lynx:

abandons retreat entirely,

becomes a spinning center of cuts and short slashes,

uses bodies of fallen foes as momentary cover,

aims Vecha'drain strikes in quick flurries to sustain themselves.

Visually: like a cat backed into a corner, exploding outward at every opening.

Wolf veterans later describe Ellendyl in such moments as:

"Everything close to her just… died."

8. Vael'Shar Rearclaw Ascent — "Pounce of the Hidden Spine"

(Rearclaw / double-blade, backflip extraction finisher)

Verse: Pounce Verse of the Third Shadow

Lyn'thyr: Starts low, behind or slightly off the enemy's shoulder.

Lýren'thal:

Shadow approach (Second Shadow / stealth from Umbral Shroud),

Sudden upwards drive — two blades stabbed in,

Rearclaw kick: both feet plant into the enemy's torso/hips,

Backflip off the embedded blades,

Blades ripped free mid-flip,

Land in a low, ready crouch behind or to the side.

Veyl'Ashar: Begins just outside Eclipse Range, ends inside it.

Catal'ri: A rising, almost playful trilling note cut off at the apex of the flip.

Effect:

Catlike, savage, and theatrical — used as:

an execution when a key target is already off-balance,

or the final kill in a multi-foe brawl.

The double-stab plus rear-kick multiplies force and ensures deep penetration; the backflip uses the enemy's body as a springboard to clear space and reset.

Ah'sin would have used a vampire-corrupted version of this in tight corridors.

Ellendyl might only unlock this in a very late book as her full Lynx echo awakens — perfect "holy crap, she's Lynx" visual moment.

Appendix 3: The Twelve Races of Vaelthara

1. Anari (Wood-elf–like people)

Core Traits: Tall, lithe, long-lived, deeply tied to forests and magic.

Culture: Clan-based society (Dragon, Griffyn, Wolf, Unicorn, etc.), with a Confederation in the future. Forest protectors.

Strengths: Magic, song, archery, linguistic gifts, and a strong oral tradition. fay beings and the forest itself are their allies. Long life span (average is 1,500 years).

Weaknesses: Pride, internal rivalries, and proven only within forests.

—Thaliryn Leafstride, Sylph Clan scout

"We don't get lost. We just discover better paths than the one everyone else insisted on."

2. Gravhal (dwarf like people)

Core Traits: Short, stocky, endurance unmatched.

Culture: Stone citadels and underground halls, strong guild traditions.

Strengths: Master smiths, rune magic, resilience in battle. Long lifespan avg. (about 740 years).

Weaknesses: Stubborn, conservative, poor adaptability outside mountain/stone environments.

—Bromdur Ironshoulder, Gravhal mason

"Aye, I'll change my mind… once the mountain does."

3. Nimvrels (Gnome like people)

Core Traits: Small, clever, endlessly curious.

Culture: Tinkerers, inventors, alchemists.

Strengths: Ingenious inventors, illusions, clockwork devices, cunning diplomacy. Long lifespan average (900 years).

Weaknesses: Physically weak, lacks military power, and overreaches through curiosity.

—Tinkletop Gearwisp, Nimvrel inventor
"Relax! I tested this device thoroughly. Only exploded twice, and I wasn't even in the room either time!"

4. Thraekars (various giant races)

Core Traits: Towering, immense physical strength, semi-nomadic.

Culture: Tribal, honor-based; keep oral histories.

Strengths: Physical might, endurance, and some storm magic. Very long lifespans (Frost giants about 15,000 years, Fire giants 12,000 years, Fomorians about 900 years, Ogres about 200 years).

Weaknesses: Slow to adapt, often manipulated by smaller races, and rare in number.

—Urmak Storm-Walker, Thraekar wanderer
"Patience is the calm before the stomp."

5. Sza'thir (Reptile bipedal race)

Core Traits: Reptilian humanoids, scaled, cold-blooded.

Culture: Marsh and river dwellers; pragmatic and survival-oriented.

Strengths: Amphibious, resilient, natural warriors, cunning hunters. Long lifespans (400 years).

Weaknesses: Distrusted by others, seen as "alien," cold pragmatism limits empathy.

—Ssilvar Yex, Sza'thir hunter
"Warmbloods panic too easily. If the water bubbles, it means lunch is coming."

6. Krikk'ar (Insect like race)

Core Traits: Carapace exoskeletons, varied insectoid forms (mantis, beetle, wasp types).

Culture: Hive societies with queens and castes.

Strengths: Numbers, coordination, tireless workers, venom or flight depending on type. Racial memory.

Weaknesses: Rigid caste system, lack of individuality, fragile diplomacy with others. Short lifespan (80 years).

—Kritt-Kritt, Krikk'ar worker drone
"Individuality is overrated. I tried it once. Terrible experience. Much confusion."

7. Zagg'rin (Goblinoid race)

Core Traits: Small, wiry, sharp-featured, cunning.

Culture: Scavengers, opportunists, live in marginal lands.

Strengths: Adaptable, tricksters, alchemy, and sabotage specialists. Rapid breeding (large birth counts).

Weaknesses: Poor unity, susceptibility to corruption, and cowardice in battle without numbers. Short lifespan (60 years).

—Zibbit the Untrustworthy (self-given title)
"Look, if I'm holding it, I definitely didn't steal it. Yet."

8. Minos (Minotaur-like)

Core Traits: Bull-headed humanoids, muscular, labyrinthine instincts.

Culture: Warrior clans, honor duels, blood oaths.

Strengths: Fierce warriors, strong seafaring tradition, labyrinth memory, infectious bite turns victims to Minos.

Weaknesses: Hot-tempered, divided into warring tribes, easily baited.

—Thalgar Redhorn, Minos war-leader
"I do not have anger issues. I have anger solutions."

9. Aeryndai (Avian people)

Core Traits: Winged humanoids, hollow-boned but strong.

Culture: Sky citadels, keen hunters, and scouts.

Strengths: Flight, sharp eyesight, aerial combat dominance. Long lifespan (about 500 years).

Weaknesses: Frail bones, isolationist, disdain for ground-dwellers.

—Skylune Sharpeye, Aeryndai sky-scout
"I'm not looking down on you. Well… I mean I am, but only because I'm literally above you."

10. Osiri

Core Traits: Tall, bronze-skinned, desert-dwelling humans with mystical lineage.

Culture: Ancient cities, sun cults, pyramids, and preservation of old magics.

Strengths: Strong in ritual magic, desert survival, and prophetic traditions. Long lifespan (about 500 years).

Weaknesses: Arrogance, bound by strict hierarchy, and insularity.

—Hesep-Amun, Osiri ritualist

"If the sun wanted you to question me, it would have blinded you sooner."

11. Veydrath (Undead)

Core Traits: Tall, pale, necrotic aura, often cloaked in shadows. Undead of various forms led by vampire counts.

Culture: Masters of necromancy, rule over undead thralls.

Strengths: Command over death, raising armies, and the feared lore of the grave.

Weaknesses: Shunned by all other races, tied to necrotic energies, fragile when cut off from their dark magic.

—Count Varis Umbershade, Veydrath noble

"Ah, the living. So dramatic about the whole 'breathing' thing."

12. Humans

Core Traits: Versatile, numerous, short-lived.

Culture: Expansive, adaptable to all lands, and empire-builders.

Strengths: Flexibility, innovation, rapid technology advancement, adaptability, sheer numbers, and quick breeding cycles.

Weaknesses: Lack of specialization, short-sightedness, hunger for expansion. No special abilities. Short lifespan (70 years).

—Captain Jalen Ward, human mercenary

"We don't need magic. We've got optimism and bad ideas in equal measure."

Appendix 4: Anari Clans

Dragon Clan — High-warrior lineage; keepers of martial traditions, draconic banners, and flame-sigils.

Griffyn Clan — Proud knightly houses, aerial cavalry, chivalric codes.

Eagle Clan — Scouts, skyward seers, farsight traditions.

Wolf Clan — Stoic defenders, cold-weather legions, survivalists; strong presence on Frostmere.

Bear Clan — Heavy infantry, guardians of taiga strongholds, craftsmen.

Unicorn Clan — Mystics and healers, linked to Verdantis and ancient rites.

White Hart Clan — Rangers and wanderers; lore of forests and liminal places.

Wyvern Clan — Fierce but more mercantile; pragmatists who balance tradition and trade.

Felhart Clan — Resilient survivalists, famed for stubbornness and unconventional tactics.

Moon Clan — Dream-seers, diviners, tied to lunar cycles and prophecy.

Owl Clan — Scholars, archivists, keepers of the Old Tongue; often allied with Kellyn's work.

Sylph Clan — Graceful wind-kin, aerial combat specialists, poets, and diplomats.

Appendix 5: The Anari Calendar

The Anari keep two principal reckonings of time. In ancient times, time was measured from the Sealing of the Chamber of Victory and expressed in divine years and animal months. In the future age, after the War of Twelve Races, time is recorded as BV (Before Victory) and FY (Future Year).

The Sealing Calendar (Ancient Anari)

Epoch: The placement of the Chamber of Victory. Dates are written as '<Divine Year> — <Animal Month>, <X> years since the Sealing.' The divine year names reflect the gods' patronage; the months honor clan totems.

Divine Cycle (Years of the Gods)

Representative entries from the divine cycle include:

• Lireal — God of Justice, Law, and Oath.

• Vaelthas — God of Shadows and Secrets.

• Nyrielle — Goddess of Stars and Fate.

• Lyrianne — Goddess of Vengeance and Redress.

• Varethor — God of Storms and Weather.

• Caelrin — God of Rangers and Tracking.

• Burk — God of Treefolk and Deep Root.

• Aelrindel — The Imprisoned Huntsman.

• Tha — God of Luck and Turning Tides.

• Fyran — Goddess of Dance and Song.

• Vecha-los — The Crone, Fate and Ending.

• Sylvara — Goddess of Forest Creatures and Growth.

Totemic Cycle (Months of the Animals)

The twelve animal months are:

• Wolf — strength, loyalty, ferocity

• Griffyn — guardianship, vision, courage

• Dragon — majesty, fire, destruction

• Owl — wisdom, silence, foresight

• Unicorn — purity, healing, grace

• Wyvern — cunning, exile, resilience

• Eagle — swiftness, vigilance, honor
• Serpent — knowledge, transformation, peril
• Stag — fertility, pride, wilderness
• Bear — endurance, patience, wrath
• Hawk — precision, freedom, the hunt
• Boar — stubbornness, battle, sacrifice

The BV/FY Calendar (Future Confederation)

After the War of Twelve Races, the futurists abandoned sacred cycles. Years are counted as BV (Before Victory), leading up to the war's end, and FY (Future Year) after. Example: BV 24; FY 3553.

Conversion Notes

Anchor points differ. By Bureau estimation, FY 3553 ≈ 25,000 years since the Sealing.

Examples:

• BV 24 ≈ Year of the Jackal, 21,423 since the Sealing.
• FY 3553 ≈ Year of Lireal, ~25,000 since the Sealing.

Appendix 6: ATLAS OF VAELTHARA

Era of Harmony Year Zero — Compiled from Bureau Reconstructions and the Codex Harmonica

"The land dreamed itself awake, and the gods wrote their names across its forests." — Lireal the Just

I. The Continent of Vaelthara — "The Land That Dreamed Itself Awake"

Vaelthara is the cradle-world of the Anari, a single vast supercontinent encircled by the Seven Seas. Its terrain forms a natural lyre-shape: mountains as frets, rivers as strings, forests as notes. Twelve Sacred Forests mark the harmonic pillars of creation, each tied to a god, a clan, and a divine Song within the Codex Harmonica.

II. The Seven Seas of Vaelthara

III. The Twelve Sacred Forests of Vaelthara

Each forest is tied to a clan, a god, and a divine Song, embodying a single note in the Twelvefold Harmony.

IV. Harmonic Structure

The twelve keys form the base Song of Twelve, the harmonic counterpoint to the Seven Null Gods of the Malloch. When sung together, the forests form a resonance field sustaining Vaelthara's life-song.

V. Cartographer's Final Annotation

"To read this map is to hear the world breathe. Each sea is an echo, each mountain a pulse, each forest a note in the long memory of the gods. And if ever the Song falls silent, so too shall Vaelthara dream no more." — Inscription on the Aetherholt Tablets.

www.ingramcontent.com/pod-product-compliance
Lightning Source LLC
LaVergne TN
LVHW010629110826
845149LV00014B/2812

* 9 7 9 8 9 9 3 9 8 3 5 3 0 *